Praise for Dianne Emley
and her novels

"Pulse-pounding prose and unexpected plot twists make this must-reading." —*Tucson Citizen,*
on *The Deepest Cut*

"Emley's solid police procedural offers intriguing insights into a killer's mind, with a few unexpected plot twists."
—*Lansing State Journal* (Michigan),
on *The Deepest Cut*

"[Dianne Emley] captures the unpredictable alchemy of human relationships . . . a fascinating look at the bizarre bond between a serial killer and one of his intended victims."
—*The Oak Ridge Observer,* on *The Deepest Cut*

"A thriller that will keep you reading far into the night." —BookLoons, on *The Deepest Cut*

"*Cut to the Quick*'s razor-sharp plot and lightning-fast pace kept me on the edge of my chair from the first page to the last. Add Dianne Emley to your list of must reads—this is one not-to-be-missed thriller writer."
—MARIAH STEWART on *Cut to the Quick*

"Diann⬚⬚⬚⬚⬚⬚⬚⬚⬚⬚ in this crime thriller. ⬚⬚⬚⬚⬚⬚⬚⬚⬚ng debut, *The First C*⬚⬚⬚⬚⬚⬚⬚⬚⬚*ut to the Quick*

"*The* ⬚⬚⬚⬚⬚⬚⬚⬚⬚⬚stablish Dianne Emley in ⬚⬚⬚ ⬚⬚⬚⬚⬚⬚ters. . . . A great read." —MICHAEL CO⬚⬚⬚⬚⬚, on *The First Cut*

"Action-packed, with plenty of suspense and enough twists and turns to keep the reader guessing long into the night." —LISA JACKSON, on *The First Cut*

Books published by The Random House Publishing Group
are available at quantity discounts on bulk purchases for
premium, educational, fund-raising, and special sales use.
For details, please call 1-800-733-3000.

Dianne EMLEY

LOVE

A NOVEL

KILLS

BALLANTINE BOOKS • NEW YORK

2010 Ballantine Books Mass Market Edition

Copyright © 2010 by Emley and Co., LLC

Published in the United States by Ballantine Books, an imprint of The Random House Publishing Group, a division of Random House, Inc., New York.

BALLANTINE and colophon are registered trademarks of Random House, Inc.

ISBN 978-0-345-49955-4

Cover design: Jem Butcher

Printed in the United States of America

www.ballantinebooks.com

9 8 7 6 5 4 3 2 1

For my husband,
Charles G. Emley, Jr.
A hand to hold when leaves
begin to fall . . .

ACKNOWLEDGMENTS

I owe a huge debt of gratitude to my editor, Dana Isaacson. Dana, I've been privileged to benefit from your keen editorial instincts, dedication, and unique perspective. Working with you on this book in particular was a supreme pleasure. We shared lots of laughs.

I'm thankful to have the wise and wonderful editor, Linda Marrow, in my corner. Thanks to everyone on the Ballantine team, especially Junessa Viloria, Kim Hovey, Scott Shannon, Elizabeth McGuire, Rachel Kind, and Lisa Barnes. Teresa Agrillo was an excellent copy editor.

Special words of appreciation for my agent and champion, Robin Rue, and everyone at Writer's House, especially Beth Miller.

My gratitude to the law-and-order professionals who help me keep it real. The fine men and women of the Pasadena Police Department were again generous with their time. Special thanks to Commander Lisa Rosales.

Steve Davidson, retired police captain, again carefully read and commented on the manuscript. Your astute observations have made my books better.

Margaret York, retired deputy chief of the LAPD and retired chief of the Los Angeles County Police, helped with some tricky police procedure questions.

Judge Karla Kerlin, Los Angeles Superior Court, again helped me sort out the legal morass into which some of my characters always stumble.

Ann Escue's comments on the manuscript were very helpful, as always.

D. P. Lyle, M.D., a fellow author, answered my medical questions.

Catherine Hamm, Toxicologist III, San Diego County Medical Examiner, aided with toxicology research.

Clyde Johnston guided me in keeping the U.S. Marines details straight.

Lynn Caffrey Gabriel and John La Barbera graciously allowed me to stroll around the grounds of their lovely home, looking for a perfect setting for an untimely death.

Bill Tata of Imagine Design and Brian Mason do a great job with my website, DianneEmley.com.

Family and friends, you know who you are. Thanks for your support in ways both big and small.

And last, but never least, hugs and kisses to my husband, Charlie, my safety net, my love.

ONE

Vince Madrigal knew all about cause and effect. Many times he'd delivered the spark, then stood back to watch the fireworks with the satisfaction stemming from a job well done. He loved his work. He'd made more enemies than friends, but hate paid better than love. Several big Hollywood names would enjoy seeing him dead. The way Madrigal saw it, if those people hadn't been doing nasty stuff that they shouldn't have, they wouldn't have dirty laundry to go through. In his line of work, secrets were money in the bank. A-list secrets had put his kids through private schools, paid a couple of alimonies, and footed a handsome lifestyle. He'd earned his moniker: "P.I. to the Stars."

Both secrets and silence were commodities. This job's client understood that ugly fact and had taken the bad news well, knowing that fame had its privileges and costs. After negotiations on that unpleasant matter, they'd quickly moved on to the next order of business: the client needing more of the rare items that Madrigal could procure. It had all been very civilized—too civilized, Madrigal thought.

It was the wee hours of the morning and raining buckets as he drove Colorado Boulevard and entered the Northeast L.A. neighborhood of Eagle Rock.

What idiot said it never rained in California?

As the windshield wipers slapped the downpour, he looked at the lonely, shiny streets of the worn-out neighborhood. He was having a dark night of the soul. He was not an introspective person, and the impulse took him unawares, like a baseball bat to the skull. It wasn't unusual for this client to arrange meetings in out-of-the-way places to elude the paparazzi, but this early-morning rendezvous in East Jesus was making Madrigal uneasy. Rather than listening to his gut, though, he anticipated the "somthin' somthin'" he'd been promised.

"I know what you like," the client had said with a snigger.

Madrigal gave his stock response, "You know what I always say, 'Faster horses, older whiskey, and younger women.'" And they'd laughed like old friends who well understood each other.

He wheeled his Midas gold Ford F-150 pickup through the deserted streets. The truck was the same color as his pristine 1975 Cadillac Eldorado in his garage at home—the car Elvis had given him. One of the few tall tales about him that happened to be true. Madrigal had done security work and a bit more for the King back in the day.

Spotting a road sign that announced that he was driving historic Route 66 prompted him to begin singing tunelessly to the old song about getting your kicks. He couldn't remember all the cities in the lyrics, so he improvised, his baritone scoured by decades of cigarettes and booze.

"Barstow, Nipomo, San Bernardino . . ."

He saw the motel's neon sign: HiWay Haven. Some of the letters were sputtering. *Of course,* he thought. The dump came into view and then blurred as the wipers batted the rain. Attached above the original neon sign was a 1980s-era backlit plastic one that boasted: "Free Cable TV."

"Don't forget Winona, by way of Pomona."

The truck idled in the deserted street as he checked out the place. The single-story motel had twenty rooms flanking a buckled asphalt parking lot. Three cars were parked there: a battered Toyota 4Runner with Mexican plates, a Nissan Maxima with California plates, and a car he recognized: a new yellow Volkswagen Beetle. The windows in all the other rooms and in the office near the driveway were dark, but a light shone dimly through a crack in the closed drapes in the room near where the Beetle was parked.

"Trendi, my love." Madrigal smiled. He'd coveted the willowy blonde, even though he thought the flowery tattoos across her shoulders and bosom were an insult to her beautiful skin. Was she his somthin' somthin'? This was a treat.

Thinking about her gave him a rise in his Wranglers.

Madrigal turned into the driveway and drove past the motel office. Cardboard Easter bunnies and Easter eggs were taped inside its windows, reminding Madrigal that it was Easter morning. He reflected on his childhood in San Antonio, Texas. His mother used to wake him and his siblings before dawn to dress for the sunrise service at Victory Baptist Church.

He improvised a hymn. "Hearts to heaven and voices tuneless . . . Alleluia!"

Madrigal parked beside the Volkswagen in front of room seven. He took out the key his client had mailed. The plastic diamond-shaped fob had "7" stamped on it in gold paint. Seven was his lucky number.

He struggled into his sport coat with its Western-style suede trim and piping. He looked thinner with it on. He worked to keep himself fit, but a belly, though not as big as the one his dad had sported in his later years, persisted in hanging over his silver belt buckle, a large oval with USMC in raised letters.

Still humming, he took a comb from his jacket pocket and ran it through his reddish-brown hair and his walrus mustache in the visor mirror. He straightened his aviator-style glasses and put on his black suede Resistol cowboy hat, also his trademarks, as were his Tony Lama ostrich boots. He guarded his image as carefully as a corporate giant protected its brands.

Into his jacket pocket went the flask of Balvenie scotch he'd brought from home. He grabbed the items he was delivering and ran through the rain, robustly singing made-up lyrics, "All along Route Sixty-six . . ."

Number 7's door was locked. One swift kick would have been sufficient to bust it open, but he used the key.

"Ahhh . . . leee . . . luiiiaaa!"

Smelling of disinfectant and stale cigarette smoke, the darkened room's furnishings were cheap pressboard, but everything looked cleaner than he'd expected—except for a stain on the carpet the size and shape of a watermelon. A dim light came from the bathroom, where the door was half-closed. The rest of the lights were off. The room was cold.

"Well, hello, Trendi."

She sat on the edge of the bed, holding a black cape closed over her torso with two pale hands. The cape was draped open over her bare legs up to her thighs. The hood was pulled over her hair. Her white face looked like a bright moon against the black fabric. Her legs were dropped open. He'd investigate further in a minute, but she appeared to be nude. That would explain why her teeth were chattering, but her face was shiny with perspiration.

She slid her eyes sideways to look at him and said nothing. It was hard to tell for sure in the nearly dark room, but her pupils looked dilated.

Higher than a kite, Madrigal thought. So much for the cocaine and X he'd brought.

He set the things his client wanted on a table beneath a window near the door. Madrigal never asked questions. He'd just opened his Rolodex—he still used one—made a few calls, and gotten the stuff: cremated human remains and a box of Cuban cigars. He'd gotten a box of cigars for himself, while he was at it. The remains were sealed inside a gallon-sized Baggie. He'd been told to procure the remains of a lawyer, overcomplicating matters, he'd thought. He'd lie if asked. They were human, anyway.

While he was locking the door, he heard Trendi say something.

"Demon."

"Excuse me, honey?"

Her eyes bored into him. She squeezed the cape so tightly that her hands looked translucent.

She moved her eyes to focus on his hat. "That's a demon's hat," she said. "It is a demon's hat." Her speech was clear, but she labored to put the words together.

"It can be any kind of hat you want, doll."

Still standing near the door, he took the flask from his pocket and set it on the table. The room was quiet except for the pounding rain on the thin roof. He sniffed the air. There was the smell of wet wool from her cape but beneath that and the disinfectant was an earthy odor he knew only too well: blood.

The girl's teeth were chattering wildly and her hands were shaking as she held the cape closed. Then blood dripped from the hem onto her bare foot and began to ooze between her fingers.

He pulled open the cape.

She didn't resist. He wondered if she'd forgotten he was there. She dropped her hands and fell back onto the bed.

She was nude, a knife embedded in her belly. Madrigal recognized the WWII-era KA-BAR knife he kept beneath the seat of his truck.

She mumbled incoherently. Her skin was smeared with blood.

He reached for the Smith & Wesson Chiefs Special that he always carried in a pancake holster.

The bathroom door was flung open. "Drop it, Vince."

He recognized the voice. Also familiar was the gun pointed his way: Vince usually kept it in his Cadillac's glove compartment. "Did you do this?" he asked, gesturing at poor Trendi.

"No, Vince. You did."

"So this is how it ends." A violent death was no big surprise. It was astonishing that it hadn't happened sooner. Of course, he would have chosen a classier joint, but all in all, it was a fitting send-off.

TWO

*T*hanks, *honey,* but I'm just going to relax at home. I've cracked a bottle of Veuve and I'm going to enjoy some peace and quiet."

Catherine "Tink" Engleford strolled around the swimming pool in the backyard of her estate in Pasadena's San Rafael hills, while talking on her BlackBerry to her girlfriend and waving a glass of champagne.

"Cheyenne didn't call you?" Tink pursed her lips. The Juvéderm treatments she'd had around her mouth allowed her fifty-four-year-old skin to crinkle slightly. "I agree. She's not the best personal assistant." She laughed.

"Well, she's had a hard life and I'm trying to give her a leg up. We can all use help now and then, right? But yes, it's time for another talk with her when she gets back. She's in Ventura for the weekend and I'm enjoying the peace and quiet."

She changed the subject. The less certain of her friends

knew about her life, the better. "Kingsley's out of town too, on a business trip to Dubai. He's great. It's too soon for us to be spending holidays together anyway. Honey, don't worry about me. I'm fine being alone on Easter. I haven't been alone until just now. I went to the ten o'clock service at Church of the Angels and then I had brunch at Annandale with golfing friends. I'm looking forward to curling up by the fire with a good book."

Tink let out a yelp when her stiletto heel teetered on an uneven piece of flagstone. "Dammit! Spilled champagne on my new St. John." She brushed her bright pink jacket with her fingers and walked across the patio to the open bottle of Veuve Clicquot in an ice bucket. She refilled her glass.

"*Darling,* I only had one tiny mimosa at brunch. Three of my four friends didn't touch a drop. Everyone was going on about how old they are. They can't touch a drop in the middle of the day, they can't wear heels anymore, blah, blah . . . It's like they're in their eighties, not their fifties. When did medical procedures become cocktail party conversation? I couldn't wait to escape and get home."

In truth, Tink couldn't tolerate the flashes of pity in her friends' eyes. The caring hand on her arm, the probing gaze deep into her eyes, and the inevitable question: "How are you *doing?*"

She'd lost her twenty-three-year-old son Derek and her husband Stan in the space of two years. Her son, the product of her first marriage and her only child, had been killed in a motorcycle accident three years ago. Her husband of five years, the love of her life, whom she'd felt blessed to meet in middle age, had dropped dead of a heart attack at the private Annandale golf course just over a year ago. Tink felt like telling the concerned souls, "How the hell do you think I'm doing?"

All things considered, she was all right. Every day she

got out of bed. Every day she did something to improve her mind, body, and spirit. She sought solace in traditional sources: her Anglican faith, good diet, Pilates, and yoga. She'd also dabbled at the fringes, into alternative philosophies and practices. She'd flirted with the occult. The pendulum was swinging back from the fringes. Lately, she'd been doing some spiritual housecleaning. Severing ties that she'd come to learn were more than simply *not nurturing,* but were downright *parasitic.*

She looked at the spot the champagne had left on her jacket. "I can't believe it's already Easter. Can you believe it? I haven't even started on my New Year's resolutions. How can you not make New Year's resolutions? Mine are the same as last year's. Lose weight. Fall in love. Meet my astral shadow."

The last one was a joke.

She paused. "Wait a second, honey." She pressed the phone against her chest and said to her guest, "What are you doing here?"

Tink moved the phone back to her ear. "Honey, I've got to run. I have an unexpected visitor. I'll call later. Bye."

She grimaced, thinking of the unpleasant business she had to take care of. Still holding her BlackBerry, she walked around to the other side of the pool, passing the chaise longues lined up side by side. "I'm not interested in hearing your explanations. I know what I know."

Tink stumbled backward and fell into the pool when a long cushion from one of the chaises hit her. Her champagne glass flew into the water. Disoriented, Tink found her bearings and started swimming for the surface. Her wool knit suit grew heavy and one of her shoes fell off.

Just as her right hand broke through the water's surface, she was again submerged. Her assailant was now in the pool, holding the cushion over her, keeping her from raising her arms. In shock, she opened her mouth and swallowed water. She began to panic.

Stay calm, Tink.

She'd always been athletic and wasn't going down without a fight. She wrenched her body and kicked viciously, touching the side of the pool with her feet. She propelled off of it, moving the two of them and the freaking cushion toward the shallow end. Her toes touched bottom. Then her feet did too.

She clawed at the cushion and felt her acrylic fingernails tearing. Her long blond hair became tangled as she thrashed. Using her hard-earned flexibility and strength, she hooked a leg around her assailant's, shifting the balance. The side of her face broke the surface of the water. She opened her mouth against the cushion and was able to take in a strangled breath. It wasn't much, but enough to keep her going. She got her other leg around, encasing her would-be murderer's other leg in a vise-like grip. They were now both sinking beneath the surface.

You're going down, too, asshole.

She knew it was false bravado as she felt herself growing weaker. Every cell in her body cried for oxygen. Then she felt herself floating off, observing from someplace that had nothing to do with water, earth, or air. The fight didn't so much leave her as it seemed silly to struggle any longer. Her legs released their grip. Her hands opened against the cushion. She was floating. She'd always loved the water. *It will support you if you only let go.* Everything except her lungs felt light and free. They burned. They were all that was holding her back. They would feel free too if she only released that last part. She saw her dead husband and son, smiling, like the last time she'd seen them together. There was something else, lurking at the edges. Was that her astral shadow? She finally let go.

THREE

Pasadena police detective Nan Vining held a dog-eared edition of *The Joy of Cooking*. She pointed to a table-setting diagram for a formal dinner and compared it with the sparkling china, crystal, and silver arrayed on her rarely used dining room table. She noticed that the linen tablecloth that had once been snowy had yellowed with age.

"See, Mom, I told you, spoons on the right and forks on the left."

Holding her glass of chardonnay by the stem, Patsy Brightly returned the forks and spoons she'd moved to their original positions. "Well, that wasn't how I was taught in Home Ec." She inspected her freshly manicured nails. "I thought Stephanie had your grandmother's tableware."

"Steph took it and had no right to." Vining perfected the spacing between a cut-crystal wineglass and a matching tumbler.

They were speaking of Vining's younger sister and only sibling, a stay-at-home mom with two little boys.

"I hope you didn't strong-arm your sister, Nan."

Vining bristled at the belief in her small family that her law-enforcement background spilled over into her personal life. She calmed herself down before responding, determined to not let her mother or anyone disturb her good mood and the festive Easter dinner she'd planned. Her boyfriend and partner at the PPD, Jim Kissick, was coming over with his two teenage boys. They'd gather around the table with her mother, grandmother, and fifteen-year-old daughter, Emily.

Vining responded calmly, "Actually, Mom, Granny asked Stephanie to drop off the tableware at my house." She warmed as she recalled the telephone conversation she'd overheard, in which Granny had told Steph, "Borrow doesn't mean keep, young lady. You can all pick over my bones when I'm dead and buried." In addition to having inherited Nanette Brown's first name, Vining also had her grandmother's flintiness.

"But Steph gives dinners and parties for her husband's business associates and the different charities and school activities she's involved in."

"And I'm just a divorced mom and a homicide detective."

"*Nan* . . . You're always so sensitive when it comes to your sister." Patsy straightened a crisp linen napkin that was edged with embroidered flowers. "I just don't know why you're going to all this trouble. We could have ordered a nice honey-baked ham with all the trimmings from Vons."

"It's fun. I've earned some fun, don't you think?" Vining began setting out the small Easter baskets she was using as place-card holders. She'd filled them each with foil-wrapped eggs, a bunny from See's Candies, and a name card she'd designed and printed on her computer.

She'd spent a week shopping, cooking, and cleaning. Earlier that morning, after the storm had passed through, she'd wiped down the big picture windows in her 1960s tract house and took in the crisp turquoise sky. The two-story home in the Los Angeles neighborhood of Mount Washington, east of downtown L.A., was perched on a hillside on cantilevers and overlooked the city's hindquarters: working-class neighborhoods; the railroad tracks of the Alameda Corridor that ran all the way to the Port of

Los Angeles; the massive County USC Medical Center; and a glimpse of the sparkling skyscrapers of downtown L.A. that peeked above the hilltops.

"Thank goodness it finally stopped raining." Patsy examined her reflection in a window. Still clutching the now-empty wineglass, she fluffed her highlighted blond hair, done in a stylish short cut. She was petite and still trim at fifty-four. It always tickled her when people thought that she and her blond, blue-eyed daughter Stephanie were sisters.

Vining had her mother's facial characteristics from the nose down, but otherwise looked as if she hadn't sprung from the same family. She was tall and lean with an athletic build and nearly black hair that she wore in a blunt cut that brushed her shoulders. Her skin was alabaster and her deep-set eyes were green-gray. Her mother said that she took after her father, of whom Vining had no memories. She knew him only as the first of her mother's four husbands and the jerk who'd abandoned them when Vining was a toddler.

"Giving a formal dinner isn't my idea of fun. I would think you'd take a vacation after everything you've been through." Patsy turned her attention from her reflection to the hems of her peach-colored pants, which matched her floral print twinset that she'd accessorized with a chunky off-white necklace and dangling earrings. "Look what the rain did to my new pants. That's mud from when I went to pick up your grandmother."

Vining was dressed simply, as was her habit, in navy blue slacks and a new argyle pullover in shades of pink and gray. Her only jewelry was silver-and-abalone-shell earrings that Kissick had bought her. "I took a vacation— a two-month unpaid suspension for conduct unbecoming."

"I can't believe the Pasadena police suspended you,

after everything you did for them. For everyone. You were nearly killed. *Again.*"

"I broke the rules. Believe me, it could have been a lot worse."

Vining kept secret the more egregious things she'd done in her obsessive pursuit of the serial killer who'd nearly made her one of his victims. Six months had passed since her final confrontation with the creep. Nearly two years had passed since their twisted relationship had begun when, while working overtime in uniform, she'd responded to an ordinary suspicious-circumstances call at a house in one of Pasadena's well-heeled neighborhoods. After he'd sliced her gun hand with a knife that he'd then buried in her neck, he'd escaped. She'd died for two life-altering minutes.

It was all behind her. She was no longer stuck in that stinking morass into which the creep had dragged her, and was at long last free of him. While the end had been less than perfect, at least it was over and she had come home at End of Watch.

After, she'd again gone through sessions with a department-appointed psychologist. This time, therapy had gone much better, perhaps because she was no longer lying to the shrink in order to be released for duty. Now she felt clear and calm. It was as if, once the creep was gone, she'd been able to unload the giant sack of paranoia and rage she'd been dragging around.

The knife scars remained. There was a long one down the left side of her neck and a smaller one on the back of her right hand. They were fading, but she'd always have them. That was okay. It would keep her from the temptation of pretending that it had never happened.

She was a different person now, but she was still Nan and she was strong and sound. Others, though, persisted in treating her as if she might again break apart along her glued-together seams. She very much wanted her loved ones and colleagues to stop walking on eggshells in her presence. As a sign of renewed vigor, she was taking on new challenges, like tonight's dinner.

Patsy persisted. "That's just what I mean, sweetie. To go to all this trouble is stressful. Plastic plates and forks would have been fine. You're trying to make it perfect. It's just family."

Just family, Vining thought. So like her mother to turn something profound, something Vining had put her heart and soul into building and nurturing, into a throwaway concept. She remembered her vow to let anything her mother might say or do roll off her.

Vining had gone all out for the dinner. The herb-encrusted leg of lamb was roasting, as was the mélange of root vegetables drizzled with the pricey balsamic vinegar that was a splurge. The creamed spinach ingredients were ready, waiting for Jim to apply his culinary magic. Her grandmother was preparing her corn casserole. Her mother was a pie-maker extraordinaire and had promised two homemade pies, but she'd shown up with two purchased from Marie Callender's.

Patsy's justification was on her lips before Vining had a chance to say anything. "When you work the hours I do, you don't have time to make pies."

Vining had decided ahead of time that she was going to remain cool, calm, and collected. Family holiday dinners ranked a close third behind weddings and funerals for bringing out the best—and the worst—in people. She'd swallowed her knee-jerk retort and had thanked her mother for the pies. Now, she again resisted temptation and remained silent instead of taking on her mother's jibe. But she did change her original seating plan and moved the small Easter basket labeled "Patsy" to Jim's right at the far end of the table and placed Granny to her own right.

"I'll uncork those red wines I brought," Patsy said. "The guy at the wine store said they need to breathe."

Shortly, she heard her eighty-four-year-old grandmother yell at her mother in the kitchen, "Why do we need so much liquor?"

"These are very good wines. Cabernet from Sonoma, pinot noir from the Willamette Valley in Washington, and I brought French champagne to have with appetizers."

"I hope you didn't spend much money, Mom," Vining shouted from the dining room. Patsy lived paycheck to paycheck from her job at the Estée Lauder counter at the Macy's in West Covina and had a history of getting in over her head with her credit cards.

The cork Patsy was pulling with the corkscrew came out with a pop. "It's my business how much I spent. We deserve a treat."

"Those wines look expensive," Vining said.

"Don't worry about it."

Granny opened a can of creamed corn. "We don't need that much wine. Nan doesn't drink much and neither does her fiancé."

"They're not engaged," Patsy retorted with a sarcastic tone that set Vining's teeth on edge.

"They will be," Granny said.

"No marriage until Em and Jim's boys are out of the house," Vining said. Jim and his ex-wife had two sons: James, seventeen, and Caleb, known as Cal, thirteen. For the first time in her on-again, off-again romance with Jim Kissick, she envisioned a happily ever after. It would be a relief to stop hiding their romance at work. This dinner was the first formal get-together of the two families.

Patsy peeled the foil from the top of the pinot noir. "I'd like to get married again."

"Thought you broke up with that man, that plastics guy," Granny said.

"His name was Harvey, and he was the Western sales

manager for a polystyrene foam packaging manufacturer," Patsy shot back. "I'm seeing somebody new."

"Why didn't you bring him?"

"He had other plans."

Granny didn't ask for details about the new beau and neither did Vining. Best not to get too attached to them.

Vining entered the kitchen, opened the oven door, and basted the leg of lamb. Out of the corner of one eye, she watched her mother pour some of the pinot noir, swirl the glass, and hold it up to the light. Patsy's newfound interest in fine wines had come with her former beau Harvey, along with golf lessons.

Patsy sipped the wine and stared off into the distance as she swished it around her mouth. She pronounced, "Black cherry and ash." She said to her mother, "Mom, you already put salt in that casserole."

"I did not."

"You did. I watched you."

Granny pointed the wooden spoon she was stirring with at her daughter. "I know that I don't hear all that well, but I am in full possession of my wits. This corn casserole recipe was passed down from my grandmother."

"We know, and you've added too much salt." Patsy downed the pinot and poured the cabernet.

Emily came up the stairs off the kitchen from her domain in the house's former rumpus room. She yanked out one of the earbuds of her iPod, and it dangled across her shoulder.

"There's our girl." Patsy set down her wineglass long enough to hug her granddaughter. "I'm so glad you're spending Easter with us."

"Wasn't my choice. Hi, Granny." Em went to give her great-grandmother a kiss.

"Where else would you be?" Granny asked.

"At the club with my dad and Kaitlyn."

The girl used to disdain what she called her father Wes's "McLife" in his mansion in a gated community with his younger, too-thin new wife Kaitlyn and their two little boys. Wes had made a fortune in property development. Lately, instead of being disdainful, Em had welcomed Kaitlyn's treatment of her as both the daughter and younger sister she'd never had. Vining had at first found Em's new distancing behavior hurtful, as they'd always been close, but she'd come to realize that it was normal. More often lately, instead of feeling hurt, she had the urge to wring the teenager's neck.

Vining had to strong-arm Em into not dressing in all black. She was wearing a soft pink sweater over pencil-leg jeans and Ugg boots. Vining had lost the makeup battle. Em's green-gray eyes, the same color and shape as Vining's, were heavily made up in smoky hues, which created a dramatic effect against her alabaster skin.

Em had an artistic nature that contrasted with Vining's practical one. Vining tried to keep the reins on Em's free spirit without squashing it. As long as Em's grades were good (they were excellent), she did her chores (barely, but she did them), and behaved herself, Vining left her dress and cosmetic choices alone, as long as they were age-appropriate.

Vining stirred her roasting vegetables with a spatula. "And what's better than a nice home-cooked meal?" Granny had never been tall and had shrunken considerably, but her gaze was still intimidating.

"I don't like Jim's sons," Emily said.

Vining closed the oven door. "I don't know why you don't like James and Cal. They're nice boys, and you'll be pleasant and polite to them."

Em shot a dark look at her mother. "We already have a perfectly dysfunctional broken family unit. Why do you want to make it even more complicated?"

Vining set her jaw and didn't respond.

Patsy straightened the gold pendant shaped like a knot with a small diamond that Em was wearing. "At least you're wearing the necklace I bought you."

"I love it. Thank you, Grandma."

"You seem like you're spending a lot of money lately, Mom," Vining said.

Patsy shrugged. "Every girl likes a little glamour now and then."

Vining heard the doorbell. "Em, can you let Jim and his sons in, please?"

Em was typing a text message into her cell phone. "One second."

Vining mustered the equanimity she'd learned from dealing with criminals. She reached over the girl's shoulder and plucked the cell phone from her hand as easily as she might have snapped on a handcuff.

Em knew that if she pushed her mother too far, she'd lose her phone privileges. Having a homicide detective as a mother was more often than not a liability for the teenager. And her mother was not just any detective. She'd become famous as the cop who'd hunted down a notorious serial killer. Em said, "Yes, ma'am."

Vining handed back her daughter's phone and resumed work on the dinner preparations, listening to the chatter of the guests' arrival at the front door. Her back was turned when she felt familiar arms around her waist. Jim Kissick kissed one ear from behind. His breath against her skin made her tingle in all the right places.

Patsy started giggling.

Granny waved her hand, clad in an oven mitt, at Jim. "You character."

Still in Jim's embrace, Vining turned to see what was so funny.

"Happy Easter, bunny." He gave her a peck on the lips

and looked at her with that silly expression he had when he was playing a joke or wanted to provoke a response from her.

She couldn't figure out what was going on until she looked up and saw the pink plush rabbit ears on his head, attached to a headband in his sandy brown hair. He laughed.

She laughed too. "You nut." She greeted his son. "Happy Easter, Cal."

Vining accepted a pot of red tulips from the thirteen-year-old. "Thank you. These are beautiful."

"You're welcome, Mrs. Vining."

She was tickled by the formal way Jim had taught his sons to address their elders.

"Introduce yourself to Mrs. Vining's mother and grandmother, Cal," Jim prompted.

The boy followed his father's instructions.

"Smells great in here," Kissick said.

"My corn casserole," Granny said. "Recipe was handed down from my grandmother."

"Don't tell me you're going to wear those the rest of the day," Cal said. He looked like a young Jim, with mischievous eyes and a quick grin. His face was still soft with baby fat, and he hadn't yet had a growth spurt.

"Better check the casserole." Granny opened the oven door and looked inside. "That corn casserole recipe was passed down from my grandmother." She closed the door.

"You just said that," Cal said to Granny.

"Cal, that's not nice," Jim said.

"Well, she did," the boy insisted.

"Cal . . ." Jim's voice was stern.

"It's all right." Vining took Kissick's bunny ears from his head and tried to put them on Cal.

"No way." The boy jerked around, colliding with

Patsy, who let out a shriek and dropped the chocolate egg she was eating on the floor. Cal stepped on the egg as he ran from the kitchen.

Jim reached for his son's arm but was too late. "Cal, get back here and clean this up."

"Good Lord," Patsy said. "I'm going someplace quieter." She left the room with her wineglass.

"Jim, it's nothing." Vining touched his hand. "Don't make a fuss."

He licked his lips, annoyed with his son, but wanting to mollify Vining. "I'll have a chat with him later." He tore off a paper towel and picked up the squashed chocolate.

"You need to get started on your creamed spinach." Vining began taking the ingredients from the refrigerator and pantry.

Kissick looked them over. "And the nutmeg. I just add a dash."

"Nutmeg?" Vining rubbed her chin. "Oops." She'd forgotten the nutmeg.

"Don't worry about it."

"Shoot. I'm sorry. I want it to be perfect." She sighed. "These are the times I wish Emily drove."

"James can make a run to the market. Speaking of James, where is he? He didn't even come in to greet you."

Vining followed Kissick from the kitchen. They found Em and seventeen-year-old James standing on the terrace. He'd seemed to have grown a foot since Vining had last seen him. He was a good-looking kid with his father's height and sandy hair and his mother's patrician nose and slightly cleft chin.

For a girl who claimed she didn't like Jim's boys, Em's body language argued otherwise. They were leaning against the railing, standing close together and laughing.

Vining went over to them. "Hi, James."

"Hello, Mrs. Vining."

Vining noticed a dreamy look in Em's eyes.

Kissick didn't mince words. "What's up with you coming into Mrs. Vining's house and not saying hello?"

"I didn't know where—"

"Don't—"

Vining put her hand on Jim's arm. "Jim, it's fine. No big deal. The nutmeg?"

An hour later, everything was ready and on the table, the serving dishes covered with aluminum foil. Granny was dozing on the La-Z-Boy. Cal was engrossed in playing a game and texting his friends on his cell phone. Patsy was into another glass of wine, lost in thought as she stood on the terrace and looked at the view, having an uncharacteristic introspective moment.

Vining and Kissick were both in the kitchen, leaning against the counter, wondering where Em and James were.

"I'll try him once more." Kissick pulled out his cell phone. "He's going to have hell to pay."

They heard the front door open.

When Vining found them in the entryway, Emily was combing her hair with her fingers. Her lips looked especially rosy and her cheeks were flushed.

Kissick snatched the small plastic grocery bag that James handed him. "Where have you been?"

James shrugged in the way that only a teenager can. "At the market."

"You've been gone for almost an hour."

Em giggled. "Has it been that long?"

"You're not exonerated either, young lady."

The girl bristled at being reprimanded by Kissick.

Vining held out her arms, trying to usher them toward

the dining room. "Let's just sit down and have a nice dinner together."

Platters were passed and plates and wineglasses were filled. Just before everyone was about to dig in, Kissick said, "Hold on. Let's say grace."

Cal said, "Good food, good meat, good God, let's eat."

James and Emily snickered.

"Children should be seen and not heard," Granny said.

"Cal," Kissick said.

Patsy's cell phone rang. "I have to get that." She caught her foot on the chair as she got up, stumbling.

James and Em, sitting across the table from each other, chuckled.

"Let's pass the food," Vining said. "Jim, would you mind serving the lamb?"

He stood and picked up the platter. "Not at all. Granny, how do you like your lamb?"

"No pink on it," Granny said.

Emily and James continued to giggle, both of them looking into their laps.

Kissick snapped, "Are you two texting each other? Stop it."

Patsy returned to the table. "Thought it was my new guy." She raised her wineglass to her lips. "He promised to call. Ha. Men are dogs. What else is new?"

Under her breath, Emily said, "The women in this family can't hang on to men."

"Emily," Kissick snapped. "Don't be disrespectful to your grandmother."

Cal ate a spoonful of the corn casserole. "This is salty!"

"Don't be rude, Cal," Kissick said.

Patsy confronted her granddaughter. "Let me tell you something, little girl . . ."

The group erupted in argument.

Vining sat in her chair with her hands in her lap, seeing her vision for her new life evaporating. She began rapping a wineglass with a butter knife. The glass broke, splattering her and the linen tablecloth with red wine.

They all gaped at her.

She shouted, "I made this freaking dinner and we're going to eat it. Happy Easter!"

She picked up her knife and fork, and began cutting into her perfectly cooked and seasoned leg of lamb.

Everyone followed, sitting in stony silence, eating to the sounds of silverware against china plates.

FOUR

The next morning, Vining drove Emily to school. The storm clouds in the sky had broken but the tension between mother and daughter had not.

Vining knew that time, the great haze-master, would blur the prickly edges of last night's dinner disaster. It was precisely the type of event that, years hence, they'd all have a good laugh over. Today was not that day.

She inched her aging Jeep Cherokee forward in the queue of parents dropping off their children at the Coopersmith School. The public high school for the arts occupied several early-twentieth-century Craftsman-style buildings on a grassy knoll above the never-completed segment of the 710 freeway in Pasadena. The fast-moving clouds had gathered and the rain had started again. Southern Californian drivers would barrel right across anything less than a 6.0 earthquake but a rainstorm incited paralysis.

There was an electronic ping on Emily's cell phone.

Emily detected the subtle change in her mother's demeanor. "I'm not responding to it. No phone calls or texting for forty-eight hours. Except to you or Dad. For an emergency."

Vining dipped her head in confirmation. Emily having cleaned up after the party and having issued a terse apology wasn't sufficient. Vining had demanded meatier punishment.

Emily gave a dejected look out the passenger window and released a melodramatic sigh. "I hate the rain."

This was something resembling conversation. Vining considered it a breakthrough. "We sure need it. They're talking about rationing water this summer."

"They're always talking about rationing water. There's never enough water. There's never enough anything."

Vining was tempted to say: *There's enough garbage . . . crime . . . negativity . . .* Instead, she said, "Seems that way, sometimes."

She finally made it inside the parking lot and stopped beneath a covered portico.

Em began waving madly at her three best girlfriends. She snatched her backpack and bounded from the car with a cheery, "Bye, Mom," her sullen mood passing with the same fickleness as the rain clouds that had again parted, revealing blue sky.

"Bye, Sweet Pea," Vining said as the car door slammed shut, adding, "Have a good day," through the windshield. She watched Emily walk backward in front of her friends as she told a story with dramatic flair. The four friends were similarly dressed and wore variations of the same hairstyle.

Vining thought of her girlfriends from her school days.

When she was Em's age, they'd been everything to her. Time passed and they'd drifted, as people do, without a real effort to stay in touch. She was terrible about that. She rarely sent Christmas cards, only acknowledged the birthdays of close family, and was often late with that.

Her mother, on the other hand, had remained close with her three best friends from the all-girls Catholic high school they'd attended. Vining recalled Patsy gossiping and bitching about her friends after a recent get-together. They would follow each other through the gates of Hell, but they were still playing out their teenage rivalries.

Her cell phone rang. The display showed: "Jim Cell."

She answered, "Good morning."

"Good morning. Are you okay?"

"I'm fine. Are you okay?"

"I'm good. Did you sleep all right?" he asked.

"I'm *fine.* I just dropped Em off at school. What's up?"

"Woman was found floating in a backyard pool in San Rafael. She's the homeowner. A widow. Her live-in personal assistant returned from a weekend in Ventura and found her. I just got the warrant to search the contents of the home. I'm headed there now."

"Why didn't you call me when you first heard?"

"I can handle it."

"Please don't coddle me, Jim. That's going to make me really angry. Okay?"

"Okay. I'll see you there." He gave her the address.

"I'll change cars and meet you there."

Within ten minutes, Vining had switched vehicles to a department-issued navy blue Crown Victoria and headed back in the direction from which she had just come. She drove across the Colorado Street Bridge, called "Suicide

Bridge" by the locals. No one knew exactly how many had plunged to their deaths off the white lacy structure that traced a gentle S shape across the arroyo floor, but it was thought to be more than a hundred.

Today, the bridge provided a lighthearted view: a double rainbow over the Rose Bowl. The lower one was big and spectacular. The smaller second one was above it and off to one side, like an eyebrow. Vining wondered whether, if the bridge's last suicide victim had seen these rainbows, he would have jumped or whether the hopefulness implicit in them would have only added to his psychic angst.

She exited the bridge, crossed over the freeway, and headed up San Rafael Avenue, which twisted past multimillion-dollar homes nestled into the hillsides, some facing the private Annandale Golf Club. Vining was familiar with this neighborhood. During her thirteen years on the force—four as a detective and most of the rest spent as a patrol officer—she'd learned every nook and cranny of Pasadena's twenty-three square miles. She'd gotten to the point where she could hardly drive down a street and not recall a crime or a situation. Like all veteran cops, she'd come to believe that she'd seen it all and that nothing about human nature—from our sparkling better angels to the depths of depravity—could surprise her anymore. It was heartening that she hadn't lost the ability to be elevated at the sight of a rainbow.

She rounded a curve and saw PPD black-and-white prowlers, white Forensic Services sedans, and Crown Vics crammed along the narrow street. Yellow barrier tape across the front of the large property marked the scene's outer perimeter.

The house was not hidden behind gates like many in the neighborhood, but was unfenced on a hilltop. The lawn looked like apple-green velvet after the spring

showers. Vining imagined Em tsk-tsking at the wasteful-
ness of such a vast lawn in arid SoCal.

The house was a two-story Cape Cod painted white
with black shutters and front door. There was no artful
landscaping, fountains, color-of-the-moment house paint,
fancy window treatments, or any type of designer stakes
in the ground. The property quietly suggested money, a
lot of it.

Flower beds were planted with local spring-blooming
favorites: yellow-orange clivia, lilac irises, mounds of
white iceberg roses, and purple pansies. They were the
same bedding plants found in the yards of both the grand
and modest homes in the area, as ordinary and comforting as a pair of old shoes and as welcome each spring as
an annual visit from an old friend.

Vining rifled through her black nylon duty bag in the
trunk for her box of Latex gloves and disposable booties.
The ground was wet, and she didn't want to leave footprints in the house. They'd assume that the woman had
been murdered until they could prove otherwise.

The overnight storm had dumped more than an inch
of rain. It wasn't raining now, but dark clouds moved
quickly across the sky. The air was crisp yet heavy with
moisture, and had a bone-chilling dampness. Birds that
had been hiding from the rain in a giant oak tree started
singing at once.

The command post was set up out of the back of a
Chevy Tahoe. Vining's friend, Lieutenant Terrence Folke,
was the Incident Commander—his first time, as he'd recently been promoted from sergeant. A large, fit, affable
African American, he and Vining had been through tough
situations together on the job.

After she'd checked in with him, she walked up a
weathered brick path that was terraced as it ascended
the hill. On the broad front porch, two white rocking

chairs were set up to take in the western-facing view. Vining snatched a private moment before she entered the dead woman's house, figuratively walked in her shoes, and immersed herself in whatever sad or just stupid circumstances had led her to end up dead and floating in her backyard pool. Soon, she'd become part of the woman's story, and the woman would join Vining's gallery of people who'd met an untimely end.

She looked at the panorama across downtown L.A. She had a hint of this view from her house but here it was unobstructed. The city sparkled after the rain, the colors pure and shimmering in the clean air. She could pick out Catalina Island, thirty miles offshore, looking like a humpback whale in the distance.

She deeply inhaled the fresh air and held it for a second, enjoying the present. She'd lived in the present a lot over the past two years, ever since the creep had stabbed her and left her for dead, but it often hadn't been a good place to be. Now, she relished a different present, the one after the nightmare, the present she'd craved yet feared would never come. Returning to a place where she felt whole had been a struggle that she'd feared she'd lose. Now, she felt truly alive. She felt good and felt no need to justify it. It just was.

Last night's dinner party came back to her. She chuckled. It was already starting to seem funny.

The front door was open. She steadied herself with a gloved hand on the door frame as she pulled the booties over her shoes. Frowning at the uncovered shoes of a uniformed officer who was leaving, she stepped inside the house onto a polished hardwood floor. The only furniture in the entry was a simple Windsor bench.

On the left was a small den with masculine furnishings—a sturdy desk, a wing-backed chair in forest-green leather, a small couch upholstered in a hunting scene print with spaniels and geese, and framed watercolors of ducks.

Built-in bookcases were crammed full. Newspapers were stacked on a corner of the desk.

Past it was a staircase to the second floor. To the right was a wide opening into a formal living room. At the end of the hall, a sunporch was lined with open French doors leading to the backyard. She heard but didn't see Kissick.

She entered the living room, which seemed little used. It had tasteful, traditional furnishings, apart from an antique couch with wood trim that was upholstered in a loud orange-and-green floral print. A baby grand piano was in a corner. There was a fireplace with a surround of weathered brick, similar to that in the outdoor walkway.

Drawn by the odor of a fire, she crossed a large Oriental carpet and maneuvered around furniture to check it out. Through a brass-framed screen, she saw ashes beneath the grate and curled fragments of partially burned white paper. There was a spattering of ashes on the brick hearth. The rest of the room was clean, with barely a hint of dust. The fireplace residue smelled fresh, not dank and musty after having sat in the damp air.

She moved the fireplace screen aside. Dropping to her knees, she grabbed the heavy iron grate and moved it to the hearth. Ashes and tendrils of burnt paper fell off. Taking a small shovel from a set of fireplace tools, she slid it beneath the ashes, lifted a mound of burnt material, and shook it. As ashes fell off, a corner of a paper was revealed. She picked it up with her gloved fingers and stretched behind her to set it on the coffee table. Shifting through the ashes again, she found another incompletely burned fragment.

The paper was off-white parchment. One piece was small, about four inches square, and burned all around. The other was about six by three inches and was not burned along the left edge. Both held strange symbols, like hieroglyphics—interconnected lines, small circles, and block letters—drawn by a fountain pen, one in black ink and the other in dark brown. The symbol on the smaller piece looked like this:

It looked as if there had been more to it, but the edges were burned.

Vining picked up *Traditional Home* from the magazines fanned across the coffee table. She placed one of the burnt fragments inside, turned a few pages, and slipped in the other.

Taking the magazine, she again stepped into the entry hall, her footsteps muffled in the booties. Past the stairway on the left was a television room with well-lived-in, slouchy furniture. On the right was a formal dining room with a table and chairs for ten.

At the end of the hall, she crossed the sunporch and went outside through one of the open French doors, passing beneath a redwood arbor with a wisteria vine. The backyard was big by L.A. standards, but smaller than one would expect for such a large house. The area's older homes had once had acreage, often with fruit orchards, tennis courts, putting greens, small-gauge railroads, or different flights of homeowner fancy. As property values rose, the land had been cobbled away. The shiny leaves of dense ligustrum planted along a fence in back blocked the view of the newer house on the other side, at least up to the second-story windows.

A lemon tree covered in fragrant white blossoms was in one corner. A fruitless plum tree with burgundy leaves was in another. Hibiscus bushes covered with pink flowers hid an enclosure that housed the pool heater and filter. The pool was an old-fashioned oval but had been resurfaced with material that looked like golden sand. It turned the water the muted blue of a Pacific wave washing across the shore. Four teak steamer chairs with striped cushions, bookended by small square tables, were lined along the side. One table held a silver wine bucket with an open bottle of champagne.

A tech from the PPD's Forensic Services Unit, a portly middle-aged Latino, was taking photos of it. Another FSU tech, a young woman with a short wedge hairstyle, was dusting for fingerprints along the steel rail that led down the pool steps. Both techs wore blue jeans and black polo shirts with "Forensic Services" across the back in gold and an embroidered badge on the breast.

Uniformed officers searched the shrubbery around the pool. A young male officer was dragging a long-handled net along the pool's bottom, focused on snaring something.

Vining saw what looked like a champagne glass on the bottom of the pool. She told the male FSU tech about the burnt material in the fireplace that needed to be photographed, removed, and examined.

An eight-foot waterfall of fake boulders was on one end of the pool. It was not running. Near it, Vining saw the victim's lower body. She had on just one bone-colored high-heeled sandal.

A coroner investigator was kneeling on the ground beside her. His back was to Vining, but she recognized Hank by his small stature and white hair. He had to be nearly sixty, and had been with the county coroner's office forever.

Two uniformed officers, one male, one female, were standing near the pool talking. Vining knew them by sight, but didn't know their names. They seemed to be gossiping and it annoyed her. The dead woman deserved respect, even if it turned out that she'd gotten drunk alone and had toppled into the pool in her mansion. Vining had to quell her own prejudices about the wealthy woman's demise. She was not alone among the PPD in having a chip on her shoulder about Pasadena's affluent denizens. The city had poor and middle-class residents, but it was also home to many rich people. Most were supportive of the police but some had attitudes about cops that would rival any gangbanger's.

Kissick stood at the far end of the pool, taking notes on his spiral pad as he interviewed a young Latina. She was statuesque, slender yet shapely in painted-on jeans. High-heeled over-the-knee boots made her nearly as tall as six-foot Kissick. Her cropped denim jacket with fringe along the arms looked like the expensive Juicy Couture model that Emily coveted and that Vining had forbidden the overindulgent Kaitlyn from buying for her stepdaughter.

Vining guessed that the young woman was the dead woman's assistant, who'd found the body. The way she was standing, or rather *posing*—her stance wide, raking her fingers through a mane of auburn-highlighted dark hair that tumbled nearly to her waist, coquettishly flicking her head—telegraphed to Vining that she approached life using sex appeal and flirtation. Vining read nervous agitation in her coltish body language, understandable since she was talking to a detective about her dead boss, but she also picked up something sad and desperate.

Kissick reached to pat the woman's jacket pocket and then started to dig his fingers inside. Vining couldn't hear what he'd said but guessed that he'd used the worn technique that citizens usually fell for—asking if he could search her and going ahead before she had time to respond. It worked most of the time. Citizens weren't well-versed in their civil rights, and were often intimidated by cops.

Not this gal. She pushed away Kissick's hand, took a

backward step, and said, "You can't do that. Give me my phone back."

Kissick held her iPhone. "Have a seat over there."

"That's an illegal search, you . . ." She turned in disgust and headed toward a patio table and chairs. As she passed Vining, she gave her an up-and-down look. She sashayed to the corner, pulled out a chair, and flopped onto it. Crossing her long legs, she raked her voluptuous hair over one shoulder, grabbed a handful, and began looking for split ends.

Vining couldn't help but notice her elaborately manicured long nails. They were polished in a dark grape color with glittery gold and silver vertical stripes.

Kissick smiled warmly as he approached Vining, who was still carrying the *Traditional Home* magazine. "That's Cheyenne Leon, who found the victim. Self-described personal assistant/actress/model/writer. One of those multi-hyphenated people."

"She's a charmer." Vining glanced at Cheyenne, who had turned her attention from her split ends to look somberly at her former employer. "Beneath the attitude, she's scared."

"She's only worked for Catherine Engleford for about two months."

"Worked for *who*?" Vining gaped at Kissick.

"Catherine Engleford. The dead woman."

Her mouth still hanging open, Vining searched Kissick's face, and then frowned at the corpse by the pool. She rushed to look at the body.

Hank, the coroner's investigator, greeted her and she muttered something in response through the fingers she'd pressed against her mouth.

Kissick came up beside her. "Nan, what's going on?"

She looked at him. Rubbing her forehead, she walked away from everyone else there.

He knew she didn't mean to exclude him and he followed.

She blew out air and for some reason focused on the woman's one bare foot. "That's Tink Engleford. She's my mother's best friend."

FIVE

S*he was* a divorced mom with her own small business, struggling along, when she married into the Englefords, who own half of Pasadena." Vining now had a hard time looking at the body. "I knew she lived off San Rafael, but I didn't know where."

She felt calm yet hazy. She'd felt this way before upon receiving terrible news. It would take about ten minutes for the reality to hit her.

Kissick raised his arm as if to put it around her shoulders.

Before he was able to follow through, she snapped, "I'm okay."

He put his hand in his pants pocket.

The two uniformed officers nearby found the huddle between Vining and Kissick interesting and shot looks their way. The detectives took pains to keep their romance a secret at the PPD. While there were a few marriages between officers at the department, couples didn't work together, and absolutely weren't detectives on the same cases.

At a look from Kissick, the officers broke up and started walking toward the house.

Kissick called out to the female officer, a beefy brunette with eyebrows that had been overly plucked into thin arches. "Campbell. I need you to run a background check on Cheyenne Leon sitting over there. Cheyenne, give her your driver's license."

Cheyenne sighed as she stood. "It's in my purse in the house."

Officer Campbell tried to take Cheyenne's arm but she jerked away and strode unassisted toward the house with Campbell trailing her.

"Make sure she doesn't touch anything," Kissick shouted after them. He shouldn't have had to remind Campbell. "Including her purse."

Vining was looking toward Tink and shaking her head. She didn't realize that she had tightly rolled the magazine and was clutching it to her chest between both hands.

Kissick asked, "Sure you're okay?"

"Just thinking about how I'm going to tell my mom." Her voice cracked. She turned to face the fence and brush away a tear.

"I'll take care of it."

"I should tell her. In person."

"I know you can, sweetheart," he said in a near whisper. "But—"

"Jim, please." If they'd been alone, she'd have melted against him, happily supported by his strong arms. But they were not alone.

"I appreciate your concern, but I'm fine. I can do this job. If people think I can't, then I'm going to have to do something else." She paused as she considered that prospect. "And I have no clue what that might be." She'd stumbled into law enforcement. Now it was the only thing she wanted to do.

"Sarge will take me off this case," she said. "It's too close to home."

"We'll let Sergeant Early make that decision. She's pulled everyone to work the Crown City nightclub shooting, which is where we'll be after we button this up, which might be quickly. Let's do what we need to do."

Well-trained at compartmentalizing her emotions, she took a couple of deep breaths.

Kissick took out his spiral pad and clicked open a pen. "How did your mother know the deceased?" His tone was all business, and she was grateful.

"Since high school. They were Ramona Girls."

"Ramona Girls?" Kissick took notes.

"Ramona Convent School in Alhambra. It's an all-girls Catholic school. My mother had three great friends from those days: Vicki, Mary Alice, and Tink. They still stay in touch. Meet for lunch or dinner a couple of times a year. When Tink was married to her first husband and her son was in school, she started a catering business out of her kitchen. It grew and she opened a storefront place in Pasadena. She got divorced. I understand it was bitter. She supported herself and her son. She catered a wedding at the Annandale clubhouse. Stan Engleford was a guest. He was one of Pasadena's most eligible bachelors. Divorced with grown kids and grandkids. They got married about five years ago. It must be just about a year since he dropped dead on the seventh green at Annandale. Heart attack. He was golfing with his friend John La Barbera. Tink was having drinks with John's wife, Lynn Caffrey Gabriel, on the terrace of their house above the green. Tink saw Stan collapse.

"Just two years before, Lynn and John hosted a reception on that same terrace after the funeral of Tink's son. The reception for Stan was held at the Valley Hunt Club. His adult kids insisted or something." She frowned, wondering why these minor details were coming back to her.

"Tink's son died two years before her husband?"

"Yep. Derek was her only child. He was twenty-three. Was on his motorcycle turning left from Glenarm onto the Pasadena Freeway. A drunk driver blew through the red light at the end of the freeway and broadsided him. Propelled fifty feet onto Arroyo Parkway. Killed instantly."

Kissick stared at her for a second, and then said, "I remember that accident. I didn't know you knew that family."

"We weren't together then." Vining looked at Hank as he worked on the body. "Tink had a terrible battle with Stan's adult children over the estate. It was ugly. His kids did fine, believe me, but they didn't want Tink to get anything. The kids claimed she was a gold digger, but it was a true love story. She came away with most of it.

"I have to hand it to my mother. She helped Tink get through both of those times. Especially after Stan's death when Tink was alone. Derek hadn't had kids. Tink was an only child. Her father is long dead, and her mother has Alzheimer's. My mom would come over here and make sure Tink got out of bed and brushed her hair and put on makeup."

Vining let out a sad laugh. "Even while my mother was being a true friend, she'd snipe about how much better she'd look if she had Tink's money to spend on dermatologists, plastic surgeons, and Pilates. Sometimes, the two of them acted like they'd never left high school. My mother . . ."

Her voice trailed off after she'd uttered those two simple and profound words. She gave a small shake of her head, as if there was much more than words could express. "The queen of spats and grudges. She'd talk about how Tink would, in her words, 'Lord her wealth over Vicki, Mary Alice, and me.' Granted, my mother tends to take things personally. She'd talk about Tink ordering expensive bottles of wine at dinner when the friends' tradition was to split the tab. Tink would say, 'I'll pay for the wine. I can't drink that cheap stuff. It gives me a headache.'

"Tink wasn't my favorite of my mom's friends. She could be shallow. Too concerned with money and labels. If she bought a new watch, it came with a pedigree, which she would describe to you. I remember a snide comment Tink made when I graduated from the police academy. It was something like, 'Now you'll never get a man, Nan.' My mother hadn't been on board with my career choice either, but boy did she land on Tink."

"I knew you got that toughness from someplace."

"For all Patsy's flakiness, she's tougher than she seems. Still, Tink was a good friend to my mother. She got her a nice used car for next to nothing through the Engleford family's Mercedes dealership. Tink was generous with her friends. She treated the girls to spa days at Ojai and to a retreat at Berryhill in Malibu Canyon." Vining stared off.

"Where'd you go, partner?" Kissick asked.

"Just thinking about my mother and her friends. I guess that's the nature of girlfriends. Complicated."

Kissick made notes. "Is Berryhill that place run by that self-help maven?"

"Yep. My mom said that Tink had bought into the whole Berryhill shtick. My mom saw it as another way for Tink to throw away money, but I think Tink was looking for ways to deal with her grief."

"How was Tink's mental state lately?"

Vining shrugged. "I don't know. My mother and the other Ramona Girls might have insight into that. Tink knew a lot of people, but I don't know who else she was close to. My mom and Tink, both being single, had drawn closer recently, but my mother complained that

Tink barely had time for her. Tink traveled in different circles."

Vining took a deep breath and then abruptly walked to where Hank was working on the body. Vining looked at Tink. She'd seen enough corpses to know that Tink had been dead awhile. She was bloated and rigid. She'd been floating facedown in the water, and her face and the front of her body were discolored.

She recalled the words of the now-retired lieutenant who was her first mentor: Think of them as just dolls. That had never worked for her. She could never separate herself from the knowledge that the victims are human, perhaps even most profoundly in their last scenes on earth. What was more human than suicide and murder? It was her job to tease the last threads of their stories from their broken bodies, to bring the bad guys to justice, and to give the victims' loved ones a modicum of comfort from knowing the facts. Not "closure." She knew from personal experience that closure was feelgood, talk-show drivel mouthed by people who didn't want to face the reality that one's life could be permanently damaged by a single event. That one never gets over it, but learns to live the rest of one's life with it, like a shadowy elephant in the room. Still, there was some comfort in being able to put a final period on a tragic story.

Hank had unbuttoned Tink's jacket, revealing a blushpink, lace-trimmed camisole with her bra beneath it. With sublime gentleness, he pulled the camisole from her skirt waistband. "I couldn't cut open these beautiful clothes."

Vining imagined Tink floating in the pool all night in her expensive knit suit beneath the pounding rain. Her earlier feelings of oneness, of being present in the world, had evaporated and were replaced with more familiar emotions: sadness and anger about a vibrant life cut short and a complex soul departed from this world.

Hank had taken a thermometer with a spiked end from his equipment bag. Instead of swinging his arm and stabbing it into her liver, like Vining had often seen done, he applied just enough pressure until it pierced her skin and went beneath the surface.

Still, Vining did something she hadn't done for years at these times. She flinched.

After a bit, Hank rolled back onto his heels. "I'd say she's been dead about twenty to twenty-four hours."

"It's ten in the morning now." Kissick looked at his watch. "So she died yesterday between ten in the morning and two in the afternoon. Any signs of foul play, Hank?"

"I don't see any defensive wounds. No bruising on her chest or neck as if she'd been held down. She might have become dizzy, maybe from drinking, or maybe she had a stroke or a heart attack, and fell in. Suicide seems unlikely. Pills are more typical for a woman like her. Found in bed in a pretty nightgown. Suicide note. Suicide by drowning like this without anything to weigh her down . . . That's rough. The autopsy and the toxicology tests will tell us the most in this case."

Vining looked at Tink's pearl earrings surrounded by small diamonds. She noticed something else. "Why is her eye makeup so smeared?"

"Wouldn't being in the water make it bleed?" Kissick asked.

"Not like that. Those are raccoon eyes, as if she was rubbing them. She could have been crying."

A uniformed officer who had been searching the grounds came over. He had brush-cut hair and his name tag said J. Garcia. He handed Kissick one of two small manila evidence envelopes he was holding. "We found her Black-Berry, Detective. It was in those bushes."

"Why was it in the bushes?" Vining asked.

"Maybe she got pissed off and threw it." With his gloved hand, Kissick took out the phone and pressed the power button. "Battery's probably dead." He dropped it back inside the envelope and handed it to Garcia. "See if you can find a charger and plug it in."

"Detective, we also found this in the pool catch basket." Garcia held out the second small evidence bag. "It's a fake fingernail."

Kissick opened the envelope and peered at the acrylic nail polished in a French manicure style with a white tip and pinky beige base.

He handed the bag to Vining, who said, "Ragged edge, like it was torn off. Not unusual. Sometimes they get caught on stuff, but why was it in the pool?"

Hank picked up Tink's right hand, which was encased in a plastic bag. "I noticed one of her acrylic nails was missing."

Vining looked at a large square-cut diamond ring on that finger. Tink had had a new ring made using the stone from her engagement ring.

Hank tugged on Tink's other nails. "Here's another one that's nearly torn off. Maybe she grappled for the side of the pool."

"Her eye makeup is smeared and her fingernails are torn." Vining planted a hand on one hip. "Maybe she struggled to get out of the pool and was too incapacitated to make it, or she could have been fighting for her life with someone who was holding her down. We can't rule out murder."

SIX

"M urdered? *No* way. Tink got drunk and fell in the pool."

They turned to see Cheyenne Leon standing behind them.

Kissick snapped, "What are you doing here?" He shouted for the officer who was supposed to be watching her. "Campbell, get out here."

Campbell bolted through the French doors. "Yes, sir. I just finished running a background check like—"

"I asked you to stay with the suspect."

"Suspect?" Cheyenne coiled her full lips, revealing pearly white teeth. Standing assertively with a wide stance, she darted her hand toward the wine bucket. "That champagne bottle is empty." She made the same gesture toward Tink's body, as if it was a garbage bin on the street that the city had neglected to empty. "She's been dead a long time. Anyone can see that. I only got back this morning. My friends will vouch for me. I'm the one who called the police."

Kissick and Vining both watched her grappling with her wall of words, knowing what the other was thinking. Cheyenne was doing a lot of explaining.

The coroner's investigator left. Vining and Kissick muttered good-byes. Vining looked at Tink's body and was glad to see that Hank had covered it head-to-toe with a thin synthetic-fiber blanket.

Officer Campbell, who was standing to the side fiddling

with her field notebook, found her opportunity to jump in. "I have the information about the friends she says she was with, Detectives." She handed Vining a piece of paper. "Her background check shows that she has a criminal record."

This news didn't surprise them. Vining held up her index finger, stopping Campbell. She told Cheyenne, "It's true that you reported finding Mrs. Engleford's body. *After* you burned papers in the fireplace."

Vining was rewarded when she saw a glint of shock flicker in Cheyenne's eyes. She unrolled the magazine she was holding and opened it to where she'd stuck one of the burnt parchment fragments.

Kissick frowned as he looked at the mysterious symbols over her shoulder.

Vining asked Cheyenne, "What is this?"

Cheyenne had recovered her tough edge, saying in a singsong voice, "I don't know."

"What about this?" Vining showed her the second burnt piece of paper, which was also covered with symbols.

Cheyenne raised an eyebrow and smirked, looking bored.

"Why did you burn these in the fireplace?"

"I didn't." Cheyenne had a second thought. "You can't prove that."

"Maybe I can't, but I know you did it." Vining met Cheyenne's insolent gaze. "You're hiding something, and I'm going to find out what it is."

As Vining flipped the magazine closed, Cheyenne retorted, "Don't flatter yourself."

Vining pointed at the patio table and chairs at the far side of the pool. "Sit down."

Cheyenne sauntered away. "Look at the detective, showing she can be a hard-ass."

"Lady, you don't know the half of it." Vining fixed

Cheyenne with the dead stare that she'd learned from Kissick, the master. The stare that gave up nothing but that sucked in everything.

While Officer Campbell was waiting for the right time to reveal her information, Kissick didn't hide his amusement over the exchange.

"Go," Vining said to Campbell, telling her to continue.

Campbell pulled herself taller and read from her field notebook. "Her address on record is on Malibu Canyon Road in Malibu. No current wants or warrants. Couple of arrests for drug possession and prostitution. Two convictions. Most recent was three years ago."

Cheyenne jumped up from the chair and whipped off her jacket, revealing her shapely figure in a tight white tank top. She slapped the inside of one arm, then the other. "I was a junkie, okay? I did heroin and turned tricks to keep myself high all the time. I've been clean and sober three years."

"Why are you living with a drunk?" Vining asked.

The question caught Cheyenne off guard. She rapidly blinked her green eyes.

Vining goaded her. "For someone whose boss just died under suspicious circumstances, you're not very upset. I would have thought that you'd at least be sad that you're out of a job. You're just ticked off about having to deal with us. I don't know why Mrs. Engleford hired you, let alone let you live in her house. Can you explain that to me, Cheyenne?"

Cheyenne again seemed sad, like she'd shown briefly earlier. She again raked her long hair over her shoulder and looked at the ends as she chewed her lip. Her shoulders rose and fell as she took in a deep breath, as if settling on a decision. "You should talk to this guy Tink was dating. King Getty."

"Getty?" Kissick asked. "Like the oil family Gettys?"

"He said he was a cousin or something." She looked up at Kissick from beneath her eyebrows and pouted.

Vining thought that she couldn't stop herself from flirting with men.

"King?" he asked.

"That's what he called himself. He wasn't a king of anything, except BS."

Kissick took out his spiral pad. "Do you know where he lived?"

"On the Westside, I think. His info should be in Tink's BlackBerry."

"What did he do for a living?" Vining asked.

Cheyenne shrugged. "Movie producer, investor . . . Whatever guys like him say they do."

"Why do you think he might be involved?" Kissick asked.

"I'm not saying he is. I'm not saying anything other than you might want to talk to him."

Vining looked at Kissick. She could tell he agreed that at least Cheyenne had given up that information. "How was Mrs. Engleford's mood lately?"

Cheyenne raised her hand as if she couldn't put her answer into words. "Tink was Tink."

"What does that mean?"

"She stayed busy. All the time. People, parties, meetings, lunches . . . She was always on. Who knew what she was really feeling?"

"You think she got drunk and fell in the pool." Kissick made a few notes in his scribbled shorthand and looked up at her. "How often did she drink?"

Cheyenne shrugged. "Most nights. She liked to drink. Too much. But that's me. I don't drink."

When Kissick paused, Vining pointed at one of the teak steamer chairs and asked no one in particular. "Why is a cushion missing?"

Cheyenne took the question to be directed at her and bristled. "I was Tink's assistant, not her housekeeper."

Vining couldn't resist. "I hope Tink had better judgment in who she hired as a housekeeper."

Cheyenne raised her index finger and shook her head, rattling the gold hoops in each ear. "There's no cause for you to talk to me that way."

They turned to see Detective Alex Caspers, who was walking across the patio as if he was entering a yacht.

The young, perennially tail-chasing detective gave Cheyenne a prolonged once-over and she did the same, twirling a lock of hair around her finger.

"Hey, Nan. Jim. What do we—"

They heard a blast of rap music.

While it played, Cheyenne propped her elbow on the patio table, put her head in her hand, and quietly cursed.

Kissick pulled out Cheyenne's iPhone that he'd confiscated from her. He read the display, "Private call." He answered, "Hello. Hello." He held out the phone to again look at the display. "Hung up."

"You had no right to take my phone and answer my calls," Cheyenne said. "My attorney's gonna know about this."

"Your attorney," Vining said.

"Whoa . . . Attitude . . ." Caspers said with admiration.

Sitting in the patio chair with her long legs crossed, Cheyenne played to the young detective's interest in her, giving him a head toss, sending her mane flying, then looking away, pretending to ignore him.

"Who was trying to call you, Cheyenne?" Kissick looked through the phone's call log. "Private call. Private call. Two other private calls this morning. No calls beyond that. And no text messages. Why did you delete your phone and text message history, Cheyenne?"

"It's none of your business."

"We can get your call history from your cell phone carrier," Vining said.

"You need probable cause to get a warrant," Cheyenne shot back.

"Oh. Said like a lawyer or a criminal." Caspers smiled crookedly, showing his bright smile, which women found adorable. He was twenty-eight with dark hair and eyes and attractive, well-balanced features, but wasn't too handsome to be intimidating. He seemed incapable of hiding the effect that Cheyenne was having on him.

"That would be a criminal," Vining said.

"You'd better get off my case or you're gonna have a big problem." With her elbow still on the table, Cheyenne lowered her arm and pointed at Vining. "You have no idea who you're dealing with."

"Oh-ho!" Caspers exclaimed. "And who might we be dealing with?"

Cheyenne raised both hands, palms up.

"I've had enough of this," Vining said. "Officer Campbell, take Cheyenne to the station."

"Station? Am I under arrest?"

Kissick attempted to tone down the animosity. "Cheyenne, we just want to sit and have a conversation with you in a quiet place."

"Unless I'm under arrest, I'm not going."

Vining shrugged. "Fine. You're under arrest."

"What charges?"

"Breaking and entering."

"*What?* I live here."

"Your driver's license has a Malibu address."

"I didn't have time to have it changed at the DMV. This is bullshit."

"Campbell, take her to the Detectives Section. Stay with her until we get there." Vining sensed that Cheyenne's bluster was an act and that she was afraid. "I need the contact information for her friends in Ventura."

Cheyenne stood, snatched her jacket, and put it on. She held her hand toward Kissick. "I need my phone to call my attorney. Carmen Vidal." She said the name as if uttering it would stop all conversation.

"Vidal." Caspers nodded. "That's high-end representation."

"I had no idea that being a personal assistant to a Pasadena socialite paid that kind of dough," Vining said.

Cheyenne leveled a gaze at Vining. "Like I told you. You don't know who you're dealing with."

"You're dying to tell us, Cheyenne," Kissick said. "Why not help us and put it out there?"

Cheyenne shook her head, her smile angled. She put her hands behind her and offered her back to Officer Campbell. "Go ahead. Cuff me. Let's get this over with. Give the officer my cell phone. I want her to call Carmen Vidal. Have her meet me at the station."

Kissick handed Cheyenne's phone to Campbell, who then pulled her handcuffs off her utility belt and went about cuffing Cheyenne. "Mirandize her. Let her call her attorney and only her attorney. Caspers, what are you doing right now?"

"Sarge sent me over here to see if you need help. I have to be in court at three."

Kissick looked at his watch. "Want to make a run to Ventura and check out Cheyenne's alibi? It'll be tight for you to get back in time."

Caspers took the paper with the contact information from Vining. "I can do it. No problem."

"The way you drive," Vining said.

Caspers shrugged. "Hey, did you hear about Vince Madrigal?"

"Caught it on the radio," Kissick said. "I'm surprised someone didn't off him long before this."

"You mean the guy with the big mustache and black cowboy hat?" Vining asked.

"Yeah," Caspers said. "The hood ornament of bull horns on his Cadillac. Supposedly Elvis gave him that car."

"What happened?" Vining asked.

"My buddy with LAPD Northeast Division told me that he stabbed some girl and she shot him. Two down at once. Happened at some dump in Eagle Rock. She was twenty-two. Priors for drug possession, prostitution, shoplifting. Madrigal could get high-end tail. Why bother with that skank? She had a porn-star name. What was it? Try Me Talbot or something."

Cheyenne stopped in her tracks as Officer Campbell was leading her from the area. She swung her head to gape at Caspers. "Trendi Talbot?"

Caspers pointed. "That's it. Trendi. You know her?"

Cheyenne let out a sound of anguish. Her legs crumpled. Campbell tried to keep her on her feet but Cheyenne dropped to her knees. She arched her back and wailed, "Trendi . . ."

"How do you know her, Cheyenne?" Vining asked.

"Not Trendi . . ." Cheyenne flopped forward, her head against her thighs.

The three detectives exchanged glances.

Campbell tried to get her back on her feet, but Cheyenne wouldn't budge. Her shoulders shook as she keened against the cement.

Kissick caught Caspers's eye and hitched his head toward Cheyenne. The younger detective moved to help.

Vining and Kissick watched them leave at the same time that two coroner techs appeared carrying a collapsible gurney to transport Tink's body.

Vining commented, "Cheyenne was right about one thing. I have no clue what we're dealing with."

SEVEN

Kissick took out his iPhone and brought up a browser. "Let's see if there're any news reports about the Vince Madrigal murder. Here's something. Trendi Talbot, spelled with an I."

Vining scowled. "Who would give their baby girl the name Trendi? Now presenting Senator Trendi Talbot or CEO of Verizon *Trendi Talbot*. I don't think so. Dooms her from birth to being—"

"A prostitute?" Kissick offered.

"Or a porn star."

Kissick brushed his fingers against the touch screen. "Nothing more than what Caspers told us. Says Trendi's last known address was on Malibu Canyon Road."

"Cheyenne's driver's license has a Malibu Canyon Road address," Vining said. "Upscale. Won't find any beach shacks there."

"And Cheyenne bragging about her big-ticket attorney, Carmen Vidal."

"Maybe the two of them are porn stars or call girls," Vining said. "But why was Cheyenne with Tink?"

The coroner techs loaded Tink's body onto the gurney, pulled up and locked the scissor legs, and pushed it across the patio. One of the techs came over to them with a clipboard.

Vining and the tech exchanged pleasantries about the weather as Kissick took the clipboard, scribbled on the form attached to it, and handed it back.

Vining watched as Tink's body was rolled away. She looked at her watch. "My mom doesn't go to work on Mondays until two. She usually does her laundry in the morning. I'd like to catch her at home before she leaves."

They were alone in the backyard. He looked at her with his deep-set hazel eyes that she loved, full of affection and concern, something she hadn't realized how much she'd craved in a man's gaze until he'd made it safe for her to feel vulnerable.

"Nan, I know you're tough, but you don't need to put yourself through having to break this to your mother. I'm more than happy to do it."

"Jim, thanks, but I'm okay. I'll let you know if and when I'm not. I now see how trapped I was when I was chasing the creep who tried to kill me. It was like I was in quicksand. But that's in the past." She looked around to make sure they were alone before she let her fingers trail against his hand. "Please believe me."

He smiled at her with closed lips. The smile crept into his eyes. "Okay."

"Okay."

Tink's bedroom shed no light on the cause of her demise but it did trace an outline of her heartache. It was the simple things. One nightstand was crammed with books and magazines, reading glasses, a box of tissues, and a clock, while the matching nightstand on the other side was bare. The three photographs in silver frames on the fireplace mantel would be nice but unremarkable family photos if one didn't know Tink's history.

One was from Tink and Stan's wedding day. Vining's mother had been a guest at the small wedding on the sand at the private Jonathan Club on Santa Monica beach. The photo showed Tink and Stan barefoot on the sand. Behind them, the sun was just above the horizon, and the necklace of Santa Monica Bay was bathed in pink and orange light.

A breeze ruffled Tink's loose blond hair and her simple white knee-length summer dress, its elastic peasant neckline pulled down to expose her shoulders. She carried a small bouquet of pale pink roses.

The groom was wearing white chinos and a Hawaiian shirt with a floral print. One hand was around Tink's waist and the other buried behind the bouquet, probably holding hers. They gazed into each other's eyes, and their joy leaped from the photo. Vining had half-believed her mother's line that Tink had married Stan for his money. This photo showed two people in love.

Another photo was of Tink's son Derek. It had been taken on a fishing trip. Derek was a toothy preteen, grinning broadly as he proudly held up a string of silvery fish in one hand, a fishing pole in the other.

The last was of Tink, Stan, and an adult Derek snapped in a restaurant booth. Derek had grown into a good-looking young man who took after his mother. He was tipping the edge of a scalloped cardboard base beneath a round birthday cake covered with blazing candles. Reading the inscription on the cake, Vining saw that it was Derek's twenty-third birthday. Later that year, a drunk driver would broadside his motorcycle.

"The most important men in Tink's life dead within two years of each other." She picked up the photo of Derek as a boy. "How do you move on with your life after that?"

Kissick had come close to experiencing such a loss. He'd sat by Vining's hospital bedside while she was in a coma for three days, talking and reading to her, living in a twilight world, wondering if she'd come back.

He clasped her face between his hands and kissed her. She was at first surprised, but was soon swept up, digging her fingers into his hair and circling her other hand, still holding the picture frame, around his back.

They parted with small pecks on the lips, like an ellipsis.

She stroked his cheek, smooth from his morning shave. She liked touching his strong jaw, which for her epitomized his inner and outer strength. She looked into his hazel eyes, always finding more colors and depths, wondering if she'd ever discover everything they held.

She released him and set the photo back in its exact spot, which she identified by a small layer of dust behind the frame, showing where the housekeeper had cut corners.

A chilly wind blew through the open windows, as if a reminder of the bleak task that had brought them there. The wind billowed the drapes and gave flight to papers stacked on the nightstand.

Kissick picked them up. "Looks like Tink was involved with something called Georgia's Girls."

"I've heard of that. I think it's a place for women prostitutes and drug addicts who were living on the streets that's run by Georgia Berryhill, the self-help maven."

He looked through the documents. "Profit-and-loss statement. Plans for a fund-raiser. Gig Towne's slated to be the emcee."

"Gig Towne the actor?"

"Must be." He shuffled through the pages. "Wolfgang Puck is going to cater."

"Fancy." Vining went to the windows and closed them. The sills were wet from rain. She reached to pick up something from the floor that Kissick had missed. "Here's the brochure from last year's Georgia's Girls fund-raiser."

On the cover of the multifold brochure was a black-and-white shot of Georgia Berryhill arm in arm with two well-scrubbed, smiling young women. On the inside cover were two more photos of young women. One was vacant-eyed and filthy on a mattress on the floor of what looked like a crack house. The other was standing on a curb tricked out in trashy provocative clothing. Captions identified them as two of Georgia's success stories who were pictured on the cover. Vining looked at the cover again. The transformation was remarkable. There were also photos of celebrity supporters, including Gig Towne, with rescued young women.

"Tink's listed as one of their top donors," Vining said. She handed him the brochure and started opening dresser drawers and rifling the contents.

Kissick looked through the other materials on the nightstand. A pair of reading glasses with purple plastic frames were on top of one of Georgia Berryhill's books: *The Method and You: Happy, Healthy, and Whole!*

In the nightstand drawer he took out a white plastic bottle with a raspberry-colored top. "Berryhill brand herbal sleep enhancer. Nighty Night." He looked at the remaining gel caps inside and dropped the bottle into a manila evidence bag.

"Her medicine cabinet is full of over-the-counter sleep aids," Vining said from the bathroom. "I'm not surprised that Tink had sleeping problems." She tossed items into evidence bags.

The well-appointed closet was packed with designer clothes, shoes, and accessories. There was a freestanding jewelry cabinet. In the lock was a small brass key attached to a fob of dangling glass beads that spelled: "Girlfriend."

Vining opened the shallow drawers, which were packed with real and costume jewelry. "Wow." She picked up a flashy cocktail ring and looked at it in the light. "Those look like real diamonds. My mother always talked about Tink's beautiful jewelry."

She opened drawer after drawer, ogling the treasures. "If Tink surprised a burglar, he hadn't gotten far. Wonder if she always left the key in the lock. Can't imagine she'd trust Cheyenne."

She shook her head and said, "I still can't figure out why she let Cheyenne live here."

They looked through the other rooms on the upper floor, finding Cheyenne's room on the opposite end of the hall from Tink's bedroom. It was cheerful and comfortable. A leather satchel was on a bench at the end of the bed. Inside was women's clothing sufficient for a weekend away. The small closet held a few garments and pairs of shoes. The contents of the dresser drawers were also sparse. The adjacent bathroom had the bare essentials of personal products.

"Cheyenne said she was living here," Kissick said. "Looks like she was stopping by."

Vining unzipped a pocket on the back of the satchel. Inside was a creased and faded color snapshot. "Look at this."

He walked over to see.

The photo showed three girls who might have been older teenagers standing on a wooden deck beside water. It looked like a party. Clutches of people were in the distance. Lit paper lanterns were strung above. The girls wore skimpy dresses in shiny fabrics and bold colors, flashy costume jewelry, and high-heeled sandals. They had their arms around one another and were half-standing and half-leaning against each other. One girl was holding a cigarette. All of them had big, loose grins and one was caught in mid-shout.

"That's Cheyenne in the middle," Kissick said.

"They look drunk." Vining flipped it over. Handwritten on the back was: "Me, Trendi, and Fallon." Also written was a date from five years ago.

"Trendi," Kissick said. "The girl who was found murdered with Vince Madrigal this morning?"

"That's why Cheyenne was upset. They were friends." Vining slipped the photo into her pocket.

*   *   *

Tink's office was across the hall from Cheyenne's room. It had a sleek black lacquered desk. The wallpaper had a design that looked like mid-century fashion sketches in charcoal on an antique brown background.

Kissick looked at the wallpaper. "Cute."

The uniformed officer had found the charger for Tink's BlackBerry and it was plugged in on top of her desk. On an upholstered chair was Tink's purse—a small white quilted Chanel handbag.

Kissick opened it and took out her wallet. "She has a bunch of credit cards and about a hundred bucks in cash."

Vining walked behind the desk. On top were loose cords for a computer. "Where's her laptop?"

She and Kissick looked around, finding no signs of a computer.

"I didn't see it downstairs," Vining said.

Kissick was running his fingers across the folders in a file cabinet drawer. "We haven't searched her car yet." He closed a drawer and opened the one below it. "Hmm." He closed that drawer and opened another.

"Hmm what?"

"The other three filing cabinet drawers are crammed full. This one has a lot of room in it. No gaping holes. The files are spaced out. I don't know if it means anything."

"Oh, my gosh." From a bookshelf beside the desk, Vining picked up a framed photograph. "The four Ramona Girls back in the day. Look at my mother. Red, white, and blue–striped bell-bottoms and big square sunglasses. Straight hair parted in the middle reaching her waist. Hilarious."

When Kissick came over to look at it, Vining picked up another photo. "Here's one of the girls today." She pointed to a woman with thick salt-and-pepper hair who was wearing an embroidered Mexican peasant blouse. "That's Mary Alice, the artist. She lives in Ojai, where she has a pottery studio and now goes by her given name, Maria Alicia. Story was that her father was Anglo, and her Mexican mother wanted her to pass for Anglo. I keep forgetting to call her Maria Alicia.

"That's Vicki. Miss No-nonsense. She's a high school principal in Claremont. Tink was the ambitious one. She went to Notre Dame. That was a big deal for a girl from Alhambra."

"How did she pay for it?"

"Family savings, I guess. Scholarships. Loans. Her father ran a local insurance agency. They weren't wealthy. None of the girls were. Tink set her sights high and made it happen. There's my mom. So pretty. Such a flirt. My mother fared the worst of the four friends. Multiple divorces. Jumped from job to job. Always having a dispute with her boss or a coworker who's supposedly out to get her. That job at the Estée Lauder counter at Macy's in West Covina is the longest she's had anywhere. Always broke. Sells JAFRA on the side. Rents the town house she's living in." She sighed.

She opened the frame and took out the snapshot. "This is a good current photo of Tink. I'm taking it."

Kissick turned on Tink's BlackBerry. "Tink kept her calendar in here. She had a full day today. Pilates at nine. Hair color at ten-thirty. Seven-thirty tonight, 'To G.T. discuss G.G. fundraiser.' Georgia's Girls? G.T.? Gig Towne?"

Vining drew her index finger across the spines of a dozen books. "Tink was really into this Georgia Berryhill. Check out these titles: *Tick-Tock Therapy—Five Minutes a Day to Heal Your Mind and Achieve Your Goals; Love Yourself Rich; You and Your Shadow—Make Friends with Your Shadow Self.*"

She pulled a slender tome off the shelf. "Here we go. Here's the gold mine. *The Berryhill Method.* It's still on the bestseller lists. Guess there's an endless supply of people wanting an easy explanation of the meaning of life. With Tink losing her son and husband, I can see how she'd be attracted to The Method. Tink treated the Ramona Girls to a retreat at Berryhill. Wasn't my mom's cup of tea. Fasting, exercise, no alcohol . . . Doesn't look like Georgia takes her own medicine."

The book's back cover had a photo of Georgia Berryhill sitting on a stone bench in a lush garden. She was in her forties with a zaftig figure, chin-length straight dark brown hair, sparkling brown eyes, and a small-toothed, almost childlike smile that revealed a dimple in one plump cheek. She had the warm, kindly mien of a sorority housemother who keeps her charges in line with good humor and by appealing to their better selves. She looked as if she had a secret that she couldn't wait to tell you.

"Found contact information for Kingsley Getty." Kissick was still going through Tink's BlackBerry. "Address on Wilshire Boulevard in L.A. Zip code puts it in the Westwood area."

"This book is personalized. 'To Catherine, my friend on The Method journey. With warmest wishes, Georgia.' " Vining put the book away and pulled out another. "This one's personalized too." She pulled out the next volume. "Looks like they all are. Georgia Berryhill has a lot of celebrity followers. Tink's money must have bought her the celebrity treatment."

"Speaking of celebrities," Kissick began, "Tink seemed to know Gig Towne pretty well. She's got his home information, office, agent . . ."

"My mother mentioned something about that." Vining was looking through the desk drawers. Arranged at the top of the desk was a collection of antique fountain pens and inkwells. "Think she tried to finagle an invitation to go with Tink to his house."

"I'd like to finagle an invitation with his wife, Sinclair LeFleur."

"Her? She's so . . . pale and wispy. Thought you liked your women more robust. I'm not wispy."

He shrugged, not offering an explanation.

She smirked at him and sat behind the desk.

"They live near here, in La Cañada Flintridge," he said.

"Odd that this drawer is empty." She rolled back the desk chair and bent over to look inside the center desk drawer. She started pulling on something. "A paper is jammed in the back." It came loose, sending her back into the chair with the momentum. She frowned at it. "Look at this."

He came around the desk to join her. "It's covered with those funny symbols, like those burnt papers you found in the fireplace."

"Whoever burned those missed this one." She carried it to the window. "One of the burnt ones was drawn in this same dark brown ink. Maybe this isn't ink. Maybe it's dried blood."

Kissick unscrewed the ornate silver cap from one of the antique inkwells. He picked up one of the fountain pens, dipped it in, and made a line on a notepad.

"Black ink." He removed the cap from another inkwell. This time, the line he drew on the pad was crimson. He picked up the inkwell and sniffed the contents. "Blood."

They looked at each other.

"Is this some sort of witchcraft, black-magic thing?" Vining again looked over the books lining the shelves. "There's nothing that suggests witchcraft here. But . . ." She pointed at spaces between books. "Books have been taken out."

*   *   *

The sunny, spacious kitchen had dozens of cookbooks, including several penned by Georgia Berryhill. A tattered copy of *The Method Feast* was on a counter as if it was in constant use. The forensics team had left sooty fingerprint dust on many of the surfaces.

A cabinet was crammed with Berryhill brand vitamins and supplements. Kissick read the names aloud. "Energy Please. Amino A-go-go. Berry Blast Antioxidant Booster."

In the living room, Forensics had removed the burnt contents of the fireplace. As Kissick and Vining headed toward the front door, she stepped inside the office off the entry. From a neat pile of newspapers on a corner of the desk, she picked up a copy of the *Wall Street Journal*. She set it aside and picked up the paper beneath it, the *Los Angeles Times*, and the one beneath that, *Investor's Business Daily*.

"They're all a year old. She left Stan's office intact." Vining restacked the newspapers as they were before she'd disturbed them.

They left the house and walked down the terraced brick path. She looked at the green lawn with its tender blades of grass and showy flowers. The sun had come out and the raindrops had dried.

They got into their cars and drove back to the station.

EIGHT

After leaving Vining's car in the PPD lot, Kissick drove them both to Patsy Brightly's town house in Monrovia.

Vining made a call and asked a Detective Section staff assistant to run a background check on Kingsley Getty.

When she'd ended the call, Kissick asked, "Don't you want to call your mom and make sure she's home?"

"I don't want to telegraph that something's up."

"She has a new boyfriend. Maybe he's there."

"Whatever." Vining closed her eyes. "I try to stay out of it. I just hope I don't have to go to another wedding."

"How many would it be?"

"Another would be five. My father was her first and shortest marriage. Stephanie's dad was the second. That one lasted a couple of years. She married number three around the time I married Wes. No coincidence there, huh?"

"You're saying your mother was being competitive with you?"

"Oh, yeah. Not so much with Stephanie, though. I don't know why that is. Anyway, number three was a nice guy. A machinist, like my grandfather. That marriage lasted ten years. It ended because he wanted to move to Vegas, where he had kids, and she didn't want to go. Ironically, she met number four in Vegas. Bill Brightly. He was a salesman for a medical supply company. I never liked him. A real ladies' man. She was the one who called it quits, and I can't blame her, even though it tore her up. She liked his last name, though, and kept it."

"Interesting that she dumped three and four, but husbands one and two, the ones she had kids with, dumped her."

"That's the story."

"What's that mean? What other story is there? You've never met your father, and neither has Stephanie, right?"

"Correct. Abandonment makes sense. But my mother recently revealed that Stephanie's father didn't abandon her. He was in jail on a drug charge and was stabbed to death. My mother made up the deadbeat dad story to shield Stephanie from the truth. And me too. I was four when it happened."

"Really." He was quiet for a while. "She could have made up stories that were kinder to her girls, like dying in accidents. Or made them heroes. Died while rescuing a child from a raging river."

"Guess my mother wasn't creative. Maybe it was simplest to say they left one day and never came back. Makes me wonder what sort of creep my father was."

"What about Granny? She must know the truth."

"I'm sure she does. When I used to ask about my father when I was a kid, she'd tell me to ask my mother, which went nowhere. I finally stopped asking."

"Why did the truth about Stephanie's dad come out?"

"Stephanie said she needed to know his medical history for the sake of her two boys, but that's just the reason she told herself. She was always asking questions about her father, long after I'd given up asking about mine. Her boys got old enough to start asking their own questions. She hired a private investigator." She chuckled. "Took him about half an hour to find out the truth."

"You never tried to track down your father? Run a background check?"

She shook her head.

"You know his name and the approximate year he was born?"

She shook her head faster, as if this was a place she didn't want to go. "I've lived this long not knowing. Even though Stephanie said she'd be okay with whatever the private detective found, she was not happy that the first photograph she'd ever seen of her father was a mug shot. Sometimes the lie is easier to live with than reality."

"Your mother doesn't have any photos of Stephanie's father or yours?"

"She claims she tore them all up." Vining looked out the window, tiring of the conversation. "It doesn't matter."

Kissick got off the freeway. Monrovia was in the flatlands of the San Gabriel Valley, south of the foothills. Like Pasadena, it had been settled by Midwesterners who were drawn by the temperate climate and open land. Once blanketed with citrus groves, the city was now studded with mini-malls.

Kissick remembered the way to Patsy's, having followed Vining here last night after she'd driven her slightly tipsy mom home.

He parked on the street in front of a sprawling complex of dark wood, sloping shingled roofs, and pine trees. The woodsy design was iconic early seventies. Clusters of two-story units were separated by tree-lined paths. The front doors were painted burnt orange. Wooden flower boxes were attached outside the upstairs windows.

Kissick parked behind another Crown Vic with chrome spotlights—an unmarked cop vehicle.

Vining met Kissick's eyes and arched an eyebrow.

At the keypad outside the front gate, Vining buzzed her mother's unit.

When Patsy finally answered, her "hello" sounded strained and tearful.

"Mom, it's me. Nan."

"Oh, Nan. Thank God. The police are here, asking me about Vince."

"Who's Vince?"

"Vince Madrigal, my new man. He was murdered last night."

A buzzer sounded, releasing the gate.

"My mother's new boyfriend was Vince Madrigal?" Vining made a sound of exasperation as she walked ahead of Kissick down a cement path that was littered with pine needles. Patchy clumps of ivy grew in the flower beds between the trees. The sweet homey aroma of baking cookies came from one of the units.

Patsy's door was ajar. Vining knocked twice, then pushed it open and entered the combined living room and dining area of the small town house.

Her mother sat on a swivel rocker in the living room, twisting a damp tissue between her hands, her face red and puffy. She was dressed for work, wearing a light blue blouse and black slacks.

"Nan, I'm so glad you're here," Patsy said, as if forgetting that she had not called her daughter.

On a couch beside the chair was a slender African-American woman who looked to be in her early thirties dressed in a navy blue pinstripe pantsuit and a crisp white shirt. Her hair was styled in a short straight bob with bangs and auburn highlights. Beneath her jacket, Vining saw a holstered gun.

Her male partner stood in the middle of the room between the living and dining areas. He was shorter, rounder, and older. Vining guessed he was in his forties, but they had been hard years. He was in a dark suit and had on a cheap stiff tie over a rumpled blue dress shirt. His brown hair had receded, and he'd closely shorn what was left.

The female detective stood and extended her hand to Vining. "I'm Detective Desiree Peck with LAPD Northeastern Division. My partner, Jeff Upton."

"Detective Nan Vining, Pasadena Police. Detective Jim Ki—"

Patsy blurted before Vining had finished, "They're asking me about Vince. He was—" She cried a stream of words that were unintelligible through her sobbing.

"Jim Kissick." He finished his name.

Vining picked up a wooden dinette chair, moved it beside her mother, and sat.

Kissick stood arm's length away from Upton with his hands behind his back and his feet apart, mirroring Upton's posture.

Peck explained, "Vincent Madrigal was found murdered this morning in a motel in Eagle Rock. There was a second victim. A twenty-two-year-old female named Trendi Talbot. Your mother was involved in a romantic relationship with Madrigal."

Vining remained poker-faced. She had many questions for Patsy, but would ask them after the LAPD investigators had left.

"Nan, I told them everything I know about Vince," Patsy wailed. "They've been here for an hour, asking me the same things over and over. Vince never talked about his business or his clients to me. He never mentioned having anything to do with cremated remains."

Cremated remains? Vining thought.

"I've never heard the name Trendi Talbot before today. I don't know what Vince was doing at some motel in Eagle Rock. I don't know. *I don't know.*" Patsy's fist tightened on the macerated tissue as her voice rose. She glared at Peck, "I don't have anything else to tell you. My daughter is a detective with the Pasadena police."

Peck's face remained deadpan but Upton rolled back on his heels and pretended to stifle a laugh. Vining was well aware of some in the LAPD having an attitude about big-city cops versus little-city cops.

Patsy swung the balled-up tissue in Kissick's direction. "That's her boyfriend. He's a detective too."

This served to further amuse Upton. Even Peck raised an eyebrow.

Vining gritted her teeth, thinking, *Too much information, Mom.* She felt her cheeks redden but said to Peck, "My mother says she's told you everything she knows. If she thinks of anything later, I personally guarantee that she'll call you."

Peck exchanged a glance with her partner before putting her hands on her knees and pressing herself up. "Okay. Mrs. Brightly, you have my card." She reached into the breast pocket of her jacket and took out more business cards, handing them to Vining and Kissick.

Vining did the same with her card. Upton and Kissick didn't participate in the formality. All of them knew how to find one another.

"I'll be right back, Mom." Vining followed the detectives outside, smelling stale cigarette smoke on Upton.

Kissick left also, pulling the front door closed but not locked.

Peck walked a distance down the path, then stopped. She asked Vining, "Did you know Vincent Madrigal?"

"No."

"How long was your mother dating him?"

"I don't know."

Peck looked deeply into her eyes. Vining knew the other detective was trying to see if she was lying. "Your mother never talked to you about Vincent Madrigal."

"That's correct." Vining didn't elaborate. "What is the significance of the cremated remains my mother mentioned?"

The LAPD detectives exchanged a glance.

Upton spoke for the first time. His voice was raspy, as if he was a longtime smoker. "Cremains were spilled in the motel room."

"Human remains?" Kissick asked.

"We don't know yet, but we'll find out," Upton replied.

"Do you have any idea what Madrigal and Trendi Talbot were doing there?" Vining asked.

Upton again was the one to quickly answer. "Not yet."

Kissick kicked away a pinecone that had fallen onto the walkway. "We heard that Madrigal stabbed the girl and she shot him."

There was a guarded silence between the partners but Vining sensed their unspoken communication and guessed they'd been partners a long time.

Peck responded. "Where did you hear that?"

Kissick made a face that conveyed that the source was of no consequence. "Around."

"We can't get into specifics." Peck took a photo from her jacket pocket. "This is Trendi Talbot. Have you seen her before?"

It was a mug shot. Trendi looked several years older and more road-hardened than in the girlfriends' party photo Vining had found in Cheyenne's room. Still, for a mug shot, it wasn't a bad photo. Trendi's straight blond hair was combed, and her makeup was on straight. Her light blue eyes betrayed her. Her gaze was piercing and fearful, much different than the happy girl in Cheyenne's photo.

The LAPD detectives had been candid with them. Vining should probably reveal having seen Trendi in the group photo and her connection to Cheyenne Leon. Still, she replied "No" and handed the photo to Kissick. They had yet to interrogate Cheyenne, their reluctant witness in Tink Engleford's mysterious death, and didn't want the LAPD to interfere.

Kissick followed Vining's lead and shook his head. He returned the photo to Peck. She and Upton turned and left without another word.

Vining looked at the dark orange front door of her mother's home. A shadow moved behind the open vertical blinds.

She lowered her voice. "How did my mother meet someone like Vince Madrigal?"

"Maybe through Tink? Tink had Hollywood and big-money connections."

"How old was Madrigal? In his sixties? My mother is fifty-four. Granted, she looks good, but Caspers captured it in his inimitable way: Madrigal dated models and starlets. Why would he drive from the Westside, where I assume he lived, all the way to Monrovia to date my mother? Last night, my mom talked as if this was an ongoing relationship. Maybe it was something more in her mind." She sighed and her shoulders slumped.

Kissick grabbed her upper arms as if to help hold her together.

Patsy opened the front door and stood in the doorway. "Are they coming back?"

"No, Mom. Not today anyway."

Patsy blew out a stream of air with relief. She nervously fumbled with a bracelet watch on her wrist. "Now I'm going to be late for work." She went back inside.

"Just a second, Mom." Vining and Kissick followed her.

"Honey, I have to go. I'll call you later, okay?" Patsy picked up a blazer from the back of a chair and put it on.

Vining knew she had to tell her about Tink, but wanted to know more about Madrigal. "Mom, how did you get involved with Vince Madrigal?"

"He's just someone I met."

"Did you meet him through Tink?"

"No." Patsy was annoyed with the question. "I meet men all the time." At first she wouldn't meet her daughter's eyes, but seemed to think better of it and faced her. "Vince stopped by the Estée Lauder counter to buy a birthday gift for his mother. I sold him a bottle of Beautiful eau de toilette."

"At the Macy's in West Covina?"

"*Yes*. At the Macy's in West Covina."

"Was he really your boyfriend?"

"I saw him a few times. I guess I exaggerated last night. He came out to have lunch with me at the mall." She quickly added, "He took me to dinner, too, to nice places."

"Where did he live?"

"In Beverly Hills."

Vining looked at her mother without saying anything.

Patsy bristled. "Men find me attractive, Nan. And fun to be with. Enough to drive all the way from Beverly Hills to take me out. I didn't know anything about his business, okay? And I never met that woman he was killed with."

"I didn't ask whether you did."

"That's all those other detectives wanted to know. I figured that's what you were getting at too."

"We didn't come out here to talk to you about Madrigal." Vining swallowed, finding her mouth dry.

"Why did you come out here?" Patsy's anger passed and she snatched her daughter's hand. "Something's happened. Is it Granny?"

Vining flashed back to when she was a child and had held her mother's hand while crossing a busy street.

Kissick saw that Vining was having trouble saying the words. "Patsy, let's sit down." He guided her to the couch.

Patsy moved tentatively, as if the world had become

fragile and a wrong step would shatter everything she knew. Now sitting, she searched his face.

Vining was grateful that Kissick had taken over. She realized how much she'd come to rely on him.

He took Patsy's hands and met her eyes. "It's not about Granny. It's Tink. She was found dead in her backyard pool."

NINE

Vining observed that news about the untimely death of a loved one was nearly always received the same way. A sharp intake of breath. Eyes boring into the messenger's eyes as if pleading for a joke or a mistake. Eyes then turning away, searching the distance while wrestling with the information. Some people screamed or cried. She'd seen a few faint. Then the practicality kicked in through the tears with questions about the facts. Sometimes those guilty of ending another's life were able to fake the emotions, but they often forgot to ask what happened.

Patsy's shock and grief were genuine. "Oh, my God, Tink!"

Vining flew to her mother's side on the couch and threw her arms around her. "I'm so sorry, Mom. I'm so, so sorry."

"In her backyard pool? How?"

"That's what we're trying to find out, Mom."

As Patsy sobbed with her face mashed into Vining's suit jacket, Vining realized that she was crying too.

Kissick sat close, doing all he could to comfort them, patting Patsy's hand and reaching across her to stroke Vining's shoulder.

After a while, Patsy got to her feet and walked as if in a trance to a box of tissues across the room. She pulled out some and dabbed her eyes. When she finally spoke, her voice was steady. "Who found her?"

Vining pulled herself together. "Her assistant, Cheyenne, came home and found her."

Patsy disappeared into the small galley kitchen.

Vining heard the refrigerator door open, the clink of glasses in a cabinet, and the small pop of a cork being removed from a wine bottle.

Patsy returned holding a wineglass filled nearly to the brim with white wine. She raised her index finger as if to forestall commentary. She lowered herself onto a chair at the dining room table. Her hand trembled as she set down the glass. She gazed out the window between the vertical blinds.

Vining knew she was sifting through her memories of the last time she'd seen or spoken with Tink. She rose from the couch, pulled a tissue from the box, and sat on the swivel rocker, wincing when it creaked beneath her weight. There was something sacred about the silence, like in church, and she didn't want to defile it.

Patsy took a long drink of wine. She raised a hand. "I'm okay." Still staring outside, she shook her head, the movement small. "I just talked to Tink yesterday."

"What time was that, Patsy?" Kissick asked softly.

Still shaking her head, she added a shrug of her shoulders. "About two, I think. She'd just come home from brunch at *Annandale*." She huffed out a sad laugh. "You know Tink. All about the big names and labels. I asked her if she wanted to come over to your house, Nan, for dinner."

Vining blinked at that news, miffed that her mother

would issue an impromptu invitation to a formal dinner without asking, as if she was having a pizza-and-beer party.

"Was Tink alone?" Kissick asked.

"Yes. She said she just wanted to stay home and relax. Come to think of it, she said she was by the pool. She'd opened a bottle of *Veuve*. Her favorite champagne. We talked for a while, and then she had to hang up because someone came."

"Someone came?" Kissick leaned forward on the couch. "Did she say who?"

Patsy shook her head. "She told me, 'Wait a second.' I guess she talked to somebody, and then she came back on and said she had to go. Said she had an unexpected visitor."

"Could it have been her boyfriend, King Getty?" Kissick asked.

"Tink told me he was on a business trip to *Dubai*." Patsy raised her eyebrows.

"Did you ever meet him?" Vining asked.

Patsy quickly shook her head. "Boy, the way Tink bragged about him. He was the most gorgeous, most wonderful man ever. The last time we had dinner, Mary Alice, Vicki, and I teased Tink. Anything she did had to be the best, biggest, and brightest. She couldn't just be dating a nice man. He had to be a *Getty*. She said we were jealous. Said King had swept her away to Paris on a private jet for the weekend. He always picked her up in a limo." Patsy's tears started again. "No one ever took me to Paris on a private jet."

Vining said, "He sounds too good to be true."

"Vicki told her to hire a private detective to check him out."

"Did she?" Kissick asked.

"I doubt it. I hadn't seen her for a month. Mary Alice,

Vicki, and I took her out to celebrate her birthday. We had such a good time, laughing, fanning ourselves when the hot flashes hit, trying to get the waiter's attention, joking that now that we're middle-aged, we're invisible. We used to be hot stuff, but now no one will look at us that way ever again." Patsy pursed her lips.

Vining went into the kitchen and filled a glass with tap water from the sink. "Where did Tink meet Getty?"

"Through friends. Her *circle*."

Vining sat at the table with her mother and drank the water. "How did Tink meet Cheyenne?"

"Same way, I guess." Patsy again looked out the window. "I think she met both Cheyenne and King at the Berryhill compound."

"What was her relationship with Cheyenne?"

"Seemed like she was always chasing after Cheyenne to do the things she asked her to do. Tink said that she was trying to help Cheyenne out. That she'd had tough breaks."

"Why did Tink let Cheyenne move into her house?" Vining asked.

"I don't know."

"Did you ask?"

"That was Tink's business."

Vining thought that was an odd response from her meddling mother. "Were you and Tink having a fight?"

Patsy looked at her. "Why do you say that?"

"You seem sort of distant about what was going on with Tink and these strange people who were recently in her life."

"Honey, I'm in shock. My head's spinning."

Kissick got up and moved to lean against the counter dividing the dining room and kitchen. "Did Tink mention having medical problems?"

Patsy shrugged. "Just being hot all the time and having

insomnia from menopause. Said her cholesterol was a little high. She was into this vitamin and supplement thing. The Berryhill Method. She spent a fortune on that stuff. It's a big racket if you ask me."

"Was she drunk when you last talked to her?" Kissick asked.

"No. She was just having some champagne."

"How about her mental state? Had she been sad?"

"Of course she'd been sad. I thought she was doing better, but you know Tink. Always putting on a good front. If she was in a really bad way, I hope she would have reached out to her girlfriends. We've always been there for each other." She finished her wine.

Kissick was still speaking gently. "Did Vince Madrigal ever ask you questions about Tink or King Getty?"

"No."

Vining thought her mother's response was unusually abrupt. "In the course of you and Vince getting to know each other, you didn't talk about the people in your lives?"

"Of course we did," Patsy said. "But not in detail. I already told you I just saw him a few times. I wish you'd drop it."

Vining raised her eyebrows and reared back a little.

Patsy glanced at a teapot-shaped clock on the kitchen wall. "Oh, crap. My boss is going to kill me."

"Mom, you're in no condition to go to work."

Patsy's shoulders dropped as if relieved that someone else had brought it up. "I really don't feel well. I have paid sick days coming to me."

"Go call your boss," Vining said. "I'll talk to her if you want."

"That's okay, hon. I'll do it."

"I don't want you staying here by yourself," Vining said.

"You think someone might come after me?"

"No, it's not that. You shouldn't be alone right now. I'll take you to Granny's."

"*Nan*. How is that going to cheer me up?"

"You could both use the company and I want to find out what's going on with her."

"Just because she put a little extra salt in her casserole? I've done that. Haven't you?"

Vining tilted her head at her mother and looked at her with dismay. Patsy, who was Granny's middle child, had never come to terms with her troubled relationship with her mother.

"Granny covers up a lot. You know how proud she is. We need to find out what's really going on with her. Go call your boss and pack an overnight bag." Vining hated handling her mother the same way she'd handle Emily, but that was reality.

"All *right*." Patsy's attitude didn't help her case. She stood and dragged herself like a recalcitrant teenager toward the stairs that led to the two bedrooms and bath on the upper floor.

"Mom, can I look around your town house?"

Patsy turned. "Why?"

"Those LAPD detectives might come back with a warrant. I want to protect you."

Patsy continued up the stairs, saying, "Go ahead and look. I've got nothing to hide."

When she was gone, Kissick stood. "Should we get started?"

Vining reached inside her mother's purse, which was on the dining room table, and took out her cell phone. "I'll come back when she's gone."

"That's why you wanted to get her out of here."

Vining nodded as she looked through the phone's call log. "Her story checks. She placed a call to Tink's cell phone yesterday at two-fifteen. They talked for eleven minutes."

She returned the phone to Patsy's purse and quickly rummaged through it. "When we're at Granny's, remind me to pick up her car keys so my mother's stranded there. My mom suddenly has extra cash to blow. Now we find out she was involved with Vince Madrigal. Something stinks. I want to find out what it is before the LAPD does. I need to work fast before Sarge takes me off this case."

TEN

K issick drove while Vining turned to look at her mother in the backseat of the Crown Vic. Patsy was examining the sheets of parchment paper with the strange symbols that Vining had found at Tink's house. Vining had put each one into a Baggie from Patsy's kitchen.

"I don't know what these are, Nan."

"Mom, was Tink interested in the occult? Witchcraft?"

"When we were teenagers, sure. Tink maybe more than the rest of us. She studied astrology and did our charts. She had tarot cards. At slumber parties, we tried to conduct séances. And the Ouija board. Tink had one and we were mad about it, scaring ourselves until we couldn't sleep. My mother wouldn't allow it in the house. Tink really had the touch with the Ouija board. When she put her hands on it, it moved all over the board like crazy."

"What moved?" Vining asked.

Patsy leaned forward and put her hand on Nan's seat back. "You never played with the Ouija board? Well, I guess it was the Age of Aquarius back then. The Ouija board is supposed to be a mystical oracle with power to connect to the spirit world. You sit facing your friend with the board on your knees and your fingers on a plastic slider thingy. You ask a question, close your eyes, and concentrate. We'd ask about who we'd marry, which guys at John Bosco liked us. That was an all-boys Catholic school. The slider moves and points to the answer. Sometimes it would spell out an answer. Very strange."

"It moved because you pushed it?" Kissick asked.

"No. That was the creepy part. The spirit world moved it."

"And you believed this?" Nan asked with a chuckle. She couldn't resist batting that ball one more time.

"I don't know why I'm bothering to tell you, Nan. You just think we were stupid girls."

Vining didn't respond but agitatedly shifted in the car seat.

Kissick sneaked his hand over to touch her thigh.

"Did anything it tell you come true?"

"Well, it told me I'd have two children that I'd raise alone. It told Tink she'd be rich. So you tell me who's crazy. One time, we really scared ourselves. Tink and Vicki were using the Ouija board, asking questions about the future. It spelled out 'war' and 'death.' Tink freaked out and threw it off her knees."

"War and death?" Vining said. "The only thing the mystical oracle forgot was taxes."

Kissick had to laugh.

"We were teenagers, Nan." Patsy looked out the window and pouted. "I don't know why I'm talking about things like this to a couple of cops. How do you know there's not something else out there, just because you can't prove it?"

Vining was the last one to argue against the existence of ghosts.

Patsy huffed out air and became thoughtful. "Poor Tink. When her son got killed, it nearly destroyed her. Then Stan died too. Vicki, Mary Alice, and I wondered if the old Tink was gone. She wasn't that different, but it was like she was playing at being Tink, if that makes any sense."

Patsy again looked at the hieroglyphics from Tink's. "If these are part of some sort of witchcraft, I wouldn't be surprised. Look at how involved she was with the Berryhill Method and all that stuff. What's their slogan? 'You can make magic happen in your life.'"

"We found a lot of Georgia Berryhill's books at Tink's house," Vining said. "Inscribed by Georgia with personal messages."

Patsy sniffed. "Georgia Berryhill should have given Tink solid-gold books for the amount of money that Tink dumped into that whole Method crap."

Kissick said, "I thought the Berryhill Method was about diet and vitamins and positive thinking."

"That's the Berryhill that Georgia sells at Costco and Wal-Mart," Patsy said. "Once you get really into it, there's this whole *advanced* program. MBS—Mind, Body, Spirit—where you integrate all the parts of yourself, especially your astral shadow or shadow self or whatever. You need to get to know it to be complete or something."

"Tink bought into this?" Vining asked. "I thought she was more level-headed than that."

"Tink loved fads. From the Ouija board to disco dancing. She knew how to do the Hustle before any of us. Georgia Berryhill is hot right now. Can't turn on the TV without seeing her on one of the talk shows.

"At dinner with the girls one time, Tink talked about taking lessons at Berryhill to meet her astral shadow. Vicki and I thought she'd lost her marbles. Mary Alice, our *artist*, defended Tink. After that, Tink only talked to us about going to the Berryhill compound like it was a spa retreat. She no longer mentioned her studies.

"Then Tink treated us to a girls' weekend at Berryhill. Vicki wondered if she did it to prove to us that it was just a nice restful place to go. Tink's favorite Berryhill treatment was the MBS Tune-Up. You're on this diet of juice and herbal tea, and you spend your days meditating and doing yoga. She claimed she felt so much clearer after. I told her, 'Thanks, but no thanks.'"

Vining squinted at her mother over her shoulder. "Where is the Berryhill compound?"

"Off Malibu Canyon Road, before you go up and over to the ocean. It's tucked back into a canyon. You wouldn't know it's there. It's lovely. Woods, rolling hills with a lake in the middle. Good food."

Kissick shot a question to Patsy over his shoulder. "What's an astral shadow?"

"Your guide in the spirit world. It's this whole Berryhill philosophy. They preach that everyone has these different shadow selves that we have to get to know before we can be whole . . . A complete person. Achieve nirvana. 'Course being rich or a celebrity gets you into Nirvana at the top of the hill more quickly." Patsy snorted.

"In the compound there's an actual place called Nirvana?" Kissick asked.

"Oh, yeah. It's like a gated neighborhood within Berryhill. No one there admits that Nirvana is for the rich and famous, or just plain rich. Or just plain beautiful. They claim that to get inside you have to progress through seven steps. Tink told me with a straight face that Georgia had put her on the fast track to Nirvana. That's how *she* got in so quickly. I told her, I could work those steps my entire life and the only way I'd get through those gates is if I won the lottery."

"Couldn't Tink get you in?" Vining asked.

"Oh, no, honey." Patsy angled her mouth, halfway sneering. "It was like the domain of the ancient Hawaiian kings that I visited on the Big Island. A commoner would be killed if his mere shadow crossed the boundary. When Tink took the girls there, she got us each a small cabin. She stayed in one too."

"How many times did you go to Berryhill?"

"Just that one time last summer. It's not in my budget. I can drink organic apple cider and herbal tea on my own. I can even buy the Georgia Berryhill brand. When I was there, I had a Shadow Symmetry evaluation, to see if I was in tune with my shadow self."

"And?" Vining asked.

"They told me I didn't have one."

ELEVEN

Kissick got off the freeway and headed toward Granny's house.

"Jim, can you pull into that Ralphs over there?" Vining pointed to a large supermarket. "Can't be sure that Granny has anything in her refrigerator."

"Good Lord, yes," Patsy said. "Let's buy the old lady some groceries before I spend the night there. I'm sure she hasn't changed the sheets in the guest room since the last time she had overnight guests, which was probably when I stayed with her after your incident, Nan."

The *incident*. That was how Vining's loved ones still

referred to the creep's knife attack on her. She hated how that situation continued to define her in everyone else's eyes and was still foremost in their minds. Not hers. She'd sent it into exile to the furthest reaches of her psyche. Not from fear, but with full will and knowledge. She'd exercised the most primitive formula known to humanity: an eye for an eye. Primitive yet eminently satisfying, emitting the clear, resounding chime of justice.

Patsy began, "Nan, I never asked you this . . ."

Vining didn't know what was coming. She felt herself hunkering down.

"The three days you were in a coma . . . Did you know we were there?"

Vining found it interesting that this *stuff* related to her stabbing and the long aftermath was coming up now. Did her loved ones feel safe because the bad guy was gone for good?

From the time that she lay comatose, she recalled half-comprehended words, the sensation of hands and sometimes lips against her skin, and lights and shapes beyond her eyelids. Sort of sadly funny for her to think of Tink dropping a bundle of cash in the search to connect with her shadow self. Vining had been in a shadow world. It wasn't anyplace she could even begin to describe, much less someplace she wanted to explore. She lied. "I don't remember anything after he stabbed me until I woke up."

She opened the car door before Kissick had set the parking brake.

Patsy also got out. "I need to pick up a few things, too."

Vining quietly groaned. She needed a break from her mother and her dramas. She yanked on a cart to free it from a row of nested carts in front of the store. As she did so, Patsy yelped, "Wait!" with such alarm that she nearly reached for her gun.

Patsy dashed toward her waving an antibacterial wipe she'd pulled from a container near the grocery carts. "Nan, don't you know that the handle of a shopping cart is one of the filthiest things there is?" She wiped down the cart's plastic handle. "Give me your hands."

Vining complied, letting her mother clean them, feeling again like she was four.

"Mom, how can you be a germaphobe and sell cosmetics?"

"I'm not a germaphobe."

"Whatever." Vining wheeled the cart through the automatic doors.

Patsy said she was going to make her meat loaf recipe, so in addition to yogurt, cottage cheese, eggs, bread, lunch meat, cereal, and fruit, into the basket went ground beef, ground pork, onion, garlic, and carrots.

While Vining was standing in line to check out, Patsy disappeared, returning with a cardboard carrier full of six bottles of chardonnay.

At a glance from Vining, Patsy became defensive. "They're on sale. If I buy six, I get an extra ten percent discount. You're the one who wants me to stay with Granny. I'm gonna need some help."

"Did I say anything?"

"You didn't need to." Patsy cocked her head to look at the cover of *People* magazine in a holder at the checkout counter. "Speak of the devil. There's Georgia."

The magazine's headline screamed: BEST FRIENDS AND PREGNANT. Pictured were Georgia Berryhill and the gorgeous young actress Sinclair LeFleur. Mugging between the pregnant women was Sinclair's husband, Gig Towne.

Vining picked up the magazine, flipped to the article, and read aloud. "Georgia Berryhill, her husband Stefan

Pavel, and Le Towne all await their blessed events in April." She winced. "Le Towne?"

"Sinclair LeFleur and Gig Towne," Patsy said. "Get it?"

"Cuuute," Vining deadpanned. She continued reading with drama, "Pavel, Georgia's younger French husband and the genius behind her Berryhill Method empire, says, 'We called Gig and Sinclair to break the news only to learn that they could hardly wait to tell us *their* news.' Energetic, forty-eight-year-old Georgia still had time to pen her latest bestseller, *The Berryhill Method of Pregnancy and Childbirth*."

Vining made a face. "Wow. She's already an expert."

Patsy shook her head. "Tink was so excited about these babies. She knew Gig and Sinclair socially. Met them at Berryhill. All she could talk about is how happy Georgia and Stefan were to be finally pregnant after all the years of trying."

"Listen to how the blessed events are going to take place." Vining read, " 'Gig and Sinclair are taking it easy at their La Cañada Flintridge estate, where Sinclair will have the baby in a pool of body-temperature water assisted by a midwife. Georgia and Stefan have prepared an identical birthing room at the Berryhill compound in Malibu Canyon.' "

She added, "These women obviously haven't had children before."

That brought a laugh from the African-American checker, whose name tag said that she was Adele and that she'd been with Ralphs for twenty-two years. She was ringing up a customer in front of them.

"Gig Towne is totally into the Berryhill Method," Patsy said. "That's what having the baby at home is about. Hospitals have bad karma. Death and sickness. The baby's self and shadow selves are just being formed, and it's important that they control the baby's environment."

"And Tink, who was no stranger to hospitals and plastic surgery, agreed with that?" Vining asked.

"Yep. She drank the Kool-Aid."

"I didn't know this." Vining scanned the article. "Gig Towne spent time in prison for running over a homeless man. He says, 'I was lost before I discovered Georgia Berryhill and The Method. Georgia and Stefan turned my life around. If it wasn't for them, I wouldn't have met Sinclair, the love of my life.' Gig, forty-four, lovingly gave his beautiful twenty-eight-year-old wife a smooch on the cheek."

She crushed the magazine between her hands, clasped it to her chest, and let out a dreamy sigh. "How romantic. I'm going to buy this, by the way," she said to the checker, who had started scanning her purchases.

Patsy took the magazine from Nan and continued reading the article aloud. "Gig Towne's recent erratic behavior on a TV interview has Hollywood players wondering whether he's lost not just his edge but his wits. He was once one of the highest-paid actors in Hollywood, hitting it big twenty years ago with his first movie, the iconic comedy *Stupid Is*. His attempts to change his funnyman image and take on meatier roles have not been met warmly at the box office. His last three mega-budget movies have flopped, while his wife's, Sinclair LeFleur's, star is soaring."

Adele the checker weighed in. "He only married Sinclair to stop the rumors about him being gay. My cousin is best friends with Sinclair's hairdresser. She said the marriage is a business deal. Gig promised to make Sinclair a big star."

"I liked him when his movies were funny," Patsy said.

Kissick found them and walked to stand at the end of the aisle by the young man who was bagging the groceries, unconsciously assuming an at-ease position with his legs shoulder-width apart and his hands clasped behind his back.

The checker spotted him. "Can I help you, Officer?"

"I'm with them." He inclined his head to indicate Vining and her mother.

Adele gave Vining a closer look and just now noticed her gun and badge beneath her jacket.

"I don't like Gig Towne's slapstick, gross-out humor," Vining said.

"That's great stuff," the teenaged bag boy opined. He was tall with thick dark hair, glasses with rectangular black frames, and patches of acne in the hollows of both cheeks. "The 'Gig giggle.' That's hilarious."

"Gig giggle?" Adele said.

"My youngest son has that nailed," Kissick said.

"I can do it." The teenager took a step back, as if to prepare, inhaled deeply, and emitted a laugh that sounded like the bastard child of Woody Woodpecker and Elmer Fudd.

Kissick laughed. "That's good. That's the Gig giggle, all right."

Vining wished the bag boy was paying better attention to packing the groceries. It looked as if he'd just set a cantaloupe on top of the carton of eggs.

"They say that Sinclair's baby isn't even his," Adele said. "That the whole pregnancy is a sham."

"My friend thought that was ridiculous," Patsy said. "She knew them, Le Towne and the Berryhills."

"Yeah?" Adele asked. "Is she in the movie business?"

"No." Patsy's shoulders slumped as she tossed the magazine onto the conveyer. "She was just a woman who was always searching for answers and found comfort at Berryhill. She just passed away."

Vining paused as she held her store rewards card over

the reader, always surprised by her frequently daffy
mother's moments of wisdom.

"I'm sorry," Adele said.

"Thank you." Patsy brushed away tears, then put out
her hand to stop Vining from running her debit card
through the reader. "I've got it, Nan."

Vining blinked when she saw her mother take a wad
of twenties from her wallet.

TWELVE

Carrying bags of groceries, Patsy led the way across
the broad front porch of Granny's modest clap-
board house in Alhambra, a city on Pasadena's southern
border. Granny's baby-blue Delta 88 was parked in the
cracked cement driveway.

The yard was in decent shape, as Granny's eldest child,
Vernon Jr., paid for a weekly gardening service. Dozens
of plants in mismatched pots were crammed onto the
wooden porch railing, mostly hearty succulents and geraniums, sprouted from clippings and planted in plain dirt
from the yard.

"Something has to be done about that peeling paint."
Vining stopped on the walkway before going up the
steps to look at the white trim on the pitched porch roof
of the yellow house. "Around the windows, too."

"I can paint it." Kissick stood behind her, holding a
plastic grocery bag in one hand and the cardboard carrier with the bottles of chardonnay in the other.

"That's kind of you to offer, Jim, but I'll speak to my uncle and aunt about it. They need to stay involved. They do, but I have to nudge them."

"What do they do and where do they live?"

"Uncle Vernon, the oldest, is a production manager at a corrugated cardboard box manufacturing plant outside Wenatchee, Washington. His wife's a part-time school nurse. They're both about to retire. The youngest is Marie, who's a high school history teacher outside San Diego."

"I'm the middle child." Patsy kept her thumb on the doorbell as she pressed her face against the panes of glass in the door, covered on the inside with lacy curtains. She'd set her two grocery bags at her feet. "Couldn't you guess?"

"My aunt and uncle have talked about moving Granny closer to one of them," Vining said, "but I'd hate to move her from the home where she's lived for sixty years until we absolutely had to."

Kissick raised his hand with the shopping bag he was holding and pointed at Patsy behind her back.

Vining leaned to speak into his ear. "Exactly. She lives paycheck to paycheck, and here's my grandmother living alone in this house and she needs help." The words spilled out faster as her anger rose. "My mother might spend a second thinking about someone other than—"

"I know what you two are whispering about," Patsy said without turning. "Finally!" she exclaimed when Granny opened the front door.

"What are you all doing here?" Granny's silver-blue hair was teased and shaped into a French twist in the back and pinned into three coils down the front. "Are you okay?"

"Granny, I called you a few minutes ago," Vining said. "Don't you remember?"

"Oh, that's right." Granny's heavy gold bangle bracelets on her arm jangled when she swatted the air. "Well, come in, come in."

Vining gave Patsy a stern look to make sure she saw the evidence of Granny's failing memory.

Patsy stepped across the threshold and went into the house.

"Your hair looks nice, Granny." Kissick leaned to give her a kiss on the cheek, the bottles in the carrier clanking together.

"It's Monday," Granny said in response to his compliment. "I always have my hair done on Monday morning. Every two weeks on Wednesday at two, I get my nails done."

"Does Hilda still do your hair?" Patsy asked.

"Hilda? She's been dead for years. I've got a new gal. Hard to find anyone who can do a set and comb-out anymore."

Patsy whispered to Vining, "I'm amazed she can find anyone who can do those turd curls for her."

Vining made a face at her mother at the word Patsy always used to describe the three long, round curls in Granny's hair that lay vertically across the top of her head. She looked around at the doily-draped furnishings that had barely changed since she'd been a child. Curio shelves on the walls held dusty porcelain Hummel figures and china teacups and saucers that she and her sister had been forbidden to touch. All the windows were tightly closed on this fine spring day. The place smelled musty and, she hated to admit, like an old lady.

Granny stood in the entry to the dining room. "Why do you have so many groceries? And that liquor . . ."

"I'm spending the night." Patsy ducked around her mother.

Granny scurried after her. "Just leave the bags on the dining room table. I'll put everything away."

"Mom, there's the mailman." Patsy jerked her head in the direction of the front door and was rewarded when Granny left to retrieve her mail.

Patsy returned from setting her bags in the kitchen. "I need a pit stop." She headed toward the one bathroom in the house.

Kissick walked into the tiny kitchen and deposited the groceries on top of a vintage Formica-and-chrome dinette table. Nearly everything in the kitchen was vintage—from the O'Keefe and Merritt stove to the Frigidaire refrigerator—and, his trained eye discerned, highly collectible. What weren't vintage were the cockroaches that dashed across the sink and down the drain from where they'd been feasting in remnants of food among a pile of dirty plates and glasses.

Vining, following him, stood frozen at the sight.

Kissick made a face as his nostrils detected a foul odor. He moved aside dingy floral-print curtains and unlocked a double-hung window over the sink, careful to avoid a scurrying cockroach. He slammed his hand up against the wooden window frame and finally got it open.

He took Vining's bags from her and set them on the table.

She finally found words. "I don't believe this."

"You didn't know?"

"*No.* I haven't been inside the house for . . . a while. Granny drives to my house. When I follow her home, she wants me to leave her at the front door. She doesn't want me to come inside. Now I know why."

She opened the refrigerator. A rank odor spilled out. She caught a glimpse of something black inside before slamming the door shut.

"I think Granny can live on her own," Kissick said. "She needs some help, that's all. We had to hire somebody to help my grandparents with the day-to-day stuff. It's worked out great."

"A stranger cleaning Granny's house? Not gonna happen." Vining pulled out a kitchen chair and sat with her legs sprawled. "And listen to them." She held her hand in the direction of the front room, where Granny and Patsy were rehashing a decades-old argument. "They are so different but so similar. One always was a child and the other is turning into one."

He stood beside her, put his arm around her shoulders, and pulled her against him. "I'll help you, honey. We'll get through this together."

Vining knew she could do this on her own but it felt great to know that, for once, she didn't have to. The weight felt less like a crushing burden and more like a problem to be solved, maybe more emotionally trying than others, but only a problem. "Thank you."

"You're welcome." Kissick took his iPhone from his pocket and put it to his ear when it vibrated with an incoming call. He saw that it was from Alex Caspers.

"I talked to Cheyenne's friends in Ventura and I'm heading back," Caspers said.

Kissick looked at his watch. "Already?" He didn't need to ask how fast Caspers had driven.

"Traffic was light. I got there in half an hour. Cheyenne's alibi checks out. Other than the friends she hung with, she stayed in the apartment of this guy named Silas Linden. Located him at his job at a local coffee and bagel place. At first, he wouldn't talk to me. I told him I'd ask his boss my questions. I didn't drive all the way up there not to talk to anybody. So then he opened up a little. Said he and Cheyenne met in Narcotics Anonymous. Cheyenne came up on Friday and she left Monday morning. He claims they were together the whole time. Confessed that he didn't know the exact time she left this morning because he had to be at work at six and she was still asleep."

"What did he have to say about Cheyenne's relationship with her boss, Catherine Engleford?"

"They got along great," Caspers said with a laugh in his voice.

"Hmm. He have a criminal record?"

"Not a long one. Misdemeanor drug- and alcohol-related stuff."

"Thanks, Alex." He ended the call when he saw one incoming from attorney Carmen Vidal. "Carmen, I've missed you," he crooned, looking at Vining with eyebrows raised. "You're on your way to Pasadena? We'll see you soon."

THIRTEEN

In the PPD interview room, Cheyenne didn't stand when Vining and Kissick entered, but fiddled with an unlit cigarette as she eyed them from her chair at the table.

Her attorney, Carmen Vidal, greeted them warmly and shook their hands.

The detectives knew Vidal from when she'd represented the troubled son of a wealthy executive. The young man, a suspect in a Pasadena murder, was not the sort of high-profile, newsworthy client that she'd built her public profile on, but the father's money was solid. Vidal always looked as if she was ready for a TV appearance on short notice. Her head was big for her petite body, a physiological stroke of luck, as the combination was perfect for the small screen. She was wearing another version of one of her many jewel-toned, collarless suits with the jacket buttoned up and a bold necklace at the base of her neck.

Today, twisted strands of gold beads complemented her amethyst suit.

For all Cheyenne's bluster when they first saw her at Tink's, she seemed reticent, staring at the table.

Vidal handed Kissick a manila envelope. "Detectives, I assume you've already verified with Cheyenne's friends that she was in Ventura, like she told you."

"Her friend from N.A., Silas Linden, said he left her sleeping when he went to work before six," Vining said. "Cheyenne reported finding Mrs. Engleford's body at nine. Cheyenne had plenty of time to drive to Pasadena."

"Cheyenne told me that, judging by the condition of Mrs. Engleford's body, it was clear that she'd been dead for much longer than a couple of hours," Vidal said. "Cheyenne's friends and her credit card receipts verify that she was in Ventura from midafternoon Saturday until early Monday morning."

"That still leaves plenty of time this morning for Cheyenne to arrive home, get rid of books and documents, and remove Mrs. Engleford's laptop computer," Vining said.

Vidal's face revealed nothing. "Also in that envelope are records of the checks Cheyenne deposited into her account from Catherine Engleford for payment for her services as a personal assistant. There are also keys to Mrs. Engleford's house and cars that she gave Cheyenne. We can provide affidavits from numerous reputable business associates of Mrs. Engleford who will verify that Cheyenne was her trusted employee. Mrs. Engleford's longtime housekeeper will confirm that Cheyenne was living in her home."

"Cheyenne, where's Tink's laptop?" Kissick asked.

Cheyenne pursed her lips and remained silent.

"Files and books are missing from Tink's office," Kissick went on. "Where did they go?"

Vidal folded her hands on the table. "Detectives, Cheyenne is only guilty of doing the right thing and calling the police as soon as she found Mrs. Engleford's body. Your allegation that Cheyenne broke into Mrs. Engleford's home is bullshit, and you know it. Let's stop wasting everyone's time."

Vining studied Cheyenne, who frowned at her and then looked away. "Cheyenne, you seem different from this morning. If you want to get something off your chest, we can talk."

Vidal shot a glance at Cheyenne, as if worried that she might start talking. When Cheyenne started playing with her hair, Vidal's face softened with relief.

"Carmen, who's paying you to represent Cheyenne?" Vining asked.

Vidal raised her hands. "Is Cheyenne free to leave?"

Kissick stood. "Where can we find her?"

"Just call me and we'll make arrangements," Vidal said. "You have my word."

Walking to her desk, Vining passed the windows of the Detective Sergeants' office and saw that Sergeant Kendra Early wasn't at her desk. She was glad, as she was certain that the next time she saw Early, the sergeant would pull her off the Tink Engleford case.

On Vining's desk was the information about King Getty prepared by the staff assistant. Kissick moved a chair into her cubicle and they went over it.

Vining looked at the copy of Getty's driver's license and handed it to him. "Handsome. Looks like an old-time movie star."

"Six foot one. One hundred seventy-five pounds. Gray hair. Gray eyes."

Vining read aloud from the materials. "He's fifty-five. No criminal record. Looks like he's been at that Wilshire Boulevard address for about eight months. Has a Florida driver's license with a Boca Raton address. Had two moving violations in the past three years. Got a speeding ticket six months ago on Malibu Canyon Road. Has a new Mercedes S six-hundred sedan registered to King G Associates in Boca Raton, Florida. Must have paid cash for it because there's no lien-holder listed."

"That's about a hundred and fifty grand," Kissick said.

"His only prior address is that one in Boca Raton, then the trail disappears. Odd for someone his age and presumably a Getty. Credit check shows an American Express black card registered to King G Associates, and a Visa, also registered to King G. Balances are current. Average balance is ten grand a month. High balance was in December. Get this . . . A hundred and seventy-five grand."

"We'll need warrants to see his credit card bills," Kissick said. "How old are those cards?"

"Barely two years. This place where he's living on Wilshire is owned by someone named Marisa de Castellane."

Vining looked at Kissick. "Here's a guy going around claiming to be a nephew of J. Paul Getty but he has no past and owns no property. He shows up in L.A. and finds a well-heeled Pasadena matron to sweep off her feet."

"Maybe literally, into the drink." Kissick looked over her shoulder. "King G Associates has a Website. Look it up."

Vining brought up a browser and typed in the address. "Movie and television production. Not much of a Website. A single page with information about how to send them a script."

They both looked up when Sergeant Early paused by Vining's cubicle long enough to say, "Can I see both of you in my office, please?"

They'd barely sat in chairs facing Early's desk when she began. "The Catherine Engleford case. Nan, you have a personal relationship with the victim, and your mother was a close friend. I can't let you continue to work this case."

Early was in uniform, probably coming from or heading to a luncheon or community event. She was African American, barely 5'4", and her waistline, a victim of middle age, was nearly as round as her hips. She never wore a scrap of makeup, and the perennially dark circles beneath her eyes didn't help her careworn demeanor. While she wasn't much older than Kissick and Vining, she treated her detectives with motherly warmth and affection. But those who mistook her nurturing side for weakness could be in for a surprising wake-up call.

"Sarge, I haven't talked to the victim in years. Yes, she was my mother's friend, but I can work this case the way it needs to be worked."

Kissick added, "While Nan's mother, Patsy, can be considered a suspect in the broad scheme of things, she's not a suspect."

"Both of your points are well-taken," Early said. "But if it turns out that Mrs. Engleford was a victim of foul play and there's an arrest, the case would be blown because of one of the investigators' personal relationship with the victim and the people close to her."

Kissick privately reflected that he also had a relationship with Patsy, through Nan, which Early didn't know about. His and Nan's personal relationship was making their professional lives ever more complicated and tenuous. They were both jeopardizing their careers. They'd been floating in a la-la land, but they needed to make some decisions before decisions were made for them.

Early looked at them with her typical tired eyes. "Caspers is in court and he might be there for a couple of days. Sproul and Jones are tied up with the nightclub shooting. What did you have planned next?"

Vining answered. "Going to West L.A. to see if we can talk to Kingsley Getty, a man Catherine Engleford was dating. Understand he's a real ladies' man." She was the only female detective in Homicide/Assault and a better choice to get information from Getty than were any of the men.

Early's phone rang. "Yes. Okay. Be right there." She stood. "Go and interview this Getty and we'll talk later."

FOURTEEN

Kingsley Getty lived in a thirty-story tower just east of Westwood. The pricey apartments and condominiums along this stretch of Wilshire Boulevard were not trendy addresses, like ones in the converted industrial buildings in eastern downtown L.A., or West Hollywood, or even in Pasadena these days. The blocky seventies- and eighties-era buildings were the sort of places where a movie star in his or her twilight years might move after unloading the Malibu Colony beachfront house. Or where an attorney at a big firm or a plastic surgeon who'd been turned out of the family Holmby Hills manse during a divorce might live until the settlement.

Kissick parked in the loading zone in front of the building. They walked to the glass double doors, where Vining pressed a buzzer. Immediately, a buzzer responded and the doors unlocked.

On the far end of a sterile lobby stood a well-dressed man behind a semicircular desk.

"Yes, Officers. How can I help you?" He wore a well-tailored dark gray suit with a black shirt and patterned gray tie. A brass name tag said: M. Rahimi. His black wavy hair was combed back from his forehead and dusted with silver at the temples. A sapphire stud earring pierced his left lobe.

Vining handed him her card. "I'm Detective Nan Vining and this is Detective Jim Kissick from the Pasadena Police. We'd like to speak with one of your residents, Kingsley Getty."

"I'm happy to help you, Detectives." He thumbed a stack of business cards in a chrome holder on the desk and handed them each one, revealing a gold watch on his wrist when his sleeve rose.

His voice was dusky and melodious. Vining thought it was the voice he might use after he'd talked a young model into a couple of cocktails and was now trying to convince her to come upstairs. As she took the card, his cologne, which had loitered in the air, hit her full force.

He introduced himself. "I'm Mike Rahimi, the assistant manager. Mr. Getty is out of town. I can try to contact him for you. Can I inquire what this concerns?"

Vining saw his eyes glint over her left hand, seeking a wedding ring. "Mr. Rahimi . . ."

"Mike, please."

She smiled. "Mr. Rahimi, a close friend of Mr. Getty's has died."

"Oh, no . . ."

"Did he ever mention a woman named Catherine Engleford? Goes by the nickname Tink?" She took out the photo of Tink with the three other Ramona Girls that she'd taken from Tink's home. She folded it so that only Tink's face was visible.

Rahimi arched one of his eyebrows as he looked at the photo. They looked better plucked and shaped than hers. His rounded and buffed fingernails were certainly better manicured.

"Mr. Getty has many lady friends," he said with admiration.

She smiled. "I hear he's very charming."

"I don't recall seeing this woman or hearing about her. Catherine Engleford, you say?"

She leaned toward him, getting another blast of spicy cologne. "Yes."

"I don't recall that name." He handed the photo back.

"It's very sad. She died under suspicious circumstances."

"How terrible."

"Her family is desperate to find out what happened to her."

"You can't possibly think that Mr. Getty had anything to do with it."

"Of course not, but he was one of her friends, and he might have information that could be useful to us. Since we drove all the way here in traffic from Pasadena, it would be great if we could at least see Mr. Getty's apartment. We can follow up with him on the phone later. We only need five minutes," she added, smiling more broadly.

Vining saw the flirtatiousness in Rahimi's eyes fade.

He tapped a key on a laptop on the desk, waking it up. "Let me call Mr. Getty on his cell phone."

Kissick had wandered away to look at a wall hanging, but now meandered toward them.

Vining asked, "Detective Kissick, will you please get the crime-scene tape?"

"Crime scene?" Rahimi said with alarm. "But there was no crime here."

"Unfortunately, we have to seal Mr. Getty's apartment. When he returns, we'll meet him here and we'll enter the apartment together."

"Seal it?" Rahimi asked. "Seal it how?"

"You've seen that bright yellow tape." Kissick opened his thumb and index fingers to show how wide it was. "Says 'Crime Scene—Do Not Cross.' We'll put it across the door."

The detectives had no legal right to seal Getty's apartment. Vining was betting on Rahimi wanting to be finished with them as soon as possible and to avoid having to answer questions from nervous residents.

Rahimi took a key from his pocket and unlocked a door in the desk that was lined with keys. "I'll take you to the apartment. I can accompany you?"

"Of course," Vining said.

Rahimi removed a key from a hook. On the desk, he set out a wooden triangle affixed with a plaque that said BACK IN TEN MINUTES.

The elevator door quietly opened and Rahimi gestured for Vining and Kissick to enter ahead of him. Vining did. Kissick held his hand against the door, high above Rahimi's head, and said, "After you."

Rahimi pressed the button for the twenty-first floor, then yanked his shirt cuffs so that they extended a half-inch beyond his jacket sleeves.

"So, Mr. Getty's quite the ladies' man." Kissick gave Rahimi a smile that was nearly a leer, like they were just two guys talking.

Rahimi drew a rounded shape with both hands, raising his shoulders. "Beautiful women, all the time. He's a lovely man. A world traveler. Speaks five languages, including a little Arabic. I'm Persian, but I speak Arabic."

"Sounds like a great guy," Kissick said straight-faced. "What's Mr. Getty's line of work?"

"Investor. Movie producer." Rahimi waved a hand as if to indicate that there was too much to put into words. "He travels a lot. He's rarely here. When he's in town, he always has a beautiful woman on his arm.

Models. Playboy playmates. He got me an invitation to a party at the Playboy Mansion."

"Really?" Kissick smiled. "Go Kingsley. When's the last time you saw him?"

"Last week. He said he was going on a business trip. Would be back in a few days."

Rahimi led the way from the elevator and down the corridor. They walked on thick Berber carpeting. Each set of walnut double doors was flanked by a pair of brass wall sconces. Vining heard only silence. Only those with money could afford that most rare commodity in L.A.

As Rahimi walked ahead of them, Kissick sang under his breath, "Just a gigolo, da, da, da, dada . . ."

Vining elbowed him.

Rahimi stopped at the last set of doors at the end of the hall and fit his key into the lock. He dramatically pushed both doors open.

The first thing that Vining noticed was the light. It was a corner apartment with vast windows and glass doors that opened onto a wraparound terrace. The apartment was as silent as the rest of the building.

The furnishings were minimalist chic of glass, chrome, and stone mixed with Asian cabinets, tables, and art. Past a white travertine tile entry was a large living room. The dining room and kitchen were through an opening lined with two pillars. Vining walked to one of the sliding doors, unlocked it, and stepped outside. The roar of traffic along busy Wilshire Boulevard filtered up. Noise, at last.

She walked back in to see Kissick scoop up a handful of mail from a round table in the entry and casually look through it as he asked Rahimi, "We understand that a woman named Marisa de Castellane owns this apartment."

"*Countess* de Castellane." Rahimi smiled. "Yes. She stays mostly in her homes in Europe."

"Does Mr. Getty rent from her?"

Rahimi raised an eyebrow. "I don't know what financial arrangements Mr. Getty has with the countess."

Vining walked into a large kitchen. It had all the requisite top-of-the-line appliances, plus a few that seemed to have some specialized function she couldn't figure out. Copper pots and pans and anodized cookware hung from an oval iron rack above an island cook station. A steel basket there held two overripe bananas and a couple of dried-up oranges. A wooden butcher block was crammed full of knives.

Her eyes lingered briefly on them. The creep who had stabbed her had used a knife pulled from a butcher block on a similar kitchen island in a different type of lavish domicile. She kept moving.

The cabinets held what Vining would have expected in a bachelor's apartment: dishes, glassware, and flatware that were nothing fancy. A drawer was crammed with the residue of many take-out meals: plastic cutlery sealed in cellophane; single servings of soy sauce, ketchup, and salt and pepper; chopsticks in paper wrappers.

The contents of one cabinet mirrored what she'd found in Tink's kitchen—it was crammed with Berryhill brand vitamins and supplements. She found the same Berryhill cookbook that Tink had. Unlike Tink's, which was splattered with food from being used, Getty's looked brand-new.

She turned to the title page. Georgia Berryhill had signed it in black pen in her distinctive angular handwriting: "To Kingsley, our new friend. Welcome to The Method. To your best mind/body health, Georgia." She hadn't dated it.

Hearing Kissick chatting with Rahimi in the other room, keeping the assistant manager busy, she checked out the refrigerator. There were plastic containers of ground almond butter and peanut butter from Whole Foods. Sprouted grain bread. Three kinds of tofu. Non-fat organic yogurt. Egg whites. Heart Beat margarine. A jar of strawberry preserves from France. The expiration dates were current.

There were packages of whole roasted coffee beans from Jones Coffee in Pasadena—a local place on Raymond Avenue. She wondered if Tink had put Getty onto it. There was a jar of Beluga caviar and two bottles of Veuve Clicquot champagne, the same brand of champagne they'd found by Tink's pool. The vegetable bin held broccoli, carrots, and spinach that were past their prime, and several apples.

She closed the refrigerator door and opened the one for the freezer. In it were a bottle of Ketel One vodka, two shrink-wrapped lobster tails, and a package of mixed berries from Trader Joe's.

She was curious about this caviar- and tofu-eating male.

She found the trash can. It was empty.

She headed down a hallway off the kitchen, passing a laundry room. She entered an office. Protruding through a hole in a built-in desk were computer cables and power cords, suggesting that a laptop computer had been plugged in there. On the desk was the same brochure from the last Georgia's Girls fund-raiser that she'd found in Tink's office.

The cabinets and drawers held nothing unusual except boxes of Crane's stationery and note cards of heavy cream-colored paper, embossed with "Kingsley Getty" in a sedate masculine font in navy-blue ink. The envelopes had this Wilshire Boulevard address on the back flap.

Magazines were scattered across a coffee table in front of a leather couch. On top was the current *People* with Gig Towne, Sinclair LeFleur, and Georgia Berryhill on the cover that Vining had bought at the supermarket. A well-thumbed copy of *The Berryhill Method* was there, along with books about the Civil War, biographies of John Adams and General Douglas MacArthur, and *Outliers* by Malcolm Gladwell.

At the end of the hallway of the huge apartment were a guest room and bathroom. Both were clean and without personal items.

She returned to the living room, where Kissick and Rahimi were still talking.

"How long has Getty lived here?" Kissick asked him.

"About two years," Rahimi replied.

"Have you ever seen this man here?" He took out a printout of a photo. "His name is Vince Madrigal."

"Madrigal. I think I've seen him on TV. Was he in the news?"

"You haven't seen him here?" Kissick folded up the photo.

"No."

She handed Kissick the photo of a younger Cheyenne, Trendi Talbot, and the unknown third girl, Fallon.

As Vining entered a hallway off the living room, Kissick asked Rahimi, "Have you ever seen any of these girls before?"

Vining entered a vast master suite. The two his-and-hers walk-in closets together were as large as her entire bedroom. One closet was empty. The other held a small collection of expensive men's clothing and shoes. There were also well-worn athletic shoes, golf shoes, tennis shoes, deck shoes, a bag of golf clubs, tennis rackets, and a case with fishing poles. There was also a smaller oblong case that wasn't familiar to her. She opened it to find the two halves of a billiards stick tucked inside a velvet-lined holder.

"Aren't we the man's man?" she mused aloud.

A king-sized bed was made up with a fluffy silk duvet and pillow shams in masculine shades of cocoa and cinnamon. Everything was as neat as a pin but the flat surfaces had a light coating of dust, as if a week had passed since the housekeeper had visited.

She was finished and about to leave when she decided to look inside the nightstands, often receptacles for little secrets like sex toys, sleep medications, and dirty magazines. She first went to the nightstand on the right side of the bed, where there was a digital clock on top. The drawer held nothing but a sleep mask to block out the light and a plastic box of silicone earplugs.

"Come on, Getty, thought you were the king. Where's your goodie stash?"

She walked around the bed and opened the drawer in the other end table. Inside were newspaper clippings and printouts of online articles. Vining was jolted when she recognized a photograph. It was of her.

She grabbed everything from the drawer and sat on the bed. All the materials were about her. Some were from seven years ago, when she'd shot a has-been rock star to death in self-defense. Some were from two years ago, when the creep had stabbed her after she'd responded to that suspicious-circumstances call. Some were recent, detailing her final confrontation with the creep, whom she'd revealed as a serial killer of policewomen.

As she looked through the articles, a buzzing noise started deep inside her ears. Sentences had been underlined, mostly quotes of things she'd said. The materials were public, in the news. Yet they felt too personal to be stashed in this strange man's bedroom drawer.

The buzzing in her ears grew louder. Her hands felt limp. She had an impulse to ball up the papers and throw them away. She fought her impulses. Best if Getty didn't know that she knew this about him. She put everything back inside the drawer.

She headed for the bedroom door and was about to leave when she spotted the indentation in the duvet from where she'd been sitting. She went back and smoothed it until no trace of her was left except for what was in the nightstand drawer, immortalized forever on the Internet.

Back inside the Crown Vic parked on the street, Kissick said, "Telling Rahimi that we'd have to put crime-scene tape over the doors was fast thinking, Nan." He cranked the ignition and looked at her. "Something wrong? You seem quiet."

She frowned. "In Getty's bedroom nightstand, there was a drawer full of dozens of articles about me."

"What do you mean, articles?"

"Newspaper articles. Clippings and stuff printed off the Internet."

She could tell he was jarred by the news.

"What do you make of it?" she asked.

"Maybe Getty's doing research for a screenplay or book."

"He'd better not write about me."

He pulled the car from the curb into traffic.

"You're okay with thinking he's doing research for a screenplay?" she asked.

"I don't know what to think, Nan."

Neither did she.

FIFTEEN

It was late afternoon, and traffic was sluggish as Kissick and Vining made the trip from congested ballsy West L.A. to the affluent refined hamlet of La Cañada Flintridge, nestled below the San Gabriel Mountain foothills northeast of Pasadena. They were surprised that it only took forty minutes.

While La Cañada Flintridge and Pasadena shared a short border, Pasadena P.D. rarely had reason to go there on police business. La Cañada Flintridge contracted with the L.A. County Sheriff's for law enforcement, but the city was so safe that some residents didn't lock their doors.

Kissick took the Angeles Crest Highway exit off the 210. "My sons are going to be impressed that I met Gig Towne and Sinclair LeFleur. What about Emily?"

"I have little clue anymore about what she considers hot or stale." Vining was using the browser on Kissick's iPhone for map directions. "You should have made a right."

"You told me left."

"No, I didn't."

"You told me to turn left, Nan." He found a place to turn around.

She wondered whether she had told him to turn the wrong way. They, like many detective partners, acted like an old married couple. Given their romantic entanglement, their conflict had an emotional aspect.

"If I did, I apologize." She was sorry for her mistake and the tension. They were facing a long night after what had been a long day. During the drive from the Westside, she'd been thinking about Tink, a woman she'd maligned over the years for her frivolity, her concern with appearances, and the flaunting of her nouveau riches. She understood Tink's search for solace after the blows of losing her husband and son so closely together. Her last stop had been The Berryhill Method. Vining wondered whether The Method had helped.

"I'm surprised there's so much traffic," he said.

As they drove on, the pines and sycamores grew denser and the houses were farther apart. They rounded a bend, entering Gig Towne and Sinclair LeFleur's neighborhood, and came upon a mob. News vans with satellite dishes were crowded onto the narrow street. Clutches of TV news crews and fans stood along the unpaved roadside. Sheriff's deputies from the Crescenta Valley Station had barricaded the street and were turning away cars.

As Vining and Kissick idled in traffic, a couple of reporters who worked the San Gabriel Valley crime beat recognized them and rushed over. The detectives cracked the car windows and said they couldn't comment.

Kissick stopped near one of the deputies and held up his badge. "What's with the crowd?"

The deputy ordered the reporters to move out of the street and said to Kissick, "This gal who worked for Sinclair LeFleur was murdered last night."

"You mean Trendi Talbot?"

"That's her. Worked as a secretary or something."

Kissick thanked him and drove on, having to slam on his brakes when a man nearly walked into his car. He was wearing a skeleton costume with a rubber mask that covered his head and was carrying a stake with a large handmade poster. On it was a black-and-white publicity headshot of Trendi with a message in dripping red paint: "Berryhill killed Trendi."

After they passed the police barricade, the street became quiet. They spotted the address on a vine-covered wall beside a set of wooden gates across a driveway. The vines had been clipped to expose four square tiles with hand-painted numbers.

Kissick parked behind a navy-blue Crown Vic. "This is déjà vu all over again. That's the car the LAPD detectives who interviewed your mom this morning were driving."

Some paparazzi had gotten through and were loitering around the gate.

Vining and Kissick grabbed their jackets from the backseat. They made their way to the call box in the wall beside the driveway, ignoring the questions lobbed at them and not making eye contact.

A male voice came through the speaker. "A family representative will make a statement at seven o'clock. Please respect the privacy of Mr. Towne and Ms. LeFleur."

Kissick spoke into the metal grate. "Detectives Kissick and Vining from the Pasadena police here. We'd like to have a few words with Mr. Towne and Ms. LeFleur."

"Stand by the pedestrian gate and I'll escort you inside."

Tucked among the vines next to the driveway was a wooden pedestrian gate. They heard locks being released on the inside. It cracked opened to reveal a familiar face.

"Officer Chase," Kissick said with surprise.

Pasadena Police Department officer John Chase stepped outside and used his body to block the opened door while Kissick and Vining hurried in. "Step back from the door." He pushed a guy away while strobe flashes from cameras blinded him. "I'm just the security guy. You don't want my picture."

He backed inside and slammed the door closed with

Kissick's help. He turned a steel bolt lock and shoved into place an iron crossbar that looked as if it had been forged early in the last century, securing it inside a bracket affixed to the opposite post.

"Detectives Kissick and Vining." Chase wiped his right hand against his jeans before offering it to Vining and then Kissick. "I'm surprised to see you here."

"We're surprised to see you, too, Chase," she said.

The young officer was in street clothes. The cuffs were rolled up on his white cotton shirt, which was tucked into blue jeans. A handgun was in a holster on his belt, where there were also pouches with handcuffs and pepper spray.

Chase was a good friend of Detective Alex Caspers. The two of them ran with a group of young male PPD cops who were single and who had started with the PPD around the same time. Vining caught wind of their fishing trips to Cabo, gambling junkets to Vegas, and other shenanigans involving booze and women when she couldn't help but overhear Caspers's telephone conversations through the thin walls in the Detective Section cubicles.

Chase had a well-earned nickname of "The Chaser" from his reputation for pursuing on foot—and catching—suspects who ran from him. Among his buddies, the nickname had an additional connotation, meaning the women he chased and often caught. He was tall and athletic and had all-American blond-haired, blue-eyed good looks. He also presented himself well and seemed like a nice guy. Vining suspected that if he'd set his sights on a woman, he wouldn't have to chase her too hard.

"I do off-duty policing for Gig and Sinclair." Chase winced as if in pain and again nervously rubbed a hand against his jeans. "I live here, on the property, a couple of days a week."

Vining knew of other PPD officers who had moon-lighted as private security for celebrities.

Cognizant of the paparazzi, whom they could hear just beyond the wall, he held out his hand. "Hop in."

He got into a John Deere utility vehicle that had two front seats. It would have been imprudent for Vining to sit on Kissick's lap, so he gestured for her to take the seat and he climbed onto the small cargo area in back, his legs dangling. Chase drove slowly down a cobblestone driveway that cut through a grove of citrus and avocado trees.

"Are you here because of Trendi?" Chase asked Vining over the engine noise.

"No. A woman who lives off San Rafael was found dead this morning in her backyard pool. She was friends with Towne and LeFleur."

"I didn't hear about that, but I've been here for the past couple of days."

They neared the end of the grove, where Vining saw a two-story Spanish-style house. The exterior was simple, with plaster walls painted the color of adobe. Above a bright blue front door, a striped cloth awning was stretched between iron spears that jutted from the façade. The second floor had two sets of windows covered with decorative black iron grills and had shutters in the same distinctive blue as the front door. The setting sun had descended past the tile roof, turning the shadows purple.

"How long have you been moonlighting here?" Vining asked.

"A couple of months. It's good. Been good." Chase seemed rattled. He again winced.

The driveway circled a large cement fountain. The tiered scalloped bowls were planted with miniature succulents. Pots of rosemary blooming with tiny blue flowers were set inside the tile pool around the fountain's base.

Chase stopped in front of the house.

"The dead Pasadena woman was named Catherine Engleford." Vining handed Chase her photo. "She went by the nickname Tink. Did you ever see her here?"

Kissick hopped off the back of the small vehicle.

Chase frowned at the photo, pressing his fingertips against his head in front of his right ear. "I don't remember seeing her."

"John, are you okay?" Vining asked.

"I've just got a headache." He agitatedly pointed toward his head and shrugged. "Been a long day."

She pocketed the photo he returned to her. "Would you like an aspirin?"

"Thanks. I took something. It should kick in soon. Two Ds from LAPD are here now, talking to Gig. You probably heard about Vince Madrigal and a woman getting offed in Eagle Rock. The woman was Sinclair's assistant, Trendi Talbot. Looks like they killed each other."

"We heard," Kissick said. "Did Gig Towne or Sinclair LeFleur have a relationship with Madrigal?"

"I don't know."

"Do you have any idea what Ms. Talbot was doing with Madrigal?" Vining asked.

"No clue," Chase said.

Kissick asked, "Is Ms. LeFleur here?"

Chase seemed pensive. "She's resting. She's really upset over what happened to Trendi."

"You must have known Ms. Talbot," Vining said. "What was she like?"

Chase sucked in his bottom lip and made a small movement with his hands as if he didn't know where to begin. "She was nice. Fun. Sinclair liked her a lot."

Vining took out the photo of Cheyenne Leon, Trendi Talbot, and the other girl. "John, have you ever seen these two girls who are with Mrs. Talbot?"

He couldn't hide the surprise in his eyes. "I couldn't say."

She wouldn't let him off the hook. "Meaning you can't or you won't?"

He hovered as if trying to decide how to respond.

"What's going on, John?" Kissick took a step closer to Chase, entering his space. "You're not being straight with us."

Chase stepped back and let out a long breath. "Look. I can't talk about what goes on here. I had to sign a confidentiality agreement. Everyone who works here has to sign one. It's got me bound so tight . . ." He held up his hands as if he was helpless.

Kissick and Vining both stared at him, unimpressed.

Chase stammered. "I'm sure Gig will tell you everything you want to know. If you have further questions, then come and ask me. Will that work?"

Vining leveled her eyes at Chase, her jaw rigid.

Kissick replied with a clipped, "Sure. Let's talk to your employer."

Chase grimaced as he took that in. He turned and started walking. "I'll show you in."

SIXTEEN

C hase mounted the two steps to the front door and turned an iron latch that served as a doorknob. He pushed the door open and gestured for the detectives to enter.

Kissick waited for Vining and then followed, stepping onto a fired tile floor in a two-story foyer.

Chase closed the door, and the latch clanked as soundly

as a jail cell door slamming shut. The vast entry with its arches, wrought iron, and tile felt as warm as a medieval dungeon. A black iron chandelier circled with dozens of electric candles was suspended from the two-story ceiling. Curved staircases ascended each side of the foyer and met at a second-floor balcony. The railings were of twisted wrought iron, the balustrades studded with iron spheres. Exposed ceiling beams were stenciled.

"This way." Chase crossed the foyer and turned down a long corridor. The walls were decorated with antique tapestries. Spotlighted cubbyholes displayed stone or metal statues of horses and warriors in armor. The air was chilly.

"You can wait in the sunroom and I'll see if Gig is available."

He led them to a room off the back of the house that was furnished with rattan couches and chairs. The outside windows were set into arches and had small panes of glass framed in iron. Through the windows they could see the U-shaped Spanish style of the house, the three wings facing a courtyard with a rectangular pool, a grass lawn, and a well-tended rose garden. A tented cabaña was at the far end.

Chase started to leave, then turned back. "Would you like something to drink?"

"I could use some water," Vining said. "Tap water's fine."

"How about you, Detective Kissick?"

Kissick turned from where he'd been admiring the view. "Water would be great. Thanks."

Chase started to leave when Kissick called after him. "Say, John, does Gig Towne know about Catherine Engleford's death?"

"I don't think so. Once we found out about Trendi, we've been dealing with that."

"Let us tell him."

"Will do."

When Chase had left, Kissick returned to gazing at the pool and the garden. The landscape lights had turned on with the setting sun. "Nice."

Vining moved to stand beside him. "The grounds are beautiful, but this house feels like a hotel to me and is about as warm."

"I wouldn't have imagined Gig Towne living in a house like this. I'd have thought he'd live in a modern place. You know, lots of glass and stainless steel, in Malibu Colony or someplace like that. A traditional house in staid Flintridge. Who knew?"

"The *People* article said Sinclair LeFleur grew up in this town."

"Nice setup Chase has got for himself, especially for a single guy," Kissick said. "Wonder what he gets paid."

"Enough to make it worthwhile for him to keep his mouth shut about what goes on here. I don't believe he's afraid of being sued. If his lifestyle's like Alex Caspers's, he rents an apartment, and the only thing to his name is his car and some clothes."

They turned at the tinkling sound of ice against glass. A statuesque older woman walked down the steps carrying a silver tray. Her short hair was dyed orange and was gelled into spikes. She said, "Good evening, Detectives," as she walked the tray to a wooden coffee table. Her smile was friendly, but her bearing was aloof. "I'm Paula Lowestoft, Gig's assistant."

She wore a long straight skirt and a short-sleeved blouse in a brown, black, and gold geometric print. Her large crystal-and-jade earrings jangled when she bent to set down the tray.

She picked up two coasters from a stack and set glasses of sparkling water on each. "Here's lime if you like." She set out a small glass bowl of lime wedges. "Gig apologizes for making you wait. He's outside, making a statement to the media. Hopefully, they'll leave after that."

Vining gaped at Paula's eyes, which were a dark amber color, like a cat's. "Thank you."

"My pleasure." She left, her flat sandals retorting softly against the tile floor.

Vining squeezed lime into her water, raised the glass to her lips, and looked at Kissick over the rim.

He raised his eyebrows and punched his wrist from his sleeve to look at his watch. Picking up his glass, he began pacing the length of the room.

Vining sat in an armchair, falling into it more heavily than she'd intended when it proved to be softer than she'd thought. She took her cell phone from the holder on her belt and began typing with her thumbs.

"I'm texting Em. See if she can get a ride home with a classmate after her photography workshop." She grimaced. "I hate having some kid who just got a license driving her."

"Can't your mother and grandmother pick her up?"

"After that six-pack of chardonnay my mother bought?"

"Sorry I brought it up."

Vining's cell phone buzzed. "Em says her girlfriend's mother can take her home. Good." She typed a response.

John Chase returned. "Gig can see you now in his office. You can leave the glasses there."

They returned to the corridor and ascended a staircase.

"Is the LAPD gone?" Kissick asked.

"Yes." At the top of the stairs, Chase rapped on a heavy door that was slightly ajar. Its iron hinges creaked with his knocking.

They heard a familiar voice sing in an operatic tenor, "Come innn . . ."

Chase pushed the door all the way open.

Gig Towne stood up at the head of a massive table. The chair he'd vacated, upholstered in red velvet and with wood carvings on the back and arms, looked like a throne. Medieval-looking straight-backed chairs lined the table. Two smaller versions of the chandelier in the entry were suspended from a crossbeam of the pitched ceiling. Bookcases and display cases filled the wall space between arched windows with small panes of glass like those in the sunroom. There was also a fireplace with a gray marble mantel.

"Detectives, please approach," Towne said in a booming voice out of a cartoon, which reverberated in the large room. He stiffly held out his right hand and robotically crooked his fingers to summon them. His rubbery face formed a stern mask with eyebrows angled up and his mouth making a perfect upside-down U, like a Kabuki actor.

Vining and Kissick remained just inside the doorway, neither one taking a step forward, needing a moment to take it all in.

Chase muttered something about being back later and slipped away, closing the door behind him. The metal latch clicked.

Towne suddenly dropped the pose, letting his shoulders and limbs go limp as if made of taffy. After a few seconds, he swatted the air and grinned in a way that was more normal, yet still exaggerated. "I apologize, Detectives. I shouldn't mess with you. Just a little humor. My twisted way of dealing with a sad situation."

He started toward them. Vining and Kissick met him midway.

She reached him first. "I'm Detective Nan Vining with the Pasadena Police Department and this is my partner, Detective Jim Kissick."

His handshake was firm and his palm was dry. His

narrow eyes were bright blue and clear, and his gaze was direct. He was shorter and thinner than Vining had thought he'd be, but looked fit. He wore a Kelly-green short-sleeved golf shirt in a light cool-weave fabric tucked into tailored black slacks. His black leather belt had a Gucci logo buckle.

Vining glanced at Kissick and saw that he was starstruck.

"What an honor to meet you, Mr. Towne. I'm a big fan and so are my two boys."

"Thank you very much, Detective Kissick. Please call me Gig. How old are your boys?"

"Seventeen and thirteen. My thirteen-year-old . . . He can do the Gig giggle perfectly. I mean, he has it down."

"You mean this giggle?" Towne took a breath and belted out a blend of braying and hiccuping.

"That's it!" Kissick laughed. "Cal . . . He's my thirteen-year-old. He can do it just like that."

"Maybe your sons would like an autographed action figure." Towne walked to a cabinet stocked with boxes of foot-tall replicas of him costumed in his different movie roles. He opened the glass door and took out a box. "Maybe one of me as the Mad Hatter."

"Thank you, Gig, but I can't accept that. But I know my boys would like an autograph."

"How about the twenty-year-anniversary edition of *Stupid Is* that's just out on DVD? They're almost worthless."

Kissick laughed at what he took to be a joke. "That would be great."

Towne opened the glass door of a cabinet and took two DVDs from a pile stacked inside. "We did a good job with this DVD. Lots of bonus features." He turned to Vining. "What about you, Detective? Would you like a signed DVD?"

Vining had been looking inside the glass cabinets. The shelves were packed with vintage lunchboxes, toys, action figures, bound scripts from Towne's movies, and other memorabilia from Towne's career. "Thank you. Maybe for my fifteen-year-old daughter. Her name's Emily."

"Traditional spelling?" Towne asked.

"Yes." She was face-to-face with a life-sized mannequin dressed like Bozo the Clown that stood in a corner.

"Your sons' names, Detective Kissick?"

Kissick told him.

Towne sat at his grand chair and began signing the paper inserts inside the DVD cases. He commented to Vining, "That costume was one of the originals worn by Larry Harmon himself."

"Huh." Vining moved to look inside another cabinet. "Crayons?"

"Unopened original Crayola crayon boxes." Towne handed Kissick the signed DVDs and walked to hand Vining hers. They thanked him. "Those boxes have discontinued crayon colors like 'flesh.'"

He opened the case and took out a box. "This is a rare, unopened sixty-four-color set, with sharpener. There are only a few known ones in existence. A box like this is in the Smithsonian."

"You learn something new every day," Vining said.

"I like having toys from my childhood around. I'm just a kid at heart." Towne again mugged, making his rubbery face and body mimic a goofy young boy's.

"Your house is spectacular," Kissick said.

"Thank you," Towne shot back.

"What's the architecture?" Kissick had put much love and countless hours into restoring his turn-of-the-century Craftsman bungalow in Altadena, the city north of Pasadena.

"Spanish Revival," Towne said. "With Majorcan influences. It was built in nineteen twenty-nine. Let's have a seat and talk."

Vining was glad to get started.

The detectives followed him to the end of the table, taking opposite sides to face each other.

Towne sat at the head and closed the lid of a laptop computer that was the only thing on the giant table.

Vining got a closer look at Towne's thronelike chair. The wood across the back was carved in the shape of opened draperies rising to a replica of a crown that was suspended above Towne's head. Above each shoulder were the heads of roaring lions with full manes. The ends of the arms were finished with giant feline paws, claws extended.

She was sure the chair had a history, but she didn't want to give Towne another opportunity to stroke his tremendous ego, wasting time while her daughter was home alone.

Kissick did it for her. "This is some table."

Gig brightened, enjoying talking about himself and his possessions. "It's from the library where I grew up in Sioux Falls, South Dakota. I spent many hours in that library when my mom was working cleaning bathrooms at the hospital and my dad was either getting drunk or sleeping one off, usually in the town jail."

He fingered graffiti on the top. "Here's where I carved my name with a Bic pen when I was ten. Miss Garner, the librarian, gave me hell. She handed me a book and ordered me to read it. It was *A Wrinkle in Time*. Changed my life. A few years ago, I helped them build a new library. Asked if I could have this table from the old one."

He seemed wistful as he traced his crudely carved name, but Vining couldn't be sure that he wasn't acting.

Towne sat back in the chair, his hands cupping the lion paws on the ends of the arms. "I just spent a long time with two LAPD detectives discussing what happened to poor Trendi. Shocking. Trendi was more than an employee. She was a dear friend. Still hasn't sunk in. I pray they find out what happened. I don't know what brings the Pasadena police to my door, but you can't be here to tell me I won a makeover on *Oprah*."

Kissick began. "Do you know Catherine Engleford?"

The look in Towne's eyes that Vining had taken for false sincerity was erased and replaced by genuine alarm. "Sure, I know Tink."

"This morning, her assistant found her dead in her backyard pool."

Towne sucked in air. He looked from Kissick to the table, to Vining, then back at Kissick.

"Drowned?"

"We're investigating the circumstances that led to her death," Kissick replied.

Towne drew his hands over the wooden lion's paws and gazed across the room. "The universe is unbalanced. Tragedy will abound until homeostasis is established."

Vining turned to follow Towne's gaze. He was looking at Bozo.

SEVENTEEN

We just saw Tink last week. Sinclair and I have been working with her on a fund-raiser for Georgia's Girls." Towne rubbed his hand over his chin. "I can't process this. First Trendi. Now Tink."

Kissick took notes in his spiral notebook. "When did you meet Catherine Engleford?"

Towne stuck the tip of his tongue between his teeth. "Oh, gosh. Must be over a year ago. Sinclair and I met her at Berryhill—Georgia's compound up in Malibu Canyon. Tink's a neighbor. Well, an L.A. version of a neighbor, meaning someone who only lives a few miles away on surface streets. Sinclair has a big heart and invited Tink over for dinner. I'm sure you know about Tink losing both her son and husband. That's what brought her to Berryhill. She worked The Method and I believe she found peace."

Kissick turned to a fresh page in his notebook. "Have you met Mrs. Engleford's boyfriend, Kingsley Getty?"

"King Getty." Towne intoned his name as if announcing the arrival of royalty. "Great guy. Sinclair and I were so happy when Tink started dating him."

"Where did she meet him?"

"At Berryhill."

"He calls himself a movie producer," Vining said. "Do you know any movies he's produced?"

Towne laughed. "That's what he puts on his business card, like some people put 'investor' or 'consultant.' He's independently wealthy."

"How do you know?"

"I haven't seen anything to indicate that he's not who he says he is." Towne became thoughtful. "I see what you're getting at. Tink is a lonely rich widow. Getty is a charming man-about-town. Look, I have a finely tuned BS monitor. When you've been in Hollywood as long as I have, you need one if you're going to survive. Actually, I'm working on a couple of projects with King right now. One is a remake of *From Here to Eternity*."

"One of my favorites," Kissick said.

"We were thinking of updating it to an army base in Iraq."

Vining considered that. She had broad knowledge of classic movies, as she frequently relaxed with the cable classic movie channel when she couldn't sleep. "That would make it hard to re-create that famous seduction scene on the beach with Burt Lancaster and Deborah Kerr in the waves."

"No one can re-create that," Towne was quick to respond. "You do something just as sexy, but different."

It was clear to Vining that Towne didn't like being challenged.

He went on. "We're also working on a modern update of *La Bohème*. Sinclair will play Mimi, and we're going to call it *Love Kills*."

Kissick raised his eyebrows. "That sounds really interesting."

Towne grinned. "It'll be a smash."

Vining cleared her throat.

Towne returned to the main topic. "King couldn't have had anything to do with Tink's death. He's much too much of a gentleman. No disrespect to Tink, but she enjoyed her cocktails. She might have had a few pops too many and tumbled into the pool."

"She might have," Kissick agreed. "How would you describe Mrs. Engleford's mood recently?"

"She was in love. She was centered, healthy, fit, and full of life and vigor. Humbled by the hard knocks she'd experienced, but grateful for all that life had bestowed upon her, and she was moving on with her life. Eager to give back to the community some of the blessings that she'd received. Working on reaching an even higher plane. Tink was not a woman who was about to commit suicide, if that's what you're suggesting."

Vining was impressed by the eloquence of his off-the-cuff eulogy. "What higher plane are you speaking of? Does this have to do with shadow selves?"

A clock on the mantel pealed a single musical chime to mark the half hour.

Towne pushed himself up from his chair, went to a bookshelf, raised the glass door, and pulled out a book. He placed it in front of Vining before again taking his chair.

It was a copy of *The Berryhill Method*, like the one they'd seen at both Tink's and Getty's homes, but this edition had a glossy cardboard cover like a textbook.

"Study that and we'll talk. I can't discuss The Method out of context, without any background. It's like telling someone that Jesus died for our sins without the backstory. You can't possibly understand. Not you personally, but anyone. You should talk to Georgia and Stefan. They'd be more than happy to answer all your questions."

Vining looked at Georgia Berryhill's plump pleasant face on the back of the book. "I couldn't help but see the new *People* magazine when I was grocery shopping. Are you and your wife really best friends with Georgia Berryhill and her husband?"

"Absolutely. Sinclair and I wouldn't have done that piece if we weren't. We've known Georgia and Stefan for years. From the beginning, when they got started with Vitamin A. Now they go all the way through Zinc." He laughed at his joke, looking at Kissick for a smile, having given up on Vining.

Kissick cooperated and grinned. "Do you adhere to the Berryhill vitamin regimen?"

"How else would I be able to keep up with a wife who's sixteen years younger than me? Berryhill vitamins and supplements are the best out there. Returning to Georgia and Stefan for a minute, we are so happy that they're pregnant. They tried for so long."

Vining knew she could be old-fashioned, but she couldn't get used to the "we're pregnant" term. She voiced some of her thoughts. "I know I'm old-fashioned, but I don't understand this trend of giving birth at home in a pool of body-temperature water. Give me a hospital with lots of doctors, nurses, and pharmaceuticals any day."

"Our midwife, Paula, will assist with the birth, but our obstetrician will be here if we need him."

"Paula?" Vining asked. "We met a woman earlier named Paula, who we understood was your assistant."

"Well, we have to give her something to do in the meantime. The point is, we have all the medical equipment and professional expertise necessary in case of an emergency, which we don't anticipate. Sinclair and the baby are in robust health. A baby's brain starts absorbing information, learning about his or her world, in the womb. At birth, the process explodes. Hospitals are treacherous places. I'm not just talking about antibiotic-resistant bacteria, which is scary, but there's the entire issue of what hospitals represent."

As Towne warmed to his subject, he started speaking more quickly and his eyes grew intense. "We bring babies into the world in this institution whose primary functions are the management of illness and death. In our so-called advanced society, we've gotten so far away from the fundamentals of birth that we consider this normal. Think about it. What is normal about bringing a new human life, a new soul, onto this planet in an environment of sickness and sadness?"

The detectives were watching him with fascination, not just because of what he was saying, but also because of how worked up he was getting. The clownish looseness was gone as he became more and more tightly coiled and his eyes grew fierce.

"As far as my role, I'll be in the birthing room and, because it's been a good-luck charm for me, I'll be wearing my vintage Bozo costume." He paused for a few beats, taking in the detectives' bewildered expressions, before laughing out loud. Thrusting both palms in front, he shouted, "Kidding!"

He smiled in the way he was famous for, scrunching his elastic face until the entire lower half was consumed by a crazy grin. The laserlike focus of his eyes dissipated and they twinkled with amusement. "Oh, boy. The looks on your faces." He let out a long, high-pitched sigh, primly crossed his legs, folded his hands on his knee, and said in the voice of a brittle, ancient spinster aunt, "So, what else can I help you with today?"

Vining squared *The Berryhill Method* on the table in front of her. "Gig, are you aware that there's a man outside your property with a sign that says, 'Berryhill Killed Trendi'?"

"Him *again*?" Towne theatrically yanked a cell phone from his shirt pocket and put it to his ear. "Dad, please stop scaring the reporters. I know you think it's funny, but not everyone is getting the joke. Please. For me."

Kissick gave a halfhearted laugh and Vining didn't even try. She was glad to see that Gig Towne's luster was wearing thin on her partner.

"Honestly, Detectives . . . When someone, anyone, becomes as famous as Georgia Berryhill, and you're inspiring people with your lifestyle and philosophy, and helping people turn their lives around, you also draw out the freaks. People condemn what they don't understand. Berryhill didn't kill Trendi. From what the LAPD detectives told me, that scumbag Vince Madrigal stabbed her."

"Maybe you can help me understand something," Vining began. "Ms. Talbot had a criminal past, but your pregnant wife hired her as an assistant."

Towne's gaze again grew intense. He turned it on Vining. "Detective, I have a criminal past as well. Trendi looked into the darkness of her soul, faced her shadows, and walked beside them into her full potential."

"Were you acquainted with Vince Madrigal?"

Towne smirked. "He was the go-to guy if you wanted to slime someone. I knew him . . . and avoided him."

Vining took out the photograph of Cheyenne, Trendi, and Fallon and set it in front of Towne. "Do you recognize the other two women with Ms. Talbot?"

Towne picked up the photo and looked intently at it. He stood and carried it to a window to study in the light. He turned it over and read the writing on the back. "Where did you get this?" His voice was somber.

"That's not important," Vining said.

"Something troubling you, Gig?" Kissick asked.

Towne shook his head. "I'm just surprised to see Trendi so young. Such a beautiful girl. What a tragedy." He returned to the table, holding the photograph out for Vining.

She didn't move to take it. "What about the other two girls? Do you know them?"

Towne seemed to be weighing his words, deciding how to respond. He set the photo in front of Vining and tapped his index finger on it. "This girl worked for Tink. Her name's Cheyenne Leon."

"How well do you know her?"

"Not well. She was helping Tink with the Georgia's Girls fund-raiser. She ran some documents over to me. That was about it."

"How long did she work for Mrs. Engleford?"

"I don't know."

"Those three girls look like they're friends. Did Ms. Leon ever visit Ms. Talbot here?"

"I don't believe so, but I'm often away."

"What about the third girl? Fallon."

He shook his head. "Don't know her."

Vining wasn't buying it. "Something about that photo is upsetting you."

Although he betrayed little on the surface, Vining felt him bristle. The clown persona was gone. He was hiding something.

"Trendi was murdered. I'm sad. Detectives, what does

this have to do with your reason for coming here, which was to talk about Tink?"

"We want to know your impressions of Ms. Leon," Vining said.

"I already told you. I only met her briefly."

"We'd like to talk to your wife," Kissick said.

"That will have to wait for another time. Sinclair is resting. She's taken Trendi's murder hard. She can't add anything to what I've already told you."

Vining pressed. "We understand that Ms. LeFleur is upset, but we need to talk to her before we leave."

"She's already tired from talking to the LAPD detectives. I don't even want her to know about Tink right now. Talk to her all you want, but I only ask that you wait until tomorrow."

"We can do that," Kissick said.

Vining glowered at him.

The mantel clock began bonging once for each hour. It was eight o'clock.

"Rise and shine!" Towne abruptly burst from the chair. He pantomimed holding a bugle to his lips as he sang reveille with his lips pursed.

Kissick chuckled.

Towne kept on, making his eyes even wilder, showing the whites all the way around as he looked at Vining, who hadn't cracked a smile.

Towne feigned collapsing, saving himself by slapping his hand on top of the table as he wheezed. "Detective Vining, you're making me work hard. What a tough audience. But seriously, Detectives, if you have no further questions, I have an engagement."

Towne walked them out, chatting with Kissick about his upcoming movie, which, Kissick was glad to hear, was a comedy.

"I'm through with trying to be a serious actor. My fans know best."

Vining was glad Towne hadn't noticed that she'd left behind the copy of *The Method* he'd given her.

When they reached the front entry, John Chase appeared from beneath an archway.

"John will see you out." Towne clapped his hand around Chase's back and onto his shoulder. "You've got a good man here."

Chase smiled wanly, looking as troubled as when he'd first met them at the front gate.

They turned at the sound of a door opening above, followed by light footsteps against the tile floor. Sinclair LeFleur stepped into the balcony at the junction of the two staircases.

Vining thought she looked even more beautiful than in her photographs. Her dark hair, a mass of spiral curls that flowed past her shoulders, was scooped back from her face and held by a white headband with a silk gardenia attached to it. Her skin was porcelain, as translucent and white as the sleeveless chiffon floor-length dress she wore, which looked like a design from ancient Rome. The low scooped neckline revealed bounteous cleavage. Below the empire waist, the draped fabric did little to disguise the fact that she was hugely pregnant. Her large eyes were as black as her hair. Her Cupid's-bow lips were rosy.

Both Kissick and Vining gasped. She took their breath away.

LeFleur grasped the iron railing with both of her fine-boned hands. She looked fragile and shaken.

Vining sensed John Chase tense at the sight of LeFleur. She glanced at him and saw him gazing dreamily at the actress.

Walking to stand behind LeFleur was Paula Lowestoft, the imperious woman who the detectives now knew was not just Gig's assistant but LeFleur's midwife.

"Funny face . . ." Towne walked to stand below the balcony. "Why aren't you resting?"

"I'm sorry, Gig," Lowestoft said, putting her hand on LeFleur's arm. "She wanted to see what was going on."

LeFleur looked at the detectives. "Are they from the police? Why are they still here?" Her voice was as soft and powerless as she looked.

"My love, they're leaving," Towne said. "It's all taken care of. You need to rest. Paula, please help my wife rest."

Standing behind LeFleur, the taller Lowestoft put her hands on her employer's shoulders. LeFleur set her perfect lips and wrenched her body. Lowestoft flung her hands off as if insulted and shrugged at Towne as if she was helpless to control his wife.

LeFleur peevishly yanked the flower-adorned headband from her hair and whirled around to leave. Before she padded away in her satin ballet slippers, she looked over her shoulder. Vining thought this parting glance was directed at Chase. She turned her head slightly so she could glimpse the young officer. He was staring at her with undisguised longing.

Chase drove the detectives back to the gate in the utility vehicle, with Kissick again sitting in the rear bed.

In the front seat, Vining had to almost shout to Chase to be heard over the engine. "Ms. LeFleur is really beautiful. She's even more beautiful in person."

Chase said, with complete sincerity, "She's beautiful on the inside, too."

"Seems such an odd match, her and Gig Towne. Don't you think?"

Chase made a small movement of his shoulders.

"Strange that they'd hire someone like Trendi Talbot—

a runaway, arrested for prostitution, a drug addict. Especially now that I see how protective Mr. Towne is of Ms. LeFleur. Did Ms. Talbot have complete access to the house?"

"She lived in one of the small rooms along the pool, where my room is. Gig was giving her a break, like someone gave him a break years ago when he was in trouble. She was cleaned up. Off drugs and all that."

He stopped at the front gate.

The detectives hopped off.

Vining said, "Chase, we want you to keep your eyes and ears open about what goes on in that house."

Chase rubbed his temples.

"You have a problem with that?" she asked.

"I guess I don't understand what your case in Pasadena has to do with Trendi Talbot or the girls in that photo, or what any of it has to do with Gig and Sinclair."

Vining couldn't have said it better herself. "We don't know either, Chase, but there's something fishy going on. Once Detective Kissick and I get to the bottom of it, then we'll decide whether we can dismiss it as the eccentricities of the rich and shameless."

Kissick spoke up. "John, what do you know that you're not telling us?"

Chase exhaled with exasperation. "I could get fired if Gig finds out I'm talking to you like this. All due respect, Detectives, but I'm between a rock and a hard place here."

"If you have knowledge of criminal activity and are covering it up, that's a conspiracy," Vining said. "We're not going to push this now, but you're going to have to answer these questions sooner or later."

"Yes, ma'am."

"Are you having a migraine?"

"No, ma'am. It's just a situation that comes and goes."

"You need to get medical attention for that," Vining said.

"I've been to a doctor. Like I said, it comes and goes."

"All right. Take care of yourself." Vining shook his hand.

Kissick did the same.

Chase unbolted the front gate.

Kissick exited in front of Vining. The paparazzi outside had left, as had the mob on the adjoining street.

As they headed toward the freeway, Vining asked, "Did you notice anything strange about that last interaction in the foyer?"

"What *wasn't* strange about it?"

"I mean, between Chase and Sinclair LeFleur."

Kissick raised an eyebrow. "As pregnant as she is? You think there's something going on?"

"Something's going on all right. He's in love with her."

EIGHTEEN

*J*ohn Chase returned to the house, securing the multiple locks on the front door. He checked the windows and began making his way through the northern wing, following his nightly routine.

Gig Towne stepped into the corridor from the media room, where he had been waiting in the dark.

Chase was startled, but managed not to show it. "Hi, Gig. Just doing my rounds. All is well. Paparazzi have split."

"Good." Gig casually slipped his hands into his slacks pockets but his demeanor wasn't relaxed. "What a shock, hearing that my friend Tink was found floating in her pool just after getting that terrible news about Trendi. I'm going to wait to tell Sinclair about Tink. She's so upset over Trendi, I don't think she could handle another blow."

"Got it."

"Your Pasadena police colleagues, Detectives Vining and Kissick, were extremely interested in Trendi. They even had an old photo of her with a couple of girlfriends. Strange."

Chase remained expressionless.

"Did they show it to you?"

He lied. "No."

"Any idea why they were so interested in Trendi? I don't see any connection to Tink's death in Pasadena."

"I couldn't say, Gig. That's above my pay grade."

"Right." Gig laughed. "Your pay grade." He gave Chase a playful punch on the arm. "You were friendly with Trendi, right?"

"Sure."

"Any idea what she was doing with Vince Madrigal?"

"No clue."

"Madrigal had a list of enemies as long as my arm. I think someone came to kill him, and Trendi was in the wrong place at the wrong time."

Chase's face betrayed the fact that he doubted the story.

"Have you heard something?"

"This is off the record, but I have a friend who has friends in the LAPD who say that it looks like Trendi and Madrigal killed each other."

"What?" Gig looked aghast. "Trendi kill somebody? No way."

"She shot him. Could have been self-defense."

"How did she die?"

"He stabbed her in the belly."

Gig wheeled around. "Oh, man. That's a bad way to go." He rubbed his face. "Wow."

"I wonder if she was using again and Madrigal supplied her."

"That must be it. Guess it'll come out in the toxicology tests. What set her off? Was she upset by anything that you know of?"

Chase shook his head. "No, sir."

"Her mother would like to know what really happened. I talked to her earlier today. Even though she was the reason Trendi ran away from home and ended up on the streets."

Chase nodded, waiting to be released.

Gig gave him a piercing look. "So you don't know anything else about what happened to Trendi?"

"No, sir."

After an awkward moment, Gig again punched Chase's arm. "John, anything you can find out through your . . . network, I'd be appreciative. Very appreciative."

Chase continued nodding. "Yes, sir."

Gig turned and headed down the corridor in the opposite direction.

Chase was glad to hear Gig's footsteps fade. He continued checking doors and windows and entered the kitchen. Gig and Sinclair's personal chef had left for the day. Chase opened one of the two refrigerators and looked through the well-organized glass containers with labels describing the contents taped to the front. Plastic food-storage containers were forbidden in the house, as Gig and Sinclair believed they leached toxic chemicals.

He took out a container of meatballs and raised the

glass lid. He would have dug in with his fingers, but he knew the kitchen was one of the areas monitored by the closed-circuit television that security-obsessed Gig had installed. He grabbed a fork and a plate and scooped meatballs onto it. He ate them cold, shoving them into his mouth whole. The chef always left some in the fridge because she knew Chase liked them.

He put the plate and fork into one of the two dishwashers and headed through a door off the kitchen and down a narrow staircase to the basement. The prior owners had turned the large space into a garage for an antique car collection. The house was built on a sloping hill, permitting one side of the basement to open to the outside, accessing the private road that went through the property.

Gig had redesigned the space, building a full gym that would rival any commercial one, a wine cellar, and a massage and meditation room. After Sinclair had become pregnant, part of the area had been taken over for the birthing room.

Chase took his time going through the subterranean rooms, checking the narrow windows near the ceiling along the outside wall. He looked through a window in the steel door to the birthing room and didn't see anyone there. He pulled down on the industrial door handle and went inside.

The pool where Sinclair would give birth was recessed into the ground. It was eight feet square, three feet deep, and lined with white tiles. There were built-in benches beneath the waterline. It was filled with purified water that was maintained at 98.6 degrees. The area around the pool had a slip-free textured surface. The floor in the rest of the room was of bleached wood planks. There were no rugs that would collect dust.

The other side of the room was furnished like a living room, in calming shades of sage green and tan. An adjustable bed was made up with fine cotton linens and blankets—nothing synthetic—for baby and parents to rest after the birth. A flat-screen television was mounted to a wall. Wireless headsets were plugged into chargers. Silence would be maintained throughout the labor and delivery.

Behind a curtain attached to a rod by rings was a fully equipped area set up for a medical emergency.

Chase hated this place. He hated the flagrant waste to have gone to all this expense building this facility, which would be used for a few hours and maybe just once. Gig was an avowed humanitarian and philanthropist. Sure, he'd done a lot of good with the fortune he'd amassed, but Chase wondered what the public would think if they saw this side of him. His publicists were already working overtime doing damage control after his appearances on *The Tonight Show* and *Ellen*, during which he was wacky, and not in a funny-ha-ha way.

That was the other thing this room represented for Chase. It was brick-and-mortar evidence that Gig Towne was nuts. The public would never find out. His inner circle was loyal and protective. If loyalty hadn't sprung spontaneously from within their hearts, Gig's attorneys imposed a facsimile of it from the outside.

None of this was Sinclair's doing. She'd gone along at first, lured into Gig's world by the white-hot glare of his fame and the seductiveness of his charm. She'd told Chase she'd felt as if she was walking deeper and deeper into a hall of mirrors. What had started as exciting, edgy fun had turned into a nightmare.

Chase stood at the edge of the pool and looked at the built-in tile chair where, any day now, Sinclair would give birth. Organic cotton cushions filled with buckwheat hulls were stacked in a stainless steel cart nearby.

The other basement rooms were always chilly—suitable for the wine cellar and the gym—but this room was kept at a comfortable seventy-two degrees. Chase knew a lot about this room. He knew that it was one of the few places on the property that was not monitored by hidden CCTV cameras.

Through the window in the door, he glimpsed an apparition of a milky-white face surrounded by a cloud of black hair. The door opened and Sinclair LeFleur padded across the floor as fast as she could manage, her legs forced wide with the baby, the soft fabric of her white dress billowing.

Chase's long legs reached her in a few steps. He took her into his arms.

Her face was streaked with tears. "Oh, John."

He wiped her flushed cheeks with his fingertips. He wanted to kiss her, but didn't. He couldn't cross that line. Not yet. He was hopeful that there would come a time when they would be together. It wasn't unheard of, the bodyguard and his charge falling in love. She hadn't expressed any feelings toward him beyond his being her trusted friend and confidant, and she wouldn't do so because it was inappropriate. He respected her for that. Still, he saw in her eyes that her feelings went deeper.

"Sinclair, were you careful?"

"Yes. I came around the back, like you said. No one saw. I barely have a moment alone anymore. I thought I was just being paranoid, but lately, everywhere I turn, there's Paula. I'm free of her for a while. She left for her scrying class."

"Scrying?"

"Learning to see visions in a crystal ball or water. The past, present, and future."

Chase didn't comment.

"I told Paula that I was really tired. I stuffed my bed with pillows and my wig." She had a natural-hair wig that looked just like her own hair that she wore for public appearances if her hair wasn't cooperating. "Gig's on the phone in his office. I heard him in there laughing. Laughing!" She released him and turned away, her hand over her mouth. "Trendi. I can't believe it."

His fingers tingled with the memory of her soft skin. "Look, Sinclair." He was calm and direct. "Trendi had a heart of gold, but she was a drug addict."

"She worked every day to stay clean."

"Once an addict, always an addict. Trendi would have agreed. All addicts aren't strung out in crack houses. They can hide it, often for a long time. Trendi had a volatile personality. It had gotten her into trouble before. She saw herself as a rebel. Who knows what she got into with Vince Madrigal?"

"That awful Vince Madrigal, of all people. None of it makes any sense." A sob burst from her. After a moment, she turned to face him. "I know what you're thinking. I was wrong to tell Trendi about our plan, but she was my friend. I wonder if she was killed because she said she'd help us."

Chase wished Sinclair hadn't confided in Trendi, but the damage was done. He wanted to go to her, to comfort her, but instead laced his fingers and tapped his thumbs together. The ringing in his ears that had finally subsided to a persistent hum again started to escalate. He hid his distress from her.

Sniffling, she took an embroidered handkerchief from her dress bodice and blew her nose. "Gig says he talked to Trendi's mother. She never had anything to do with Trendi. Trendi had little love for her, that's for sure. But she kept the connection with her mom, making sure she called her on her birthday and Mother's Day and sending her money. So what does her mother want? Money. Gig told her we'd pay for Trendi's funeral. You know what she told him? Have her cremated and send me the money you would have spent on the funeral."

Sinclair laughed through her tears without mirth. She sat on a glider, lowering herself with hands on both chair arms. "Those other two detectives, who were they? Why were they here?"

"Gig will talk to you about that."

She turned her dark eyes on him. "I want you to tell me now."

He again gritted his teeth, making a dimple form in his cheek. "It doesn't matter."

She balled her fists and pounded the chair arms. "I hate being patronized like this! Why does everyone act like I'm going to fall apart? Nobody knows the real me. Don't worry. I'll behave appropriately when Gig breaks the news. I've gotten good at putting on an act."

He took in a breath and told her about Tink Engleford's death and the photograph with Trendi, Cheyenne, and the girl named Fallon.

After her initial shock, Sinclair listened to his recounting of the events with steely detachment. "Poor Tink. She was a nice lady. Cheyenne had been here before but I don't remember Trendi mentioning a friend named Fallon. All these tragedies seem tied together somehow. It confirms that I'm right to be scared."

Her eyes lingered on the pool. The surface of the water rippled as the filter cleaned it.

He saw where she was looking. "Gig and this Berryhill birthing bullshit. I know Georgia's your friend and all, but I'm sorry . . . Some things you don't fool around with."

"I brought up to Gig again about having the baby at Huntington Hospital and having her delivered by the obstetricians my girlfriends swear by. Dr. Janus could even be the attending physician, but Gig won't budge."

"But this is your baby too."

"John, I'm so afraid all the time for me and my baby." She looked at a schoolhouse clock on the wall. "I'd better get out of here."

She started to press herself up from the glider.

He moved to help her up with his hands beneath her armpits.

They were facing each other, standing close.

"John, nothing's changed, has it? Even with what happened to Trendi, it's going to be all right, isn't it?"

"Sinclair, you'll have your baby in the hospital like we planned. Nothing's going to happen to you or your baby." He squeezed her delicate fingers. "It's going to be all right. I'll make sure of it."

She put her hand against his cheek. "You're sweet. I wish you could save me. It feels very much like it's all beyond our control."

NINETEEN

At the PPD station, Kissick dropped Vining at her Jeep. He took off to observe Tink's autopsy at the county coroner building east of downtown L.A. Vining promised to return to the station and work on their reports once she got things squared away at home. Emily had sent her a text message that she'd had her friend's mother drop her off at Granny's, as Patsy had summoned her there.

At Granny's, the front drapes were still drawn, but it looked as if all the lights in the house were on. Granny's Delta 88 was in the same spot in the driveway. Parked at the curb in front were two cars Vining didn't recognize, a Toyota Prius and a newer Acura sedan.

As soon as Vining opened her car door, she heard music

and laughter. Walking up the front path, she recognized the song that was playing. It was one she remembered her mother singing along with when she'd tune to KRTH, K-Earth 101, the oldies station, in the car. She heard her mother's voice ring out above the din coming from the house, "I was sooo in love with Davy."

Vining rang the bell and knocked on the front door, but no one responded. She peered through the folds of the lacy curtains that covered the narrow windows in the door and saw shapes moving. People dancing. In unison, several female voices sang but mostly shouted, "I'm a believer . . ."

A woman yelled over the music, "Every Monday night at seven-thirty, we were all glued to Vicki's TV. Remember?"

Vining pressed the thumb latch on the front door handle. The door was unlocked. She opened it to see her mother, her two girlhood friends, Vicki and Maria Alicia, and Emily and Granny too dancing in the middle of the living room. All the furniture had been pushed out of the way. Emily was synchronizing her movements with Vicki and Maria Alicia, who were twirling their hands. Vicki, who'd always been the group leader, starting moving her arms as if she was swimming while shimmying her body. The others followed.

Patsy, as expected, was doing her own thing—a frenetic version of the pony, pumping her knees, toes pointed, imitating a prancing horse. Granny was stepping side to side and clapping her hands. Maria Alicia, still the dark, sultry, artistic one who had always had leading roles in the school plays, was by far the best dancer.

Patsy's vinyl record albums were strewn across the floor beneath a console that held Granny's stereo. Propped on top was the one that was playing now: "More of the Monkees." Red plastic drink cups were scattered around, as were bowls of potato chips, Cheetos, Fritos, dips, and paper plates with the remnants of pizza. Apart from the recent clutter, the room appeared to have been dusted and vacuumed. The place smelled of booze.

Vicki spotted Vining first and boogied over to her, pulling her by the hand into the group. Granny drifted away to collapse onto her Naugahyde recliner. Patsy gave Vining a tipsy hug and wet smack on the cheek, as did the other women. Emily waved before following Vicki's lead, drawing her index and middle fingers over her eyes, as if making a mask. Maria Alicia, always the hippie, her thick hair still falling to her waist, the black now streaked with gray, only half-jokingly pointed at the gun on Vining's belt and made the shaming gesture of rubbing one index finger across the top of the other.

After eating a slice of cold pepperoni pizza while standing, Vining tried to escape from dancing, but the other women wouldn't let her. The album scratched when Patsy picked up the needle to start "I'm a Believer" over again. Someone shoved a plastic cup into Vining's hand. She set it down.

"Come on, Nan," her mother said. "You're off duty."

"Yeah, Officer Nan," Maria Alicia said.

Vining smiled. "That's Detective Corporal Nan."

"Wait, wait, wait . . ." Vicki had slipped into the kitchen and returned with more plastic cups. She responded to Vining's glance when she handed a cup to Emily. "That's orange soda, Miss Police Lady."

Maria Alicia leaned toward Em and said, "I thought I had it hard growing up."

"I heard that," Vining said.

"Ignore Mary Alice, Nan," Vicki said. "The old Marxist socialist. She still has a poster of Lenin leading the proletariat in her house."

"Times are a-changing." Maria Alicia raised her plastic cup. "You'll see."

"Maria Alicia," Emily began, using her preferred name

that her old friends wouldn't use either out of forget-fulness, habit, or spite. "Someone has to get the bad guys."

Vining put her arm around Em's shoulders. "That's my girl."

"Yeah, Mary Alice," Vicki said. "Weren't you bitching about your studio being broken into and you called nine-one-one and you were pissed off when the police didn't show up for five minutes?"

"Because they were probably out busting some home-less guy sleeping in a doorway." Maria Alicia took a drink. "No offense, Nan. The police usually do a good job."

Vining shrugged. "Fresh doughnuts had probably just come out of the oven at Winchell's."

Vicki bent over, laughing, nearly spilling her drink.

"Ladies!" Patsy shouted. "Set aside your petty squab-bles for two minutes."

Vining thought the noise in the place was so loud, she wouldn't be surprised if the neighbors called the cops.

Patsy held her cup high. "Ramona Girls and honorary Ramona Girls, let's raise a glass to our friend Tink."

Everyone shouted. "To Tink!"

Vicki added, "She was the only one out of all of us who thought Mike Nesmith was cute."

Maria Alicia yelled, "Even at thirteen, she picked the rich one."

The three remaining Ramona Girls laughed and wiped away tears.

Vining made a face when she took a sip of the contents in the cup. "What is this?"

"Boone's Farm Strawberry Hill," Patsy said. "They *still* make it."

"I'll never get through my day tomorrow if I drink

this." Vining walked into the dining room and set the cup down on the table, where there were more plastic cups, many with dregs of wine, margaritas, or flat soda. Spread across the table were open shoe boxes crammed with mementos, piles of faded color snapshots, photo albums, and yearbooks from Ramona Convent School.

With trepidation, she continued into the kitchen, hoping that Vicki and Maria Alicia hadn't gone in there. She was happy to find it clean. Not spotless, but as clean as the tired linoleum floor and cracked tile counters could get. The air smelled of Raid. She opened the refrigerator door and saw that it had been emptied of rotten food and scrubbed.

She turned to see her mother behind her.

"I know what you're thinking." Patsy carried an empty pizza box and shoved it inside a large green garbage bag on the floor near the back door. "I spent the whole day cleaning. I wasn't going to let Vicki and Mary Alice see it that way. Give them something else to gossip about in relation to me."

Vining was glad to see the house looking good, even if her mother had made the effort out of vanity rather than concern about Granny's well-being.

"Come and join the party, Nan. Whatever you have in mind, it can wait."

Her mother had guessed correctly. She had been thinking that she needed to interview Vicki and Maria Alicia about Tink. Patsy was right. It could wait until tomorrow.

"Just so you know," Patsy began, "they're not driving home. We're having a slumber party, like the old days. Vicki's taking tomorrow off from her job at the high school. Tomorrow is my day off and Mary Alice doesn't work. I mean that ceramics stuff she does. It's not like she has a real job."

"The way you women snipe at each other . . . I'm amazed you're still friends after all these years."

Patsy looked at her with surprise. "Still friends? We *love* each other." She tugged Vining's arm. "Come on, Nan. 'Daydream Believer' is playing. That was my favorite Monkees song. Davy Jones sings."

She scooted from the kitchen, pulling Nan by the hand. In the living room, Maria Alicia and Vicki were arm in arm and drunkenly swaying as they sang along. Emily sat cross-legged on the carpet, reading the liner notes of Cream's album *Disraeli Gears*. Granny had thrown in the towel and was asleep in her recliner. Seeing her, Vining was envious. It had been a long day.

Patsy joined her friends, breaking into the middle between Vicki and Maria Alicia, swaying and singing.

Vining leaned over and asked Em, "Ready to go home?"

The Ramona Girls followed them out the door, sending them off with heartfelt if inebriated hugs and kisses. As Vining and Em got into the car, they watched the Ramona Girls with their arms across one another's shoulders, doing a strange sort of synchronized marching across the front lawn, swinging their legs stiffly up and around to the right and then to the left.

"This is the Monkees' walk. They used to do this on their TV show," Patsy said in response to her daughter's and granddaughter's surprised expressions. "We did too, when we were younger than you, Emily."

"Go, Grandma," Emily said.

The Ramona Girls broke up laughing, and the impromptu chorus line ended. Maria Alicia and Vicki said good-bye again to Vining and Em and headed into the house.

Patsy remained in the front yard with a loose grin on her face.

"You okay, Mom?" Vining stood with her hand on the open driver's door.

"I'm fine. Makes me feel like a teenager again, when I had my whole life ahead of me." She looked up at the moon.

Vining saw her mother become wistful.

"Lots of water under the bridge." Patsy looked at her daughter and granddaughter. "I bet you girls think you know everything there is to know about old Patsy." She leaned her head back and laughed at the moon. She straightened, too quickly, taking a step to steady herself. "You just might be surprised."

She jokingly saluted and turned to go back inside. Marvin Gaye's "I Heard It Through the Grapevine" was playing. She put a Motown groove into her step.

At home, Vining took out the autographed DVD from Gig Towne.

Emily sneered, "That freak."

"I thought you liked him."

"Like him? He's old. He's strange. I think *you* like him."

"I don't think he's so old, but he is strange. You don't want this?" When Emily shook her head, Vining opened a drawer in the dining room china cabinet that had turned into a receptacle for odds and ends and shoved the DVD inside.

" 'Night, Mom." Emily started heading downstairs to her room.

"It's not that late. Do you want to watch some TV with me?"

"I was going to go on YouTube and look for videos of The Monkees. I like their clothes, the Nehru jackets and the long scarves and that knit hat with the pompom that Mike, the rich one, wore. Vicki told me his mother invented Liquid Paper. Can you believe that?"

Vining put on her pink thermal-weave pajamas that were printed with a snowflake pattern and her fleece robe. While the temperatures were inching up during the day, the nights were chilly.

She made a mug of chamomile tea. She was still hungry, so she foraged through the Easter dinner leftovers, making a plate of roast lamb and Kissick's creamed spinach. She didn't take any of Granny's too-salty corn casserole. She didn't have the heart to put it down the garbage disposal while Granny was helping her clean up. She'd scoop it out of the Pyrex casserole tomorrow.

Sitting at the dinette table, she felt lonely. It wasn't a feeling she had often. She was usually too busy. Em used to take a lot more of her time. The teenager's new independence was bittersweet. She thought about her mother and her friends. Vining had never been one to have a lot of friends. She had a few, mostly women she'd met at the PPD. Tara Khorsandhi, the Forensic Services Supervisor, was her best female friend. She realized that Kissick was her best friend.

She finished her food and put the plate and fork in the dishwasher. It was so quiet in the house, she heard the kitchen wall clock clicking off the seconds.

She grabbed her cell phone and sent Kissick a text message: *In PJs. Not typing my reports! Hope all is well.*

She didn't expect him to respond right away, as he would be in the middle of observing Tink's autopsy, but he did, texting: *Good for U. Relax. Love U.*

Smiling, she texted back: *Love U 2. Nite.*

Now, she no longer felt lonely.

She put more hot water into her mug of tea and took it into the TV room. On her La-Z-Boy, she pulled up the chenille throw, and clicked on the classic movie channel. They were broadcasting *North by Northwest*. It was one of her favorite Alfred Hitchcock movies, in which

Cary Grant plays an advertising executive who is mistaken by bad guys for a spy.

She made it to the part where Grant is at a hotel bar and he inadvertently stands up at the same time the bad guys have the spy paged. She clicked it off and went to bed.

TWENTY

The next morning, Vining arrived early at her cubicle. The three-story police department was on the corner of Garfield and Walnut in the city's civic center. Kissick's cubicle was next to the windows and larger than Vining's, in accordance with his seniority, and gave him a view of the pretty, Spanish Renaissance–style Central Library across Walnut Street. At least hers was close enough to the windows so she could see sunlight.

She grabbed her favorite coffee mug to head for a refill. The mug had been a Mother's Day gift from Emily five years ago. It was decorated with a photo of toothy ten-year-old Em and Vining with their heads pressed together and Em's hand-painted: "I love you Mom." When she stood, she saw Kissick, who was just arriving.

"Morning, Jim."

"Good morning, Nanette." He winked at her.

She gave him a warm smile. She was always happy to see him, but lately, her first glimpse of him in the morning had made her heart leap on little wings.

She followed him to his desk. "I called over to Granny's, and the Ramona Girls are moving slowly. Maria Alicia was making breakfast. She said they're going to see Tink's mom, who's in an assisted-living facility. That gives me at least until noon to search my mom's place. I called in a favor with a buddy who runs a spy shop who'll meet me there and sweep for bugs.

"I talked to Maria Alicia about Tink. She didn't have any new information. She hadn't seen or talked to her since the girls last had dinner a few months ago. Vicki was close with Tink. She's going to meet me at Jones Coffee Roasters later. Want to take a drive out to the Berryhill compound after that? That is, if I'm still working the case."

"You might have dodged that bullet for now. Just saw Caspers in the hall. He's due in court again today. Sproul was on-call last night and was sent out to investigate a suspicious death. Found a dead guy sitting in a desk chair in the middle of Colorado Boulevard."

"Have a feeling that will be my case. Did you find out anything at Tink's autopsy?"

"She had water in her lungs. She drowned. No evidence of heart attack or stroke. Her blood-alcohol content was point zero seven, so she was tipsy, but not drunk. The toxicology reports will tell us more when they're completed in a few weeks. Forensics tested the liquids in Tink's inkwell. One is ink. The other is blood, but not human."

"Creepy," Vining said. "I'm surprised Tink was involved in that woo-woo stuff."

"Woo-woo?"

"Witchcraft, occult, whatever . . ."

"You think that's creepy, listen to this," he said. "Remember the LAPD detectives said they found cremated remains in the motel room where Madrigal and Trendi were killed? I did some research on the Net and found out that cremated human remains are used in witchcraft to cast spells. The dead person's spirit is used to help solve someone else's problem."

"Ugh."

"Get this. The remains' former human entity can be brought to bear on problems in the earthly plane."

"Translation, please?"

"Say you're having legal problems, you'd steal the cremains of a lawyer. If you're having family problems, you steal a therapist."

"If you're having car problems, you steal a mechanic?" she joked.

"I guess. Witchcraft stuff seems contrary to Madrigal's cowboy image."

"Maybe they were Trendi's."

"Possible," he said. "I also did research on symbols drawn in blood. Didn't turn up much of anything."

Vining held up her index finger. "There's that bookstore on Lake that specializes in mystical stuff."

"That's a great idea. While you go out to your mom's, I'll take Tink's symbols over there and see if someone knows what they are."

"Sounds good. I'm going to get more coffee before I head out to my mom's."

While she was in the small coffee room, pouring Irish Crème–flavored Coffee Mate into her coffee, Alex Caspers came in.

"Morning, Nan." He pulled a molded foam cup from a stack and filled it with coffee.

"Hi, Alex. How are you?"

"Livin' the dream."

She laughed.

"What?" He grinned, a mischievous look behind long curled eyelashes.

"Hey, guess who Jim and I ran into yesterday over at Gig Towne's and Sinclair LeFleur's place in La Cañada Flintridge?"

"John Chase? He's got a nice off-duty gig there." He

stirred his coffee. "FYI, Chase keeps that on the QT around here. I mean it's perfectly legit, it's just that . . . Working for *Le Towne* and all. Such big stars, he doesn't want people asking him to get autographs and stuff."

"Have you ever been there?"

"Once. I met *Gig* and *Sinclair*." He bobbled his head, mocking the significance. "That place is something, isn't it?"

"It is. I wonder what goes on behind the scenes."

"I wonder too. Gig Towne's supposed to be kind of a nut."

"Is that what Chase told you?"

"That's what I see on TV." Caspers made a noise through his teeth. "The Chaser can't talk about what happens with those people. Confidentiality agreement."

"You guys are buddies. He doesn't even say anything to you?"

"Nope. He won't talk about it other than to say that it's a good gig and they treat him well."

"Why is he working two jobs? He's not married and raising kids."

"He's paying off student loans. He went to USC for his B.A."

"They have a criminal-justice program there?"

"John studied ancient history."

"Ancient history?" Vining was surprised to learn that about the first-on-scene, throwing-them-down young cop.

"The Chaser is a real egghead."

"Huh." Vining sipped coffee and lingered for a moment. "When we saw him yesterday, he seemed like he was in pain from a headache or something. Do you know anything about that?"

Caspers shrugged. "Maybe he did have a headache."

"Alex, are you holding back?"

He looked at her. "He doesn't talk to me about stuff like that, Nan. We're men."

Vining took a sip of her coffee and nodded. "You're right." She left the coffee room, vowing to bring the issue up to Chase's commanding officer, Lieutenant Terrence Folke.

She met Kissick walking the other direction.

"Guess who's in the lobby?" He didn't wait for her response. "Kingsley Getty."

Vining raised her eyebrows. "That was easy."

TWENTY-ONE

Vining and Kissick took the stairs to look for King Getty. The open staircase gave them a view of the lobby, where a few people were waiting on the Mission-style benches against the wall. King Getty was easy to spot standing in the middle of the floor. Vining thought the tall, broad-shouldered, silver-haired man would have stood out anywhere.

His stance was relaxed, as if he owned the place, yet there was something formal and vaguely military about him, to Vining's eye. He spotted them right away and smiled easily, his white teeth bright against his tanned face, as he watched their descent. His light gray suit and silver-blue tie complemented his silver hair.

Vining thought of the press clippings about her that she'd found in his nightstand drawer, making his sharp gaze feel disturbing. He was smiling at both of them, but Vining felt that he was especially scrutinizing her. Mike

Rahimi, the assistant manager of his building, had probably told him that she'd gone through his apartment. Did Getty suspect that she'd searched his nightstand?

When she and Kissick reached the lobby floor, she was disappointed in herself for feeling reticent when Getty stuck out his hand.

He shook Kissick's hand first. "Kingsley Getty. You must be Detective Kissick." He turned to her. "And Detective Vining."

He surprised her by grasping her fingers and pulling her hand to his lips. Once she saw where this was heading, she tried to pull back, but he held on more tightly and planted a kiss on the back of her hand. She saw his eyes glint over the scar there where the creep who had ambushed her had sliced her.

"Delighted to meet you, Detective." His head still bowed, he looked up into her eyes.

She sensed Kissick struggling to hide his amusement.

"Nice to meet you, too, Mr. Getty." She pulled her hand free and dropped it to her side, resisting the impulse to wipe off his kiss against her slacks.

As he straightened, his gaze flitted across the long scar on the left side of her neck that started behind her ear and disappeared beneath the collar of her shirt.

She again thought about the stash of clippings beside his bed and felt like squirming.

Getty was still smiling as if he was at a cocktail party. "You are much too pretty to be a homicide detective."

She didn't care for that comment. Her eyes were frosty as she met his. She didn't respond.

Getty moved on. "I was horrified to hear the news about Tink. Please tell me what happened." The sadness that dimmed his dark gray eyes seemed genuine.

His lustrous eyes looked to Vining like a clear, cold pond. He had a slight accent that she couldn't place. A whiff British but not quite. A gold ring set with a big diamond glittered on his pinkie finger. Everything about him seemed clean, except his motives.

"Let's discuss it upstairs." Kissick held out his arm.

Getty inclined his head.

Vining led the way to the elevator.

Getty looked around. "This is a *gorgeous* building for a police station. So fitting with the Spanish and Mission architecture in Pasadena. When was it built?"

"Nineteen eighty-nine," Kissick replied.

The elevator doors opened. They stepped back to let two uniformed female officers exit. Vining and Kissick gave them quick nods. They nodded back, gave Getty a glance, and then, as if choreographed, did double takes.

He smiled with closed lips. "Good morning, ladies."

They replied, "Good morning."

Kissick again looked amused, to Vining's irritation. Both men waited for her to enter first, so she did.

"Dear Tink." Getty clasped his hands behind his back. "She loved showing me around Pasadena. Such a beautiful city. We shared lovely meals at the Valley Hunt Club and at Annandale," he said, dropping the names of the city's exclusive private clubs. He emitted a small moan. "My gosh . . . It's still sinking in. Poor Tinker Bell."

Vining couldn't tell whether he was lying, which troubled her.

The elevator doors opened. Getty swooped out his arm as if to keep the dangerous door from injuring Vining, provoking an angled smile from her.

She led the way into the Detectives Section, crossing the small waiting room where Getty garnered the attention of the two female staff assistants at desks there.

Getty never let an opportunity pass. "Good morning, ladies."

Passing the Detective Sergeants' office, she saw Sergeant

Early spot them from her desk through the large window there that overlooked the suite.

Kissick had Getty wait while Vining made sure the interview room was empty. By the time she'd returned, Getty was asking Kissick about the organizational structure of the Detectives Section, listening with rapt interest whether he was in fact interested or not.

"Mr. Getty, please." Inside the interview room, Vining held up her hand, signaling Getty to take a chair.

"Call me King." He uttered the ridiculous statement with complete sincerity. He pinched his pant legs and sat, crossing his legs, looking as comfortable as if he were waiting for his favorite waiter at a club to bring his cigar and snifter of brandy on a silver tray.

Still standing, Vining said, "Would you like some coffee . . . King? Water? Soft drink?"

"A cup of coffee would be great, Detective Vining. Thank you. Cream and a little sugar, the real stuff, if it wouldn't be too much trouble."

"No trouble at all." She ducked into the adjacent observation room and made sure the video recording system was on. Through the one-way glass, she saw Getty again chatting with Kissick, who'd sat across from him.

She went to her desk, where she grabbed her coffee mug and the file folder with Tink's strange drawings.

In the coffee room, she ran into Sergeant Early, who asked, "Kingsley Getty?"

Vining dumped an unhealthy dose of sugar into a Styrofoam cup she'd filled with coffee. "His friends call him King."

"He's not hard on the eyes."

"And doesn't he know it." Vining poured coffee for herself as Early took out one of the yogurt smoothies she kept in the refrigerator, shaking it as she left the room.

When Vining placed the coffee in front of Getty, he said, "You're too kind, Detective Vining."

"You're welcome." She set down the file folder and her coffee mug on the same side of the table as Getty but with a chair between them. "For the record, this interview is being videotaped." She announced the date, time, and people present. "Please continue."

"I was explaining my family background to Detective Kissick. I'm a distant nephew of J. Paul Getty. My father is Reginald Getty, a bastard half-brother. In those days, especially in England, an illegitimate child was scandalous. My mother was sent away to live with her grandparents at Lake Windermere, and that's where I grew up. But the Getty family stepped up and made sure Reggie was taken care of."

He picked up the coffee and sipped, half-closing his eyes and opening them to smile at Vining. "Perfect. Thank you, Detective Vining. Good brew, too. I attended Eton, of course. Where all our family went." He lazily turned the cup on the table. "I began at Oxford, but was lured away by a fetching Française. Ended up spending a couple of years and most of my tuition in Cap d'Antibes, which did not make my father too happy." He pronounced Cap so that it sounded like a clipped-off "cop."

"But, through connections I made in Cap, I invested the money I had left in a newly discovered South African diamond mine. This was decades before DeBeers had cornered the market. In fact, our little syndicate sold our interests to DeBeers. Was able to pay my father back the tuition I'd borrowed." He winked. "And then some."

"You made your own money on top of your family fortune," Vining said.

He turned to her. "My side of the Getty clan never had what I would call a fortune, although I'm sure some would. We lived comfortably. I went to good schools. But there really wasn't enough to properly support me. I had to make my own way."

Getty reached toward Vining's "I love you, Mom"

coffee mug with its five-year-old photo of her and Em on it. "Hello, Beauty. Is this your daughter, Detective?"

Vining protectively pulled the mug toward her and turned the side with the photo away from him. She felt foolish for bringing such a personal item into an interview and ignored his question. "So you've done all right for yourself."

Getty tilted his head back and peered at her. "That's a fair statement."

"So, King, help me understand something," Vining began. "Why are you living in the Countess de Castellane's apartment? Why don't you have your own place?"

He laughed, giving her a full view of his rugged jaw and white teeth. "Detective Vining, do you think I'm a gigolo, preying on lonely rich women?"

"I'd like you to answer my question."

"You are correct, Detective, that the Wilshire Boulevard apartment belongs to Marisa. It sits vacant most of the year. The countess also has an apartment in London and a villa in Portofino. I have an apartment in Paris and a place in Majorca, both of which I rarely use. I've known the countess for years, since my Cap d'Antibes days, and we've traded properties for years. The countess is staying at my Majorca villa now. Would you like to talk to her?"

He reached into his jacket pocket, took out an iPhone, and held it up.

Vining said, "Sure."

Getty found the number and held the phone to his ear. After a moment, he said with a big smile, "*Buona sera, Contessa.*"

He carried on in Italian, fluently to Vining's ears. After a while, he returned his gaze to the detectives and switched to English. "Marisa, guess where I am? In Pasadena, California." He chuckled. "No, *bella*, the Rose Parade takes

place on New Year's Day. I'm at the police department."
He laughed again. "No, no. It's not what you think. I'm
being interviewed by two detectives. Sad news. A dear
friend of mine was found dead. No, no one you know. The
detectives are doing God's work in trying to find out what
happened. One of them is an attractive young woman
named Detective Vining, and she'd like to talk to you.
Well, she wants to ask you about me, of course. *Grazie*,
Marisa. Here she is."

Vining took the phone and said, "This is Detective
Nan Vining."

A woman with a sultry voice trilled, "Oh, Detective,
please tell me. What has that bad boy King gotten into
now?" She followed with throaty laughter.

Vining carried the phone into the observation room
and shut the door. She asked the countess how long
she'd known King, about their relationship, his finances,
his background, and so forth, trying to corroborate
what Getty had told them.

The countess punctuated her speech with robust
laughter. She said she and Getty had been lovers long
ago, but were like brother and sister now. Her answers
jibed with Getty's. Vining ended the call and returned to
the interview room.

Getty took the phone from her and slipped it back inside his pocket. "So, you see, Detective, I really am just
a pussycat."

Vining took her seat and gave Kissick a look.

He picked up her cue and took over. "King, when and
where did you meet Catherine Engleford?"

"Last New Year's Eve. She was spending a few days
alone at Berryhill and so was I. Instead of engaging in
forced gaiety or staying home alone, we both went there
instead to nourish our spirits and bodies. We bonded
immediately."

"And when was the last time you saw her?"

His fingers went to his chin. "I left for Dubai on Saturday. Tink and I had dinner at the Parkway Grill the night before I left. That must have been Friday night."

"Was it just the two of you?"

"Yes."

"What happened after dinner?"

"I drove her home around nine o'clock. I had an early flight the next morning, so we made it an early evening. I saw Tink inside her house, gave her a good-night kiss, and drove home."

"Did you have a sexual relationship with her?" Kissick asked.

"No." Getty's eye contact with Kissick didn't waver.

"You never had sexual intercourse with Catherine Engleford?"

"There are still a few gentlemen left in the world, Detective. I was fond of Tink. Our relationship might have become intimate one day, but both of us were content to have fun. To share big events and quiet moments. Tink was a sweet, dear person with a troubled soul. I felt that she kept herself so busy to try to keep from feeling lonely. She was lucky to have a few true friends, but they had busy lives, too."

Kissick asked, "What was Cheyenne Leon's relationship with Mrs. Engleford?"

"Cheyenne?" Getty stared off as he thought. "Cheyenne and Tink were fond of each other. Cheyenne had a troubled past and Tink helped her. Do you know where Cheyenne is?"

"Is she missing?"

Kissick's question threw Getty for a second. "I . . . I wouldn't know whether she's missing. I assume she's not allowed to stay in Tink's house while the investigation is going on. I'm wondering where she might be."

"What's your relationship with Cheyenne?" Vining asked.

"Friendly. Paternal."

Vining rested her hands on the table and tapped her fingertips together. "I can understand Mrs. Engleford being generous with her time and money in helping others, but wasn't letting someone with Cheyenne's background live in her house a risk? Why did Mrs. Engleford do that?"

"Tink was generous, as you said."

Vining opened her hands toward Getty. "You said that Cheyenne was fond of Mrs. Engleford. That wasn't my take. She was disrespectful and even hateful about Mrs. Engleford."

Getty widened his eyes in surprise followed by a knowing smile. "That's Cheyenne." He shook his head with amusement. "Her modus operandi is 'the best defense is a good offense.' Façade as tough as nails. Core of marshmallow. No doubt she is deeply upset by Tink's death."

Kissick asked, "Do you know where Cheyenne met Mrs. Engleford?"

Getty didn't answer right away. Vining wondered if he was trying to remember or measuring his response. "I don't know exactly. Possibly at Berryhill."

"Cheyenne was able to afford retreats at Berryhill?"

"Georgia and Stefan are generous with people who want to participate in The Method, but who may not have the financial means."

Vining took out the photo of Cheyenne, Trendi, and Fallon. She placed it in front of Getty.

He picked it up.

Vining observed his jaw tighten for a fraction of a second.

"Cheyenne must have been a teenager here. Even then a raven-haired beauty." Getty turned over the photo and read the handwriting on the back. "Me, Trendi, and Fallon." He looked the photo over again. He slid it in front of Vining.

"Do you know who those other two girls are?" she asked.

He met her eyes. "No, I don't."

She held up the photo. "Are you sure?"

He didn't look at it again. "I'm sure."

"This girl, in the middle . . ." Vining tapped the image with her other hand. "Her name is Trendi Talbot. Did you ever see her at Mrs. Engleford's house?"

"No. Do you consider Cheyenne and those other two girls suspects in what happened to Tink? Is it your opinion that Tink met with foul play?"

"We have to consider all possibilities," Kissick said. "The Berryhill Method and the Berryhill compound were a large part of Tink's life. Help us understand that."

"The Method and the Berryhill compound gave Tink a modicum of tranquillity. It's a holistic, healing environment. Georgia and Stefan are generous in spirit and heart." He widened his eyes. "Do they know about Tink?"

"I couldn't say," Kissick said.

Getty grimaced. "They'll be crushed. What about Gig and Sinclair? Have they heard about Tink?"

"Yes," Kissick said. "We paid them a visit."

Getty stared at the glass wall. After a few seconds, he returned his attention to them. "Forgive me. It's still sinking in. Poor Tink."

Vining took out the photocopies of the papers with the strange symbols and placed them in front of Getty. "Do you know what these are?"

Getty cocked his head as if to make sense of the drawings. "No. Are they some sort of hieroglyphics?"

"Did you ever see Tink drawing anything like this or talking about any such thing?"

"No. Did you find these at Tink's house?"

Vining put the symbols away and drummed her fingers against the file. She was dying to ask Getty about his file of clippings about her. Instead, she asked, "Have you ever heard my name before today?"

"No, I have not. My apologies, but is there some reason I should have?"

They stared at each other, neither wanting to look away first. She knew he was lying.

Vining gave a careless shrug. "No reason." She looked at Kissick and raised an eyebrow, signaling that she was finished.

Kissick pushed back from the table and stood. "King, thank you for coming in today. You've been very helpful."

Getty stood as well. "It was my pleasure." He anticipated Kissick's next comment. "If I think of anything else, I will call you."

"Excellent." Kissick took a card from his jacket pocket and handed it to him.

Getty reached into his inside jacket pocket and produced a silver business card holder. He flipped it open and peeled off two cards.

"Are you planning on staying in town?" Kissick opened the interview room door.

"Yes, I am." Getty walked out ahead of Kissick. "All my contact numbers are on my business card. Please keep me in the loop if you learn anything about what happened to Tink."

Vining carried her coffee mug with the photo on it turned against her slacks. She didn't offer her hand. "Detective Kissick will see you out."

Kissick returned to find Vining at her desk typing up a report of the interview on her computer.

"King Getty . . ." she sneered. "Uses names like a salesman. That shameless flattering. What a bullshit artist."

"He's smooth. That upper-crust, prep-school, lockjaw way of talking. Hail-fellow-well-met. I can see why Tink found him attractive. He is charming. Polite. Good conversationalist. He'd mix easily in her world. She could bring him to a dinner party and he'd know the fish knife from the butter knife."

"As long as you don't scratch the surface, everything is beautiful," Vining said. "But maybe that's what Tink did, and it got her drowned."

TWENTY-TWO

*V*ining parked in front of her mother's town house complex. A black SUV at the curb was tricked out with windows that were tinted too dark and wide chrome wheel rims. Magnetic signs on both front doors said:

SPOOK NOOK
SECURITY AND SURVEILLANCE EXPERTS
CALL FOR FREE CONSULTATION

Vining walked up to the driver's window, which was part-way down, and tapped on it, startling a man in his late thirties behind the wheel, who was dozing.

"Sir, your windows are illegally too dark. I'm going to have to cite you."

His hand moved to his waist as if instinctively reaching for a firearm. His jolt of surprise turned into a warm smile. "Hey, Nan Vining."

She grinned. "Hey yourself, Chad Preston."

He got out of the car. There was an awkward moment as if he didn't know whether to shake her hand or reach for a hug.

She helped by opening her arms.

He squeezed her, a little tightly, smashing her breasts against his chest.

Stepping back, she saw a partial tattoo beneath his open shirt collar—two twiglike shapes that she knew were the legs of a black widow spider inked onto his chest. He leaned against the car, his posture relaxed and flirtatious.

They'd had a romantic relationship when they were both at the police academy. She'd been divorced and had been working as a citizen jailer in the Pasadena P.D. jail when she'd applied and was hired as an officer. She was soon at the Orange County Sheriff's Academy, where the PPD sends many of its recruits. There she met Chad, who'd been hired by the O. C. Sheriff's Department. They dated off and on after graduation. Conflicting schedules, geographic challenges, and Vining's decision to stop dating until Emily was older had ended their romantic relationship. They hadn't been in contact for a couple of years, but they'd kept tabs on each other through mutual friends.

As for Chad, after three years as an O. C. sheriff's deputy, he decided that Orange County wasn't big enough for him. He joined the Secret Service and worked in Criminal Investigations, on the trail of money counterfeiters, and then transferred to the White House, where he worked the presidential detail. He was injured while pursuing a homeless man who had aimed what looked like a handgun at the president. All the homeless man had been holding was a dead and rigid snake he kept as a sort of pet. After his injury, Chad was offered a desk job, but he took early retirement instead and started his spy equipment and consultation business in Hollywood.

"You're looking good, Nan."

"Thanks. You look well."

He sucked in air through his teeth as he took in the long scar on her neck. "Yikes."

She self-consciously turned her left side, with the scar, away from him. "You should have seen the other guy."

"So I heard. You're a hero."

She allowed a lackluster shrug. The topic had become tiresome for her. "What about you? Doing a double gainer off a flight of steel steps in pursuit of a homeless man who was trying to show the president his danger-ous petrified snake."

He grinned. "Just protecting the commander in chief. Did you get the message I left on your house phone? I called after that thing with your bad guy came down."

"I got your message. Thanks. I wanted to call back, but had a lot going on." That wasn't why she hadn't re-turned his call. She hadn't wanted to open a dialogue with him, even though she'd heard he'd gotten married. She'd only called him now because she needed a favor. He owed her one, as she'd done him a big favor years ago when they were both rookies.

"You look happy," he said.

"Things are good. You don't look too worse for wear yourself."

He patted his firm midsection, emitting a solid thump. "Try to keep things in shape. Someone might want it one of these days."

"I heard you'd gotten married."

"I did." After a few seconds, he held up his fingers as if conceding that he couldn't come up with a clever response or deciding not to BS her. "It didn't work out."

His demeanor had turned almost sheepish. She didn't

pursue it. "What's this?" She pointed at his shaved head, which had a shadow of new growth, showing the map of his receded hairline.

"Argh . . . Losing my hair. Looks better with it shaved off." He tilted his head. "Rub it. It's good luck. Go ahead."

She laughed and didn't move to take him up on the offer.

He straightened, his eyes sparkling. "What?"

"You're hopeless."

"So are you dating anyone?" he asked.

"I am."

He waited a second for more, and then asked, "What does he do?"

"He's a cop."

"I could have figured that one. Is he with Pasadena?"

She turned up her hand. "Does it matter?"

"That's a yes." When she didn't elaborate, he moved on. "How's Emily?"

"She's great. Just turned fifteen."

"No way. Where does the time go?"

She took out her wallet and showed him Em's latest school photo.

He seemed remorseful. "She's gorgeous. She looks just like you." He handed the photo back.

"Thanks. She's a great kid. Kind. Smart. Too smart, sometimes. How's biz?"

"Fantastic. It's a great time for surveillance and countersurveillance. So who lives here?"

"My mother. She was dating Vince Madrigal."

He made a face. "I'm sorry to hear that."

"You know him?"

"Oh yeah. I have a couple of high-profile clients who kept me busy removing bugs and other surveillance equipment that Madrigal installed. Heard he was about to be indicted for illegal wiretaps, among other things. He was friends with a dirty LAPD sergeant who did illegal background checks for him. Madrigal used to hire thugs to intimidate his clients' enemies. Tough-guy Mafioso stuff, like leaving dead fish wrapped in newspapers with messages: 'Drop the lawsuit or else.' Why was your mom mixed up with him?"

Vining rolled her eyes. "I don't know. A good friend of hers, a well-connected Pasadena socialite, drowned in her backyard pool under suspicious circumstances. I'm thinking the dead woman might have had damaging information and someone hired Madrigal to find out about it. Madrigal might have used my mother to get access to her friend. We'll head over to the friend's house after we're done here. Thanks, Chad, for coming out, especially on such short notice."

"You're welcome. I owed you one."

"We're even."

He went around to the front passenger door and picked up a briefcase from the floor. "Does this mean you won't call me anymore?" He locked the car. "What am I saying? You don't call me now."

"Come on. We're friends." She'd mentioned to Kissick that she'd dated a few guys in the early years after her divorce, but had never named names or gone into specifics and he hadn't asked. Chad had been her only semi-serious relationship.

Holding the briefcase, he locked the car door. "Nan, we'll never be friends. Not that way, meeting for coffee and chewing the fat."

He gave her a look and she knew he was right. There was too much sexual tension between them. She felt it now.

"So we're professional colleagues."

"If that's what works for you, Nan."

She led the way to the town house complex gate, unlocked it, and went through first. Standing there joking with Chad was like old times. While she knew herself and knew she wasn't in danger of stepping over the line with him, the small, fun flirting felt like a betrayal of Kissick.

While she was unlocking her mother's front door, he moved to stand close behind her. He wasn't touching her, but was close enough for her to feel his breath on her hair and to sense a vibration from him.

"Nan, for me, you'll always be the one who got away."

She opened the door. Before she went inside, she turned to face him. They were nearly nose-to-nose. "Chad, I'm in love with my boyfriend."

He stepped back, putting a polite distance between them. "He's a lucky guy."

She said, with sincerity and for the first time ever about a man, "I'm the lucky one."

TWENTY-THREE

*C*had began sweeping for bugs in the living room, pacing with an electronic device about the size of a DVD player slung by a strap over his shoulder and waving a wand across the walls, ceiling, and inside cabinets.

Vining went upstairs to the smaller bedroom Patsy used as a guest room and office. She hooked up an external disk drive she'd bought at Best Buy on the way over and started copying the hard disk of her mother's old desktop computer. She began searching Patsy's bills and bank statements. She wasn't completely surprised when she found a stack of overdue credit card bills, notices from collection agencies, and a dozen presumably maxed-out credit cards wrapped with a rubber band, but it was jarring to hold evidence of what she'd suspected and to see how bad the problem was. The interest and fees the credit card companies tacked on had made the balances ratchet up quickly.

While she was sitting there, Patsy received several phone calls from collection agents, some leaving threatening messages. That explained why Patsy would only pick up her home phone after Vining or Em had started to leave a message, giving an excuse that she was in the shower or on the patio.

Vining was horrified. Patsy had always been a spendthrift, but she had no clue that her mom was in this kind of trouble. In a closet, she found boxes of old financial records. Pulling some at random, she saw that Patsy had skirted the edge of financial disaster for years, but had managed to keep it at bay. Things had started to go out of control about two years ago.

That was when the creep had attacked Vining, sending her into a three-day coma and a yearlong leave of absence. Had that been the tipping point that had caused Patsy to lose her bearings? Vining had always felt like the glue that held their little family together. She now saw the extent to which she was.

She thought back to her mother pulling out a wad of twenties to buy groceries and the expensive necklace she'd bought Em. In the bank statements, Vining saw the direct deposit of Patsy's biweekly Macy's paycheck but didn't see evidence of other income. She remembered her mother's tipsy hint last night about having surprising secrets. Had she been working for Madrigal?

The bank statements had images of paid checks that

the bank provided in lieu of returning the actual cancelled checks. Granny had written some checks to Patsy, a couple of hundred dollars here and there. This made Vining more mad than anything she'd seen so far. She didn't see any checks written by Tink or her other friends. It made sense. Patsy would have been too proud to reveal her dire financial situation to her friends.

Angry tears burned Vining's eyes as the phone rang yet again. A collection agent began leaving a hostile message. She couldn't resist picking up the phone.

"This is Detective Nan Vining of the police department. You are in violation of the California Fair Debt Collection Practices Act. You cannot make threats during a call to collect money. Consider this your first warning." She slammed down the phone.

She bundled up her mother's phone bills for the past six months, rubber-banded them, and did the same with her bank statements. She'd planned to be more discreet, rushing out to photocopy documents and returning them before Patsy was the wiser, but she was so ticked off, she didn't care.

She heard Chad's steps on the stairs.

"I'm in here," she shouted when she heard him go into the other room.

He found her and approached with his open palm held out. In it were several small black objects the size of dimes.

"I found these in your mother's downstairs phones and in the wall behind that art print over the couch. They're components of a hook-switch bypass. It's a common way to bug a telephone and one of Madrigal's signature surveillance methods. I can't tell you how many of these I've pulled out of homes and offices that Madrigal bugged."

"How does it work?"

"When a telephone has been bypassed, it becomes 'hot

on hook.' The handset is modified so that even if the phone is hung up, it can intercept conversations in the room and pass them down the phone line to a listening post. The components cost about forty-five cents. Turns the telephone into a room bug. It's a parasitic eavesdropping device, meaning it pirates its operating power from a source such as a telephone line or the house wiring. It doesn't need its own battery."

"Is someone listening to us now?"

"Maybe. An off-site listening post could be anywhere. You just need a telephone landline."

Vining lined up the bugs on the desk, wondering if Madrigal had been eavesdropping on Patsy to make sure she was holding up her end of the deal, whatever it was.

Chad picked up the handset of the cordless phone on the desk and started removing the plastic case.

Vining checked the progress of the auxiliary drive's backup of the computer's hard disk, gathered up the documents she was taking, and went into her mother's bedroom.

Patsy's bedrooms through the years and across different locations were always outfitted the same. King-sized beds with frilly coverings, copious throw pillows, and tattered childhood toys: a Teddy bear, a Winnie the Pooh, and a stuffed doll with round sunglasses, purple and black striped legs, and black vinyl boots. Vining wondered whether her mother's husbands having to sleep in such an overly feminine and juvenile environment had contributed to her many failed marriages.

Jane Fonda's autobiography was on the nightstand. A price sticker showed that Patsy had bought it at Costco. She'd used the front book jacket flap to mark the page. She was halfway through. Beneath it were several tabloid gossip magazines.

Vining went to the closet, which was jammed with clothes and shoes. Some garments still had price tags on them. Boxes held shoes that had never been worn. Clothes had fallen off the packed closet rod and were crumpled on the floor.

Patsy shopped to feel better.

On top of the dresser was her mother's jewelry box, which she'd had as long as Vining could remember. She opened it and poked her finger around the mounds of mostly costume jewelry and few pieces of fine jewelry, but nothing grand. She found some that she and her sister Stephanie used to play with when they were kids. Patsy had never gotten rid of any of her jewelry, and the box contained a forty-year fashion retrospective.

She carried the box to the bed. From a tangled mound of necklaces, she freed one that used to be her mother's favorite. It was a gold-filled medallion of Taurus the bull on a heavy twisted chain. Taurus was an apt Zodiac sign for Patsy. Vining put on the necklace. She followed it with a peace symbol on a leather cord and a gold Italian horn on a serpentine gold chain from Patsy's disco days in the seventies.

Taking off her own simple pearl earrings, Vining donned drop earrings with dangling mirrored disco balls. She found a mood ring. Her hands were larger than her mother's and it only fit on her pinkie.

She lifted out a panel in the box, revealing a lower layer, and found dozens of slogan buttons: Boycott Grapes/Support United Farm Workers; Out of Vietnam; McGovern for President; happy faces. The three ring boxes were still there with Patsy's rings from her previous marriages. While her diamond engagement rings were far from Elizabeth Taylor caliber, each subsequent marriage had brought a bigger stone.

Vining took out a small box covered in fake red leather embossed in gold. The inside was lined with gold velveteen, just as Vining remembered. Rings from Patsy's first two marriages shared the box. A slender, plain gold band from her marriage to Vining's father, her first and briefest, was crammed into the padded velveteen slot with the white-gold wedding set with the quarter-carat diamond from her second marriage, to Stephanie's father.

When playing dress-up, Stephanie would claim the wedding set, leaving Vining the Spartan gold band. Patsy explained that when she'd married the first time, they had been very young—she had just turned eighteen—and the gold band was all they could afford.

Vining slipped the band over the first knuckle of her ring finger, as far as it would go, and recalled her disappointment. A plain gold band that didn't even have its own box was all that was left of Patsy's marriage to her father. A man so rotten, Patsy had always claimed, that she would not even speak his name.

Vining twisted the ring on her finger and traveled to a place she rarely went, thinking about the passive-aggressive cruelty in her mother's refusal to even reveal her father's name. Vining used to press her for information about him when she was little but gave it up. When she grew to be tall and dark, so different from her blond, petite mother and sister, Patsy confessed that Vining took after her father. That was the sum total of what Vining knew about him: he was tall and dark; he'd given her mother a gold wedding band; and he'd abandoned his wife and infant daughter and disappeared.

Granny hadn't been any help in clarifying things. In response to Vining's questions, she would only say, "You have to talk to your mother about that." Her tone was so bristly, Vining had been intimidated to ask further.

Later, she'd married young herself, right after her high school graduation, and soon had a daughter. In a few years, she was a divorced single mother. For a while, she'd had a chilling thought that, in spite of her fervent desire not to emulate her mother's life, she had done just that. She'd steeled herself and vowed that Emily would not grow up in the same environment she had—not knowing her father and with a trail of men coming in and out of the house.

Even though she'd wanted to kill Wes for leaving her and two-year-old Emily to take up with Kaitlyn, his young Super Cuts hairstylist, she made sure she kept their relationship civil. Wes was committed to being in Emily's life.

As far as her thoughts about her own father, she'd been too busy to dwell on them. Now though, again wearing the thin gold band she'd played with as a child, she found herself with space in her life for new challenges—and for old hurts. She was again angry at her mother for many things, past and present, and the issue of her father again bubbled to the surface.

"Found the same setup in the office." Chad entered the bedroom, holding the bugs he'd pulled out of the office phone. "What are you doing?"

She glanced in a mirror over the dresser. She looked ridiculous. "Fooling around."

She took off the necklaces and earrings, and crammed the gold band back inside its shared space in the ring box. Pulling the mood ring off her pinkie, she noticed that the color had turned black.

Later, at Tink's house, Chad found hook-switch bypasses in all the landlines, including the separate phone line in Cheyenne's room.

Vining walked him to the door. "I wish I could find Madrigal's listening post. Love to get my hands on the recorded conversations."

"I'll put in a few calls and see if I can get any information for you."

She didn't prolong their good-bye and held out her hand. "Chad, thanks a bunch."

He got the message. "No problem. See you around, Nan. Take care."

"You too."

He walked out the door and she closed it, also feeling as if she were closing the door on her years as a single divorcée. She was with Jim Kissick now. She knew that that fact had not been hazy for him, but it had been for her. That was no longer the case.

She called Desiree Peck, one of the two LAPD detectives investigating the Vince Madrigal and Trendi Talbot murders. She reached her right away and told her about finding Madrigal's signature wiretaps at her mother's town house and Catherine Engleford's home.

"He had a listening post set up in the back of a North Hollywood nightclub that a mob-connected buddy of his owned," Peck said. "Someone cleaned out all the video and audio recordings and computers in the early morning after Madrigal and Trendi were killed. Madrigal's Beverly Hills office was cleaned out too. Computers, cameras, files. Everything."

"Hmm."

"Do you have any idea why Madrigal bugged your mother's place?"

"No." That was mostly true.

"We're trying to find a friend of Trendi's, a woman named Cheyenne Leon," Peck said. "She worked for your deceased woman, Catherine Engleford. Do you have any idea where she is?"

Vining told a white lie. "We interviewed her yesterday morning. We haven't eliminated her as a suspect in Mrs. Engleford's death. We don't know where she is now." She left out the information about Carmen Vidal promising to make Cheyenne available. Cheyenne didn't like talking to cops, and Vining didn't want to sic the LAPD on her and have her disappear.

"The way our investigations overlap, working together we'll close them that much more quickly."

"Absolutely." Vining didn't feel too bad lying to Peck.

TWENTY-FOUR

K issick pulled into the parking lot behind the Transformation Bookstore on South Lake Avenue. When he got out of the car, the aroma of cooking meat wafted toward him from Burger Continental a few doors down. A wooden staircase led to the Yoga Kingdom studio above the bookstore.

California Pharmacy, a longtime local Pasadena business, was shuttered. Its customers' prescriptions had been transferred to the new Walgreen's across the street. It was another gong of the death knell for small businesses in Pasadena, slow erosion that was largely going unnoticed except by its graying residents.

The cooking smells made Kissick realize he was starving. He entered Burger Continental from the parking lot through the back, crossing a tented outdoor space with tables and plastic chairs. There were a few tables in the front and on the sidewalk, but on the weekends, the action was in the back, where musicians played Armenian songs, and a belly dancer who was getting up in years shimmed for tips around the regulars at this family-owned eatery.

Kissick polished off a lula kebab of ground spiced lamb and beef on pita with French fries and a wedge of baklava.

Leaving the domain of savory meats, he entered a world of incense in the bookstore. Wind chimes were displayed on a hat rack. There were yoga clothes, mats, crystal balls, candles, and even voodoo dolls. Bookshelves divided the space into nooks. Calligraphy signs designated the topics: New Age Spiritualism; Eastern Philosophy; Western Philosophy; Occult; Diet and Health.

Two young women with no discernable body fat and yoga mats in cases slung over their shoulders were looking over the incense display. When Kissick approached, they looked at him, their eyes bright and faces calm, as if they were still blissed out from their yoga class and on another plane.

While the yoga gals seemed to be walking in the light, the clerk was drawn toward a darker world. Her hair was dyed jet black and asymmetrically cut, with tendrils like spiderwebs against her face. Her eyebrows were plucked into a clownish arch. Among her many piercings was a piece of silver shaped like a tiny dagger through her lower lip. She wore a white starched blouse with ruffles down the front and on the sleeves, the ruffles nearly covering her hands.

A winsome smile framed by black-cherry lips was incongruous with the dark image she sought to create. She stood from her chair and asked, "Can I help you?" She wasn't very tall, and her round figure was on display in a pair of peg-leg jeans.

He saw the yoga gals glide from the store as he handed the clerk his card. "I'm Detective Jim Kissick with the Pasadena police. I was hoping you might be able to help me with some items that might be related to the occult."

"Sure. I can help you." Her ease in his presence told

him that she'd not been in trouble with the law or had negative experiences with cops. "I'm a practicing witch," she informed him.

"Oh . . . Great." Just when he thought he'd heard everything. "What's your name, please?"

"Magick with a K."

"Last name." He jotted on his spiral pad.

"Just Magick."

"And your given name?"

"I don't need it anymore." She made a motion with both hands, as if parting the waters and putting the past behind her.

She observed him with the same calm, open gaze as the yoga gals, as if she could see through him. It was a technique he'd mastered.

"You know how us cops are, by the book. Could I have your given name, please?"

"My parents named me Sarah Meacham." She shrugged as if the name was of no consequence. "What did you want to ask about?"

He took out the originals of the papers with the weird symbols that Vining had put in the Baggies and set them on the counter.

"Sigils," she said. "Nice ones."

"Sigils?"

"It's a type of spell-casting from combining symbols and letters. Each person builds their own. No two are alike. They're designed to convey a specific intent. Something the person wants to manifest. This one looks like it's drawn in blood." She picked it up and held it in the light.

"Does that mean anything?"

"Sigils are often anointed with blood or sexual fluids to increase their power. These two are burnt. Burning a finalized sigil is a way of charging it or imbuing it with power."

Kissick still thought that Cheyenne had burned these papers to destroy evidence. Even though he thought this witchcraft business was nonsense, he found it ironic that perhaps Cheyenne had inadvertently given power to Tink's wishes by burning them.

"What would a person want to manifest, for example?"

"Any of your heart's desires. Love is a big one. Looking for love in general or wanting someone in particular to fall in love with you." With her finger, she outlined the symbol on one of the burnt pages. "Or it could be something mundane, like, 'Heal me from the flu,' or 'Guide me to the right new car.' If you want to find out what these mean, why don't you ask the person who drew them?"

"She's deceased."

"Oh." Magick looked at the sigils more intently. "Murder?"

"Her death is under investigation."

"I see." She compared the three pages. "These look like variations of the same message."

"Can you read them?"

"No, but I can see that the style is similar." Magick stepped from behind the counter. "We have books on sigilry."

He followed her as she went to a cubbyhole between bookshelves in the Occult section. She took down a large paperback and carried it to the counter.

"There are lots of ways to create sigils." She flipped through the pages and then held the book open on the counter.

"Here's one way. You start by writing your intention in a single line. Let's say it's: 'Guide me to the right new car.' "

She grabbed a notepad and wrote the sentence in block letters.

"Then you cross out all the vowels." She drew slashes through the vowels. "Then you cross out any letters that repeat. You have a few letters left."

She rewrote the letters that she hadn't crossed out on a new line.

"Then you lay the letters on top of each other, transforming them, moving them . . . You can make them masculine, with no curves and all angles. Yours look feminine with all the circles and curves."

Taking a fresh piece of paper, she started drawing her set of letters, overlapping the edges, forming a W on the back of an N, tacking a C atop the N's arm. "You follow your intuition."

"When is it finished?"

"When you feel that it's finished. You should draw the finished form only once and put it in a sacred, secret place. Some people have tattoos done of their sigils."

"Do you have any idea of the message in these?"

Magick shook her head. "They're like snowflakes. This magic belongs to that individual."

He gathered up the sigils. "Thank you. I'll buy this book."

While he took out his wallet, she picked up a deck of tarot cards and started shuffling them, pulling the deck apart and weaving it back together. She tapped the cards against the counter and slid the deck toward him. "Would you cut the deck, please?"

He reached toward the deck without thinking but stopped before he touched the cards. "Why?"

"It might guide you in your quest."

Against his better judgment, he cut the cards.

She put the two halves together and slid off the first card. "The Queen of Swords. A courageous, smart woman who's suffered deep sorrow or loss." She slid off the next card and placed it beneath the first card. "The Ten of Pentacles. Signifies wealth. Family fortune."

When she turned over the next card, she hesitated before setting it sideways below the other two. "The Devil. Its position means uncontrolled ambition. Greed. True evil."

She moved her hands away from the cards and lowered them to her sides. "While I was shuffling the cards, I tried to manifest the intent of the person who created those sigils. I would say that it's a woman. Someone of wealth and intelligence, and she's mixed up with evil." She looked somberly at Kissick.

He picked up the book. "Thank you, Sarah . . . er, Magick. You've been very helpful." As soon as he was outside, he muttered, "What a crock."

TWENTY-FIVE

Vining arrived to meet Vicki Hotchkins at Jones Coffee Roasters, which was tucked into a small industrial park on South Raymond in Pasadena. Vicki was ensconced with her laptop in an overstuffed chair, sitting with both legs tucked beneath her gauzy skirt.

A coffee bar and a wall of Plexiglas dispensers stocked with roasted beans were across from the seating area. In the back was a giant stainless steel roaster. The shop's beans were grown on family property in Guatemala. During roasting times, the aromatic fumes wafting from the rooftop chimneys scented a several-block radius.

On a couch, a young man in a shirt and tie was manically tapping his thumbs on a PDA that he held between both hands. His head of spiky gelled hair moved in time with his efforts.

Vicki reached for a large container of coffee on an end table and noticed Vining coming in. She set the laptop aside, unfurled her legs from beneath her skirt, slipped her feet into sandals, and rose to greet her.

Vining was amazed that Vicki could sit comfortably with her legs twisted beneath her—something she couldn't do, especially after years of police work had taken its toll. Unlike her mother and Tink, who both dieted relentlessly to stay rail-thin, Vicki had eased into comfortable acceptance of her middle-age spread.

"Hi, honey." Vicki gave her a warm hug. She'd stopped dying her hair back to brown in her forties when the gray became overwhelming, and switched to a silvery blonde that made her gray roots less obvious. She wore it in a short, chic style, long on top and feathered at the sides. Her eyes were bloodshot, betraying the Ramona Girls' late-night slumber party and reacquaintance with Boone's Farm.

Her necklace of multicolored beads matched her skirt. Her earrings, with a shower of small beads, and her beaded bracelet matched her necklace.

Vining reflected that this generation of women loved their matching jewelry. She lingered as she returned Vicki's hug, enjoying this affectionate embrace from a woman her mother's age who embodied qualities that Vining longed for in her mother: warmth, wisdom, fairness, and fierceness. She needed such a hug right now, after having done what she'd long dreaded, but knew she'd have to face eventually—pulling back the veil on Patsy's life.

Vicki held her at arm's length, smiling with her lips closed. With her high-heeled sandals, the top of her head was eye level with Vining eyes.

"Oh, honey . . ." Vicki saw the distress in Vining's face and hugged her again, stroking her back. "This must be so hard on you. Tink drowning. You just don't get any peace, do you?"

"Seems that way sometimes."

"How about a coffee? I could use a fresh one. What would you like?"

"Just a small black coffee. Thank you." Vining understood why Vicki was a much-beloved high school principal. There was warmth, but the strength behind it came through too.

Vicki returned with the coffees and handed one to Vining. She slipped her feet from her shoes, again tucked them beneath her as she sat, and smoothed her skirt over her legs.

The steam from the coffee felt good against Vining's face. "How is Tink's mother?"

Vicki pursed her lips. "She has moderate Alzheimer's. Tink moved her into an assisted-living facility in Pasadena. Gorgeous place. We told her about Tink. We explained what happened and she understood. She cried. Her short-term memory is gone. Actually, by the time we'd left about an hour later, I don't think she remembered why we'd come. We girls were talking after and decided that it could be a blessing to forget certain things."

Vining pulled back a corner of her mouth, thinking she could be right. "Did Tink have any other relatives?"

"Her brother Greg. Tink's relationship with him and his longtime girlfriend was cordial but distant. He lives on a houseboat in Sausalito in San Francisco Bay. Gets by as a housepainter. He had little contact with Tink, and I don't think he's called his mother for years. When I called him to tell him about Tink, he was more upset about being left in charge of his mother than he was about Tink's death. Bastard was relieved when I told him that Tink made me her mother's guardian. I'm also executor of Tink's will. She made her final wishes clear. The funeral will be at the Church of the Angels with Father Bob officiating. She'll be buried beside her son and husband in the Engleford plot at San Gabriel Cemetery in the dress she wore when she married Stan. After, there'll be a reception at Annandale with mariachis."

"Mariachis?"

"Yep. That's what she wanted." Vicki smiled and shook her head.

Vining thought about the conflicting picture she had of Tink. There was Tink the socialite party girl. There was responsible and generous Tink, raising funds for good causes, taking care of her mother, and making sure her final wishes were taken care of. And there was Tink's dark secret side. For Vining, it called to mind her experience at the Le Towne mansion. All the gaiety and joking in Gig Towne's office was undone by the sight of a very troubled Sinclair LeFleur.

"Nan, have you found out what happened to Tink or can you say?"

Vining took a sip of coffee before saying, "The autopsy is complete. The medical examiner said she drowned. No evidence of a physical event, like a stroke, that would have caused her to topple into the pool, but she was slightly drunk. The toxicology workups take a couple of weeks, so the coroner won't issue a final report until then."

Vicki suddenly lost her composure, looking away with her hand over her mouth and her eyes pressed shut. After a few seconds, she said, "Sorry."

"It's all right."

"I miss her so much. It hasn't really sunk in, that I can't pick up the phone and say, 'Hey, Tinker Bell.' And she'd say, 'Hey, Stinky. What's shakin'?'"

"Stinky?"

Vicki waved off discussion. "Don't ask. And I'd say, 'Too much is shakin'.'"

They both laughed.

Vicki rested her coffee cup against her thigh. "In Tink's will, she amply provided for her mother. She left Mary Alice a painting she'd admired. Left me one also and a portrait of her when she was twelve that her mother had painted. It used to hang over the fireplace in her parents' home. She was very generous with your mother too. She left her nearly all her jewelry. It's appraised at close to a million dollars, Nan."

Vining gasped.

"I was surprised, too. In her will, Tink said she was leaving Patsy her jewelry because Patsy had helped her get through the black times after her son and husband had died. We have to give your mom credit for what she did to help Tink hold it together. She got Tink out of bed. Made her put on clean clothes and brush her hair. We all helped, but Patsy really stood by her. Tink said she was leaving Patsy her jewelry because Patsy had admired it and had always wanted beautiful jewelry of her own."

"I'm speechless. Does my mother know?"

"Not yet. I need to go over the documents with Tink's attorney. Tink kept a few pieces of jewelry that she wore a lot at home, but the rest is in a safe-deposit box." Vicki set her coffee cup on an end table. "She left most of the rest to charities, her church, and her schools. Ramona Convent and Notre Dame are each getting seven figures. She left money to more than a dozen charities. The way Tink lived and breathed Georgia Berryhill, I had a nightmare that she'd leave her everything. I hoped that Tink had better sense and I was right, although she did leave two million to Georgia's Girls." Vicki smirked. "Tink's bequest is set to fund a new Engleford Wing in the dorm."

"Where is the Georgia's Girls facility?" Vining asked.

"It's on the grounds of the Berryhill compound. Big white house. Tink showed us around during our girls' weekend there. I guess it's all right. I just don't like the whole slick Berryhill thing."

Vining thought about her mother and Vince Madrigal. "Vicki, are you sure my mother didn't know about the jewelry Tink was leaving her?"

"I don't think so. Unless Tink told her, but I doubt that. You know your mother can't keep a secret. We all would have known about it."

Vining wondered if somehow Vince Madrigal had found out about Tink's large bequest to Patsy. "Did Tink ever mention someone named Vince Madrigal?"

She shook her head. "Hasn't he been in the news lately?"

Vining nodded but didn't explain. "What about Tink's new boyfriend, King Getty? Did you meet him?"

"Just once at Tink's annual Oscars party. After, my husband and I couldn't believe how slick he was and how Tink had fallen for him."

"Vicki, when Tink took you to the Berryhill compound, did you see anything that suggested that they might practice the occult?"

"You mean like witchcraft? I didn't see anything like that, but there is a sort of cultish feeling to the place. Who knows what goes on in the inner sanctum? I can understand how Tink might have been tempted. But no, Tink never talked about anything like that."

Vicki grew sad. "It's strange. You think you know somebody as well as you know yourself, then you find out that they had a secret life. You realize they showed you the part of themselves that they wanted you to see, or how they wanted to see themselves. You try to trace back the thread through your entire relationship, all the way back to childhood, looking for the moment the disconnect started. Certainly, you tell yourself, you *knew* them at one point, and then they changed. But you have to wonder, did you ever really know them?"

Vining understood what she meant. When she was tracking the man who had knifed her, at times she had felt that she barely recognized herself, given the lines she was crossing in her obsession to get him. Now, she was having the same unsettled feeling about her mother. She'd long known that Patsy would spin the truth and tell fibs out of pride, but now she wondered if her mother had something sinister going on and she'd never seen it.

Vicki looked at Vining with a bemused expression. "My life is so simple. I don't have time for a secret life."

She chuckled and Vining did too, waiting for a time to ask what was on her mind. There was no good time. She steeled herself and went ahead.

"Vicki, can I ask you something?"

"Sure, doll. Anything."

"Did you ever meet my father?"

Vicki was taken aback by her question. Her eyes softened. "No, honey. When your mom got married and had you, I was away at U.C. Santa Barbara. I stayed there during the summer between my freshman and sophomore years. Got a job as a waitress at one of the restaurants on the pier. Spent all my spare time at the beach. The next time I saw Patsy, she was bouncing you on her hip."

"What about Maria Alicia or Tink?"

"You'll have to ask Mary Alice, but I suspect it was the same as with me. She was studying art at Otis near downtown L.A., sharing an old Victorian house with a bunch of students. Tink was at Notre Dame. That first summer, I think she did an internship with a publisher in New York."

"And then there was my mother, dropping out of Pasadena City College after one semester, having a baby at nineteen."

"You know Patsy."

Vining smirked. "When you came home and saw my mom, where was my father?"

"He was gone. Back to Vietnam."

"*Vietnam?*"

"He was a marine officer. Your mother never told you that?"

"She told me he abandoned us when I was barely three. She wouldn't even speak his name."

"He was shot down in Vietnam. MIA. They never found a trace of him."

Vining put a hand to her forehead. "That doesn't make any sense. If she was married to him, she could have had him declared dead after seven years and received survivor benefits. She married my sister Stephanie's father when I was four. She didn't even wait seven years. He could have been in some POW camp. She even tore up all her pictures of him."

"You've never seen a picture of your father?"

She nearly shouted, "I don't even know his name!" Calming down, she whispered, "Do you?"

Vicki was leaning forward with her elbows on her knees, both hands over her mouth. She parted her hands and said, "David."

"David?"

Vicki nodded.

"No last name?"

"Honey, I don't remember. How many years ago was this? Thirty-five?"

"Why would my mother lie to me? She probably got knocked up and the guy split."

"Honey, I love your mother like a sister, but . . ."

Vining was growing to hate that "but" word.

"I wouldn't put it past Patsy to make up a story about being married to a war hero to tell her girlfriends who were away at college making something of their lives."

"That would explain the gold band in her jewelry box," Vining said. "For each of her other marriages, even if the rings were inexpensive, she had a proper wedding set. For her so-called marriage to my father, all she had was a simple gold band, which she only produced after I got old enough to ask about it. It's time she came clean with me."

"I agree. You have a right to know."

"Please don't tell her we discussed this."

"Of course I won't. Do you want me to be with you when you talk to your mom?"

"Thank you, Vicki. I think I'll be okay. I need to pick a time and place. There's too much going on to bring it up to her now."

They hugged goodbye. Vining headed back to the station.

TWENTY-SIX

*J*ohn Chase arrived at Gig Towne and Sinclair LeFleur's home to start his shift. The previous night, he'd gone home to the small rental house he shared with another cop rather than stay in his room in Towne's house. He'd needed a break.

He drove on a private road, slowing at a gate that was already rolling open. A guard sitting outside it on a lawn chair to take in the morning sun had opened it when he saw Chase's truck. A couple of young male paparazzi who were hanging around lost interest when they saw who it was and that he was alone.

Chase worked twelve-hour shifts for Le Towne on his three consecutive days off from the PPD, giving him no days off. His superiors at the PPD didn't know how many hours he was here, as they wouldn't approve. But the Le Towne job wasn't hard. He was young and energetic, and long hours didn't faze him, plus the money was great. After he'd paid off his student loans, he could start socking money away, hoping to save enough for a down payment on a house. He was twenty-eight and not ready to settle down, but the idea of being a family man had started to seem comforting rather than confining.

His parents were concerned about his long work hours, but gently suggested that he might be maturing, at last. Gentle was a key word when dealing with their son, as he'd indulged in hot-headed flashes that had earned him a couple of formal reprimands at the PPD. His parents had also treaded lightly when suggesting to Chase that he patch things up with Alison Oliver, his girlfriend of nearly a year. They were certain that Alison was "the one," and were upset when Chase announced several weeks ago that they'd broken up. It had happened after a rift that he wouldn't discuss. He didn't reveal that Alison had complained that he was distracted and inattentive, and had accused him of seeing someone else. He'd sworn that he wasn't, but that wasn't completely honest. While he wasn't actually dating another woman, he was emotionally entwined with one: Sinclair LeFleur.

Chase used to drive Gig and Sinclair and act as a bodyguard when they went out in public, but now that Sinclair was in the latter stages of her pregnancy, she rarely left the house. Her obstetrician, Dr. Janus, came there to see her. She'd told Gig that she preferred having Chase with her at the house, so he had other bodyguards drive and travel with him. Since the estate's security system was excellent, his job was easy: walking the property and making sure Sinclair felt safe.

While he initially loved working there, as Sinclair's anxiety and distress grew along with her unborn child, he'd found the job increasingly troubling. It made him feel powerless, a feeling that used to be foreign to him. The tinnitus, the ringing in his ears, that had plagued him since he was a child had flared as it tended to do when he was under stress. It could get bad enough to force the thoughts from his head, leaving only something that sounded like a school bell or a fire alarm that wouldn't stop ringing.

The road circled behind the property and led to a second, rarely used gate at the back. He parked in a small lot by the northern wing near his room. Chase had chosen the smallest of the rooms Gig offered—a single, furnished with a twin bed, easy chair, desk, bookshelf, and TV. The other rooms were suites with kitchenettes, but he'd chosen the small room because it was farthest from the main house, which he secretly called "the mausoleum."

Gig had said that he could stay at the estate full-time and save the rent he was shelling out, but Chase had felt a tentacle snake around him. He breathed more freely after he declined, and the sticky suction cups lost their grasp. Sometimes when he thought of Sinclair, which he did often, in his mind's eye he saw her encased in milky white tentacles that spewed from a leering Gig Towne, who was roaring the Gig Giggle over and over.

As soon as Chase unlocked and opened the door to his room, he saw a note on top of his bed. He recognized Gig's "From the Desk of . . ." notepaper and could read his sprawling handwriting from the doorway: "Come see me. G."

Chase dropped his duffel onto the bed and snatched the note, which he crumpled and tossed into the trash bin. He unzipped the duffel and took out a white pharmacy bag with the Xanax prescribed by his doctor. He'd finally sought medical help for his tinnitus. It was one of those bedeviling conditions with the cause hard to pin-point. After the doctor had ruled out physical causes, he'd concluded that it was caused by stress.

In the tiny bathroom, Chase grimaced at his reflection in the mirror. The sound in his head felt like pain. He ripped the stapled receipt from the bag and took out the plastic bottle. The little white pills rattled like teeth. He tapped one into his hand. He was reluctant to take it, not knowing how it was going to affect him, but he was desperate for relief. He tossed it down his throat and followed with a tumbler of tap water.

Opening the medicine cabinet door, he set the Xanax on a shelf. Two shelves were filled with Berryhill brand nutritional supplements—white plastic bottles with dis-tinctive raspberry-colored lids and labels. The expensive products were terrific job perks for Chase, who was a health-and-fitness enthusiast. He worked out almost every day, and was fastidious about his diet. The estate's full gym was another perk.

He opened the bottles one by one, ending up with a handful of tablets and capsules. He skipped the vitamin E, as his doctor had told him that it could aggravate his tinnitus. He picked up the bottle of multivitamins and read the label. It contained 30 milligrams of vitamin E. While he hated interrupting his vitamin regimen, he thought it wise. He returned the multivitamins to the shelf. He filled a glass with water, pounded the pills into his mouth, and swallowed them all at once.

Starting to leave the bathroom, he had second thoughts. He returned to the medicine cabinet and took out the Xanax bottle, and also gathered the pharmacy bag and receipt. Sinclair's conviction that she was being watched was rubbing off on him. Before now, he hadn't cared whether Gig was searching his room or not, as he'd had nothing to hide. Now he did. He'd heard Gig's diatribe about the evils of pharmaceuticals often enough to worry that discovery of his Xanax prescription would be grounds for termination.

Gig had quizzed him about his diet and exercise habits before hiring him. It was inappropriate, but the entire interview had been unusual. It had been held in Gig's office with Gig seated at his throne. Paula had been there too, in a chair off to the side turned to face Chase. After Gig had introduced them and they'd exchanged pleasantries, she hadn't spoken a word. All she'd done was sit and watch him, her face cryptic, her catlike amber eyes glittering.

Gig had asked him personal questions about his family, childhood, and social life. That was eight months ago, when he was still dating Alison. Their relationship had seemed serious at the time, and he'd told Gig so. He'd asked Gig about the personal nature of the interview. Gig didn't apologize and said that because of his and Sinclair's public profiles, he had to feel extremely comfortable with whomever he brought into their lives. While he didn't look for pedigrees, far from it, he did look for character and mental and physical integrity. Gig had gone so far as to ask him about his medical history and drug use, including prescription drugs. The only drugs Chase had ever taken were antibiotics for an ear infection he'd had as a child. Gig had tsk-tsked about how antibiotics were overprescribed, especially to children, and how there were excellent holistic remedies, specifically mud packs for earaches.

At that time, Chase had wondered if this job was really something he wanted to pursue. Then Sinclair had been summoned to meet him and he'd had no further doubts. He used to think that love at first sight was something from fairy tales for adolescent girls and bored housewives who read romantic potboilers. He hadn't known then that Sinclair was pregnant. After he was hired and had signed the confidentiality agreement, the pregnancy was the first Le Towne secret he was made privy to. It was a big one. Worth a bundle. He'd kept that secret even after the tabloids had offered him a pile of money, as Gig had warned they would. Chase had thought the pregnancy, strange eating habits, preoccupation with security, and Gig's sometimes nasty disposition would be the extent of the A-list secrets he'd have to keep. He'd had no idea what he was in for.

He hid the Xanax and the packaging inside a gym sock, which he crammed into a zippered pocket of his duffel where he kept dirty socks. He left and walked down the colonnade toward the main house.

TWENTY-SEVEN

After knocking at the door of Gig's office, Chase was summoned inside with a jovial, "Avante!"

Gig was on his throne at the head of the giant library table, his laptop computer in front of him. He exuded energy, as always. That was one thing Chase could say about Towne—he was the picture of vitality. He held up his hand and crooked his fingers, summoning Chase toward him.

Chase moved to stand near the middle of the table and clasped his hands behind his back, a good ten feet from Gig.

Gig's bright eyes darkened and he frowned with concern. "Why so glum, chum?"

Chase shrugged. "A little headache."

Gig morphed his rubbery face into a comically overdone

look of concern, frowning severely while at the same time arching an eyebrow impossibly high. He did a spot-on imitation of John Wayne. "Looks like more than a little headache to me, pilgrim."

Chase grinned at Gig's antics because he knew that that's what his employer sought. Gig craved attention like a needy child. During Chase's first few months there, he didn't have to fake amusement, but Gig's act had grown tired as Chase began to glimpse the darkness behind the clown mask. Sinclair's distress had done much to color his view, but the bloom had begun to fade from the Towne rose even before she'd started confiding in him.

"It's nothing, Gig. I'm fine."

"Your spine is probably out of alignment. Would you like my chiropractor to adjust you?" Gig took out his iPhone.

"I'm good. It's already going away. Umm . . . Thanks. Thank you for offering."

Speaking normally, Gig asked, "Did you take something?"

Chase wondered if there was a CCTV in his room that he hadn't detected. "I laid down for a few minutes with a warm towel over my forehead."

"You might try a cold compress on the back of your neck. Right here." Gig placed his hand on his neck. "Right at the back of the skull."

"I'll try that. Thank you."

Gig leaned back, his hands resting on the lions' paws at the ends of the chair arms, and silently stared at Chase.

Chase remained standing with his legs shoulder-width apart and his hands behind his back. He met Gig's gaze for a few seconds, then looked at the ground, not wanting to appear rude by staring back at him. He recalled that in certain ancient cultures, looking the king in the eye was grounds for death. While Gig continued his mind game, which was all it was, in Chase's view, he looked at the patterns in the antique Persian carpet and listened to the sound that only he could hear—the incessant ringing in his ears. The Xanax must have started to kick in because the noise was fading, losing its iron grip on his mind. He had the welcome sensation of walking away from it, leaving it at the end of a long corridor.

He deepened and slowed his breathing, trying a calming method he'd learned from Gig. Gig remained silent. Chase didn't know if he was still staring at him, but suspected he was. A compelling thought entered the newfound space in his mind: *Resign. Quit.*

He would have done it on the spot, but Sinclair's face from the last time they'd met came to him. He thought of her full, pink lips and the softness of her skin, which had a luminous quality, as if lit from within, and had grown more so as her pregnancy advanced. He thought of the tears on her cheeks and how easy it would have been to kiss them away. He recalled the surprising firmness of her round belly against him. When he'd found out she was pregnant, it hadn't stanched his desire for her. It made her more of an enigma, more fragile, and more dependent upon him. She would be lost without him. He knew it was his ego talking, yet . . . Who would watch out for her if he wasn't there?

"John."

Chase looked up at Gig.

"Why are you talking to my wife in secret?"

It was easy for Chase to lie to him. He'd come to despise Gig Towne and his juvenile and cloying need for attention and his mania to control how the world saw him, which spilled over into micromanagement of his environment and all the human beings in it.

The best way to answer Gig's question was with another question. "What do you mean by 'in secret'?"

"You've been secretly meeting Sinclair in the birthing room."

The Xanax had not only toned down the ringing in his ears, but had also changed his perception of everything. He boldly met Gig's eyes. The clown mask was off. Rather than seeing an overdone expression of sadness wrapped around a joke, he saw shark-like coldness and determination. He'd seen the same look in the eyes of hardened gangbangers who had turned over everything to the life, even their soul.

This little meeting in the master's office was a power play. Chase owed Gig no explanation. It was Gig who should explain why he was keeping his pregnant wife a prisoner in a gilded cage. As the situation at the estate had become more bizarre and unpalatable, Chase had considered revealing the truth behind the Le Towne facade. What could Gig and his attorneys do to him? He didn't own anything except debt. The Le Towne secrets would be worth a lot of money. But before he went down that path, he needed to gather irrefutable evidence, photos and videos, about Le Towne's sordid underbelly. He also needed to make sure that Sinclair was protected, that she wasn't smeared with Gig Towne's mud.

"I've run into Sinclair while doing my rounds in that part of the house. We've chatted. There's nothing secret about it."

"You seem to care for Sinclair."

"Who doesn't? She's called America's Sweetheart for a reason."

He gestured as if the point was well-taken.

"Gig, just come out and tell me what you're getting at."

Gig drummed his fingernails against the wooden paws and exhaled noisily as if searching for the right way to begin. After a few seconds, he sat straighter, showing that he'd come to a decision. "Sinclair is a beautiful person, inside and out. The public loves her because they sense her pure and kind spirit. Her essential *joie de vivre*. Women feel that they could be her friend. Men . . . Well, she's attractive to men. She can be a lady in the street and there's an understated sexiness about her that suggests that she can be a whore in the bedroom." He leered at Chase. "I'll only say this about that . . . It's true."

Chase could have slugged him.

Gig picked up on his anger and his eyes sparkled. "John, here's something else you don't know about my wife. That same duality carries through Sinclair's personality." He stroked one of the paws. "How do I say this . . . ?"

He looked at Chase apologetically, as if there was no good way. "Sinclair is not emotionally stable. I don't know what she's told you about having the baby at home. Anyone can see that everything has been put in place with the utmost care and concern for both baby and mother. Sinclair and I would like to follow The Berryhill Method of childbirth, but that is not the primary reason I've set things up the way they are. I did it to protect Sinclair. She's never been . . ." Gig clicked his tongue against his teeth. "Mentally fit, to put it gently. She's been diagnosed as bipolar."

Chase knew he couldn't hide his surprise about that revelation. He found it hard to believe. He'd thought that Sinclair's fragile, bruised-lily persona was part of Le Towne's carefully crafted image. Even with the flights of emotions he'd witnessed in Sinclair lately, he sensed a core of iron running through her.

"We've managed her disease naturally and holistically. She's responded beautifully. But the stress of the pregnancy has taken a mental toll. That's why her doctor and Sinclair and I decided that given all the risks, it was best to have the baby here, in a controlled environment and out of the public eye.

"I'm confiding in you, laying my heart on the table." Gig pantomimed throwing down his heart. "You deserve to know the whole picture. Yes, we're adhering to The Berryhill Method of childbirth, but the reasons for it go deeper than some fanatical attachment to a fad, like the media accuses us. Sinclair and our baby are my primary concerns. Sinclair is my life."

Chase couldn't dispute that. Gig's marriage to Sinclair had quieted rumors that he was a nutcase. He nodded.

"John, I have something else I want to talk to you about." Gig again paused as if gathering his thoughts. "I'm concerned about you. Lately, you seem to be in physical pain. You spoke of a headache. What's going on?"

"It's just a small headache, like everyone gets. It's not impacting my ability to do my job."

"Is everything okay between you and your girlfriend? What did you say her name was?"

"Alison." Chase thought it was none of Gig's damn business how things were going and hadn't told him that they'd broken up, but were still friendly. "Things are great."

"Glad to hear it," Gig said with excessive enthusiasm. "It's so important to have someone in life you can count on, who you can reach out to in the middle of the night. I'd like to invite her over for dinner with Sinclair and me."

"That would be great. She'd enjoy that."

"I'll have Paula set it up."

"Terrific."

"So your headaches aren't being caused by what my father used to call terriblelackanookie."

Chase smiled at the thin joke because that's what Gig expected. He thought about Gig's pointed references to sex. Gig's hints of prowess were probably covering for a lack of it. He'd love to ask Sinclair about that, but while her husband wasn't a gentleman, Chase prided himself on being one. He wondered when Gig was going to let him get the hell out of the room.

"John, I highly recommend my chiropractor or my acupuncturist. They can do miracles."

"I've seen my own doctor, thanks."

"Did he give you pharmaceuticals?"

"All due respect, Gig, but that's between me and my doctor."

With a smug expression, Gig pushed away from the table and went across the room to a cabinet that was crammed with the familiar white-and-raspberry containers of Berryhill brand supplements. He fished around, moving bottles, finding what he wanted in the back. He approached Chase, holding out the bottle.

Chase had no choice but to accept it. The label said Headache Handler.

"Take one of those three times a day. You'll see relief in two days, or your money back."

Chase again managed a limp laugh. "Thanks, Gig."

"Georgia Berryhill didn't build an empire on BS. She and Stefan know their stuff. Even if you don't subscribe to the complete Method, their products have helped millions around the world."

Chase nodded. "Great. Thank you. I'll try it."

Gig slapped him on the arm. "You're a good man, John."

"Thanks. Just doing my job."

"Take it easy and remember what I said." Gig returned to his throne and touched the laptop's keyboard, waking it up. He began typing and didn't look up when Chase left. "Close the door on your way out."

Chase returned to his room. He was about to throw away the Headache Handler, but thought he should wait until he was off the property. He thought of Sinclair, wondering where she was, wanting to see her, but he didn't dare. Not now. He opened the Headache Handler. The protective liner over the cap had been removed. He tapped out a gel capsule that was full of a brownish material. He smelled it. It smelled like dirt. He dropped the capsule back into the bottle and set it inside the medicine cabinet.

He again looked at himself in the bathroom mirror and thought about Gig's revelation concerning Sinclair's mental health. Things at this place kept getting stranger. Maybe he should walk away. As much as he'd grown obsessed with Sinclair, he had to admit that he was flattered by her attention. He knew that Gig was a manipulative megalomaniac, but what were Sinclair's motives? She'd been an unknown starlet before she'd latched onto Gig Towne. Gig had launched her into superstardom, and she'd given him the aura of normalcy that his public persona had needed.

They had a sort of unholy alliance, Gig and Sinclair. She wasn't a naïve victim in all this. Yet, Chase knew she hadn't expected the situation she found herself in now. Her fears were valid, and he knew she wasn't playing him. She truly was depending on him to help her.

He felt bad about quitting his job here, but he had a sense of foreboding that if he didn't get out now, something terrible would happen to him, and then where would Sinclair be? Their plan was in place. He'd designed it so that she could execute it on her own, as there was no guarantee that he could be there when the time came. She'd be fine. He had to reassure her of that.

He got his duffel and began scooping in the contents of the medicine cabinet and the toiletry items on the sink. He packed his few garments from the dresser and closet. Tossing key cards and keys for the Le Towne estate onto the bed, he slung the duffel over his shoulder.

After he was off the property, he'd call Gig and tell him he'd quit.

He put his things into his truck. He had to let Sinclair know what was going on, but couldn't risk seeing her. The safest way to communicate was to send a text message to her cell phone. He kept it cryptic: *All OK. All in place. No worries.* ☺

TWENTY-EIGHT

I'm glad that Princess Cheyenne conceded to meet us at her attorney's office, but why does it have to be at eight tonight?" Vining was driving Kissick, making slow progress on the hour-long trip from Pasadena to the Berryhill compound in Malibu Canyon. "The mother of Emily's friend will pick up the girls after rehearsals for the school musical and take them out for dinner. I owe her big-time."

"Em is singing and dancing?"

"*High School Musical.* She has a small role, but she has a solo. She's actually good."

"I have no doubt. I'm just surprised that she's putting herself out there like that."

"Transferring to this arts magnet school has been great for her. It keeps her busy. It's a good thing."

"Her romance with that boy is no more."

"Yes, thank goodness. They're 'just friends,' she says. He's graduating in two months and headed to Stanford. Can't happen too soon for me."

"What did you find out today after the bug sweep?"

Vining took a breath before filling him in on what she'd learned from searching her mom's home. She also told him about her conversation with Vicki and how Patsy was about to become wealthy.

"Vicki said she doesn't think my mother knows about Tink leaving her jewelry to her. My mom can't keep a secret. Certainly not one as big as becoming rich overnight."

"But you told me that at the girlfriends' party at Granny's house, your mom was hinting about a secret life. She's flush with cash from somewhere. Madrigal would want to keep Patsy happy if he was in fact using her to get to Tink. But after he'd had his bugs in place, why would he need your mom? Unless he prompted her to ask Tink questions about her will."

Vining shook her head. "When Tink drowned, my mom would have blubbered everything to me. Maybe Madrigal found out about Tink's bequest and was laying the groundwork to later rob my mother of the jewelry, maybe convince her to put it into a shady investment. My mom would be an easier mark to steal from than Tink. But Madrigal was murdered hours before Tink died."

"King Getty and Cheyenne are still our best suspects," Kissick said. "They were close to Tink, and may have found out about her leaving her jewelry to Patsy and hired Madrigal to do his usual dirty P.I. work and plant the bugs. He could have made a move on your mother, just as she described. Maybe he gave her a couple hundred bucks as a gift, because that's the kind of guy he was. And Patsy's not guilty of anything other than being Patsy."

"That's a scenario I can believe. She hasn't flashed that much cash or bought a new car or something. In the emotional state she was in when we talked to her, she probably forgot some of what she and Madrigal talked about. You need to interview her."

"Yes, I do. Without you there."

"I know," Vining said. "That LAPD detective, Peck, told me that Madrigal's office was ransacked around the time he was murdered. All his recordings and computers were stolen. He had information that someone didn't want getting out."

"That was worth killing for."

"I am worried about my mother's safety. She doesn't seem to be, though." Vining slapped the steering wheel. "There are so many pieces to this that make no sense. Even what Vicki told me about my father makes no sense. If he was a marine officer who was MIA in Vietnam, why would my mother keep it a secret and tell me he was a rat?"

Her voice grew loud. "I'm probably the product of a one-night stand with some Joe Blow she met somewhere, conceived in the backseat of my grandfather's Chevy Malibu at a drive-in movie. My mother told me she used to go to double features at the drive-in. She made up a war hero for the benefit of her friends."

"The finger bowl." He grinned at her.

"The finger bowl?"

"The drive-in. That's what my father used to call it." He playfully pinched her arm. "Come on, Nan. Sure, you want to know the truth about your father, but it doesn't impact your life now. Your mom did the best she could with what she had. Patsy is Patsy. She raised you and fed you, and kept you clean and in clothes and shoes, and kept you safe, and made sure you went to school."

"You're right."

"She didn't hit you or abandon you or let harm come to you."

"I know. I remember that there was one guy she dated who seemed a little too interested in me and my sister and she got rid of him right away."

"See? Whose childhood is perfect?"

"Yours?"

He smiled. "Well . . . Other than mine."

She made a face at him.

They drove in silence for a while, then he said, "This is way too close to home for you."

"I'm surprised Sarge hasn't taken me off the case already. On or off the case, I can and will get to the bottom of what my mother's up to."

She got off the freeway and started the winding ascent through the Santa Monica Mountains that would come out onto Pacific Coast Highway and the ocean on the other side. The hillsides were covered with poppies, lupines, and wild mustard. Impulsively, Vining pulled into one of the lookout points along the road. The sky was clear, as the storm clouds had blown east from the coast and were now moving across Pasadena and the San Gabriel Valley.

Kissick looked at her with surprise.

"It's just so beautiful today."

He joined her at the railing along the edge of the cliff.

She spread both arms open. "Look at this view. The sky is so blue. The ocean too. And the air . . ." She inhaled deeply.

"It is a gorgeous day."

"I just had a thought about Gig Towne."

"Oh, no . . ."

"Not him actually, but his vintage box of sixty-four Crayola crayons."

"With sharpener."

"I remember a crayon color called Sky Blue. It's that color." She pointed at the sky. "That color is so special there's a crayon named for it. Through the decades, children have used that color to depict the clear skies of their imaginations."

"That's beautiful, Nan. Very poetic." Standing behind her, he slipped his arms around her waist and kissed the tip of her left ear, which was peeking through her hair. "A day like this makes me want to just take off and drive up the coast. Stop in Morro Bay or Cayucos. Spend the night. Have drinks and fried calamari at Schooner's Wharf."

She leaned back, enjoying his solidness as she let him support her. He responded by cinching his arms more tightly around her. She put her hands on top of his. "That sounds nice."

"Really?"

She turned in his arms to face him. "Why are you surprised?"

"Do you realize we've never gone away together?"

She thought about that. "There was that time we worked that case by the Salton Sea."

"Yeah, and some nut was shooting at us. That wasn't what I had in mind."

"You're right. A few days away would be nice. But we can't request vacation at the same time."

"We could do a long weekend. Go someplace close. San Diego."

She reached to take his face between her hands. She loved feeling his square jaw and the planes beneath his cheekbones. She ran her fingernails against his stubble.

"I should have run a razor across my face before heading out here."

"Makes you look rugged. Bet it will turn on Georgia Berryhill. She likes younger men."

He pulled her closer, widening his stance so that his face was even with hers. "What about you?"

"I like you."

"Yeah?"

"Yeah." She slid her hands into his hair and pulled his face toward hers. The spring breeze rustled their hair while they kissed. With her eyes closed, the cars passing on the highway sounded like waves crashing on the beach. Sometimes when she kissed him like this, spontaneously and deeply, she tried to pretend it was their third kiss. Not the first one with its hyperexcitement and newness. Not the second, which was still tentative, searching for the right groove. But the third one, fresh enough to be enthralling yet she could set aside her mind and let the sensations move through her, carrying her away while at the same time roiling the depths of her core.

She was able to recapture that now. Their breathing grew more intense and the cool breeze did little to dissipate the heat rising from their bodies. They knew there was no time or place for anything more than a kiss right now, so they gave it everything, their belts, badges, and guns digging into each other.

Someone in a passing car leaned on the horn and whooped from an open window. It was like an alarm clock, waking them from their dream.

He looked at her with his hands laced behind the small of her back and sighed.

She taunted him, and herself, by reaching down across the front of his slacks and giving his erection a squeeze.

"I just had a thought."

"You mean there's still blood in your brain?" she teased.

"This meeting with Berryhill will take less than an hour. We're meeting Cheyenne and her attorney in Century City. No point in going all the way back to Pasadena."

"A motel?" Her eyes widened. "I've never had a tryst in a motel. Have you?"

He narrowed his eyes.

She held up her palm. "Sorry I asked."

"What do you think? Or we could just grab dinner at this little seafood joint I know on PCH."

"A motel does sound a little . . ." She searched for the right word. Only one came to mind. "Nasty."

"It can be as nasty as you want."

"Why, Detective . . ." She fanned her face with her hand. "I do believe you're making me blush."

TWENTY-NINE

It was hard to miss the entrance to the Berryhill compound. The drive was lined with graduated walls of sand-colored stone blocks that led to an arch over the front gates, where "Berryhill" was written in mosaic tiles. The sign was in the same raspberry hues and script used on all Berryhill products, from nutritional supplements, baby food, and pet food to popcorn and salad dressing. The iron scrollwork gates were open. A tall fence surrounding the compound was cloaked with dense oleander shrubs that almost covered the barbed wire strung along the top.

Vining turned into a road bordered with a white picket fence covered with raspberry vines.

The property looked open and welcoming, but as Vining drove, Kissick spotted CCTV cameras tucked by the front gates and in trees.

"I remember this property." He looked at a lake surrounded by a hodgepodge forest of pines, junipers, sycamores, and eucalyptus. "It's one of the few privately owned parcels in the state forest. It used to be a Buddhist monastery. Look over there."

He pointed at a golden Buddha nestled in a clearing beneath a canopy of trees. A semicircle of backless wooden benches faced it. An individual of indeterminate sex and age wearing loose white clothing sat cross-legged on a bench, hands palms up on top of his or her knees.

Vining slowed at an intersection marked with a signpost on which white placards, the ends cut into arrows, bore hand-painted directions in the trademark Berryhill script and reddish-purple color. The arrows pointed to Reception, Home Base, Gift Shop and Cafe, Quiet Space, Georgia's Girls, Nirvana, and Rest Rooms. Smaller lanes off the main road disappeared into the rolling hills.

On a deck beside the lake, a class was under way. A small group of people in white garments sat on folding chairs facing a woman who was scribbling on a whiteboard.

The main road led to a mid-century ranch-style split-level house. It was plain but solid-looking, comforting in its homeliness. It was painted bright white, trimmed with raspberry-colored shutters and front door. Its two overlapping pitched roofs had probably had wood shake shingles when the house was new but were now covered with fire-resistant composite.

A turnabout in the driveway was planted with berry-colored petunias. Flags flew from each of three poles: the stars and stripes, the grizzly bear California state flag, and a white flag with the Berryhill logo.

"This looks like a country inn," Vining commented. "I can see why Tink liked to come here to get away."

"I was thinking the same thing. I wonder how much they charge."

"Hard to believe that anything sinister like witchcraft could be going on here, but we've been surprised before."

"Georgia Berryhill is such a brand name with all her

books and products. You'd think she'd work to keep her image as squeaky-clean as possible." Kissick turned to watch several young women walking along the road carrying wicker baskets on their arms. They wore simple blouses with short sleeves and loose ankle-length skirts. Their hair was braided and pinned up in back. "Squeaky-clean like the young women around here."

"Looks a little cultish to me, like sister wives in a polygamist compound."

"Not everyone's on board. Two gals with tight jeans, right there."

"You couldn't help but notice."

She parked in a visitor lot with about a dozen other cars. On the other side of the lot was the gift shop and café in the same ranch-house style. A few people were dining outdoors at white wire mesh chairs and tables shaded by berry-colored umbrellas.

Vining and Kissick climbed the wooden steps of the main building and crossed a wood plank porch that was painted white. Cushions on the white wicker settees and rockers had a pattern of berry vines.

He opened the front door and they entered a two-story foyer. Area rugs on the hardwood floor had a berry-and-vine pattern. Chamber music was playing. The reception desk was straight ahead. To the left of a staircase was a reading and game room. An elderly man and woman, both in white T-shirts printed with the Berryhill logo, were at a round pedestal table playing Scrabble. At their elbows were stoneware mugs printed with the Berryhill berry-and-vine pattern.

To the right of the reception desk, a river rock fireplace served as a room divider between the lobby and a small white-tablecloth dining room. The fireplace was open all the way through, with stone hearths on both sides. A wood fire that was mostly embers threw off gentle heat.

Berryhill books and products, including jars of berry jam made from the property's vines, were displayed on a table with a sign: Don't Forget to Visit Our Gift Shop.

Vining approached the reception desk. A woman stood with her back to the counter, working at a photocopy machine. She was slender and wore loose garments similar to the ones they'd seen on the women outside. Up close, Vining saw that the fabric had a nubby, natural texture and looked like unbleached cotton. Over her loose pants, the woman wore a long-sleeved shirt with the cuffs rolled up, printed with the berry-and-vine pattern. Vining wondered if Georgia Berryhill had trademarked the design.

Vining tapped a silver bell on the counter. The woman flashed a broad smile as she turned. Her blue eyes were clear and bright. Her long brown hair was braided and streaked with gray. She appeared to be in her forties. A plastic tag with the Berryhill logo pinned to her blouse identified her as "Lucretia." Beneath the open mandarin collar of her blouse was a rectangular hunk of unpolished crystal attached to a black cord.

"Welcome to Berryhill. How can I help you?"

Vining glanced around for Kissick to find that he had wandered away, as was his habit. She handed Lucretia one of her cards. "I'm Detective Nan Vining of the Pasadena police. My partner, Jim Kissick, is around somewhere." She stepped back to look into the game room and didn't see him. "We'd like to see Georgia Berryhill."

Lucretia looked at the card with interest and again at Vining's face, as if trying to reconcile the two. "I'll see if she's in. What can I say this concerns?"

"We'd like to discuss that with Ms. Berryhill in person."

"Let me make a call." Lucretia's voice was calm, as were her movements, neither slow nor rushed.

While she picked up a phone, Vining walked into the game room. The couple playing Scrabble nodded and smiled at her. She said "Hello" and saw Kissick at the far end of the large room, standing in front of a fireplace, holding a mug. Carafes of coffee and hot water and baskets of Berryhill-brand teas and hot chocolate were on a library table behind a sofa.

"Enjoying yourself?"

He nodded, a satisfied smile on his lips. He held out the mug, from which a tea bag string and small label dangled. "Berryhill Blast tea. It's good."

"Not right now, thanks. Care to join me?" She hooked her thumb to indicate the lobby.

He took a gulp of the tea and set the mug on a butler's tray.

When they returned to the desk, Lucretia said, "Asia will be down shortly to take you to Georgia."

"Thank you." Vining thought that had gone easily. "How long have you worked here, Lucretia?"

"Nearly two years. When my husband passed on a few years ago, I was ready for a new life. I was terribly depressed. A friend brought me here and I never left. It's changed my life."

Vining took out the photo of Tink at a recent Ramona Girls dinner. "Do you know this woman?"

"Of course. That's Tink. She lost her husband also. She and I had long talks together."

"I'm sorry to tell you that she passed away on Sunday."

Lucretia inhaled sharply. "Oh, dear." She pressed Tink's photo against her chest and with her other hand grabbed the crystal around her neck. She closed her eyes and moved her lips as if in prayer. When she opened her eyes, they were damp in the corners. She said to the photo, "Rest well, sweet lady," and returned it to Vining. "Is that why you're here? Can I ask what happened to Tink?"

"She drowned in her backyard pool."

"Oh, my."

"When was the last time Mrs. Engleford was here?"

"I don't know."

Vining pointed to a computer monitor on the counter. "Wouldn't you have the records?"

Vining saw Lucretia's blue eyes withdrawing. "You'll have to ask Georgia about that."

"All right," Vining said amiably.

Kissick left Vining in charge, as having two detectives descend on the reception clerk would have been overkill. He was flipping through *The Berryhill Method of Training Your Pets* that he'd picked up from the table of Berryhill products.

Vining put Tink's photo away and took out the one of Cheyenne, Trendi, and Fallon. "Do you know these girls?"

Lucretia tentatively took the photo. Her high-on-life attitude had dimmed. "Poor Trendi. Look how young she looks here."

"Did you know her?"

"A little."

"What about the other two girls?"

Lucretia clasped the photo to her chest, as she had done with Tink's, and was reaching for the crystal on its black cord when she turned toward the stairs at the sound of footsteps.

Also turning toward the stairs, Vining saw bare feet in Birkenstock sandals with clipped unpolished toenails. A chunky ankle beneath a flowing hem was adorned with a strand of beads on a leather cord. Soon, the rest of the woman appeared. She was tall and sturdy. Her straight blond hair fell past her shoulders and was pulled away from her face and fastened on each side with small butterfly clips. Her long dress had a simple scoop neck and cap sleeves.

"Here's Asia." Lucretia said.

"I'm Detective Nan Vining and this is my partner, Detective Jim Kissick."

"Welcome to Berryhill." Asia's smile was enigmatic.

She wasn't wearing makeup, and her cheeks and chin looked chapped. Her face was as plain as her dress. Her brown eyes were sharp, the whites bright and healthy, which also seemed to be part of the Berryhill brand. Vining pegged her to be in her mid-thirties.

"Detective, your snapshot." Lucretia handed the photo of the three girls back to Vining.

When Asia caught sight of the photo, she cast a look at Lucretia that made the other woman take a step back and reach for the crystal around her neck.

Vining held up the photo for Asia. "Do you recognize these women?"

She gave it a perfunctory glance. "I couldn't say." She turned and headed toward the stairs. "Follow me. I'll take you to meet Georgia and Stefan."

THIRTY

V ining and Kissick followed Asia up the stairs, down one corridor and then another, entering an addition to the original building. The floors here were not warmly aged hardwood, but linoleum that looked like hardwood. The berry-and-vine pattern was stenciled along the walls.

The cozy reception area and public rooms were a faux front, disguising the industrial wheels that powered the Berryhill empire. The offices housed hives of cubicles emitting a steady tapping of computer keyboards and the hum of people talking into telephone headsets. From what Vining could see, people in the back office were dressed in typical business casual garb.

The hallway was decorated with an odd combination of artifacts from an eclectic mix of spiritual traditions: a golden Buddha on a pedestal; a silk-screened mandala; yin and yang symbols in black watercolor; a painting on wood of Jesus Christ placing his hands upon the afflicted. Interspersed were framed magazine covers featuring Georgia Berryhill. She was with Oprah on the cover of *O: The Oprah Magazine*. She was with Stefan Pavel on the cover of *BusinessWeek* under the caption "America's Top Entrepreneurs." She was on the cover of *Cooking Light*.

Asia silently walked ahead of them, keeping a steady brisk pace.

Kissick asked the back of her head. "Asia, are these the Berryhill corporate offices?"

She cocked her head over her shoulder and didn't slow when she answered. "These are the business offices for the compound only—the guest facilities, gift shop, restaurant, wellness center, and spa. The Berryhill-brand books and products are run out of a building adjacent to the gift shop."

"Do Georgia and her husband live in the compound?"

Asia didn't bother looking back, but said only, "Yes."

Near the end of the corridor, Asia put up her hand, signaling Vining and Kissick to stop. She leaned into an open doorway, gently rapped on the frame, and spoke in a soft voice that was much different from the all-business tone she'd used with the detectives.

"Hi, Georgia. The detectives from Pasadena are here."

"Please show them in, Asia dear."

Vining recognized Georgia Berryhill's honeyed voice from her television appearances and commercials.

Asia held her hand toward the door. Without a parting word, she left.

Vining entered the office first, and Georgia rose to greet them. She looked just like she did on TV: plump and apple-cheeked. Her facial features were small but well proportioned, and reminded Vining of chubby baby dolls she'd had as a child.

Georgia's straight black hair was in a blunt cut that brushed her shoulders. Her loose dress of burgundy raw silk had raglan sleeves and a hem that nearly touched her black patent-leather flats. Her voluminous dress didn't disguise the fact that she was very pregnant.

"Welcome, Detective Vining." She took Vining's hand between both of hers. Her hands were warm and slightly moist. "And Detective Kissick." She gave him the same two-handed clasp. "Please sit."

There was natural, easy warmth about her that Vining found appealing. She hadn't expected her office to be so cluttered. An inexpensive round table that might have come from Ikea was crowded with what looked like projects in progress: sketches of advertising campaigns on whiteboard; fabric swatches; a thick stack of white paper bound by rubber bands that might have been a new Berryhill book.

In a shallow basket on the floor, a silver-gray terrier dog with a face like a gremlin and dark circles of fur around both eyes sleepily raised his head from a red plaid cushion.

Georgia gestured toward a small couch while she lowered herself onto an armchair. She rested her feet on an ottoman. "Forgive my casual pose, but my doctor told me to keep my feet elevated. My husband Stefan will be here soon. I'd like him to join us, if that's okay."

"Absolutely," Kissick said.

Georgia picked at her dress, gathering it so that it didn't drag on the floor, and then laced her hands on top of the shelf formed by her belly. She let out a long sigh and smiled. "That's better."

"When are you due?" Vining asked.

"Three weeks." Georgia beamed. "Stefan and I can

hardly wait to finally be a family. I have to admit that I'm getting a little tired of being pregnant." She crinkled her petite nose. "Other pregnant women told me this would happen, but I didn't believe them. I was so thrilled to be pregnant after all the years of trying. But now . . ."

A tall reedy man breezed into the room. "What's this? You don't want to be bloated and swollen forever? I'm Stefan Pavel, Georgia's husband." He clasped first Vining's hand and then Kissick's as they introduced themselves.

Vining found his handshake unnecessarily bone-crunching. He was the most formally dressed of anyone they'd seen in the compound, wearing charcoal-gray slacks, a white dress shirt, and a hand-tied bow tie in navy blue and yellow paisley. He wore bookish round tortoiseshell glasses. As if to underscore his nerdy image, his thinning blond hair had a deep part along the side and was slicked down.

From the article in *People,* Vining knew he was thirty-five—thirteen years younger than Georgia, and he was French. His continental accent fit with his Old World persona. She wondered if it had been as carefully crafted as the other facets of the Berryhill brand.

"Hello, my love." He leaned down to give Georgia a kiss.

Her lips touched the edges of his and she made a smacking sound.

Stefan darted his eyes around the room, his movements jittery. He raised his index finger, said "Another chair," and dashed out with a couple of long-legged steps in his cordovan dress shoes.

Georgia stared at the doorway through which he'd gone, shaking her head with loving amusement. "He tires me out. He has so much energy. I used to. But lately . . ." She raised her eyebrows as if she barely recognized herself.

"Being pregnant for the first time at forty-eight is a challenge."

"I imagine it is." Vining found Georgia's voice as soothing as a lullaby.

"We tried for so long. Finally, we had to face reality and started looking into adopting and . . . we got pregnant. We were cautious because we'd been down that road before, but this little one here decided that he or she wanted to be born. We don't know the baby's sex. We want to be surprised."

Beaming, she rubbed her belly. "I'm nearly finished with my new book: *The Berryhill Method of Being an Older Mother.* Of course I had to share what I've learned with other older mothers and women who want to be older mothers."

Of course, Vining thought.

The small terrier slowly stepped from his basket on stiff arthritic legs. He stretched, pressing his front paws forward and his tail end into the air. He hobbled to Kissick, who offered his fingers for the dog to sniff. Having passed muster, the dog allowed Kissick to scratch his head.

"Poor old Mr. Peepers," Georgia said.

The dog presented his snout on his smashed-looking face to Vining, who stretched out her fingers. The black circles around his eyes did make him look as if he was wearing glasses. His left eye was clouded by a cataract. Both eyes were runny. Yellowed front teeth were visible beneath his fur mustache.

Vining scratched his head. His fur was silky, but his bony skull was prominent beneath his thin skin.

The dog moved to Georgia, making a halfhearted attempt to jump up, his front paws only reaching her thighs. She scratched his ears. "He's almost sixteen years old, nearly blind in one eye, and partially deaf. But you're my special little boy, aren't you, Mr. Peeps?"

The dog dropped to the carpet and began slowly making his way back to his basket.

Stefan returned carrying a wooden straight-back chair. "Oh, Mr. Peepers."

Georgia looked at the dog and broke out laughing.

"I'm glad you find the dog's rude behavior in front of guests so amusing, darling." Stefan snatched tissues from a box on the desk.

Vining leaned to look. On the floor were a couple of small turds. Another one fell from the dog's behind as he jerkily walked to his basket.

While Stefan picked up after the dog, Georgia continued laughing, her belly bouncing. "I shouldn't laugh."

"No, you should not, dear heart." Stefan followed the trail to the dog, who had settled back onto his cushion. He examined Mr. Peepers to make sure the dog had finished his business. "So embarrassing."

He dropped the mess into a trash can, which he set in the hallway. Squirting gel from a bottle of hand sanitizer on the desk, he rubbed it over his hands as he sat on the chair he'd brought in. He blurted, "Please tell us what happened to our friend Tink."

"What have you heard about Mrs. Engleford?" Kissick asked.

Stefan blinked rapidly. "She was found floating in her pool. Our friend Kingsley Getty told us this morning, as soon as he'd gotten in from Dubai."

"Mr. Getty told you?" Kissick said.

"Of course. Tink was our great friend," Stefan said, as if the reason should be obvious. "And so is King. They met here, at the compound. It did our hearts good to see Tink enjoying life again. Naturally, King called us as soon as he'd learned the terrible news. Poor man was devastated. He said that two detectives from Pasadena, I'm assuming you, had been to his apartment, asking questions, as if you thought that he had something to do with Tink's murder."

Vining tried not to react when he said "murder." She recalled Getty's casual behavior when they'd interviewed him at the PPD. He'd seemed far from devastated.

Stefan began speaking faster, "You can't think that King had anything to do with Tink's death, can you? Wasn't he out of the country when it happened?"

"King Getty told you that Mrs. Engleford was murdered?" Kissick stretched his legs out from where they were cramped behind the coffee table.

Stefan widened his eyes. His thick glasses distorted them, making them look bigger. "I just assumed, you being homicide detectives, that she was murdered."

"We investigate all suspicious deaths in Pasadena," Kissick said.

"So it could have been an accident?" Stefan's hand flew to his chest as he exhaled. He wore a wide gold wedding band. "That's a relief. Murder is much different cosmically than an accidental death. If Tink had been murdered, she would have been a lightning rod for negative energy. It would have radiated to anyone linked to her spirit, including Georgia and our baby. A purification process would be necessary. But maybe she just fell and hit her head. Had she been drinking alcohol?"

"We can't discuss the circumstances of Mrs. Engleford's death," Kissick said.

"She struggled with a compulsion to consume alcohol to excess." Stefan crossed his legs. "Georgia and I enjoy a fine wine and a touch of cognac every day, but never to excess. Georgia is not consuming alcohol for the time being, of course. I miss our sherry and Stilton parties." Stefan leered at his wife, as if a party around sweet wine and stinky cheese was the height of decadence.

Vining didn't know what to make of him.

Georgia sat like a sphinx with her hands clasped between her breasts and belly, listening. She'd spent years as a psychiatrist before expanding her horizons. She raised a shoulder and closed her eyes as if the solution was simple. "Sage."

"Yes, yes." Stefan nodded, looking at the detectives as if they'd be pleased. "We'll burn sage."

Kissick stood, unable to tolerate sitting cramped on the couch. He took out his spiral pad. "When was the last time you saw Catherine Engleford?"

"We last saw Tink . . . It must be how long ago, darling? Last month?" Stefan again looked at Georgia.

"We can check her account records." Georgia waved in the direction of the computer on the desk and said, "Stefan, dear."

Stefan leaped to his feet and went to the desk.

Vining asked Georgia, "What were your impressions of Mrs. Engleford the last time she was here?"

"Well—" Georgia began. "She came for her periodic MBS Tune-Up. That's our trademark Mind/Body/Spirit program. Tink was religious about having a periodic tune-up for rejuvenation and restoration. She stayed in the Rainbow Cottage, her favorite. We had tea on her patio. She seemed happy."

Stefan typed on the keyboard. "Yes, Tink was here six weeks ago. She had an MBS Tune-Up, a massage, and a guided-imagery session. I'll print the details for you."

"Mrs. Berryhill, you said Mrs. Engleford *seemed* happy," Vining said. "You're not sure. Was something on her mind?"

Georgia angled her lips. "Tink often seemed a bit off. She struggled to achieve symmetry. She could not integrate her shadow self, which manifested a tendency toward addiction that damaged both her physical and spiritual beings."

"What does that mean?" Kissick sounded as if his patience was growing thin.

"One's shadow self is composed of repressed tendencies, both weaknesses and strengths. A person in symmetry can achieve any dream. Nothing is beyond her grasp."

Stefan added, "We've helped millions come into their full selves and a new way of living."

"In searching for one's shadow self," Vining began, "is witchcraft or the occult used?"

"The occult?" Georgia raised her eyebrows. "Is that a joke?"

Kissick took a Xerox of the unburned, full-page sigil and handed it to Georgia. "What do these symbols mean to you?"

Holding the pages of Tink's records that he'd printed, Stefan moved to look over Georgia's shoulder. He frowned, shaking his head.

Georgia's eyes widened as she examined the mysterious images. "This means nothing to me. What is this?"

"It's a sigil," Kissick said. "We found that in Mrs. Engleford's house. Creating sigils is a way to cast a spell, a form of witchcraft."

Stefan handed Kissick the copies of Tink's records. "How curious." He took the sigil from Georgia. "May I keep this? I'd like to research it."

"I'll see that you get a copy later." Kissick held out his hand and returned the sigil to his inside jacket pocket. "Cremated human remains are also used to cast spells. What do you think about that?"

"Cremated human remains?" Georgia again burst out with her infectious laughter. "We promote healthy living through a fully integrated mind/body/spirit. There's nothing to do with the occult here."

Stefan began massaging Georgia's shoulders.

Georgia closed her eyes. "Thank you, sweetheart. That feels wonderful."

"Did you know Vince Madrigal?" Vining asked.

"Just socially." Stefan focused his efforts on the right side of Georgia's neck. "He was here on occasion as a guest."

"He was a mass of negative energy," Georgia said. "We tried to isolate him to keep him from spying on our celebrity guests, which was, I'm sure, the only reason he was interested in the compound." She cringed. "Ow."

"Sorry, darling, but you're all knotted up. I don't wish ill on anyone, but I'm not sorry that Vince Madrigal won't be visiting us again."

"Speaking of that terrible double homicide . . ." Vining took out the photograph of Cheyenne, Trendi, and Fallon and handed it to Georgia.

When Stefan saw it over Georgia's shoulder, he stopped massaging.

Georgia clucked. "Look at Trendi, so young. And Cheyenne."

"How do you know those girls?" Vining asked.

"They were my girls. Georgia's Girls." Georgia turned over the photo and read the handwriting on the back. "Fallon . . . That's right." She handed the photo up to her husband. "It's my special project, the one dearest to my heart. I have an open door at the compound for young women who have lost their way. Who are on a path of self-destruction. You see, I was once a lost girl, and someone gave me a helping hand. Pay it forward."

Vining's antennae went up. "How old are these girls?"

Georgia waved dismissively. "I just call them girls. I think of them as my girls. They're young adults. Much as I'd love to help younger teens, for legal reason I can't let them come here unless they're eighteen. They come to me. Tink was a big supporter of Georgia's Girls." Sadly shaking her head, she added, "Tink did so much for the girls. Such a loss in so many ways."

"Mrs. Engleford was so involved with Georgia's Girls,

I imagine she left something to the organization in her will." Vining was testing to see if Georgia knew about the large bequest.

"I have no idea," Georgia said. "I imagine we'll hear soon if she did. Tink was so generous with her time and money on the earthly plane, we expect nothing more."

Vining felt that Georgia was being truthful. "The Georgia's Girls facility is here, in the compound?"

"Yes. The girls live together in a lovely restored ranch house. I warn them that this is no picnic. I commit to giving them room and board and professional help to get clean and sober. For their part, they have to work to change their lives. It's a sort of boot camp. They have chores. They go to class and study. They have jobs on the compound and they work The Method. I even have a wonderful woman teach them etiquette. These poor girls were living on the streets. After they graduate—meaning clean and sober for a year and they've achieved their high school equivalency—I find them jobs. *Good* jobs."

"We'd like to see the facility," Vining said.

"Oh . . ." Georgia looked at her husband.

"We're redecorating," Stefan said. "The whole house is at sixes and sevens. When it's done, we'll be happy to give you a tour."

"So did you place Trendi as Sinclair LeFleur's assistant?" Vining asked.

"Yes. And I got Cheyenne the job with Tink Engleford. These are not jobs you'll find listed in the classifieds. Only a couple of my girls so far have made the grade and graduated. Sadly, all too many float through and move on."

"You recognized the girl named Fallon," Vining said. "Tell us about her."

"I don't remember much about her. She wasn't here long. I don't even remember her last name, do you, dear?" Georgia looked up at Stefan.

"No, I don't. My wife is a saint, working with these young women. They're not debutantes, that's for sure. Especially these three—Cheyenne, Trendi, and Fallon. Boy, were they rough when they first arrived. To use that quaint American term that describes people like them—" He tapped the photo against his thumb. "Poor white trash." He grinned, pleased with himself.

"Stefan! Shame on you." Georgia slapped her hand over her shoulder at him.

"Cheyenne is Mexican." Stefan was on a roll, finding himself amusing. "So that would make her what, then? Poor Mexican trash?"

Georgia playfully smacked him on the butt. "Go sit down and shush."

Stefan trudged back to his chair, hanging his head in mock shame. "Oops. I'm being sent to the doghouse. That's another American colloquialism of which I'm fond."

"My rather blunt husband studied mathematics at the Sorbonne. I would still just be a psychiatrist with a small practice if it wasn't for Stefan." She wagged her finger at him. "But subtlety is not his strong suit."

Stefan laced his hands behind his head. "That's why I love mathematics. It's black and white."

Vining wasn't particularly fond of Cheyenne Leon, but found Stefan's cracks offensive. "How long had Cheyenne been working for Mrs. Engleford?"

Georgia thought for a minute. "Not long. Two or three months."

"How would you describe her?"

"She struggled with a disadvantaged childhood. She's a tough young lady. She can be a handful."

"Does she have a short temper?"

Georgia breathed out heavily. "I see where this is going. You think Cheyenne might have had something to do with what happened to Tink. I can't speculate on that."

"My wife is reluctant to speak ill of Cheyenne, or anyone, for that matter," Stefan said. "Cheyenne is like a daughter to her. But darling, we must be realistic. Clearly, based upon the detectives' line of questioning, they don't think that dear Tink's death was an accident. If Cheyenne's responsible, her actions are indefensible. She must take responsibility."

"Stefan, have you ever seen Cheyenne become violent?" Vining asked.

"No, but I heard through the grapevine that she'd slapped Fallon and that Cheyenne's bullying was why Fallon chose to leave us."

Vining turned to Georgia. "What do you think about that?"

Georgia's eyes were downcast. The levity and calm she'd shown before had evaporated. "It makes me sad."

"But you still promoted or graduated her from your program," Vining said.

"Cheyenne refocused her efforts on working The Method," Georgia said. "We all deserve second chances."

Vining paused to gather her thoughts and Kissick jumped in. "Naturally, we interviewed Cheyenne because she was living with Mrs. Engleford. We were surprised when Cheyenne quickly hid behind a prominent and pricey attorney—Carmen Vidal. Do you have any idea how Cheyenne would be able to pay for an attorney that costly?"

"I couldn't say," Georgia replied.

"And Trendi Talbot?" Vining asked Georgia. "What was she like?"

"No breeding," Stefan said. "That wasn't exclusive to drug-addled Trendi. I saw that with most of Georgia's girls. It's like they were raised by wolves."

Georgia leveled a gaze at her husband. "Stefan, it's true that they can be coarse sometimes. But everybody has their challenges."

"Indeed, Georgia. You're right, as always." Stefan raised his index finger. "Darling, we should have thought to burn sage because of what happened to Trendi, let alone Tink."

"Yet you recommended Trendi to work as an assistant in the house of your friends Gig Towne and Sinclair LeFleur," Vining said.

"When Trendi left us, she was clean, sober, and healthy," Georgia said. "My dear Sinclair adored Trendi. I'm sure she told you. Sinclair and Gig have big hearts. Gig had his own troubles at a young age, which is no secret. He's been forthcoming about his past in the hope that other troubled souls might take strength from his journey. In that same vein, Gig and Sinclair wanted to give Trendi a chance."

Georgia's eyes welled with tears. They looked genuine, but Vining wasn't exactly sure what had provoked them.

Stefan was quickly out of his chair and at his wife's side. He kneeled beside her chair and grabbed her hand.

Georgia pressed tissues to her face. "Sorry. It's just so much loss to handle at once."

Stefan, still on his knees, asked, "Detectives, have we answered all your questions? My poor wife . . ."

Vining looked at Kissick. He turned up his hand, indicating that he was finished.

"Thank you both for your help," Vining said. "If you think of anything that might help us with our investigation into Mrs. Engleford's death, please call."

Kissick added, "All the best for your upcoming parenthood."

"Thank you so very much," Georgia said. "Forgive me for not getting up."

Stefan jumped to his feet. "I'll walk you out."

THIRTY-ONE

After they'd said their good-byes to Pavel at the front door, Vining stopped at the signpost and looked at the arrow that pointed to Georgia's Girls. "Want to take a stroll?"

"Sure," Kissick said. "Stefan Pavel really gets into his role of the slobbering lapdog to the great diva."

"The earth mother empress and the geek. Talk about an odd couple." Vining put her hand on his arm, stopping him from walking. "Do you think Georgia was lying when she acted like she didn't know anything about sigils?"

"I think both of them are a big ball of PR bullshit. Their images are so carefully crafted and polished, it's hard to tell where the commercial ends and the show begins."

"How about the way Stefan was talking about Trendi and Cheyenne, calling them trash? Nice way to talk about Georgia's beloved girls. What was up with that?"

"He probably came on to them and they told him to take a hike."

"I feel like taking a shower," Vining said.

They walked down a lane that twisted through woods and shrubs. After a ten-minute walk, they reached a locked gate. Beyond it was a white two-story house on the lake. Kissick stretched to get a better look at young women in bikinis lounging on patio furniture on a wooden deck.

"That must be one of their etiquette classes," Vining said.

"They look well behaved to me."

"Tink wouldn't have given her name and money to this place if it wasn't on the up-and-up."

In the drive were workmen's trucks. There was the distant sound of hammering.

Vining pressed the call button on the gate. No one answered.

Kissick looked up at a CCTV camera above the gate.

While Vining pressed the button again, they turned as a bicycle approached. It was Asia with her long skirt tucked up around her legs.

"Can I help you, Detectives?"

"We'd like to look around," Kissick said.

"We're undergoing renovations," Asia said. "But I can give you a tour, if you like."

Kissick and Vining looked at each other. She made a small movement of her mouth, showing that she didn't care.

"We'll come back another time," Kissick said.

"Okay, then," Asia said. "Anything else I can help you with?"

"You had berry tea in your lounge," Vining said. "Can I buy some?"

"Of course. The gift shop's still open. To the left of the parking lot."

The detectives turned to walk back and Asia rode off.

"Tea?" Kissick asked.

"I think Em would like it." After Asia was out of sight, Vining said, "They keep it low-key, but the compound is highly secured."

They headed across the main drive toward their car and the gift shop beyond.

"I can understand why," Kissick said. "The Berryhills have their naysayers. Accusations that The Method is a cult, that people have died undergoing the more-extreme procedures, but nothing has stuck so far. The bigger the Berryhill brand gets, the bigger a target it becomes. The employees here aren't any more guarded than any other corporations where we've asked hard questions. Look at those people. They seem peaceful, don't they?"

Vining turned to look at a group of people sitting in a circle beneath a giant oak, cross-legged on mats with their eyes closed. "After a week on juice and herbs, they're probably hungry."

"Communing with their shadow selves."

Vining sneered. "I know something about encountering your shadow self. I met mine and now he's six feet under. Looking at that granite headstone, I found myself in perfect symmetry. Speaking from personal experience, I don't recommend getting in touch with your dark side. Not healthy."

"I'm thinking of a side of you I want to get in touch with." He let his hand brush her butt and sneaked a quick pinch.

She squealed.

He looked at his watch. "Three hours until we meet Cheyenne at her attorney's office. Do you want to go see if that dive seafood place out in Malibu is still there?"

She slipped her hand around his waist. "I thought you wanted to go to a motel."

He looked at her out of the corners of his eyes. "I didn't think you wanted to. You want to?"

"I've never done anything like that before. It's been a while since we . . ." She arched an eyebrow.

"Since we . . ." He toyed with her. "Since we what?"

She dreamily closed her eyes. "Made love."

"It was only last weekend. You making a habit out of me?"

"Maybe it's all this fresh air. It's making me kind of . . . I don't know."

"Think sex is allowed at the Berryhill compound?"

She held him tighter. "If it isn't, I can't imagine why people would pay so much to stay here."

She passed the gift shop and went to the car.

"Thought you wanted to buy some tea."

"It can wait." She unlocked the doors.

"Eee-ow. I don't think I've seen you like this before." He climbed into the passenger side.

"Fasten your seat belt and hold on."

"Oh, baby baby."

They found a Quality Inn in West L.A., not far from their appointment in Century City—nothing fancy, but it was clean. They picked up some Mexican food from a hole-in-the-wall place that Kissick knew on Pico Boulevard from his UCLA days.

Vining stayed in the car munching tortilla chips while Kissick got the room, asking for one in the back. While he fumbled with the electronic key, first putting it in upside down, she nervously glanced around even though the odds of anyone recognizing them were remote. The light on the door lock flashed green and he opened the door.

She dropped the bag with the food and sodas onto a narrow table beside an in-room coffeemaker.

As he was sliding the security chain into place, she leaped on him from behind, hooking her right leg around his waist, and standing on her other leg.

"Whoa! Careful . . . My sciatica."

"Sciatica?"

He pulled the chain to shut the vertical blinds, then turned and lifted her off the floor with both hands beneath her butt.

She clasped his lower body between her legs and his neck with her hands. Their noses were touching. "When did you come down with sciatica?"

"Hey! It's gone!" He staggered as he carried her to the

bed. When he leaned over to set her on it, she dropped backward, making him tumble on top of her.

As they kissed, he worked at her blouse buttons and she unbuttoned his shirt. He reached behind her and fiddled with her bra hooks before giving up and pulling her bra up over her breasts. He grabbed her breasts in both hands. They fit easily. He sucked on one nipple and nibbled the other. She arched her back.

"Wait." Panting, she pushed him off and stood. She took off her badge and tossed it on the nightstand, followed by her Glock in its Velcro holster, and he did the same, the equipment landing heavily on the table. Sitting on the bed, she ripped open the Velcro on her ankle holster and added her backup Walther to the pile.

They quickly stripped off their clothes and hung them in the closet, both mindful of their next appointment.

While he was still hanging up his clothes, she grabbed the bedspread, thin blanket, and top sheet and flung them to the side. Nude, she slid onto the bed, piling pillows behind her back and watched him, propped up on her elbows with one foot flat on the mattress and her leg bent.

Also nude, he stood by the bed, hovering for a moment as he took in the sight of her.

She smiled crookedly, waving her bent leg. She let her head fall back and looked at him through slit eyelids. She made larger arcs with her leg and finally let it fall open.

"You witch."

She slid back into the pillows and reached out her hands for him. He joined her.

THIRTY-TWO

Attorney Carmen Vidal's office was on the thirtieth floor of the thirty-five-story Fox West tower in the Century City area of L.A. The building was on Avenue of the Stars, which had been patterned after Paris's Champs-Élysées when the "city within a city" west of Beverly Hills had been constructed in the early 1960s on a 260-acre Fox Studios back lot.

A security guard had to unlock the tall glass doors to let Vining and Kissick inside the building. The guard made a call to Vidal before directing them to the express elevator. The elevator silently zoomed up toward the heavens.

A brass plaque outside Vidal's suite showed that she shared the offices with two partners. The suite's doors were unlocked. As the detectives walked through, they passed junior associates working late, squirreled inside windowless offices in the center. The suite had calming, plush, and impersonal décor. Like all offices, the worker bees eventually didn't see their environment, but only felt it crushing in on them.

A corner office had the door open and the lights on. The detectives heard Vidal and Cheyenne talking. They suspected that with Vidal there, this was a pointless exercise, as they wouldn't get anything out of Cheyenne, but they had to try.

They stopped at the open doorway. Their approach had been silent and startled Cheyenne, who was leaning against a credenza in front of a darkened window, causing her to jolt to her feet. The stiletto heel of one of her strappy sandals caught in the thick carpet, making her stagger. She wore a white miniskirt and a long-sleeved sheer blouse with a floral print. Underneath, a red bra peeked. The fringed denim jacket she'd worn when they'd first seen her at Tink's was tossed across a chair.

Vining saw Kissick glance at her long tanned legs. Even after their just-completed motel tryst, he still couldn't pass up a chance to admire a sexy, long-legged woman. Vining suppressed the urge to slug him.

Vidal rose from her chair and circled her desk with her hand held out. "Detectives Vining and Kissick. Welcome."

As at their prior meeting at the PPD station, Cheyenne didn't greet the detectives but eyed them with her face turned away.

Vidal ushered the detectives to a round table with rolling chairs. She held out her hand, signaling for Cheyenne to join them.

The young woman stomped across the room, her high heels leaving indentations in the carpet.

When she passed in front of her, Vining noticed tattoos of shooting stars on the backs of both toned thighs.

Cheyenne pulled out a chair and dropped onto it. When she crossed her legs, her skirt hiked up, leaving little to the imagination. As she had done by Tink's pool, she examined her split ends with fascination.

"Detectives, why did you want to meet with Cheyenne again?" Vidal took a seat. "Surely there's no problem with her alibi?"

"Cheyenne still hasn't told us where Mrs. Engleford's laptop and missing documents and books are," Kissick said.

Vidal looked at him as if she didn't understand. "Cheyenne doesn't know anything about that."

"We think she does," Kissick said.

"Detectives, we've been cooperative. Cheyenne has nothing to hide. You wanted to have another meeting and here she is." She held her hand toward Cheyenne as if she'd made her materialize.

Cheyenne laconically slid her eyes to look at Vidal.

Kissick took out the Xeroxed sigil and set the page in front of Cheyenne. Vidal was good at hiding her thoughts, but Vining detected heightened interest, as if she hadn't seen this before. It looked to Vining as if Cheyenne was trying to read the symbols.

Vining pointed at the sigil. "You missed this one. It was stuck in the back of Tink's desk drawer."

Cheyenne's expression darkened.

Kissick spoke to Cheyenne as if carefully reasoning with her. "Mrs. Engleford drew these in her office. She either studied sigils on her own or someone taught her about them. We didn't find books about sigilry at her home, and someone cleaned out her office desk and burned the sigils, except for this one. What are you hiding, Cheyenne?"

Cheyenne glanced at Vidal.

"She isn't hiding anything," Vidal said. "Is that paper the reason you wanted this meeting?"

"We'll leave it here for you," Kissick said, pushing up from the table. "You think of anything you'd like to tell us, give us a call."

Cheyenne smirked and shook her head as if the detectives were clueless.

Vidal stood. "Thank you, Detectives. A pleasure, as always."

"One more thing." Vining took out the photo of Cheyenne, Trendi, and Fallon and set it in front of Cheyenne.

"What're you doing with that?" Cheyenne grabbed it

and turned it over, seeing the writing on the back. "You stole this from my room in Tink's house."

"It's evidence," Vining said coolly.

Vidal reached to take the photo from Cheyenne.

"Evidence of what?" Cheyenne glared at Vining. "That I had friends?"

Vidal tried to calm Cheyenne by touching her shoulder, but the younger woman bolted from the chair.

"Yes, you *had* friends, Cheyenne," Vining said. "Trendi's dead. And Fallon . . . What really happened to Fallon, Cheyenne?"

"Who's Fallon?" Vidal demanded.

"She was one of Georgia's Girls, Carmen," Vining said. "Just like Cheyenne and Trendi. Georgia's Girls is Ms. Berryhill's pride and joy. Her way of giving back for all the wonderful things she's attained in life."

Cheyenne snorted derisively.

"Ms. Berryhill even sent the three girls to charm school." Vining added a jab. "Those lessons really took hold."

"What does this have to do with Mrs. Engleford?" Vidal asked.

"Mrs. Engleford was very involved with Georgia's Girls." Vining stared at Cheyenne. "She gave them a lot of money and left them a fortune in her will. What do you think about that, Cheyenne? You don't seem to have a high opinion of Georgia's Girls."

"This has nothing to do with Cheyenne." Vidal took a step toward Vining. "This conversation is over."

"It has everything to do with Cheyenne," Vining said, instincts aroused. "I'd like to know how you benefited from being one of Georgia's Girls, Cheyenne."

Vidal started to speak and Cheyenne gestured for the attorney to shut up. She looked angrily at Vining. "Did you talk to Georgia about this picture?"

"Yes, we did." Vining slipped a hand inside her slacks pockets. "Ms. Berryhill told us that you three girls were hard-luck cases that she took under her wing. She singled you out as an especially difficult case."

"Yeah?" Cheyenne snorted again. "What else did she say?"

"Ms. Berryhill said that you have anger issues and a volatile temper. And her husband said that after an argument you had with Fallon turned violent, Fallon took off. Mr. Pavel described Trendi as a drug-addled nutcase."

Cheyenne balled her fists. "What else?"

Vidal put her hand on Cheyenne's arm. "There's no point—"

"What else did they say?" Cheyenne demanded.

Vidal persisted. "Cheyenne, if you're not going to take my advice, I can't represent you."

"What else?"

"Ms. Berryhill didn't say too much after that, but her husband sure did. When he looked at that photo, he laughed and called the three of you trash. Said you were raised by wolves."

Cheyenne's eyes bored into Vining. "And Georgia was there?"

"Of course. Sitting with her feet up. Chuckling with her hands clasped across her big pregnant belly."

Cheyenne turned and walked a few feet, her back to them, fists clenched.

Vining spoke softly. "Cheyenne, do you want to tell us something? We can help you."

Vidal moved to put herself between Vining and her client. "We've answered your questions, Detectives. It's time for you to leave." She held out her arms to try to usher them out, stopping short of touching them.

Vining didn't move. "What's Fallon's last name, Cheyenne? Just tell us that."

Cheyenne turned.

Vining was surprised to see tears in her eyes.

"Price. Her name is Fallon Price."

Vidal tried again. "This conversation is over."

Vining refused to stop. "Cheyenne, people you know keep getting killed. Tink, Trendi . . . Your good friend Fallon's been missing for years."

Cheyenne hung her head. Tears fell onto her blouse.

Vining kept on. "Why are you crying, Cheyenne? Are you scared or do you feel guilty?"

"Detective Vining," Vidal said, "don't make me report you to your police chief. We're good friends, you know."

"We'll see ourselves out," Kissick said.

"Cheyenne, call us. Day or night." Vining followed Kissick out.

THIRTY-THREE

As *Vining* and Kissick got out of the car at the PPD garage, they saw Sergeant Early walking toward them, leaving for the day.

They greeted her. "Hi, Sarge."

"Good evening, Jim and Nan. Jim, Patsy Brightly is waiting for you in the second-floor lobby. Nan, you're off the Catherine Engleford case. She was your mother's good friend. Finish your reports tomorrow. I'll assign Alex Caspers to assist you, Jim. Have a good evening."

She got in her car and left.

Vining and Kissick looked at each other.

Vining said, "I guess that's that. Good luck with Patsy."

"I'm too close to this case to be handling it either."

"I know," she said. "If there's a trial, could be a problem. Unless you want to come out about our relationship right now, we'll have to take that risk."

"See you tomorrow."

They parted without a touch or lingering look.

An hour later, in the interview room, Patsy wailed to Kissick, "Jim, I told you, I don't know why Vince Madrigal would bug my house and Tink's."

"Did Madrigal probe for information about Tink or the people she knows?"

"No."

"What did the two of you talk about?"

"Just whatever." Patsy fluttered her hand. "Whatever people on a date talk about. Movies. The news."

"How did you meet Vince Madrigal?"

Patsy groaned. "Jim, I already told you that. Why do you keep asking me the same things over and over? I was at my job at the Estée Lauder counter at Macy's. He came in to buy perfume for his mother."

Kissick sat quietly, looking at her. Finally, he said, "Patsy, look . . . I know you're in bad financial trouble. I saw all the credit card bills and letters from collection agencies."

Patsy gaped at him. "I gave Nan permission to look around. I didn't mean she could go through my desk. I didn't know she'd do it when I wasn't even home."

"You gave permission to search your house. That's what 'search' means."

Patsy turned away, shaking her head.

"Patsy, look at me. You're in financial trouble. You're vulnerable. Lately, Nan's noticed that you have a lot of extra cash. Where did you get the money from?"

"I sold some things on eBay."

"Did Vince Madrigal ever ask you about Tink's will?"

"No."

"Do you know what was in Tink's will?"

"Nooo. Why? Do you?"

Kissick wasn't going to get into Tink's bequest to Patsy right now. He didn't think she was lying, but many things he'd thought about Patsy were being turned upside down and he couldn't be sure.

"Where have you been getting all the extra cash?"

Patsy hit the table with her fist. "I told you. I sold some things on eBay. Old clothes and stuff."

"Did Vince Madrigal ever give you money?"

"No."

"At your mother's house, Nan said you were talking about how she doesn't know everything about you. What did you mean by that?"

"She told you that?" Patsy rolled her eyes. "I was drinking. I don't know what I was saying."

"Patsy, you're holding back. I know you are. Spill it!"

Her blue eyes became shot with red, and her fair skin flushed pink. "Stop badgering me!" Big tears popped into her eyes and ran down her cheeks, cutting rivulets into her makeup. She let out a heartrending moan. Her open mouth was turned downward, as were her eyes.

Kissick thought her face looked like the mask of tragedy he'd seen on a poster for a play at his eldest son's school. Usually he considered it a triumph when he'd made someone he was interviewing cry. It meant he was breaking him or her down and the truth was close. Instead, he suddenly felt exhausted. "How much money did you make on eBay?"

Patsy said through her sobs, "Not a lot. Two hundred dollars."

He asked again, "Did Vince Madrigal ever give you money?"

She sniffed and said in a small voice. "Yes."

"How much?"

"Five hundred dollars."

"Why?"

"Not for any reason you might be thinking of, Jim. It was a gift. He saw that I was always broke and he gave me a gift." She held up her palm. "He was from Texas."

Kissick later called Vining at home and told her about his interview with Patsy. "Your mother was consistent. I questioned her for nearly two hours. She finally told me that Madrigal had given her five hundred dollars as a gift. After that was on the table, she didn't waver from it. She and Madrigal talked about current events and that was it."

"Do you believe her?"

He paused before answering.

"That's a 'no,' " she said.

"Not necessarily. It was just sort of un-Patsy, if that makes sense. Her responses were brief, with no elaboration or gossip."

"Or self-pity, like 'Why do you think Madrigal had an ulterior motive in dating me? Don't you think I'm attractive enough for him?' "

"Exactly. What do you think?"

"I don't know what to think. I'm going to bed."

"See you tomorrow. Love you."

She smiled. She loved it when he told her that. "Love you, too."

Later, after Emily had gone to bed, Vining was bedeviled by the sleeplessness that would hit her when she was the most tired. She made chamomile tea, which helped. Instead of watching a classic movie on television, as was her habit, she went into her bedroom and turned on her laptop.

She researched the J. Paul Getty family. The information was scattered and unofficial, but she pieced together a family tree going back a few generations. She didn't find any mention of a Kingsley Getty or an illegitimate Getty brother.

Then, for the first time ever, she Googled herself. She was shocked by the number of times her name was listed.

THIRTY-FOUR

John Chase and his housemate, Kevin Ramirez, were hosting the bimonthly poker game with their group of cop buddies. Tonight, six had made it, including Alex Caspers, Chase's best friend at the PPD.

Chase and Ramirez rented a house in San Dimas, one of the San Gabriel Valley's plain-vanilla bedroom communities. San Dimas was between Pasadena, where Chase worked, and Pomona, where Ramirez worked, and far enough away from both cities so that they wouldn't run into people they'd arrested or knew from the streets while going about their personal business in the grocery store or Home Depot.

Chase was telling the guys how he'd quit his job with Le Towne earlier that day. "So Gig Towne calls me and just about begs me to come back, but I told him, 'Gig, I'm done.' "

They were sitting at a dining room table set that had been a castoff from the Le Towne household when Sinclair had gone on a redecorating binge. The pieces were formal and fancy, reflecting Gig's tastes, and had garnered ridicule from Chase's friends. It hadn't taken long for the bachelors' rough usage to rob the furniture of its pedigree.

"That was a good job," Ramirez said. "What tore it?"

Chase raised a bottle of Sam Adams lager to his lips. "It was just a weird scene. Let's leave it at that." He was wearing his lucky shirt, which his ex-girlfriend Alison had bought him on a weekend trip together to Vegas. The rayon shirt had a loud pattern of playing cards, poker chips, and greenbacks.

"You're still holding to that confidentiality agreement?" Caspers threw down three cards. "You can trust us."

"It's not that." Chase frowned as if struggling to focus on the cards he held in his hand. "It's too long to get into."

"I wouldn't mind that gig. Would you put in a word for me?" one of the other guys said. He had a prominent nose and small eyes—a combination that had earned him the nickname "Ratso."

"No problem, dude. I'll call Gig and put in a word." Chase finished his beer. "I'm getting another one. Anybody want something?"

A couple of guys put in requests.

Caspers pushed up from the table. "I'll help."

Chase opened the refrigerator door and began moving bottles around. "There's only one Sam Adams left. I'm taking it."

"Chase, what's going on?"

Chase looked behind Caspers to make sure they were alone. "That Ratso is a jackass. I'll put in a word for him but he wouldn't last five minutes with Gig."

"Forget Ratso and Gig. What else is going on? Something's bothering you."

Chase handed him bottles of beer. "It's this tinnitus. Keep it between us, will you?"

"Sure. Especially because I don't know what the hell it is."

"It's like a ringing in my ears. Sometimes I can hardly think."

"What's it from?"

"My doctor's ruled out everything physical. That only leaves stress. I've had it since I was a kid, but never like this. I didn't want to say anything in front of the guys, but the stress of working for Gig Towne is why I bailed out of there. Gig acts like he's the freaking puppet master."

Chase was quick to add, "Understand that I'm not putting myself or anyone else in danger. Ditching the off-duty gig should help."

"No one will hear it from me," Caspers said. "But I have to tell you, it hasn't gone unnoticed. Nan cornered me and asked if you were having some sort of a physical problem."

Chase loudly exhaled. "Crap. I couldn't believe it when she and Kissick showed up to ask Gig about some old rich bag who'd drowned."

"Nan's buddies with your C.O."

"I know."

"Be better for you to be up front about what's going on." Caspers twisted the cap from a beer bottle. "I'm just sayin' . . ."

"You're right. Now that I'm not working two jobs, I should start feeling better. If I don't, I'll come clean to Folke. I won't put you in a position of getting called on the carpet because you knew and did nothing."

Caspers slapped his back. " 'Nuff said."

"Where are those beers?" a guy shouted. "We're dying of thirst."

Chase and Caspers grabbed the bottles by the necks and carried them in.

As the dealer started a new round, Chase's cell phone

rang. He took it from his shirt pocket and looked at it. "I gotta take this."

The guy next to him looked at the phone's display and said, "Sinclair's calling."

"You in or out?" the dealer asked.

"Out." Chase got up and headed toward his room to a chorus of guys giving him grief.

When he answered the phone, she said only, "John."

He closed his bedroom door. "Sinclair, is it time?"

"No. Not yet."

He wouldn't relax until he'd rescued her and she'd delivered her baby at the hospital, safely away from the clutches of Gig, Paula, and Dr. Janus.

She was crying. "John, how could you just leave like that?"

Her anguish cut him. "Sinclair, please don't worry. You and your baby will be fine. I'll make sure of it. I had to leave. Gig was suspicious. He knew about our meetings."

Her weeping turned to sobbing.

He was firm with her. "Sinclair, you need to calm down. Trust me, okay? Do you trust me?"

She sniffed and said meekly. "Yes, I trust you."

"Good. Everything will be fine as long as you stick to the plan. Okay?"

"Yes. Okay."

He heard the resolve in her voice and felt better. "Call me whenever you want. Just be careful."

"Okay. John?"

"Yes?" He loved it when she said his name. "Thank you. You're my best friend."

He swallowed the lump in his throat. "No problem."

He returned to the poker table and his buddies' ribbing. As soon as he sat down, his phone beeped, signaling that he had a text message.

"She really wants it," one guy said.

"Won't that poke the baby?" another joked.

Chase looked at the phone display. "It's Alison. She's texted me twice. Guess I didn't hear it."

"At midnight?" a guy said. "Can only mean one thing."

"Booty call!" Ratso yelled and the others joined in. "Booty call!"

Chase made a face as if it was out of the question. "She's dating some cop with Glendale P.D."

"She lives in Glendale, doesn't she?" one guy asked.

"She hooked up with another cop? Did he pull her over or something?"

Chase ignored the questions and read the message. "I don't know why she's texting me instead of him. Her sink's backed up. It's always backing up in that old place where she lives."

"Booty call," Ramirez said.

Chase texted a response, then slapped the phone closed.

"Why doesn't she call her new boyfriend?" one of them asked.

"She wants something more than her sink fixed," Ramirez joked.

Chase tossed in his cards and headed toward the bedroom.

"You're down a hundred bucks," Caspers said. "You don't want to try to win it back?"

"No."

"Gig Towne's money," one of them spitefully said.

"He is so not over Alison," Ramirez said while Chase was still within earshot.

Caspers didn't comment, not wanting to gossip about his friend.

After a few minutes, Chase returned. He wore the same jeans but had changed from his lucky shirt. He was now wearing a blue V-neck sweater over a crew-neck

T-shirt with a khaki zip-front jacket over it. "I'll get my tool kit from the garage and go over there."

One of the guys cracked, "The tools she wants aren't in the garage."

The others laughed.

He tried to be game. "Yeah, yeah . . ." He headed for the back door through the kitchen. "See you guys later. Caspers, mañana."

"Take it easy, buddy." Caspers watched him disappear through the doorway. He was concerned about his friend.

Alison Oliver lived on a quiet street in the flatlands of Glendale, a city a short drive west of Pasadena and about the same size. It was another of the foothill cities that abutted the San Gabriel Mountains along the 210, aptly named the Foothill Freeway.

Chase parked on the street in front of a courtyard complex of ten Spanish-style bungalows with tile roofs set in pairs around a center walkway. Each unit had a tiny front yard, a minuscule porch with a light, and a backdoor off the kitchen. All the porch lights were turned off, as was the norm, as the tenants paid for their own electricity and cut corners where they could.

Chase grabbed his tool kit and walked to Alison's bungalow in the back. He saw lights through the closed blinds over her living room windows. The bungalow had just one adjoining wall with the unit next door, which was occupied by Art, a bachelor in his fifties who was a crew manager at Trader Joe's. He spent his weekends refurbishing a 1963 Chris-Craft cabin cruiser that was docked at the Long Beach marina.

As Chase walked past the darkened bungalows by the glow of ground lights dotting the front yards, he saw that Art's 1992 Saab 900 Turbo convertible was not parked in its spot beside his unit, meaning he was probably staying on his boat. Art had helped Alison with small household repairs before.

Chase walked up the single step to Alison's front porch, which was lined with pots of geraniums, two red and two pink. He opened the screen and rapped lightly on the door, not wanting to wake the neighbors, who were mostly college students and young singles who put up with the tiny bungalows because of the cheap rent and retro charm.

"Alison," he said softly. "It's me. John."

The blinds over the windows moved. He heard the security chain being slipped off the door, which cracked open. He stepped inside.

At ten o'clock the next morning, when the reliable Alison hadn't shown up for work or answered her phone, her girlfriend from work came to her front door. Her knocking and calls roused Alison's neighbor. Art had been sleeping in, having the day off from his job.

Art knew where Alison kept her spare key, poorly hidden beneath a rock in the boxwood near her door. He unlocked the door and went in first. The tiny living room was neat as usual. A metal tool chest was on the floor inside the door.

With Alison's girlfriend behind him, Art crossed to look inside the small kitchen, then walked through the living room again and entered the short hallway. At the end, the bedroom door was ajar. He smelled the gunpowder and blood before he'd fully pushed open the door.

It took him an instant to take it all in. Alison and Chase lay on top of a white chenille bedspread. Blood had spread in a dark crimson halo around their heads and shoulders. She was wearing a pink terry-cloth bathrobe.

Pink-and-green striped pajamas extended beneath the bottom hem. She was barefoot. He was fully dressed, still wearing a zippered jacket over his sweater and loafers on his feet.

There was a single gunshot wound between Alison's open eyes. It had done little damage to her face.

Chase was on his back, clasping her right hand with his left. His right hand was curled on his chest, holding the Beretta he carried off duty. The muzzle was beneath his chin. Hair, skull, and brains were splattered against the headboard, wall, and ceiling.

After looking at the scene for two seconds, long enough to imprint the image in his mind for the rest of his life, Art pulled the door closed and blocked it, not allowing Alison's frantic friend to get any closer.

THIRTY-FIVE

Vining was at her desk the next morning, finishing typing her reports on the Catherine Engleford case, when she received a return call from the Department of Homeland Security. She didn't see any problem in taking down the information, even though the case was no longer hers. The caller told her that there was no record of Kingsley Getty having traveled to Dubai or anywhere outside the country during the prior week. The only overseas travel on record for him over the past two years was a round-trip from L.A. to Paris the previous month and another to Madrid with a connection to Palma, Majorca, a year ago.

Getty had taken the trouble to lay the groundwork that he was going to be out of the country at the time of Tink's death. But Dubai? That was baffling. Travel by airline, especially overseas, was easily verified. A cagier move would have been for him to have driven someplace close to L.A., like Palm Springs. Check into a hotel. Be seen at the bar. Buy gas. Slip out and make a quick trip back to Pasadena. Maybe Getty, the slick con artist, had never dreamed that Tink's death would be considered anything but accidental and thought that his story would never be questioned.

Vining rested her chin against her fist with her elbow propped on the desk and stared at the cubicle's gray fabric wall. When she thought of Getty as Tink's murderer, she saw it as a crime of passion. Maybe Tink had turned down Getty's request for money or called him out as a sniveling con artist. But Getty telling people in advance that he was going to be out of town suggested premeditation. Had Getty been paid by someone to sidle up to Tink and find out how much she knew about something or someone? Had Vince Madrigal learned the same information that had caused Tink to be eliminated? Vining thought of the bugs planted in her mother's home. Patsy claimed ignorance but had she heard something that could put her in danger? Even if she hadn't heard anything incriminating, it was enough if someone *thought* she had.

She took out photocopies of Tink's sigils. Was the deadly secret encoded in them? She'd accused Cheyenne of having burned them, but maybe it had been Getty. Maybe they'd both been involved in bringing Tink down.

She spread out the pages and studied them. There were similarities between the three sets of symbols.

She went to Kissick's cubicle. He wasn't around. The book he'd bought about sigilry was on his desk. She took it, telling herself this was just a little research. Sergeant

Early shouldn't have a problem with that. She couldn't conceive of Caspers wanting to bother with this.

Back at her desk, she skimmed the descriptions of the mystical underpinnings of sigil-making, discussing how the sigil traps the expression of a desire into a powerful symbol, and found the nuts-and-bolts section. She first needed to come up with a statement about something she wanted to manifest and then write it in a line, spacing the letters evenly.

An intention popped into her head. She wrote it out:

F I N D O U T W H O K I N G G E T T Y I S

As per the instructions, she crossed out the vowels and the letters that repeated, and then began to superimpose the letters. They could be reversed, overlapped, or written inside other letters. Lines sticking out could be topped with a circle, a feminine symbol, to give power to something to be changed internally, or an arrow, a masculine symbol, to manifest something externally.

It didn't take Vining long to come up with her sigil. Now she understood why each sigil is unique. It's a product of the sigil-maker's inspiration.

Vining again studied Tink's three sigils. She now saw that Tink hadn't densely overlapped her letters. She could pick out F, S, and G. She could see W, N, T, V . . . Since letters could be superimposed, it was hard to know which ones had actually been incorporated. The F, S, and G gave her an idea. She turned her pad to a clean sheet and wrote:

G E O R G I A S T E F A N

After removing the vowels and duplicates, she compared what remained with Tink's sigils. She could make a case that Tink had crafted an intention about Georgia Berryhill and Stefan Pavel. She found a P but nothing that resembled a B, which led her to think that if the sigils were about Georgia and Stefan, Tink had used just their first names. The P pertained to a different message.

She tried to guess what Tink's intentions might have been about Georgia and Stefan. She considered her own questions about the couple. A phrase popped into her head. She wrote it down and reduced it according to the sigil formula. She found evidence of these letters in Tink's sigils:

H P M F D T R B G N S

The letters were derived from this simple wish:

H E L P M E F I N D T H E T R U T H
A B O U T G E O R G I A A N D S T E F A N

What she'd come up with felt right.

She had long ago grown adept at shutting out the phone conversations and sometimes loud jiving among the detectives. The noise level had risen. She'd tuned it out until she detected a tone of anguish that was roiling through the section. She rose and saw Sergeant Early leading Caspers to his cubicle, which was adjacent to hers. Early's no-nonsense face looked graver than Vining had ever seen it. Caspers trudged as if in a daze.

Detectives were standing in their cubicles and murmuring to each other. Vining's heart fell to her stomach, yet her head felt as if helium was pulling it from her body. Something terrible had happened.

Caspers heavily sat in his chair and covered his face with his hands. His chest rose in a staccato motion. He might have been crying or gasping for breath.

Vining looked at Early, who told her, "Officer John Chase and his ex-girlfriend were found in her apartment in an apparent murder/suicide."

Vining didn't need to fill in the blanks. She knew the drill. The male cop had shot his girlfriend, then himself.

From between Caspers's hands came a low moan and a barely decipherable, "Oh, God."

Early rested her hand on his shoulder.

At her touch, Caspers moved his hands from his face. He wasn't crying, but his hands trembled, and he was doing all he could to maintain control. "I was just with him last night. It was our poker night."

Kissick came in. It was clear that he'd heard the news. Those in the Detectives Section had moved from their cubicles and offices into the common areas, where they stood in stunned silence. Ringing phones went unanswered.

Early told Caspers, "Lieutenant Beltran is at the scene. Investigators from the Glendale P.D. will want to interview you, but Sergeant Folke and I want to talk to you first in my office. We'd like to do that now. Would you like to get some water or coffee before we begin?"

Caspers wiped his eyes and nodded. "I'll get a Coke and be right there."

Early left.

When Caspers rose to follow, Vining grabbed his arm. He touched her hand, nodded, and moved on. Other hands reached out to touch him.

Vining lowered herself back into her chair. Kissick moved to stand in the entrance to her cubicle. She rocked her chair, the tips of her steepled fingers pressed against her lips. She slid her eyes to look at him.

"Murder/suicide?" he said. "Bullshit."

She again stared straight ahead.

"First Tink, then Vince Madrigal and Trendi. Now John Chase and Alison Oliver."

Vining spoke through her fingers. "They're all less than six degrees from the Berryhills."

He reached to pick up the yellow pad from her desk. "Help me find the truth about Georgia and Stefan?"

"I don't know if that's exactly what Tink intended, but I can make that sentence fit into her three sigils." She reached for the pad and turned to the first sigil she had created, based on the phrase "Find out who King Getty is." She tore out the page. "Getty wasn't in Dubai. As far as the jet-setter he claims to be, he's only made two overseas trips in the past year, one to Paris and one to Majorca."

"Where he thinks it would be nice to own a house," Kissick said. "So he pretends that he does. I think we have probable cause for a search warrant for his phone and financial records. I'll get started on it."

"Wouldn't you love to get your hands on the Berryhills' records?"

"You were ready to buy their herbal tea."

"I changed my mind."

He put his hand on her shoulder. She briefly grabbed his fingers.

He turned and left.

She started to throw her sigil about Getty away but instead folded the paper in half and put it inside her top desk drawer.

THIRTY-SIX

Sinclair LeFleur was resting on a divan in her suite, her back propped against pillows, watching her girlfriend, a fellow actor, talking about her new movie on *The View*. The program was interrupted for breaking news. A stiff-haired female anchor began talking at a breakneck pace, her eyes boring holes through the TV screen, as she reported a murder/suicide in a courtyard apartment in Glendale. The station cut away to a reporter standing on a street crowded with the usual gawkers, police, and coroner personnel and vehicles.

Sinclair muted the television, not wanting to expose herself and her baby to the negativity. When it seemed that the news broadcast would continue indefinitely, she started to get up. It was tough for her to rise from the low divan.

Earlier, Paula had huffed that if Sinclair insisted on reclining on the divan, she should use a chair to help hoist herself up. Paula had dragged a yellow silk boudoir chair that had a low round back from the makeup table and placed it beside the divan.

Sinclair grabbed the back of the chair and started to stand. She felt swollen and heavy, and was amazed that her body was capable of stretching to the size it had.

She was nearly up, pushing against the chair back, when, out of the corner of one eye, she saw a photo of John Chase on television. It was his official PPD portrait.

She gasped and swung around to grab the remote control from the divan, throwing off her already tentative balance. She toppled backward, pulling the chair over with her. She fell onto her back, slamming her head against the hardwood floor.

The fall stunned her. It took a moment for her to realize that she was looking at the ceiling. One leg was over the fallen chair and the other was painfully bent beneath her.

The suite's door flew open and Paula rushed inside, Gig at her heels.

"Funny face, what happened?" Gig kneeled beside her.

"I told you not to lay on that thing." Paula helped Sinclair get untangled from the chair while Gig straightened her leg and examined it for breaks. Paula draped Sinclair's arm over her shoulders and helped her to her feet.

Sinclair was still clutching the TV remote. She was barely aware of them or the pain from her hard fall. As they fussed over her, she turned up the TV volume. A reporter was speculating about the motives of the alleged perpetrator, Officer John Chase.

"John Chase?" Gig's attention was drawn to the flat-screen TV on the wall.

"John . . ." Sinclair swooned as everything went black.

A pall fell over the PPD, as if the station were draped with a black shroud. Officers took from their lockers the small black bands kept there for the inevitable occasion of a fallen brother or sister and affixed them diagonally across their shields.

In the Detectives Section, work continued at the plodding pace of a funeral dirge. Undercover officers had reported that King Getty was in the Beverly Hills office of his so-called film production company. Kissick sent a plain-wrap car to keep tabs on him and to try to obtain something with his fingerprints and maybe his DNA. Hoping he could show sufficient probable cause for a judge to issue a search warrant for Getty's telephone and financial records, and his apartment and office, Kissick was preparing an affidavit contending that King Getty had incriminating information about Catherine Engleford's death.

Sergeant Early sent Caspers home.

Vining knocked on the doorframe of Early's office. Early was sitting her in her chair, thinking. She gestured for Vining to come in.

"Sarge, I finished my reports and was going to go over everything with Alex."

Early's face conveyed that Vining didn't need to say more.

"I was planning on researching the Berryhills on the Net. I can have Alex—"

Early waved her on. "I can't have you interviewing witnesses or suspects, but anybody can look at stuff on the Internet. You want to have a staff assistant or cadet do that?"

"Thanks, but I'm focused about what I'm looking for. It shouldn't take long."

Vining returned to her desk. She started with the official Berryhill Website, which was an amalgam of Georgia's folksy warmth and corporate polish. The site had chat rooms where monitored discussion groups hashed out everything from diet tips to dealing with problematic shadow selves. Vining learned nothing of investigative value.

The anti–Berryhill Method sites presented a vastly different perspective. The Berryhills were targets of angry bloggers and others claiming to have been damaged by The Method and that the whole thing was in fact a cult. On YouTube, she found a clip of one of Georgia and Stefan's TV appearances on a morning talk show in which they and the unctuous female host had a hearty laugh about The Method being dangerous and even deadly.

Two sites in particular, BerryhillKills.com and TheMethodCult.org, looked as professional as the official Berryhill site. Each claimed to present the dark side of Berryhill that Georgia and Stefan had spent millions to keep buried.

It was no secret that Georgia had once been a well-known Beverly Hills psychiatrist with a celebrity clientele. The Berryhill corporate patter described Georgia's dissatisfaction with treating her patients' mental turmoil through traditional psychiatry. She came to see those methods as mere Band-Aids to these troubled people's psyches. While in a therapy session with a patient, Georgia had an epiphany. She visualized her patient breaking into three components—mind, body, and spirit or shadow self. All three needed to be nourished as a unit in order to achieve wellness. The Method was born.

The anti-Berryhill sites told a different story. Georgia was a Beverly Hills psychiatrist, they conceded, but the success of her practice was based upon her willingness to prescribe psychotropic drugs. She had been investigated in the death of a patient, a former runway model, who'd died from an accidental overdose of prescription drugs, some of which had been prescribed by Georgia and other notorious "pill doctors." Rather than subject herself to an investigation by the state licensing board, Georgia turned in her license and reinvented herself as a Mind/Body/Spirit maven.

Stefan Pavel had an equally checkered past, or so his enemies said. According to them, his given name was Stefan Pavel Vladimirescu. He was not from France, as he claimed, but hailed from Bucharest, Romania, where his father was a butcher and his mother worked in a bakery.

In Romania, he began a college degree in engineering and then, at age nineteen, moved to Paris, where he studied mathematics at the Sorbonne for less than a year.

He came to the U.S. on a student visa and reinvented himself as Stefan Pavel, French mathematician and bon vivant. Pavel's nerdy charm, eclectic knowledge of obscure French and Dutch artists, fondness for fine wines and cheeses, and continental manners, plus his natural ability as a con artist, gained him entry into the highest social circles in Manhattan and the Hamptons.

He married vitamin heiress Abigail Chambers. Three years later, she mysteriously drowned when she fell off her yacht during a New Year's Eve trip they'd taken with a group of friends to the Bahamas. Pavel was awarded only $750,000 from Chambers's vast estate. Rumor had it that he accepted the settlement and released all claims on the estate in exchange for the powerful Chambers family making the criminal investigation into his involvement in the heiress's death go away.

Fate made Georgia Berryhill and Stefan Pavel's paths intersect. She was looking to expand into vitamins and other nutritional supplements. He knew the business. Together, they bought the former Buddhist monastery in Malibu Canyon for a song during a real-estate slump. The rest was Mind/Body/Spirit history.

Vining found it strange that Pavel's first wife had died from an "accidental drowning," similar to Tink's death.

She also learned that a few years earlier, the Berryhills had been sued in a wrongful-death case. The parents of a young woman accused Georgia and Stefan of killing their daughter through starvation and dehydration during an MBS Tune-Up. Defense attorney Carmen Vidal had represented the Berryhills, who had settled out of court for an undisclosed sum.

Since Carmen Vidal was also Cheyenne Leon's attorney,

Vining was now convinced that Berryhill was footing Cheyenne's legal bills.

Digging deeper, Vining was shocked to come across a familiar name. Five years earlier, Georgia and Stefan had been implicated in the disappearance of a teenage runaway from Las Vegas named Fallon Price. Fallon's mother had tracked her to the Berryhill compound, where the trail went cold. While at Berryhill, Mrs. Price was told about the fight Fallon had had with one of Georgia's other "girls." Around the compound, "Georgia's Girls" were called "Berryhill's babes." Mrs. Price heard whispered rumors that the girls did more than study etiquette and do odd jobs. It was alleged that sex orgies were held at the compound, but this couldn't be substantiated. "Girls" from Georgia's program who had gone on to jobs on the outside dismissed such allegations as anti-Berryhill venom.

Vining looked at a photo of Fallon on the Website. She took out Cheyenne's photo of her with her two friends. Trendi was dead. Fallon was likely dead. They were all Georgia's Girls. Fallon was seventeen when she disappeared. If true, then Georgia Berryhill lied about taking in only wayward young women who were at least eighteen. It appeared that Georgia had lied about many things.

THIRTY-SEVEN

*S*inclair had strange dreams of being tied down mixed with images of John Chase's suicide and his girlfriend's murder. In the background, she always heard a steady electronic beeping noise.

"She's waking up, Doctor."

Paula was in her bedroom? And why was her bed so hard? Her back hurt. It felt as if someone was fooling around with her down there.

"Let her wake up. We're dilating nicely. The oxytocin is doing its job."

Sinclair opened her eyes and saw a white sheet. She realized she was looking at a sheet covering her bent knees. She saw Dr. Janus's face down there. She felt him pull his fingers out of her.

He smiled as he stripped off his latex gloves. He was wearing green surgical scrubs. "You're going to be a mother soon, Sinclair."

With a bald head, pointed nose, and broad, lippy smile, he'd always reminded her of a fish. He especially did so now as Sinclair blinked to clear her vision.

"What's going on?" she asked. Her voice was weak. She was thirsty.

Paula stood to her left, also dressed in green scrubs, tapping a keypad on an IV infusion pump. Her hair was covered by an elastic cap.

"Contractions should start soon," Dr. Janus said. His bald head was not covered.

With a start, Sinclair saw the IV needle taped to her left arm. "What's this? What are you doing?"

She was on the adjustable bed in the birthing room. The back was elevated. Pulling up the U-neckline of the white gown she was wearing, she saw elastic straps crossing her belly. The beeping of the fetal heart-rate monitor was what she had heard in her dreams.

She raised herself to her elbows and slid her legs flat. "You're inducing labor?"

Only then did she see Gig standing beside her, also in green scrubs, his hair under a cap. He reached over and tenderly stroked her head. "Hear that, funny face? We're going to be Mommy and Daddy soon."

She glared at him. "Why are they inducing labor?"

"It's all for the best, funny face."

"But *why*?"

Paula sternly repeated Gig's words. "It's all for the best."

Dr. Janus smiled like a toothy shark. His head looked small on his round body. "We're concerned about your and your baby's welfare, Sinclair."

"What time is it?" The schoolhouse clock on the wall showed two-twenty. In the windowless basement room, she didn't know if it was day or night. "How long have I been here?"

Dr. Janus kept smiling. Sinclair suspected that he was trying to look reassuring. "Long enough."

Sinclair gaped at the liquid being infused into her vein. "I don't want that. That's not good for the baby."

"It won't harm the fetus," the doctor said.

"There's no reason to induce labor. This is crazy!"

"You're in good hands, sweetness," Gig said. "Don't worry."

Panting, she looked up at him standing over her. She used to think his high-pitched, nasal voice was funny, but now it made her cringe, as did his long, probing fingers on her hair and forehead. His gaze was impassive, as if he was not looking upon his wife who was about to give birth but at a stranger, maybe someone he'd happened upon by the side of the road after an accident and whom he was trying to comfort because it was the right thing to do, while at the same time praying that professional help would arrive quickly so he could get the hell out of there.

Paula and Dr. Janus were near the end of the bed. Paula regarded Sinclair blankly while Dr. Janus maintained his simpering smile. Sinclair blinked and their faces morphed into demons with black holes for eyes and sunken cheeks. Breathing even harder through her mouth, she frantically looked at Gig.

"What's wrong, baby?" he asked. "You okay?"

She was overwhelmed with fear. John said he'd be there to make sure that nothing happened to her and her baby. She was to call him as soon as she went into labor. Now he was dead and she was trapped.

Gig, Dr. Janus, and Paula all stared at her with cold, clinical eyes. She had to get out. She had to get her baby out.

She grabbed the edge of the bed and started to swing her legs over.

"Honey, where do you think you're going?" Gig asked.

Paula rushed to her side. "Do you have to use the bathroom? I'll help you."

Sinclair pushed herself up into a sitting position. She slapped away Paula's hands. "Don't touch me!" She set her bare feet onto the floor. "Get away!"

Paula again approached and Sinclair madly swatted at her.

"That's okay, Paula." Dr. Janus intervened, extending an arm between Sinclair and the midwife. "Let Sinclair walk around."

She whipped her head around to stare at him. "Stop talking like I'm a child. Worse than that, you're treating

me like I'm a bred show dog about to birth prize pup-
pies, and you just can't wait to see how perfect they
are." She cradled her belly and stepped back from them.
"You're not getting my baby."

"Sinclair, now you're acting like a child." Gig put his
hands on his bony hips.

Dr. Janus motioned Gig to remain silent. "Sinclair, we
understand how frightening this is for you, but after it's
over you'll be able to hold this perfect little baby in your
arms, and you'll forget all this."

She stepped backward, stretching the plastic IV tube.
Behind, her hands touched a metal floor lamp. She
grabbed the pole with both hands. With a jerk, she pulled
the plug from the wall. She turned the pole so that the
frosted glass bulb faced out, holding it like a battering
ram. "He promised to watch over me."

"Who did?" Gig's top lip was raised, making him look
like a chipmunk.

"John." Sinclair couldn't say his name without crying.

"Who's John?" the doctor asked.

Gig turned to him. "That cop we had working here.
He just killed his girlfriend and then killed himself."

Sinclair yelled, "What did you do to him? What are
you doing to me?"

She yanked the IV needle from her arm.

Paula moved toward her. "I'm just going to have to
stick you again."

"Stay back." Sinclair made a ramming motion toward
Paula with the lamp.

Paula made a grab for the lamp. Sinclair swung both
arms back and hit her in the stomach with it.

Paula doubled over with the blow. "You bitch! You
think you're gonna hit me?"

Gig threw up his hands. "I don't believe this. Sinclair,
you're about to have a baby. Stop this ridiculousness
right now."

Sinclair's eyes were wild. She was shaking her head as she backed toward the door.

As the situation escalated, Dr. Janus grew calmer. "Let's everyone relax. Sinclair, if you want to leave, feel free to leave."

"You think I won't?" Sinclair backed toward the door, still holding the lamp in both hands. "You act like I've lost my mind, but I've never seen things more clearly. I see evil."

"Evil? Sinclair, c'mon," Gig said imploringly.

He, Dr. Janus, and Paula inched toward her.

Sinclair bared her teeth. Her cheeks were flushed, and her long hair was mussed as if for a romantic film's bedroom scene. "First Trendi and now John. That's not evil?"

Gig widened his eyes. "All that means is that we have to do a better job at screening the people we hire."

"People around me are dying and you think this is a joke." Blood ran down her arm.

Gig stopped mugging. "It's no joke, Sinclair."

On the floor against the wall was a tall ceramic vase that held broad stalks of dried bamboo, a decorative touch intended to be calming and Zen-like. Holding the lamp in one hand, Sinclair pulled out one of the stalks, which was about three feet long and two inches in diameter, with a hollow core but about a half-inch thick and heavy.

She threw down the lamp. Its glass orb shattered, sending glass shards across the floor. With both hands, she grabbed the bamboo stalk near the end like a bat.

"Look at the mess you made." Paula darted her hand toward the floor.

Sinclair waved the stalk back and forth as she headed toward the door.

"She's the Ninja pregnant woman," Gig mused. "A new superhero—Ninja preggers."

"Oh, Gig," Sinclair said. "If people only knew how *funny* you are." Her eyes challenged him.

That wiped the smile off his face. "Dr. Janus, let's put an end to this."

"No need to traumatize the baby unnecessarily unless we have to." Dr. Janus watched Sinclair exit the room while filling a syringe from a vial. "She won't get far."

Moving more quickly than she thought possible, Sinclair reached the institutional-style door, pressed down the lever, and squeezed out.

Gig bolted toward the door.

The heavy door slammed closed on its own. Sinclair wedged the bamboo stalk beneath the lever. She slowly backed away, not sure the bamboo would hold. When she saw them through the window in the door and heard them pounding and yelling, she started giggling as she walked as quickly as she could down the hallway, holding her belly with both hands.

She cried out when a contraction hit, grimacing and leaning against the wall. Her knees buckled, but she didn't go down. She rapidly inhaled and exhaled through her teeth, like she'd been instructed to do when she'd played a woman giving birth in a movie. The pain subsided. She was able to open her eyes. She kept moving down the dimly lit hallway that Gig had designed to give the feeling of walking through catacombs. While she still heard them pounding against the door, trying to break through the barrier, Sinclair wondered why she'd given in to Gig on so many things. She'd always felt like a visitor in his life, like a guest leery of asking for more towels or special food lest she be thought a pest and not invited back.

It had been the same with the pregnancy. She'd wanted birthing classes, to commune with other expectant mothers, to see her doctor in an office and not in what she'd come to think of as a basement laboratory. She wanted her pregnancy to be normal. Gig had patiently explained that once she had become half of Le Towne, being "normal" was no longer an option.

When the baby started to grow and move inside her, everything changed. It was as if the scales had fallen from her eyes. But by the time she saw what a fool she'd been, she was trapped. John Chase had showed her that she wasn't trapped. He'd helped plan an escape. They'd worked it all out to the smallest detail. She'd check in under an assumed name at Huntington Hospital. She'd been in touch with an Ob/Gyn in Pasadena whom she'd seen since she was a young adult. She'd explained to the doctor that she and Gig preferred to have the baby at home because of the media frenzy that would ensue, but she wanted a backup arrangement and it needed to be kept hush-hush.

She'd trusted John and Trendi. Sinclair had trusted them with her secret and they'd both promised to help her. Now they were both dead. That's what their loyalty had cost them. But she was still alive and so was her baby. The escape plan was still in place.

There was an exit outdoors from the basement level through the gym. From there, it was a short walk to the garage. Inside a storage cabinet, behind Gig's collection of vintage lunchboxes, was a tote bag that held clothes and copies of her ID and insurance information. There was a spare key to the Mercedes SUV and an inexpensive prepaid cell phone that Chase had bought.

The hospital was just a few miles away. She'd check herself in and would refuse to be moved until the baby was born. She would pitch a fit if anyone tried to get her to come home. She'd banked on Gig not wanting a scandal like that showing up in the tabloids.

A contraction hit right when she pulled open the gym door. She clutched the doorframe, pressing her head against it. The pains were coming more closely together.

* * *

In the barricaded birthing room, Dr. Janus had an idea. He slipped a wooden tongue depressor into the door to hold open the latch. Gig and Paula hoisted an easy chair onto its side and used it to batter the door. The bamboo stalk splintered. Bursting through the door, the three of them ran into the corridor, not finding Sinclair and having no idea where she'd gone.

Wiry Gig sprinted ahead. Paula ran up the stairway while the rotund Dr. Janus jogged after Gig, his medical bag swinging from its handles in his hand.

The doctor heard Gig let out a wail. Janus moved as fast as he could, gasping for breath, as he was woefully out of shape. When he got to the gym door, his heart leaped into his throat at the sight of Gig kneeling over Sinclair, who was stretched out on the rubberized floor.

Gig turned at the sound of the door opening, moving out of the way to reveal a perfectly formed baby lying on top of Sinclair's belly and her soiled white gown.

Sinclair turned her head toward the doctor, a blissful look in her eyes, a familiar expression he'd seen on the face of every mother he'd assisted when she'd first laid her eyes upon her newborn.

Gig had tears in his eyes. "She's beautiful."

Sinclair was cradling the baby atop her stomach. "She's sleeping." The baby was very still. The umbilical cord was still attached. "Sweet little thing's tuckered out. You should have heard her crying before."

Dr. Janus came closer and Gig moved out of the way, avoiding the fluids and by-products of the birth. He set his bag on the ground and took out a hypodermic needle.

Sinclair rubbed her hand against the baby's slimy hair. "She's sucking on her fingers. Are you hungry, baby?"

Dr. Janus took the cap off the needle. "Hold her," he

ordered Gig when Sinclair tried to get away. He jabbed the needle into Sinclair's arm.

"I have to feed my baby."

Gig braced her on the other side. "Honey, the baby's not breathing."

"Of course she's breathing." The tranquilizer started to take effect right away. Everything turned hazy. Sinclair felt them taking the baby from her. She tried to get up but felt as if velvet ropes had lashed her to the floor. "Give me my baby."

Through the fog, she heard the baby crying.

"Hear that? She's fine. My baby's fine. Give her to me!"

"Honey, the baby's not fine."

She felt Gig again stroking her hair. She wanted to break his fingers. She tried to grab them but could barely raise her hand. Looking around, she didn't see the baby or Dr. Janus. Still, she heard the baby crying and crying, the sound growing fainter.

"She is too fine. My baby is fine!" Sinclair could fight it no longer. She slipped into blackness.

THIRTY-EIGHT

*A*lex Caspers pulled up in front of the house that John Chase and Kevin Ramirez had shared. Their poker game last night seemed as if it was a lifetime ago.

Ramirez opened the front door before Caspers knocked. He was dressed in sweatpants and a torn T-shirt printed with the logo from a local gym. He held an open bottle of Dos Equis by his side between his fingers and a frosted unopened bottle in his other hand. Without a word, he raised the unopened bottle of beer toward Caspers.

He took it, twisting off the cap as he followed Ramirez inside. He took a long swig, the cap still in his hand. When he saw that the house, which had never been pristine to begin with, had been tossed, he chucked the bottle cap into a pile of books, magazines, and DVDs that had been yanked from bookshelves and strewn across the floor.

"They had drug-sniffing dogs through here." Ramirez swung his hand, still holding the bottle, indicating the mess. "Fucking Glendale P.D."

He walked into the kitchen, kicking a path through the mess on the floor. The kitchen was worse than the living room, with everything thrown from the cabinets combined with the remnants from the poker night that hadn't been cleaned up.

"Chase was a cop, just like them. Show some respect." Ramirez kicked an empty cardboard cylinder. There were paw prints in the oatmeal strewn across the floor. "Look at what those jackasses did. This was spiteful. I'm filing a complaint." He finished his beer and set the bottle on the counter.

"You should," Caspers said. "I just finished spending a few hours with a couple of their detectives. They were assholes."

Ramirez found an unbroken bottle of beer on the floor. He used the end of his T-shirt to clean it off and opened it.

"I'm going to check out John's bedroom, okay?"

"Knock yourself out."

Caspers picked his way through the living room and down the small hallway. In the middle was the bathroom the two guys shared. At the end of the hall was Chase's bedroom. The Glendale cops had dragged his clothing and sports equipment from the drawers and closet. An empty leather shoulder holster hung from a hook on the back of the door of the small closet. The shotgun that Caspers knew Chase kept in a corner of the closet was gone.

Caspers frowned at the beige fiberfill comforter on the bed. It was covered with muddy paw prints from the drug-sniffing dogs.

The bathroom had an old-fashioned pedestal sink with a medicine cabinet above it. The mirrored door was open. Some items were still inside the cabinet, but most had been scooped out into the sink and onto the floor. It was the usual stuff: shaving cream, deodorant, mouthwash, toothpaste, aspirin, Alka-Seltzer, Visine. There were also dozens of Berryhill-brand vitamins and nutritional supplements. The dog had been through here too; there were paw prints on the beat-up linoleum floor.

He went back to Chase's room and grabbed a gym bag he'd seen there. He dumped everything out of it, returned to the bathroom, and started tossing the Berryhill products into it.

Ramirez stood outside the door, drinking his beer.

Caspers asked, "You don't mind if I take this stuff?"

"Be my guest. John got 'em for free from Gig Towne. They have Berryhill herbal supplements for everything from keeping your hair from falling out to making your dick stay hard. Those bottles cost twenty-five or thirty bucks a pop. I was like, 'Hey man, don't they have any cigars or booze at that place?' " Ramirez huffed out a laugh that quickly faded.

Caspers wondered if Towne had spiked Chase's supplements with something that had made him sick.

After Caspers had finished, he shook Ramirez's hand. "See ya."

THIRTY-NINE

*S*tefan Pavel tried to clear Georgia Berryhill's way through a crowd of fans in the lobby of the Beverly Hills Hotel following a sold-out event benefiting a free medical clinic in Venice, California. Walking on the other side of Georgia, Kingsley Getty moved her forward with a gentle hand on her back.

Georgia had been the luncheon keynote speaker and was interviewed onstage by the health commentator of a local evening newscast, an emaciated forty-something blonde who ran a rehab clinic popular with the Hollywood crowd. Her new book was out: *Normalizing the New Normal*.

Georgia signed copies of her own latest books, taking time to chat with every fan who wanted to speak with her or snap a photo. She treated each book buyer as if he or she was her dearest friend. The Berryhill contingent could have left by the back way, as the hotel's celebrity guests usually did, but Georgia relished contact with her fans. The baby's arrival would change everything, and she wanted to prolong the love she received from her public as long as she could. She slowly made her way toward the Lincoln Town Car waiting at the curb.

There was just one paparazzo in the crowd—a greasy-haired young man in jeans and tennis shoes, ready to dash to the next possible celebrity sighting. As famous as Georgia was, photos of her didn't sell for much unless she was with a celebrity friend, like Sinclair LeFleur.

The opportunistic photographer's digital camera also recorded videos. When Georgia passed nearby, he started recording, shouting, "Georgia! Any comment about Sinclair and Gig's baby?"

Georgia turned toward him and said, "It's so sad. My heart goes out to them."

Getty veered close to the sketchy guy, waiting for an untoward question. He was soon rewarded.

"Tell us how the Berryhill Method killed Le Towne's baby."

Georgia's hand flew to her mouth. Nearby fans in the crowd protested. Stefan put his hand over the camera lens, but the nimble photographer slipped from his grasp.

"Don't rough me up, man."

"You stop this, now," Stefan said.

Getty grabbed his arm. "Let me handle it, Stefan."

The intrepid photographer asked, "So Georgia, what really happened to Le Towne's baby?"

"Okay, pal. That's enough." Getty placed his broad chest between the camera and Georgia. He spread his arms, avoiding touching the photographer, but moving in tandem with him so that he couldn't get around.

Two hotel security guards entered the fray and escorted the loudly complaining photographer out of the area.

As Georgia took her time signing a book, Stefan opened the car's rear passenger door. He climbed inside, leaned out, and called to her, "Darling, we're going to be late. That's the last book you sign, please, my love."

A young man who'd been loitering near the hotel entrance approached the car. When Getty saw him reach inside his overcoat, Getty's hand darted inside his jacket. He relaxed when he saw that the young man had pulled out a rolled canvas, which he unfurled and held above his head. Painted on it in uneven block letters was BERRYHILL KILLED FALLON.

Getty left the guy alone. Tussling with him over the sign would only draw attention and suggest that the guy's protest had validity. With video capabilities of cell phones, the scuffle would be recorded, uploaded onto YouTube, and immortalized.

While Getty was distracted by the protester, a Cadillac Escalade with darkened windows sped toward Georgia's car from behind, causing a valet to jump out of the way and shout, "Watch it!"

Getty turned as the Escalade screeched to a stop just past Georgia's car. The driver's window began rolling down. Getty caught a glimpse of someone wearing big sunglasses and a watch cap. A blue kerchief hid the lower half of the driver's face.

Getty reached inside his jacket, but the Escalade's driver was already aiming a handgun.

Everything happened at once.

Shots rang out. A window of a car at the curb shattered. People screamed and scattered.

Georgia hunched over, clutching her belly. Getty shielded her body with his and shoved her into the Town Car. He rose, using the vehicle for cover, and aimed his gun at the fleeing Escalade. He didn't fire, not able to get a clean shot through the hotel employees and guests who were running wildly.

He watched the Escalade speed off, swerving around cars and bouncing over a curb. It turned right and disappeared.

Getty slapped the Town Car and shouted, "Go!" to Georgia's driver. After the car took off, an adventure-loving cabbie pulled out of the taxi line and screeched to a stop beside Getty. He opened the front passenger door and hopped in. The cabbie took off after the Escalade before Getty had closed the door.

The cabbie was a tanned and blond young man wearing sunglasses who looked as if he should be surfing. He made a sharp turn, tires squealing, onto the street in the direction the Escalade had gone.

They reached a red light. Getty knew the cabbie would have run it, dodging cross-traffic, but he told him to stop.

"The Escalade's gone," Getty said.

FORTY

Sergeant Early's Homicide/Assault detectives were having a briefing with their boss in the Detective Section conference room. Doug Sproul and Louis Jones were going over their progress on the Crown City nightclub shooting when Alex Caspers, whom Early had sent home, blew in. He was excited about his visit with Donna White, a toxicologist he was friendly with at the L.A. County Crime Lab.

"I told Donna how Chase had this tinnitus, this ringing in his ears all the time." Caspers was holding a bottle of Berryhill Headache Handler. "So Donna opened one of the gel caps, put the powder in a test tube, and then put in this liquid called Trinder's reagent. She shook it and it turned purple, indicating the presence of salicylates."

He paused for effect, opened his hands, and said, "Like in aspirin."

"Aspirin?" Early asked.

"It can aggravate tinnitus," Caspers said. "Donna said it would take more tests to determine the exact dosage, but she thought the capsules held much more aspirin than you get in an over-the-counter tablet."

Vining reached for the Headache Handler bottle. "This doesn't say anything about having aspirin in it. Chamomile, lemon balm, ancient Chinese herbs."

"Is aspirin an ancient Chinese herb?" Kissick asked.

Early rubbed her eyes. "Alex, you're saying that somebody spiked Chase's vitamins with aspirin? Why?"

"Gig Towne did it to fuck Chase up," Caspers said. "To make him behave strangely, to stress him out so that this murder/suicide wouldn't look like it came out of nowhere. Chase wouldn't say much about what went on at Gig's place, but he did say the dude was obsessed with security. Gig could have spied on Chase and overheard him on a phone call with his doctor."

"Why would Gig Towne do such a thing to one of his own security staff?" Sproul asked.

"Well, the way Chase talked about Sinclair LeFleur, it was like he had a crush on her," Caspers said. "It wasn't like John to kiss and tell, but I don't think they were really involved. The whole enchilada, if you get my drift. He told me that Sinclair used to talk about how much she depended on him. I think he got off on being her knight in shining armor.

"I thought she might have been playing him. Getting off on him looking at her a certain way. Why be a movie star if you don't crave attention? I thought he was nuts, with her being all pregnant with Gig Towne's kid. But then, she did call him last night at our poker game."

"Anyone follow up on that?" Early looked at Kissick.

"I tried to reach Sinclair today," Kissick said. "Spoke to Gig's assistant, that creepy Paula Lowestoft. The Le Towne estate is on lockdown, and Sinclair's in seclusion after the death of her baby.

"Why would Sinclair need to depend on Chase?" Vining asked. "Was she afraid?"

She recalled the only time she'd seen Sinclair in person on the balcony inside the Le Towne mansion, looking like an ethereal apparition that might fade away if one stared too hard.

"I wonder what happened with her baby," Early said. "I know babies die at birth sometimes, but you'd think that people like Gig and Sinclair would have turned over heaven and earth to save theirs. They certainly had the resources."

"I have a friend who's a sergeant with the sheriff's department out of the Crescenta Valley Station, which has jurisdiction over La Cañada Flintridge," Vining said. "Sinclair's doctor, a Dr. Janus, signed the death certificate. Cause of death suffocation. But that's all she was able to find out. The lid on that story is down tight."

"They didn't call nine-one-one," Jones said. "Even people at Michael Jackson's house called nine-one-one."

"They had their own medical team there and their own hospital setup right on the property," Vining said. "All in accordance with The Method."

"Chase told me about that," Caspers said. "Le Towne called it the birthing room. It was in the basement, near the gym."

They shook their heads at the foibles of the megarich.

"For people who are so into this Berryhill wellness method, the folks over there aren't too healthy," Sergeant Early said. "There's Trendi, Chase, and now Sinclair LeFleur's baby."

"And Tink Engleford," Vining said. "And Vince Madrigal. We don't know how he's involved."

"Who's killing and why?" Kissick asked. "I don't see Gig Towne being good for all this. How does King Getty figure in?"

"He lied about being out of the country during the time Tink was murdered," Vining said. "I can almost guarantee that he isn't related to J. Paul Getty."

"Our undercover team got his water glass after he had

lunch at a Beverly Hills café," Kissick said. "We got good fingerprints off it."

"And?" Early sat straighter.

"Nothing came up in any of the criminal databases," Kissick said. "We have his DNA from saliva."

Early put up her hand. "Let's hold off. No budget for that unless it's absolutely necessary."

Caspers stood and began pacing. "I'd love to get a search warrant for the Le Towne home. Send a SWAT team in there. Haul Gig Towne's behind onto the street and toss that place."

"We have nothing that incriminates Gig Towne," Vining said. "No one forced Chase to take those supplements. He might have put aspirin into those gel caps himself."

"Alex, I know you're worked up over what happened to John," Sergeant Early said softly. "But you can't get a search warrant because you think people or their lifestyles are strange. If you can come up with evidence of something criminal going on at the Le Towne property, then we can talk."

Early again began rubbing her eyes with the fingertips of both hands and started talking before she was finished. "We need to rethink this investigation. Our communications with the LAPD investigators have been informal. We now see the extent to which our interests overlap. Glendale P.D. has the John Chase incident."

She took her fingers from her eyes, which looked redder than before. "The Berryhill compound and the Le Towne home are both in the L.A. County Sheriff's jurisdiction. Rather than everyone flying off in different directions, it's time to form a multiagency task force and gather around a table."

"I agree," Kissick said.

"Alex, please sit down," Early said. "You're rattling my nerves."

The young detective pulled out a chair a few seats away from the rest of them. "I have an idea. We know that Gig Towne likes to hire cops. He's got a job opening." He gestured toward himself.

Kissick took notes. "Georgia Berryhill takes in these young women who are on the skids. We could send in an undercover officer who fits the profile."

They all turned when one of the staff assistants leaned into the doorway. "Georgia Berryhill was just shot. It's on the news."

Caspers leaped up and grabbed the remote control for the TV in the room. The Berryhill shooting was on the first network station he clicked. A female reporter that the detectives recognized from news conferences at the PPD was broadcasting in front of the closed gates of the Berryhill compound, where a crowd had gathered. Behind her, people were weeping.

The reporter said, "Georgia Berryhill was rushed not to a hospital, but back here to the secluded Berryhill compound in Malibu Canyon. Fans and Berryhill Method advocates have traveled here, and are anxiously waiting for news about Georgia Berryhill and her baby's condition. As you can see, some people are praying and singing."

The crowd noise dropped to an anxious murmur. The reporter peered through the gates. "Here comes Georgia's husband, Stefan Pavel. Let's hope he has good news."

Vining frowned at the screen. "King Getty's with him." She looked at Kissick, who raised his eyebrows.

Getty opened the gate and stepped out ahead of Pavel, clearing the crowd.

Bookish Pavel wore his trademark bow tie and round tortoiseshell glasses. He was dressed as if he'd walked out of a Brooks Brothers catalog, wearing a pink shirt, maroon sweater vest, camel sport jacket, navy-blue slacks, and a bow tie. In spite of his power clothes, he looked wan and shaken.

While he unfolded a sheet of paper, the reporters jockeyed for position.

Pavel began. "I'm going to make a brief statement. My dear wife, Georgia, was not shot."

The fans let out an audible sigh of relief.

Pavel repeated, "Georgia was not shot. However, she is in labor and we expect the birth of our baby soon."

The fans whooped and clapped. Many stood weeping, clasping their hands or one another.

"Georgia is under the care of her personal physician, Dr. Janus."

Vining shot a look at Kissick. "That's Sinclair's doctor."

"Georgia and I are so grateful for the outpouring of love and support we've received from the friends of Berryhill and The Method," Pavel said. "Your love permeates the compound and lifts us up. We will make a statement as soon as our baby is born. Thank you."

He turned on his heel and headed back inside the gates.

Getty staved off the surging reporters and groupies, saying, "No questions."

"Getty and the Berryhills are supposedly good friends," Vining said, "but he's surveilling the crowd like a trained bodyguard."

"Even has the wraparound sunglasses," Kissick commented. "Is he on their payroll?"

"Look at this," Early said.

The television was broadcasting a video of the shooting. The paparazzo who'd been lucky enough to have recorded it was jostled during the chaos, but there was decent footage of Getty covering Georgia with his body and hustling her into the car, and a close-up of the shooter's getaway. As the Escalade sped off, the camera caught Getty standing in the driveway in front of the hotel, his gun aimed at the fleeing car.

"I'll call the TV station and ask for a copy of that video," Kissick said.

A reporter commented that the unidentified shooter was still at large. Witnesses were able to provide a partial license-plate number. The TV broadcast a still photo from the video showing a close-up of the disguised shooter.

"Am I seeing things or does the shooter have a kick-ass manicure?" Early asked.

Vining had noticed the same thing. The shooter's nails were polished in a dark grape color with glittery gold and silver vertical stripes. "I've seen those nails before. It's Cheyenne Leon. She went gunning for the Berryhills."

Kissick came closer to the TV. "Don't mess with Cheyenne. Well, she was really worked up last night after you told her what Georgia and Stefan had said about her and her friends."

"We need to tell Beverly Hills PD that we have a person of interest in the Berryhill shooting," Vining said.

"People, we'll pick up this meeting later," Early said.

Vining called Beverly Hills PD and told them she was confident that Cheyenne Leon was their shooter at the Beverly Hills Hotel. They thanked her and said they'd put out a BOLO—Be On the Lookout—right away.

She'd just hung up when her cell phone rang. It was a number she didn't recognize. "Detective Vining."

"Detective, King Getty here. You've been asking questions about Georgia's Girls. I strongly suggest that you stop."

"Stop?" Vining asked with a chuckle in her voice.

"Look. I have an important reason for asking you that. Come meet me in Malibu Canyon and I'll tell you everything."

That surprised her into silence.

Before she could formulate a response, he said, "Don't

come to the compound. There's a lookout point about a quarter mile north. I'll meet you there in an hour."

"All right."

He hung up.

She was officially off the case, but nothing was going to stop her from meeting Getty. She was again considering going rogue, like she had when she'd pursued the creep who'd stabbed her. She was still holding her phone when Kissick came to her cubicle.

"What's going on?" he asked.

He knew her too well. He saw in her face that something was wrong. She told him what had happened.

"You're not thinking of going out there alone, are you?"

"I was."

"No, you're not. I'll get my jacket."

FORTY-ONE

*S*inclair *LeFleur* lay in bed in her bedroom suite, curled into a fetal position and wearing a white cotton nightgown decorated with handmade lace. Her lush dark hair was the only color in the sea of white bedding. Her complexion was paler than ever. The TV was tuned to a cable movie station that had no commercials and, more important, no breaking news broadcasts. The volume was turned down low. She wasn't aware of it, but the Julia Roberts romantic comedy she'd tried to watch had ended. Now, a slasher bloodfest was on. Bursts of screaming rose like the caws of a flock of enraged crows.

She'd managed to hold it together during her parents' and her best friends' visit. She'd put on makeup and fixed her hair. She knew how to look good on the outside. She'd dragged herself out of bed and they'd sat on the loggia off her suite for the tea with scones, homemade kumquat jam, and finger sandwiches the chef had prepared. She'd allowed some of the flowers that she and Gig had received to be set around the room. She'd cried. They all did. It was expected, but her despair was much deeper than her loved ones could ever imagine. She'd bucked up and carried on while glancing at the clock and waiting for the time when she could crawl back beneath the covers of her bed.

Gig had stopped in and visited with the group for a while, then claimed to have an appointment. He knew that her parents and girlfriends had never approved of their marriage. Didn't think he was right for Sinclair. Were suspicious of The Method and his conversion of impressionable Sinclair into its practices.

Sinclair remembered her enthusiastic declarations to her parents after her first Mind/Body/Spirit Tune-Up. "I've never felt more centered. More alive. I'm present in the world in a way I never was before."

She also remembered her father's penetrating and disapproving stare. He was a physicist at the nearby Jet Propulsion Laboratory—a genuine rocket scientist—and distrustful of things that he couldn't see, measure, and quantify. She recalled her surge of anger at being subjected to that stare yet again, like she was still an adolescent. She'd smiled and hugged and kissed him, even though the two words he'd spoken had cut her as much as if he'd whipped a lash at her judgment: "Be careful."

During the visit, she'd made sparse and rehearsed statements about what had happened the night the baby was born. How the baby wouldn't breathe. Dr. Janus had tried everything. There was nothing to be done.

How she'd never heard her infant daughter cry. This line made her burst into tears. It provided good theatrics for the story, but whenever she said it, she heard her baby's cry ringing in her ears. Gig, Dr. Janus, and Paula insisted that it was all her imagination. Maybe it was, but the sound seemed so real, like an actual memory.

Gig's version of the story was the same, almost word for word. Her parents asked probing questions, but they'd stuck to their story. Sinclair had been a fixture on the Hollywood gossip circuit for long enough to know that if she didn't deviate and if she, Gig, and their people remained on-message, no one could prove that the truth was something different. The truth would leak out only if someone broke ranks.

After her guests left, she'd ordered the flowers removed. Their cloying odor and insipient gaiety sickened her. She knew they were intended to cheer her up, but she saw them as another representation of young death, the blooms snipped from the plant, severed from that which had given them life.

She'd wiped off her makeup, ostensibly to keep from soiling her snow-white bedding. Secretly, she wanted to look into the mirror and see her unadulterated ghostly complexion and vacant eyes. Even as muddled as her mind was now, she saw some things more clearly than before. Her mind wasn't foggy. She'd refused the herbal aids that Gig and Paula had tried to foist on her, even if taking something might help her nightmares.

Once, during a particularly hellish dream, she'd run from the room, only to be grabbed by Paula, who was keeping watch outside her door. Sinclair had fully awakened to find Paula holding her. Sinclair would have gone over the balcony banister if Paula hadn't stopped her.

Sinclair had looked down at the tile floor many yards below. She knew it was bad thinking, but part of her wished she'd flown headfirst over the railing. She envisioned her body lying on the tiles—white night-gown, black hair, red blood. It would be a fitting legacy. Her fans had always liked her depictions of the tragic heroines the best. Her life would be defined by her tragic death just like Elvis, Marilyn, and Michael. No one would see her grow old. She would be young and beautiful and sad forever.

She lay in bed with her eyes closed, afraid to drift to sleep lest the bad dreams come. She heard a light knocking at the door. It was too soon for Paula to come in and help her pump her breast milk. She fluttered her eyes open just enough to see Gig entering, carrying a bed tray.

He spoke softly. "Sinclair . . . Funny face . . . You awake?"

She opened her eyes halfway and looked at him as if she hated him.

He set the tray on the bed. On it were glasses of orange juice and milk and two silver domes covering dishes. "Come on. Let's sit up. You need to eat something."

He started to slide his arm beneath her, but she shoved him away and pushed herself up.

"Let me fluff your pillows."

She gave in, leaning forward. After he'd finished, she'd leaned back against the pillows and tried to comb her tangled hair with her fingers before giving up. She didn't protest when he set the tray over her legs.

He removed the domes with a flourish. "Chef made chicken soup with her homemade stock. Mmm . . . Smell that."

She took a sniff, placating him. The sooner she ate a few bites, the sooner he'd leave.

"And . . ." He took off the other dome. "Your favorite. Popovers. Homemade blueberry jam."

A smile played at the corners of her lips. In another life, she had loved popovers.

He ladled soup into a spoon and started to move the spoon to her mouth when she took it from him.

"I can do it," she said.

His expressive face showed annoyance, but just briefly, quickly grabbing control and donning a textbook example of a concerned expression.

She sipped the hot soup. It tasted good, but she was happier not eating, not having her senses stimulated in any way. She'd feign eating, until Gig was satisfied enough to leave. She was a pretty good actor herself.

"You feeling better?" he asked.

"Yes," she lied without missing a beat.

"You look much better."

She knew that was a lie. She reached for the popover and peeled off a layer of flaky crust. "Gig, I want to see my baby. I want to see Liliana's body. Where is she?"

"Oh, honey." He stroked her hair.

She wanted to recoil, but didn't. "I don't even have a picture of her. I want a picture of her in the casket. I want a tiny white casket, lined with pink satin."

"Sure, baby. Anything."

He sat beside her on the bed and slid his arm around her waist. She retracted, ever so slightly. He got the message and let her go.

"What happened to my baby?"

"She suffocated, honey." Gig looked genuinely anguished. "She choked on amniotic fluid. I know this doesn't help you right now, but we can have another baby, okay? You're in perfect health. You can have lots of kids."

"But I heard her crying."

"That was a lovely dream you had, nothing more." He toyed with the lace edging on the duvet. "Sinclair . . . I hope you don't blame me for what happened. I mean, having the baby here, following The Method. We both agreed on that, right?"

Her dark eyes grew darker until they looked like fathomless pits. She didn't respond.

"What are you watching?" He picked up the remote control from the nightstand and clicked the Information button. "*Freddy Versus Jason*. That's nice and cheerful." He channel-surfed, stopping on a gossip program that was broadcasting a story about the birth of the Berryhill baby girl.

Sinclair stared into the bowl of soup.

He turned up the volume. "I sent flowers to congratulate Stefan and Georgia. I called, too. Talked to both of them."

"What did they name the baby?"

"Simone Marie. Stefan's mother's name and Georgia's mother's name."

"That's right. I remember now. Those were their choices for a girl. I can't see them for a while. I can't see their baby."

"I understand. They understand, too. It's gonna take time, sweetheart." He paused.

She sensed a tremor in his silence, like a violin string still vibrating after the tone had faded into a range beyond human perception. It was the proverbial pregnant pause and she had no patience for it. She cut it off. "Who's called for an interview?"

He bit his lip as if sharing the pain. "Everyone. The *Today* show. *Good Morning America*. Larry King. Oprah is making a big play to be first. She'll come here. I know it's too soon to make any decisions, but we have to think about it at some point."

"What if we just said no, Gig? No to the cameras. No to the intrusion into our private life. No, no, no."

"We'll talk about it later. I'm sure you'll feel differently."

She shoved at the tray, but it got caught on the thick bedding and didn't budge.

He got to his feet and picked up the tray. "You didn't

eat very much. I'll set it over here. Maybe you'll want some later."

"Take it, please. I don't want it if it's cold."

"You might change your mind." He headed toward the door without the tray.

"Gig . . ."

He turned with a hopeful look on his face.

"Thank you. I am feeling a little bit better."

He beamed. "That's great, Sinclair. I'm glad."

"I'm going to sleep now."

"Okay. I'm heading out. Brian has courtside seats for the Lakers game."

Brian was his agent. Drinks would follow the game. Gig would be out late. She didn't care.

"Paula will check in on you later. She's having a guided-meditation session at six."

When she heard the door close, Sinclair sighed in relief. She pulled down the pillows from where they were piled behind her back and was slipping her arms around them, curling into a fetal position, when she heard Georgia Berryhill's voice on television. Sinclair looked at the TV and saw that it was an old interview. Suddenly, she wanted to talk to her friend Georgia. Georgia lived in the same celebrity universe as she and Gig. She understood the pressures of being under the public eye every second. Through her pain, Sinclair was happy about the birth of Georgia and Stefan's baby.

She climbed out of bed. Standing, she felt woozy and put her hand on the bedpost until her head cleared. She walked to the secretary on the other side of the room, where she'd left her iPhone, turned off. She powered it on and watched the message count on the icon for her e-mail in-box grow higher and higher. She ignored it and looked up the listing for Georgia's private landline.

Stefan answered the phone and knew it was Sinclair from the Caller ID. "Sinclair, *cherie*, how are you?"

"I'm doing okay, Stefan. May I talk to Georgia?"

"Of course, you may, Sinclair. Georgia will be delighted you called. We both desperately wanted to chat with you, but . . . It was awkward. She's in the baby's room, feeding her."

Sinclair heard a rustling noise through the phone line.

"I'm walking the phone to her right now." After a few seconds he said, "Georgia, it's Sinclair."

Through the line, Sinclair heard Georgia exclaim. "Wonderful! Can you take her, please?" She came on. "Sinclair? Hi, honey. How are you?"

"I'm doing all right. Congratulations."

"Thank you. It's . . ." Georgia's voice trailed off as if she'd been about to gush but thought better of it. When she next spoke, her voice was calm. "We're very happy. But I want to hear all about you and how you are."

"Well, I'm all right." Now that she was talking to her friend with whom she didn't have to keep up the good face, she felt tears welling. She took a deep breath, preparing to reveal the depth of her despair to Georgia, when she was struck silent by the sound of the baby crying.

Her eyes widened and her lips parted. She pressed the phone against her ear, trying to hear better.

"Healing takes time, honey," Georgia said. "In the meantime, you mustn't neglect yourself."

Sinclair felt as if she couldn't breathe. "That's her." Her voice was strangled. She cleared her throat and tried again. "She has strong lungs."

"Yes, she does."

The crying grew fainter as if the baby had been removed from the room.

Sinclair's heart began pounding and her hands grew clammy. She had a hard time grasping her breath. "Who does she look like?"

"She looks just like Stefan."

"Send me a picture." Sinclair was panting. "Please. I'd like to see a picture."

"Sinclair, are you all right? You sound short of breath."

"I'm fine. Take a picture on your cell phone and send it to me."

"Oh, honey. Soon. Don't concern yourself with things here. Take care of yourself. Give yourself time to grieve."

"I won't give it to the media."

"Sinclair, that's the least of my worries. How's this? You can take a picture when you're well enough to come see the baby. We'll take pictures of all of us, okay?"

"Okay. That sounds good." Sinclair's voice had become wooden. "All right. I'll let you go, Georgia. Give my love to Stefan. Kisses. Bye now."

She ended the call. Her hand holding the cell phone dropped to her side. "That's my baby."

She was wobbly as she headed toward the closet, but she felt stronger with each step.

FORTY-TWO

Sinclair pulled the drapes closed, turned off the lights, and climbed into bed, pulling the bedclothes up around her neck. She left on the TV. She usually left it on all the time now.

Shortly before 6:00 p.m., she heard faint rapping at the door. It opened a crack and a slash of light fell across her face.

Sinclair heard quiet yet firm footsteps that she could

tell were Paula's, as the open-backed shoes she always wore slapped against her heels. The footsteps moved toward the table where Sinclair had left the tray. There was a small clang when Paula raised the metal dome covering the plate. She heard Paula utter an appreciative "Hmm," finding the food gone.

Earlier, Sinclair had wolfed down the cold food, feeling surprisingly hungry. She hadn't bothered with the spoon, but had raised the bowl to her lips and drunk down the soup.

She waited a couple of minutes after Paula had closed the door before throwing back the bedcovers. Sinclair was wearing jeans, a long-sleeved T-shirt, and tennis shoes. She didn't dare walk through the house, not knowing where Paula and her spiritual coach were having the guided-meditation session Gig had mentioned.

From beneath her bed, she retrieved a box with a flexible ladder. They were supplied in all the second-floor bedrooms, to be used in case of a fire or an earthquake. The ladder was made of two nylon straps with plastic rungs strung between them. Carrying it to the windows, she pulled open the drapes, opened one of the French doors, and went out onto the loggia. Setting the ladder on a metal patio chair, she crossed to the wrought-iron railing and looked across the courtyard.

It was dusk and the garden lights had come on. She looked at where John Chase's room had been. Now, she could only rely upon herself.

She went inside her large closet, where she'd hidden her Sig Sauer pistol inside a plastic storage box where she kept yarn, needles, and unfinished projects from her fling with knitting between takes on movie sets. Her father had given her the gun when her fame had started to rise and she'd attracted a few creepy fans. Gig had been decidedly anti-gun until a scary stalker began troubling them. After that, Gig brought armed off-duty police officers to live in their home. Still, he wanted Sinclair to get rid of her gun. She hadn't, mostly because it had been a gift from her father. But also, she had resisted Gig's squeezing her entire persona into his vision of who or what she should be.

As she shoved the cold steel beneath the waistband of her jeans against the small of her back, she recognized the wisdom in that small act of defiance. A corner of her psyche had accepted what the rest denied.

While she was in the closet, she remembered that it was chilly outside. She grabbed a hooded, zip-front sweatshirt printed with a crazy design of skulls in Day-Glo paint.

Again listening at the door of her suite, she heard only morguelike silence, which is what the house had come to seem to her with its chilly tile floors and iron fixtures. She slipped her iPhone into her jeans back pocket. She took her keys, driver's license, a credit card, and a wad of cash from her purse and put them into her other back pocket.

She hurried back outside onto the loggia, not feeling completely her old self but buoyed by adrenaline. Her mind felt crystal clear, unnaturally so, with only one thought that caromed around unobstructed and unchallenged: *Get my baby*.

She fastened the top of the ladder around the railing and unfurled it. The last rung was a few feet above the grass. She pulled a patio chair beside the railing, stepped on top, and swung her leg over, avoiding looking down. She got one foot and then the other on one of the rungs. She started climbing down.

She descended in front of the windows in the first-floor sunroom, where she saw Paula on a rattan easy chair. Instead of her spiritual guide, Paula had invited a girlfriend, who was on the rattan couch. The fully stocked bar cart had been rolled out, making it easy for them to refresh their drinks. Paula held a glass of red wine and the girlfriend was drinking from a martini glass. It was dark where Sinclair was hanging from the ladder, but they could have easily seen her if they'd looked up, but they were too busy laughing.

Guided meditation my ass, Sinclair thought.

She felt the heft of the gun against the small of her back and for a wild moment, thought of turning it on them. It was a crazy idea, she knew, but in the clear arena of her mind right now, it made perfect sense.

But she had more important business.

She reached the bottom rung and dropped onto the grass on all fours. She kept low, letting her black hair form a curtain to hide her white face from the sunroom windows. There was a pause in Paula and her friend's lively chatter and Paula said something about hearing a raccoon.

When the chatter started again, she crawled on her hands and knees until she was around the side of the house. She got up and ran to the garage, which was in a separate building.

Inside the garage, she found the tote bag with her escape clothes, money, and documents that John had helped her hide. She pulled the hood of her sweatshirt over her head, shoving her hair inside it. From the tote, she took out a ball cap and pulled it on over the hood. The tote held sunglasses too, and she put them on to further disguise herself.

There were several cars in the garage. The Mercedes SUV was "her" car and the one she felt most comfortable driving. She used the keys she'd taken from her purse, got inside, started it, and clicked open the garage door. When the door had rolled up just enough for the car to clear it, she threw it into reverse and backed out. In the driveway, she made a snap decision to exit through the back gate, as paparazzi and fans might be hanging out at the front. Paula and her friend were at the rear of the house and might see the headlights. She doused them and had to take off the sunglasses in order to see. Even though her heart was racing, she kept the car at a steady, moderate speed. Once she was off the property, she knew the back roads to take to the freeway, having driven these roads for years.

She didn't know what would happen at the gatehouse, if the guard would give her any problems, if Gig had told him not to let her out. She stopped and gave him a wave. He released the gate. She was miffed. Gig didn't think she'd try to leave. He was in for a surprise.

FORTY-THREE

*K*issick *and* Vining were traveling north on the 101 and were close to the exit that would take them to Malibu Canyon Road when Vining received a text message from Getty. She read it aloud, "Can't meet. Will contact you later."

She let her hand with her cell phone fall into her lap and looked at Kissick, who was driving. "Crap. He doesn't want me asking about Georgia's Girls, he wants to meet away from the compound, and now he doesn't want to meet at all?"

"We're almost there," Kissick said. "Might as well see what's going on. Wonder if there's still a big crowd at the gate."

She picked up her phone. "I'll text Getty, saying, 'Got your message. Already here. Can you meet?' See what he says."

They headed into the canyon. There was even more traffic than when they'd made the trip yesterday. The expensive housing developments on the lower part disappeared and the terrain became rugged, with a rocky mountainside to their right and, across the opposite lane, a sheer cliff on the left. Around some of the curves, they caught the blanket of lights of the northwestern corner of L.A. County. A jagged line of lights outlined the coast. The Pacific was cast in purple twilight.

A sign announced a lookout point a quarter mile ahead.

"Is that the one Getty was talking about?" Vining asked.

"It would be about the right distance from the compound."

He rounded a bend and hit his brakes hard. The road was clogged with a long line of cars that were nearly stopped.

"Is this for the Berryhills?" Vining asked. "Who would waste their time?"

"People who need a life."

"The compound is locked up. I don't know what they think they're going to see."

"They just want to breathe the same air as Georgia and Stefan."

The traffic inched forward.

Kissick steered the car with two fingers of his right hand, which was resting in his lap.

Vining pointed at the lookout coming up on their left—a packed dirt and sand turnoff with a drive-through entrance and exit. It was jammed with cars, people, and TV news vans with satellite dishes on top.

Vehicles were parked along the narrow shoulder leading to the lookout, crushing the wild wheat, mustard, and foxtails. After a few yards, the shoulder disappeared, leaving no place to park off the road, as there was a steep cliff beyond the pavement. A stream of people walked along the shoulder.

A beleaguered sheriff's deputy stood in the middle of the road, trying to keep traffic moving.

Vining glowered at the mob scene. "Getty picked a public place to meet. I doubt he was planning an ambush."

After a few minutes of little progress, Kissick said, "Code Two and a Half?"

"Absolutely."

Code Three meant using both lights and siren, and was to be used only in an emergency. Officers sometimes ignored regulation and used just the light bar to cut through traffic, which was jokingly called Code Two and a Half.

He was about to switch on the light bar when he caught sight in his rearview mirror of a car driving erratically. "Look at this guy. Passing on the left. Leapfrogging over cars. Yikes . . . That was close."

She twisted to look through the rear window. A cream-colored Mercedes SUV took advantage of a small break in the oncoming traffic to pull across the double yellow line, pass two cars, and then barely squeeze behind the Crown Vic. The driver of a pickup truck coming from the opposite direction leaned on his horn.

The driver in the Mercedes behind them flashed its high beams.

"Asshole," Vining said.

Kissick peered into the rearview mirror. The driver was wearing a baseball cap over a hoodie and had on sunglasses in the dark. "Why the disguise? That driver looks like a woman."

"Didn't we see an SUV like that parked at the Le Towne home?" Vining again turned around. The SUV was on their rear bumper. She got a glimpse of the driver before she was blinded by flashing high beams. She blinked away the effects of the bright lights. "It's Sinclair LeFleur."

Kissick looked into his rearview mirror. "I think you're right." He yelped when she again flashed her high beams.

Sinclair began honking the car horn.

"What's she doing here?" Vining asked.

"Maybe she's on a pilgrimage to Berryhill, like the rest of us. She probably could have taken a helicopter or at least had a driver."

"I thought she was in seclusion. She's sure agitated." Vining turned the rearview mirror so she could watch the car behind them. Between flashing the high beams and blasting the horn, Sinclair was raising her fists, pounding the steering wheel with both hands, and leaning out the open window to watch for a break in the oncoming traffic.

"She's going to hurt herself or somebody else," Vining said. "The traffic's moving so slowly, I can get out and ask her what's going on."

"Be careful." He stopped the car.

In response, Sinclair leaned on the car horn.

Just as Vining opened her door, Sinclair pulled into the opposing traffic, forcing an oncoming car to swerve, coming perilously close to the cliff.

Vining shut the door. "That's one way to cut through traffic."

Turning on the lights and siren, Kissick pulled out onto the Mercedes' bumper.

Cars in both directions tried to squeeze out of the way, creating a narrow path down the middle of the road.

The unexpected police escort emboldened Sinclair. She turned on the Mercedes' flashing emergency lights and kept up the pressure on the car's horn.

Vining gritted her teeth as Sinclair wove in and out, alternately speeding up and slamming on her brakes.

Kissick kept up with her, navigating the obstacle course. Most drivers pulled as far to the sides as possible but some ignored the lights and siren.

A road sign warned of a hairpin curve and recommended a reduced speed of fifteen miles per hour. Sinclair was doing close to fifty. As the Mercedes entered the curve, they briefly lost sight of all but the car's rear end. The tires skidded, leaving marks on the asphalt, while an oncoming Honda Accord was forced onto the narrow shoulder.

Ahead was the entrance to the Berryhill compound.

An L.A. County Sheriff's Department cruiser was parked across the broad driveway blocking the locked gates. A deputy in the street signaled drivers to keep moving. Another deputy in front of the gates was trying to manage the crowd.

Sinclair slowed to make a left turn into the driveway when the deputy who was directing traffic moved in front of her car with his hand raised. He walked up to the driver's window.

Kissick pulled up behind Sinclair. Vining got out.

"You can't go in there, ma'am," the deputy told Sinclair through the car window she'd rolled down. "Keep moving."

"I'm a friend of the family. I came to congratulate Georgia and Stefan on the birth of their baby. I'll call Georgia and tell her to let me in."

Vining approached the deputy, shield in hand. She kept her eye on the paparazzi and reporters who hadn't yet noticed the SUV driver's identity. "Detective Nan Vining of the Pasadena police. I'll take over from here."

Sinclair snapped at her. "What do you want? Leave me alone!"

"You're upset, Ms. LeFleur." Vining remained calm. "Climb over into the passenger seat and I'll drive you home. The reporters haven't spotted you yet."

Sinclair looked at Vining as if she'd threatened to harm her. "Did he send you to follow me?" Her voice had a manic edge. "He sent you, didn't he?"

The altercation attracted the attention of the paparazzi. Somebody shouted, "It's Sinclair!" A stampede started.

Sinclair screamed, "He sent you!" She gunned the accelerator and took off, nearly clipping Vining's toes.

While some paparazzi ran for their vehicles, others swarmed Vining, peppering her with questions. "What was Sinclair LeFleur doing here?" "Is she all right?" "How did she look?"

Vining shoved past them and ran to the Crown Vic. Kissick took off before she'd closed the door.

The road leading away from Berryhill was clear, and Sinclair easily put distance between herself and the detectives. She also had a lead on the paparazzi, who'd lost time rushing to their cars, but a couple of guys on motorcycles were closing in.

Kissick drove as fast as he dared, watching Sinclair's taillights in front and the single headlights of the motorcycles in the rearview mirror. He shut off the light bar and siren.

The Crown Vic's tires squealed as Kissick took another hairpin turn at high speed just as Vining was putting on her seat belt. She held on to the dashboard as the car fishtailed. He cleared the curve in time to see a stretch of straight road and the Mercedes making a wild left turn onto an almost invisible lane.

Kissick floored the accelerator, trying to hit the lane before the paparazzi saw him around the curve. The lane was unmarked, cut into a brushy hillside with no streetlamps nearby. He almost blew past it, slamming on his brakes at the last minute and again fishtailing, the car's tires tearing through grass and mud alongside the narrow road.

They saw only darkness on the lane ahead of them.

Kissick again checked the rearview mirror. "I think we beat the photographers."

"Where the hell is she?" Vining frowned into the darkness beyond the headlights.

"What did she have to say?"

Vining recounted Sinclair's words, adding, "She sounded on the edge."

Kissick slowed the car as they approached a wood-plank fence strung with barbed wire on top. The headlights illuminated a sign: PRIVATE PROPERTY. NO TRESPASSING.

A gate across the fence had been busted open. The frame was splintered, and the gate, smeared with cream-colored paint, was hanging by a single hinge.

FORTY-FOUR

K issick stopped the car outside the broken gate and put it in park. "I think this is the back of the Berry-hill property."

"Sinclair crashed through. She might be injured. We have to look for her."

He took out his cell phone and called the PPD watch commander. "Someone should know we're here. I'll ask whoever's on the desk to give a heads-up to the Sheriff's Lost Hills station."

While he made the call, she unfastened the strap that

secured her Glock in her belt holster and tugged the gun butt, reassuring herself that she could draw it smoothly. She reached under her right pant leg and did the same with her backup Walther PPK, the gun that had saved her life more than once.

Kissick pocketed his phone, put the car in drive, and crossed onto the property.

The paved lane cut through a dense forest. There were no lights.

They rolled down their windows, but all they heard were the sounds of a spring night in the chaparral: crickets, birds, coyotes.

Vining squinted and whispered. "A car engine. Hear it?"

He slowed. "Yeah. Straight ahead. Traveling fast."

"Sinclair apparently knows the lay of the land."

He started moving again, ramping up the speed.

"Sinclair had that look in her eye," Vining said. "Like she just had one foot in reality."

"And the other on a banana peel?" Kissick countered. "She didn't seem exactly all there the other day either."

"Something sad about her. When you imagine that certain people have everything . . ."

They came upon a prefabricated warehouse. Pickup trucks and ATVs were parked in a concrete lot. The vehicles were painted white with the raspberry Berryhill logo. Motion lights kicked on as they drove past. The area looked deserted.

Farther on, they passed cabins nestled among the trees. Paths off the main road meandered into the rolling hills, where ground lights lit the way. Larger cabins were on higher ground. It looked like a plush country resort. No lights were on in any windows. No cars were in the parking spaces.

"Guess they told the guests to get the hell out," Vining said. "Doesn't jive with the Berryhill Mind/Body/Spirit, let's gather round the campfire and sing 'Kumbaya' program."

"They locked this place down fast."

He stopped at a crossroads. "I don't hear the car anymore."

"If my orientation is correct, the lake is over there and the offices and shops are on the other side."

He turned right.

After they'd traveled a few hundred feet, they heard the unmistakable twisting metal sound of a vehicle colliding with a fixed object. It came from the other direction. The night sounds hushed.

Kissick whipped the Crown Vic around, speeding as quickly as he safely could on the narrow dark road. They reached a T-intersection where a giant oak tree had yellow reflectors nailed along its trunk. Behind it, almost hidden in the bushes and small trees, were red taillights.

"Holy crap." Kissick stopped the car and jumped out.

Vining grabbed a flashlight from the glove compartment and followed him into the brush. She fought through thorny bushes, scratching her hands and face.

Sinclair had missed the turn and gone off the road. The SUV's headlights were still on, and its engine was running. The passenger side was crumpled. The driver's side was relatively unscathed, with just a few scratches. The driver's door was open. Sinclair was gone.

Kissick reached inside and cut the ignition.

The night sounds returned. Frogs croaked a short distance away.

With the flashlight guiding her, Vining walked a few yards through thick brush. Kissick followed. They stepped into a clearing. The moonlit lake was in front of them. Nearby, ducks and swans nestled in coops, safe from coyotes.

The vista of the lake let them better see the property's layout. The main gate was diagonally across. The administration building and gift shop were a football-field length away.

Everything looked closed and abandoned. They heard the low roar of traffic from Malibu Canyon Road, the crowd gathered there, and the angry voices of the deputies keeping it all under control. Headlights flickered through dense oleander bushes planted along the fence.

They turned to look up at the ridge behind them and were surprised to see a large house high on the hill. The lights in its many windows were ablaze. The stately mansion was in stark contrast with the woodsy, pseudo-hippie design of the rest of the compound.

"There's the party," Kissick said. "It must be Nirvana."

"It looks like the White House plunked in the middle of Woodstock Nation."

They ran back to their car.

FORTY-FIVE

The wide road to the hilltop manse was lined with white Corinthian columns lit by floodlights. An arch above locked gates had "Nirvana" written in lights.

Kissick stopped at the gates as they took in the spectacle. A bright crescent of a new moon was rising in the dark sky behind the gleaming bright mansion.

"It's like a Disney animator's idea of Heaven," Kissick said.

"All that's missing are angels lounging around on clouds strumming harps."

Kissick looked at the keypad outside the driver's door. "If Sinclair went in there, she has the gate code or knows a back entrance."

"The gate code to Nirvana. Key in GBSP. I found the code in Tink's BlackBerry."

"Georgia and Stefan's initials. No ego there." He rolled down the window and punched in the code. The gates parted.

"Sad that Tink loved being allowed in here," Vining said.

"All she needed was the right bank balance."

"She was no dummy. Maybe she just liked having the better-quality sheets and towels that I'm sure the rooms here have."

They drove past the colonnade, not seeing a soul. At the top, the driveway circled a large metal fountain forged into an abstract interpretation of the entwined nude bodies of a man and woman. Water spouted and flowed provocatively around the forms, splashing into a pool. Hundreds of coins had been tossed inside.

Kissick turned the car so that it pointed back down the driveway. They got out and looked around. The only noises were the songs of night birds and a chorus of croaking frogs rising from the lake.

Kissick sniffed the air. "Wood smoke. Fireplace."

A woman's scream pierced the silence.

Both turned to look into the dark grounds to the left of the mansion when they heard another scream.

Guns out, they started running, one looking forward, and the other keeping an eye on the rear. They passed through a formal rose garden and darted around flower beds. At the edge of the garden, the ground lights disappeared and there was dark forest. They jogged along

an unlit gravel path that twisted through the trees alongside a babbling creek. Lights through the trees came from
a small log cabin. Smoke curled from its chimney.

Vining held up her hand, signaling Kissick to stop. She
cocked her head, listening.

There was music coming from inside the cabin, Nancy
Sinatra singing "These Boots Are Made for Walkin'."
It was turned up loud and muffled the sounds of a
party. There was another scream, followed by a woman's
laughter.

There was a distinctive odor above that of the wood
smoke. She sniffed and whispered, "Cigar."

Kissick pointed for her to go around one side and gestured that he'd take the other. As they were heading off,
they heard footsteps crunching on the gravel path. Turning, guns out, they saw Kingsley Getty approaching. He
had on a light suit and a golden tie and walked with the
casual ease of a trust-fund scion welcoming houseguests
to a weekend party at his country home.

"Detectives Vining and Kissick. This is a pleasant surprise. Welcome to Nirvana." He spread his arms.

Vining and Kissick got closer but kept their distance.

He stood smiling, his white teeth and silver hair gleaming in the moonlight. "To what do we owe—"

"Cut the shit, Getty," Vining said. "Or whoever you
are. We heard a woman screaming inside that cabin."

"Hands behind your head," Kissick said.

"Detectives, this is ridiculous. There's a private party
going on. It's a little boisterous."

"Hands behind your head," Vining ordered. She wondered if Sinclair was in there or if he even knew she was
in the compound.

Getty complied with a put-out attitude. "What in the
world are you doing here?"

Not answering, Vining started patting him down. She

took a handgun from a shoulder holster and handed it to Kissick, who put it into his jacket pocket.

Getty stood calmly, as if he was patted down at gunpoint every day. "Didn't you get my message that I couldn't meet you?"

An earphone and a curled wire leading from it disappeared beneath his collar. Vining removed his earphone and the transmitter inside his jacket. "Who's on the other end of this?"

"I strongly advise that you leave now," Getty said.

"Where's your wallet, Getty?" Vining asked. "You go around without ID?"

"Who's in that cabin?" Kissick asked. "If it's just a little party, what do you care if we take a look?"

The amusement had left Getty's eyes. "This is private property, and I want you out of here now."

"Are you the property owner?" Kissick asked.

"I said now."

"We're not leaving," Vining said. "Call the sheriffs to have us removed. A couple of deputies are directing traffic outside the compound gates. They'll be here in no time."

Nancy Sinatra finished walkin'. There was a break in the music and they heard loud talking and party sounds from inside the cabin. A distinctive laugh rose above the noise: the Gig Giggle. They heard the familiar strains of the old cowboy standard "Back in the Saddle Again."

Vining and Kissick looked at the rustic front door. Beside it was a window with a lacy curtain.

Kissick asked, "Is Gig Towne in there?" He made a move toward the cabin.

Getty stepped in front of him.

Kissick aimed his gun at Getty's chest.

"Detective Kissick, you are not going to shoot me," Getty said, as if chiding a schoolboy.

"Try me."

Vining bolted to the window and peeked through a break in the curtains. She'd expected something illicit since Getty was being so protective, but it took her a few seconds to process the sordid scene.

"Nan . . ." Kissick called over his shoulder. "What's up?"

Gig Towne was nude except for cowboy boots, a toy holster and guns around his hips, and a comically gigantic cowboy hat on his head. He held leather reins attached to a harness with a bit in the mouth of a nude young woman who was on all fours on top of a bed, her rear end to him. He was thrusting into her and slapping her butt. Her neck was arched back by the harness.

Gig shouted along to the song's chorus, "Whoopie ti-yi-yay!"

There were two other girls on their hands and knees similarly harnessed, pawing the bed with their hands as if they were horses. Gig pulled out of the first girl and went on to the next, who made a noise like a horse's whinny when he jammed into her and then laughed when he flicked the reins and yelled, "Giddy up!"

Stefan Pavel was observing from an easy chair across the room, nude beneath an open blue silk robe. Smoking a cigar, he seemed more interested in Gig's antics than in the young woman on her knees in front of him, giving him a blow job, or the one standing behind him who was rubbing his shoulders.

Vining stumbled as she moved away from the window and returned wide-eyed to where Kissick still held Getty at gunpoint. "Gig Towne and Stefan Pavel are having an orgy in there with a bunch of girls. Towne's trussed up like some X-rated cowboy."

"And to one of my favorite songs." Kissick scowled at the cabin.

"Look, you two," Getty began. "You don't know what's going on here."

Vining squared her shoulders. "No, *you* look King Getty, or whoever the hell you are. I have a fifteen-year-old daughter. Is this why you told me to stop asking questions about Georgia's Girls?"

Getty turned away and took a deep breath. "Those girls . . . Those *women* are of age and willing participants. You have to trust me."

Vining said, "We don't trust you, and we're not going to trust you. What we're going to do is—" She stopped at the sound of a shotgun being racked.

"Drop your weapons. Clasp your hands behind your heads." The voice was female and unhesitant.

The detectives tossed their guns on the ground and raised their hands. Asia, the stern young blonde who'd showed them into Georgia and Stefan's office, walked from the woods, holding a Winchester shotgun between both hands.

A woman's panicked voice suddenly rang out from the house on top of the hill. "My baby!" It was followed by indistinct shouting and screaming.

Asia was startled and distracted just long enough for Vining to deliver a roundhouse kick, knocking her to the ground. To subdue her, Vining pounced.

Getty took off into the woods.

Grabbing his gun from the ground, Kissick ran after him.

The party in the cabin obliviously continued, the blaring music drowning out the drama outside. A girl shrieked and shouted, "Gig, you crack me up!"

Vining wrestled in the dirt with Asia. Her backup Walther PPK was still in her ankle holster, but she couldn't grab it. Seeing Asia reaching beneath her skirt, Vining clamped onto her hand just as Asia managed to seize the butt of a small pistol in a thigh holster. They struggled for the weapon. Vining got hold of Asia's fingers and bent them back. Asia cried out and Vining pried the gun from her. She pressed the barrel against Asia's thigh.

"Get up," Vining ordered.

The drama in the big house on the hill continued. There was a bitter shriek. An infant started wailing. Vining thought she heard Georgia Berryhill scream, "Sinclair, stop!"

Vining felt a surge of adrenaline. Her hands trembled as she patted Asia down while she looked around for Kissick. She didn't find more weapons on Asia. She picked up the shotgun, cleared the shells from it, and picked up her Glock, returning it to her belt holster. She checked the bullets in Asia's small pistol and put it into her slacks pocket.

"Walk." Vining gave her a shove out of the woods, away from the cabin.

"That was not necessary."

"Shut up." Reaching a wooden bench in the rose garden, Vining said, "Sit."

She flipped open the leather case on the back of her belt and took out her handcuffs. She snapped a handcuff on one of Asia's wrists and locked the other end to an arm on the bench.

"I'm no danger to you," Asia said.

"That's why you were holding a shotgun on me."

The ruckus at the top of the hill was escalating. Vining heard Sinclair scream, "Stop! You're hurting her!" Then Georgia yelled, "She has a gun! Help me. Somebody help!"

The baby's wailing continued unabated.

Vining looked around for Kissick. "Jim!" She didn't see him or Getty. "Dammit."

Leaving Asia secured to the bench, Vining ran up the hill toward the house.

FORTY-SIX

While *Vining* ran, she pulled out her phone and speed-dialed Kissick's cell. No answer. She pressed the speed-dial numbers for the PPD Watch Commander's office. She gave the lieutenant on duty a clipped update and requested backup.

Gun in both hands, she ran up the steps and pressed behind the front door of Nirvana, which was ajar. She darted her head around it and saw a sliver of the interior. No one was in sight. She pushed the door, opening it a few inches. The women were still fighting and the baby was still crying.

Sparkling lights from a crystal chandelier were reflected on a polished marble floor. The foyer was furnished with fussy chairs, parlor benches, and giant mirrors in ornate gold frames. There was a grand marble staircase that reminded Vining of the classic movies she loved where the female star made her entrance descending the steps wearing a satin ball gown. As she looked over the shiny, white, and frigid area, she thought that this wasn't her idea of nirvana.

She dashed across the foyer to the staircase and took the steps two at a time, following the screaming and crying. She ran down the hallway toward a room where the commotion was.

Her heart leaped into her throat when she heard a gunshot. She quietly prayed as she approached the room, "Keep crying, baby. Please keep crying."

The infant complied, wailing, stopping only to take a choking breath before beginning again.

Vining flattened against the wall beside the door, holding up her gun. Georgia and Sinclair's argument had deteriorated into grunts and cursing. A physical struggle was going on.

Vining took a breath and spun inside a nursery, gun out in a two-handed grip. "Hands! Hands! Show me your hands! Drop it! Drop it!"

Georgia and Sinclair were wrestling over a gun. Sinclair was holding the baby against her chest in her left arm. She was bleeding from a gash in her forehead, and her face and hands were scratched, presumably from crashing her car and escaping through the brush. She had both hands on the gun, as did Georgia. They grimaced and circled around, their bodies pressed together, squeezing the wailing baby.

"Stop her!" Georgia yelled. "This lunatic is trying to take my baby."

Vining kept her aim steady, shifting between Georgia and Sinclair. "Drop the gun. Show me your hands. Drop the gun before somebody gets hurt."

Sinclair released her grip on the gun and raised her right arm, still clutching the baby with her left.

Georgia didn't drop the gun, but aimed it at Sinclair. She nervously slid a finger around the trigger, the gun shaking in her trembling hands.

The three women were suddenly silent but for heavy breathing. The baby's cries subsided to whimpering. Sinclair shifted the baby over her shoulder, out of Georgia's direct line of fire.

Vining aimed her gun at Georgia's heart. "Ms. Berryhill, very slowly, set the gun on the floor."

Georgia's eyes were wild as she continued to aim the gun at Sinclair. "She brought this instrument of destruction into my home. She threatened to kill me if I didn't give her Simone."

Sinclair's T-shirt beneath her open sweatshirt had wet patches over her breasts where her milk was seeping through. The baby began gnawing on the curled fingers of one of her own tiny hands.

Vining could tell that Sinclair was afraid, yet the mania she'd shown on the road had disappeared.

In a calm voice, Sinclair said, "She's not your baby, Georgia. She's mine, and her name is Liliana."

"She's *my* baby and you can't have her." Georgia punctuated her words by moving the gun up and down. Her tone was hysterical. "Detective, make her give me Simone."

Vining spoke evenly. "Georgia, put the gun down and we'll figure this out, okay?" She moved toward her.

"You don't understand."

Vining kept her gun on Georgia. "I want to understand, but I can't talk to you while you're holding a loaded weapon." She was close enough to reach Georgia's gun. Had she been wearing her Kevlar vest, she would have tried.

Sinclair carried the baby to a rocking chair and sat.

Georgia aimed the gun at Sinclair's head. Her hand was still trembling, and she started to cry.

"Just walk away, Georgia." Sinclair pulled up her T-shirt and exposed a breast. "You'll think of a way to spin it and you'll be just fine." The baby made grabbing motions with her hands as Sinclair moved her to her breast.

As Georgia watched the baby latch on to Sinclair's breast, she began crying harder. Vining grabbed the gun barrel and pushed it down. Georgia limply opened her hand and released it.

The baby was nursing. Sinclair smiled down at the fuzzy dark head and rocked the chair. It was the first time Vining had seen Sinclair at peace.

FORTY-SEVEN

Good job, Detective Vining."

Vining bristled when she heard King Getty behind her. She wheeled around only to do a double take when she saw a shield around his neck on a thin chain. Peering more closely, her mouth gaping, she saw that it said FBI. She'd been so focused on the drama in the nursery, only then did she notice the commotion on the compound grounds and the crowd of law enforcement personnel in the hallway.

Kissick entered the room and was visibly relieved to see that Vining had the situation under control.

Georgia had recovered her composure and was again the diva in charge of her empire. She took the words from Vining's mouth as she ran her fingers through her hair and straightened her dress. "What the hell's going on, King?"

"I'm not Kingsley Getty. My name is David Scarbray, and I'm a special agent with the FBI. You're under arrest for violating the Mann Act." He took out handcuffs and grabbed Georgia's right wrist. "A federal crime."

"The Mann Act? What's the Mann Act?"

"Transportation of a female across state lines for immoral purposes. Specifically a seventeen-year-old named Fallon Price."

"Fallon." Georgia looked at Scarbray as if he was an idiot. "You don't even know where she is. How can you accuse us of transporting her across state lines?" She tried to pull her arm away from him as he cuffed her.

Vining looked at Sinclair, who was rocking the chair as she nursed the baby, lost in another world. Looking at the gash on Sinclair's head, she said, "We need paramedics up here."

"I'll take care of it." Kissick slipped from the room.

Georgia started walking toward Asia, who'd entered the room, also with a badge hanging around her neck. "Asia, call my attorney, Carmen Vidal."

"My name is Jeannie Brasfield. I'm a detective with the L.A. County Sheriff's Department. You're under arrest for the murder of Fallon Price."

"Fallon? She ran off years ago."

"We believe she's buried on your property, Georgia. You knew about it, which makes you guilty of murder."

"I knew no such thing."

"And you're under arrest for the sexual abuse of a minor."

"I didn't sexually abuse any minors," Georgia spat. "That's ridiculous."

"You knew about it happening here," Brasfield said. "We might be adding kidnapping to the charges."

They all stared at what Detective Brasfield was holding between her hands, taking a second to process what they were seeing. It was a pregnancy suit made of foam rubber covered with cotton, designed to imitate a woman's torso and breasts in pregnancy. Brasfield was holding it by the Velcro straps that would attach it to one's body.

Georgia coiled her lip. "I've never seen that before. *You* brought that into my house. I'll have all of *you* arrested."

Vining walked closer and fingered the bullet hole that went straight through the belly.

Getty started to laugh. "I don't believe it. You *faked* being pregnant?"

Georgia pouted. "You can't prove that."

"Maybe we can't, but DNA can." Vining pointed at

the now-sleeping baby, whom Sinclair was cradling in her arms. "That hair color didn't come from a bottle."

"Georgia, anything you say can and will be used against you . . ."

As Scarbray Mirandized her, Georgia sniped, "King, how dare you do this to me? After everything I did for you."

Scarbray handed Georgia over to Brasfield. "Jeannie, get her out of here."

"With pleasure."

Georgia snapped at her. "Stop pulling on me. I'm injured. I think my wrist is sprained. These handcuffs are too tight."

Kissick returned with two teams of paramedics.

Brasfield directed one team to Georgia.

Georgia brushed them off. "No one touches me except my personal physician, Dr. Janus." She continued barking orders as they removed her from the nursery.

Vining went to the rocking chair. "Sinclair, you need medical attention. You were in a car accident. You're bleeding."

Sinclair stood, cradling the sleeping baby. "I know, but I'm not letting go of her. Understand?"

"I'll take care of her." Vining held out her arms. "Trust me. Your baby needs to be looked at too, okay?"

Sinclair nodded and handed over the baby.

Vining took the infant into her arms. "She looks just like you, Sinclair. What did you say her name is?"

"Liliana." Sinclair smoothed the baby's hair and kissed her forehead. "Mommy will be back soon, sweetheart." Tears welled in her eyes. "That's the first time I've ever said that." She let the paramedics lead her from the room.

Kissick looked over Vining's shoulder. "She's beautiful."

Vining looked down at the perfect rosebud lips and the fringe of long dark eyelashes on Liliana's closed eyes. She drew her fingers across the tiny velvety head covered with black hair. She inhaled a shuddering breath. "It was close. Too close."

Kissick put his arm around her and pulled her against him. "Everything turned out fine. No second-guessing yourself."

She sniffed and nodded. Raising her gaze from the baby, she saw Special Agent David Scarbray standing across the room, watching.

FORTY-EIGHT

Vining, Kissick, and David Scarbray wove through dozens of law enforcement and forensic personnel who had swarmed Nirvana.

"This was a multiagency operation that's been in the works for more than two years," Scarbray said. "FBI agents and L.A. County Sheriff's investigators infiltrated the Berryhill organization at different levels. Some posed as clients. Some were hired as employees. I penetrated the client inner circle. Kingsley Getty was Georgia and Stefan's kind of guy—well-connected, rich, and possibly dangerous."

They went down the marble staircase, walking outside onto the mansion steps. From their hilltop view, it looked as if the entire compound had been turned into a crime scene. It was organized chaos.

"Thanks to both of you," Scarbray said, "we were finally able to bust this place wide open." He surveyed the goings-on with pride. "Detective Vining, when you called Beverly Hills PD and ID'd Cheyenne as a suspect in the

Beverly Hills Hotel shooting, we'd already asked them to keep us apprised of any developments. They put out a BOLO, and Santa Monica PD found Cheyenne at the edge of the pier, just looking out at the ocean. She didn't resist and was ready to talk. We cut a deal. In exchange for leniency on the shooting charge, she told us everything that went on at the Berryhill compound. Cheyenne said the intense grilling in Carmen Vidal's office got her really thinking. Kudos to you, Detective."

Vining tipped her head, acknowledging the praise.

Kissick grinned.

"Further," Scarbray began, "Cheyenne shooting at Georgia gave me the chance to show my loyalty and value to the Berryhills in a tangible way. Tonight, we closed the deal."

They watched as the young women who'd been cavorting with Towne and Pavel in the cabin, now dressed in street clothes, were led into an SUV by a man wearing an FBI Windbreaker.

"Two of the participants in the orgy you saw, Detective Vining, are informants," Scarbray explained. "All those women are of age. They just look young. We expect that more victims—more of 'Georgia's Girls'—will likely come forward."

Kissick watched as the SUV drove off. "So Georgia's finishing school for lost girls was a means to supply sexy underage girls to her husband and his friends?"

"Procuring women for orgies with his good buddy Gig Towne was certainly one of its purposes," Scarbray said.

Vining cringed at the thought that Towne was as creepy as she'd thought.

Scarbray went on. "Georgia's Girls was also a source of free labor to help run the compound. They cherry-picked girls who were vulnerable to being emotionally and sexually manipulated. Built them up with promises of show-business careers if they cooperated."

"But it was also a PR vehicle for Georgia," Vining said. "Gave her an opportunity to throw big fund-raising parties with lots of celebrities."

"We're looking into the finances now," Scarbray said. "Millions of dollars are unaccounted for. This whole compound is built on BS. The Berryhills performed carnival-style fortune-telling rip-offs. The rooms where the MBS Tune-Ups are conducted have hidden video cameras to record clients' most private secrets. Pavel hired Vince Madrigal to build dossiers on the Berryhills' richest clients. Pavel also had Cheyenne and the other Georgia's Girls who'd moved on report on their employers. Once he had the information, he and Georgia could satisfy clients' every desire, no matter how ridiculous or depraved. They have rooms for fake séances with projectors to make spirits appear. Madrigal supplied them with materials, like cremated remains, for the witchcraft Georgia dabbled in and apparently believed in. He also kept Pavel supplied with Cuban cigars."

A burly man with an FBI badge embroidered on his polo shirt came over to Scarbray. "Excuse me, sir. You'll be happy to see these." He handed him a pair of men's loafers inside a plastic bag.

Scarbray took it and smiled. He looked at the label inside the shoes. "Pavel's Brooks Brothers loafers. Thanks." He sent the agent on his way. "I'm confident those will match footprints left in the cremated remains that were spilled at the Madrigal and Talbot homicides."

"Stefan Pavel was involved in that?" Kissick asked.

Scarbray made a noise as if that wasn't the half of it. "Madrigal found out about the underage girls. He was blackmailing Pavel for ten million dollars and thought he was collecting the night he was murdered. Near as we can figure, Pavel loaded Trendi up on LSD, stabbed her in the belly, and used her as a distraction."

"Trendi was more than just a distraction," Vining said.

"She'd become a liability for Towne and Pavel and their plan to steal the Le Towne baby. Georgia must have been green with jealousy when Sinclair got pregnant. I'd be interested to know which one of these nuts—Stefan or Georgia—hatched the baby-napping plan. Georgia probably thought she'd get more PR mileage if she actually gave birth. I had a few minutes with Sinclair in the nursery and she told me that she'd enlisted Trendi and our Officer John Chase to help her have her baby in a hospital and not in that disgusting birthing room in the basement of the Le Towne home. Perhaps Trendi was found out and Chase too. Chase sent Sinclair a text message after he quit his job at Le Towne, telling her that everything was still in place. It was probably intercepted. Could Pavel have murdered Chase and his girlfriend Alison?"

"We're confident that we'll find evidence linking Pavel to the John Chase and Alison Oliver homicides," Scarbray said. "Pavel is a calculating sociopath. A cold-blooded assassin who kills people that get in his way."

"Upstairs, Sinclair told me that Gig is Liliana's father," Vining said. "Why would he conspire to kidnap his own baby and give it to the Berryhills?"

"Maybe the Berryhills had something on him beyond sex with underage girls," Kissick said.

"We're hopeful that Cheyenne can explain a lot of what's been going on in *Nirvana*." Scarbray said the name sarcastically.

They turned at the sound of a commotion inside the foyer. A woman yelled, "Get him!" followed by a man shouting, "That way!" all accompanied with barking from a small dog.

Two deputy sheriffs, one holding a blanket between both hands and the other with a leash, were chasing Mr. Peepers. After clearing the stairs, the dog darted wildly through the foyer before running outside. Kissick, Vining, and Scarbray jumped back as the enraged cur bolted in their direction, snapping and snarling.

The female deputy threw the blanket over the little dog and the other deputy helped her scoop him up into it.

Vining had pressed her hand against her chest. "I'm amazed that Mr. Peepers could even move that fast."

Scarbray watched the deputies struggling with their difficult bundle and shook his head. "That dog . . ."

"So Stefan Pavel is likely responsible for the murders of"—Kissick began counting on his fingers—"Madrigal, Trendi, Chase, and Alison."

Vining added, "And very probably the drowning death of his first wife, the vitamin heiress. What happened to Fallon Price?"

"That's the only one we're not sure about. We'd long suspected that something deadly had happened to Fallon at Berryhill and that she's buried here," Scarbray said. "An agent posed as a client and came with his cadaver-sniffing dog. We identified a suspicious area not far from the party cabin in the woods. We have yet to complete our interviews with Cheyenne, but she claims to have information."

"Did Pavel murder Catherine Engleford?" Vining asked Scarbray.

"He may have. I don't know what his motive would have been. I hope that Cheyenne can help you close that case."

"Did you become involved with Mrs. Engleford to learn secrets about the Berryhills, putting her life in danger?"

"No. I never thought she had inside information about the Berryhills. Tink was another wealthy client whom they kept stringing along as long as the money kept coming. Spending time with Tink was a way to move the investigation forward, and I enjoyed her company. The

Berryhills were intrigued by King Getty, but they'd seen guys like him before. My relationship with Tink gave me legitimacy with the Berryhills."

Vining became angry. "If you thought Mrs. Engleford was in danger, you should have warned her."

"I already told you, I don't know any reason Tink would have been in danger from Pavel." Scarbray's eyes shifted briefly before returning to meet Vining's.

It was only a split second, but it was enough for Vining to tell that he was lying.

He seemed to sense this and tried to explain further. "Look, an investigator takes some risks—but that's not what I did with Tink."

"You know how I've pushed the envelope in investigations." Vining was glad to see that her comment caught him off guard. "You know all about me. You have a stack of articles about me in your apartment. Why?"

Again his eyes darted away for a second. "This is neither the time nor the place for such a discussion."

"How about this then? My mother was dating Vince Madrigal. I swept her house for bugs and found some. Did you also have her under surveillance and why?"

Georgia Berryhill, her hands still cuffed, was guided by Detective Jeannie Brasfield down the steps of the house. A jacket was thrown over Georgia's shoulders. Brasfield gestured for one of the unmarked black SUVs to drive forward.

"I truly can't talk now," Scarbray said. "I have some pressing matters to attend to."

"I need answers," Vining said.

Scarbray was already walking away when he said, "And you'll get them. I'll call you."

Vining frowned at his back.

Kissick said, "He was forthcoming about their investigation. He didn't need to give us all that information."

"Maybe he felt that he owed us something."

"In my experience, that's not how the FBI works."

Vining watched Scarbray conferring with officers and agents. She couldn't hear what he was saying but he was clearly in charge. "He hasn't told us everything."

Stefan Pavel, fully dressed, his hands cuffed behind his back, was led across the driveway by Lucretia, the Berryhill acolyte who'd greeted Vining and Kissick at the front desk when they visited Berryhill. An L.A. Sheriff's Department shield dangled around her neck.

Following Stefan was Gig Towne, also now clothed and in handcuffs, being led by a tall man wearing a black polo shirt with an embroidered FBI shield above the pocket.

Seeing his wife, Stefan Pavel lunged at her. "This is your doing, you foolish bitch. You just had to have a baby."

"Keep your fat mouth shut, Stefan." Georgia took a step toward him before being restrained by Brasfield.

"Get moving," Lucretia said, pushing her supposed former boss ahead of her, making him stumble.

"They're already turning on each other," Vining said.

Gig Towne, hearing Vining, turned to look at her and Kissick. He gave them a maniacal grin. Vining couldn't tell whether it was a joke or real. He stopped and suggestively pumped his hips in their direction. Noting their shock at his vulgarity, he laughed in a way that sounded like the Gig Giggle blended with pure evil.

This time, even Kissick didn't find him funny.

FORTY-NINE

Vining was in the PPD detective's conference room watching a DVD of Kissick's interview with Cheyenne Leon that had taken place at the FBI's Westwood office. After a while, Vining turned her chair to look out the window and she just listened to their voices.

Cheyenne was composed and spoke from the heart with none of the attitude she'd shown before. "I really liked Tink and I think she liked me. That job as Tink's personal assistant was the first real job I had ever had. Tink helped me grow professionally and personally. I feel bad for being so snotty with you and Detective Vining after I found Tink's body, but I was so afraid. Plus, I felt guilty, like maybe it was my fault that Stefan killed her."

"How did you know that Stefan Pavel had murdered her?" Kissick gently asked.

Cheyenne drew in a long breath. "I didn't know for sure. I just felt it in my gut. I was helping Tink plan this big party to raise money for Georgia's Girls and I just couldn't stand it. I knew what went on there. Good people like Tink were giving their money to Georgia and Stefan so they could take advantage of girls. I told Tink, I said, 'Stop giving them your time or money. You don't want to be involved with that place.' I told her, 'That's all I can say, understand?'

"She looked at me and the color went out of her face. She didn't ask me any questions. She didn't mention it to me again, but I heard her on the phone telling Stefan that she was through with Georgia's Girls. She was going to cut them out of her will and she didn't intend to keep her mouth shut."

The recording went quiet. Vining turned to see Cheyenne staring down at her hands.

"A couple of days later, Stefan called me. I was in Ventura. Turns out, it was the morning after it happened. Stefan told me I had to return to Pasadena right away. He said he'd stopped by Tink's and found her floating in the pool. He told me to take Tink's laptop, her Georgia's Girls files, and anything having to do with Tink playing around with the occult. He didn't want anyone to find out about Berryhill's dirty little secrets."

Vining knew that all the materials Cheyenne had taken had been found by investigators during the compound bust in a back closet in Pavel's office. Investigators had also found the evidence they sought that tied Pavel to John Chase and Alison Oliver's murders. Among Pavel's papers were maps of Chase's house and Alison's courtyard apartment and logs of their, their neighbors', and Chase's roommate's comings and goings. Fibers matching one of Pavel's sweater vests were found on Alison's body.

"I took everything except Tink's sigils," Cheyenne said. "I went to a gas station by the freeway, and some flunky who worked for Stefan was there to pick the stuff up. I went back to Tink's. Before I called the police, like Stefan told me to do, I burned Tink's sigils. Tink and I had studied sigilry. We'd burned others before. These were new. I'm sure she was asking for guidance about Stefan and Georgia. Burning them released their power."

"Cheyenne, why didn't you tell us all this before?"

"I was afraid Stefan would kill me. He'd killed Tink, and she was way more important than me. Then when I heard about Trendi, I knew I could never say anything. I'd been afraid for Trendi. I knew Trendi and John Chase were planning to help Sinclair give birth in a hospital. One night, Gig Towne wanted Trendi to party with him and she wouldn't do it. Trendi told me she'd mouthed off, saying, 'You're gonna be sorry. You'll never see Sinclair and her baby again.' That was the end of her. When Detective Vining was tough with me at Carmen Vidal's office, I realized how really wrong it was to let them get away with everything. After I shot at Georgia, I no longer cared if Stefan came after me or not."

"Cheyenne, what happened to Fallon Price?"

She sucked in air through her teeth. "Gig Towne liked rough sex. Maybe it was the only way the perv could get off. One night, we were partying in the cabin in the woods. It was me, Trendi, Fallon, Gig, and Stefan. Gig was screwing Fallon and he had this cord around her neck, from behind. You know . . . I saw her go down on the bed. She didn't look like she was breathing. Trendi and I were screaming. Stefan got us out of there. The next day, Fallon and all her stuff were gone.

"Stefan pulled me and Trendi over and told us that Fallon had drunk too much. He said that she woke up and went to her room. She must have left the compound during the night. Trendi, with her big mouth, was like, 'Gig strangled her. We saw.' Stefan denied it. Then he said, 'Too bad Fallon left because I got both of you great jobs. You'll need cars, so you'll be getting brand-new BMWs and new wardrobes and you'll be earning money.' And then he said, 'Of course, if anyone asks about Fallon, you'll say she got in a fight with you, Cheyenne. You slapped her and she left. All right? Because we wouldn't want the two of you just disappearing like Fallon.'"

Earlier that day, Vining had heard that sheriffs investigators had found Fallon's body in a shallow grave in the compound. The hyoid bone in her neck was fractured, indicating that she'd been strangled.

While it had taken Georgia Berryhill and Gig Towne about five minutes after they were arrested to offer to rat out everyone in exchange for a plea bargain, Stefan Pavel had remained as silent and inscrutable as one of the Buddha statues in the Malibu Canyon compound. To Vining, news of his equanimity in the face of the charges against him revealed his heartless, sociopathic core. The only information that Pavel offered was "I did not kill Fallon." He would say nothing more.

Vining stopped the DVD and sat quietly thinking.

In a brief but furiously busy period of deadly house-keeping, Stefan Pavel had murdered Madrigal, Trendi, Tink, Chase, and Alison, methodically killing as a by-product of doing business and protecting his interests. Vining thought he must have enjoyed the wet work, since he hadn't hired it out. She'd discussed the cases with a prosecutor friend in the L.A. District Attorney's Major Crimes Division. With all the first-degree murder charges, conviction on just a couple would guarantee Stefan a spot in a state penitentiary for the rest of his natural life, which might be shortened with a death penalty conviction and a date with the needle.

Gig Towne wouldn't admit to knowing anything about the murder of Fallon Price. Since it was allegedly committed during a sex crime, Vining's Deputy D.A. friend told her that, if it could be proven, it was a special circumstances homicide, and what would have been a second-degree murder charge with fifteen years to life could become life without the possibility of parole, or even the death penalty. Much hinged on the credibility of Cheyenne's testimony. Gig was also charged with Un-lawful Sexual Intercourse, or statutory rape.

Gig was silent regarding his role in the kidnapping of his own baby. Prosecutors alleged that when Stefan helped Gig cover up Fallon's murder, he set the stage to later demand a favor in payment. That obligation would come due several years later when Stefan demanded that Gig hand over his newborn to mollify his baby-lusting wife.

Dr. Janus and the midwife, Paula Lowestoft, were also charged with kidnapping of a child under age fourteen. Sinclair's testimony would help in the kidnapping case against them and Gig, which brought a sentence of five to eleven years in state prison.

Regarding the kidnapping, Georgia claimed ignorance. She insisted she thought her husband was arranging a black-market adoption, saying, "I would never steal a baby, and most certainly not from my dear friend Sinclair."

Stefan, again, maintained his silence.

Sinclair, in exchange for her testimony about the kidnapping plot, was facing misdemeanor charges of aggravated trespass and carrying a loaded firearm. She might serve three months, if that, in county jail.

Regarding Cheyenne's shooting from her car in front of the Beverly Hills Hotel, Carmen Vidal negotiated a deal for her client to be charged only with misdemeanor unlawful discharge of a firearm. She might do six months in county jail.

Cheyenne and Gig both claimed that Georgia Berryhill knew everything that went on behind the scenes at the Berryhill compound, even as Georgia held to her story that she was Stefan's pawn and as much of a victim as the clients he ripped off and the young women he abused. There was little solid evidence to prove that she knew of any crimes being committed. She would face an assault with a firearm charge for having aimed a loaded gun at Sinclair, but it was a wobbler—meaning it could be charged as either a misdemeanor or a felony—plus she could argue self-defense. Vining doubted she'd spend more than a few months in county jail.

Kissick came into the conference room and interrupted Vining's reverie, asking, "How about some lunch?"

They went to Green Street, one of their favorite local restaurants.

Vining spoke between bites of her Dianne salad, the restaurant signature dish of iceberg lettuce, shredded chicken, toasted almonds, and a sweet dressing. "My prosecutor friend says that, sadly, all the serious charges will slide off Teflon Georgia. She was cagey enough to hide or eliminate evidence of her involvement."

Kissick was having a Big John's Meat Loaf sandwich, his favorite Green Street lunch. "Just a wrist-slap for the firearm charge. Amazing if she walks away from this whole thing."

"She'll write a book about it," Vining added. "Make the talk-show circuit and rise from the ashes. Whaddya bet? Get away with stealing Sinclair's baby. 'Course, faking a pregnancy isn't a crime."

Kissick wiped his mouth with a napkin. "Georgia's damage-control people are already working overtime to gloss over that entire incident as a PR stunt that went awry. Smart move for Sinclair to have filed for divorce from Gig Towne right away. She needs to distance herself from that nut and fast."

Vining started to laugh. "I was thinking about your taped interview with Cheyenne when she said that Gig and Stefan would get off on watching each other with those girls. She used to feel like telling them, 'Why don't you guys get a room?' In that little glimpse I had of their orgy, Stefan seemed more interested in what Gig was doing than in the young gal who was blowing him."

"It was hilarious when Gig denied having sex with Cheyenne," Kissick said. "She told the prosecutor that Gig can deny it all he wants, but how else would she know that he has a gherkin penis? Now he has to reveal his private parts to prosecutors."

Vining reached to pick up a gherkin pickle from Kissick's sandwich plate. She held it up. "As I remember it, I'll give him a little more than gherkin. Let's call it a baby dill."

FIFTY

*P*atsy Brightly set one of three bags of groceries she was carrying on the ground and unlocked her town house door. She banged it with her hip to push it open, as it had become sticky after the last earthquake. Moving through the doorway, she dropped a bag on the parquet tiles inside, which was accompanied by the sound of shattering glass.

"For crying out loud, Nan," she said to her daughter, who was sitting at the dinette table. "You scared me within an inch of my life."

"Sorry, Mom, but you won't return my phone calls."

"I've been superbusy, honey." Carrying the other bags into the kitchen, Patsy returned to look inside the one she'd dropped. "Ugh. That was a jar of salsa. It's all over everything."

She looked at Nan, who hadn't budged, and asked with annoyance, "Could you get the broom and dustpan for me, please?"

Stifling a sigh, Vining got up and went into the kitchen.

When she returned, her mother was taking canned goods flecked with red goop from the bag.

Vining helped clean up the mess and put away the groceries.

After they were finished, Patsy announced, "I'm having a glass of wine. Don't worry, Detective. It's after six o'clock in the evening. I assume you won't have any."

"No, thank you." Vining took the same chair at the dinette table.

"I have Coke and orange juice. You want anything?"

"Nope."

In the galley kitchen, Vining heard the clinking of glass and the pop of a cork being pulled from a bottle.

"Nan, is this about your grandmother? I'm sorry, but I can't live in that house with her."

"It's not about Granny, although we're going to have to have a family meeting about that soon."

Patsy carried a brimming glass of white wine to the table and sat. She took a healthy sip and asked, without looking at her daughter, "So what's this about?"

Vining answered without hesitation, having planned what she was going to say. "Your house was bugged, Mom, and so was Tink's."

Patsy puckered her lips.

"Mom, look at me. Please."

She reluctantly met her daughter's eyes.

"Did Vince Madrigal pay you to get access to Tink's house?"

Patsy's eyes reddened. She brought the wineglass to her lips, slowly sipped, and just as slowly set it down. "Nan, I spent hours talking to Jim about this right in your police station."

"I know you did. Jim and I both think that you weren't being honest. Please tell me what happened."

Patsy frowned and then sighed. "Okay, Nan. I'll tell you. But it wasn't that cut-and-dried. You make it sound like I sold my friend out for money. It didn't happen that way. It's more complicated."

"More complicated how?"

"It just is."

Vining sucked in air through her teeth. "How did it happen? How did he approach you?"

"Like I said." Patsy's voice turned small. "He came to the Estée Lauder counter and told me he wanted to buy perfume for his mother. Then he asked me out to dinner."

"How long before he revealed his true motives?"

She lazily raised a shoulder. "A couple of nights later, I met him for dinner at a restaurant near here. We were chatting and having drinks. We ordered dinner and then he started with this strange conversation. He told me he knew I was in trouble with my credit cards. I asked him how he knew and he said he had friends who knew things. He said he could help me out."

Vining grimaced. Madrigal had used his dirty law-enforcement connections to illegally access Patsy's financial records. "What did he want you to do?"

"Spy on Tink. He said it like it was no big deal. Get her to talk about her life, her regrets, any secrets she might have. Just normal girl talk. See if I could get inside her house and take any diaries she might keep. And he said, 'By the way, if you can get to know Cheyenne better, that would be valuable.' He was especially interested in things that were going on at Berryhill. He made out like he was trying to help Tink. Thinking about it now, it was all a bunch of double-talk that didn't make sense."

"Did he want you to get him inside Tink's house?"

"Not specifically. He said that was taken care of."

"How did he plant the bugs?"

"I'd found out later that he'd already put them in place. He'd messed up the external wires to Tink's cable TV. Tink told me she'd had problems with her cable. Guys in a van had showed up to fix problems they'd detected with her service and they were in the house. I asked Vince if they worked for him."

"How much did he pay you?"

"Five thousand dollars."

"You took five grand from a dirty P.I. to give him access to one of your best and oldest friends? Five grand for information that probably got her murdered. Did he want information about Georgia's Girls?"

"No, no." Patsy covered her face with her hands. "It wasn't like that, Nan."

"So tell me what it *was* like."

"Nan, I loved Tink like a sister. I helped her survive the worst time of her life. I was there for her every day. I would never hurt her."

"Then why did you?"

Patsy turned her head, moving her hands to cover her mouth, as if restraining the words inside. Her eyes were red, but she wasn't crying.

"Why'd you do it, Mom?"

Patsy shook her head, her hands still over her mouth. She peeled away a couple of fingers and raised them, still shaking her head, as if struggling with an internal debate. "It's all over. They're all in jail. I don't see the point in having to keep this a secret."

"Keep *what* a secret?"

"I didn't do it!" Patsy shouted, letting her fists fall to the table with a bang. She fiercely stared at her daughter. "I told Vince Madrigal to go to hell. That I wouldn't betray my friend like that."

Vining raised her hands, not knowing what to think. "If you told him no, then why did you continue seeing him? Why is your place bugged? Why did you take his money?" She shot her hand toward her mother like a dagger. "You have extra money, Mom. Everybody's noticed the way you've been throwing cash around."

"The FBI approached me and asked me if I would play along with Vince. They offered to pay me and said I could keep Vince's money too."

Vining's mind was spinning. "FBI . . . You mean the man who was posing as Kingsley Getty?"

Patsy sipped wine and nodded with the same casualness as if she'd just told her daughter that she'd decided to dye her hair a different color.

Vining rose from the chair in slow motion and took a few steps in the small living room. "You're telling me that you were a double agent for the FBI?"

"I guess you could call it that."

Vining had to laugh, slapping her thigh and holding her ribs.

Patsy was offended. "Is it so surprising that your mother can be a hero too, Nan? You think you're the only one in this family who's capable of doing big things?"

Her comment took Vining aback. Was her mother that competitive with her? Vining realized that it had been insensitive for her to laugh. She calmed down. "The real name of the FBI special agent who was posing as Kingsley Getty is David Scarbray."

Patsy's gaze darkened. "I know that, Nan." She held the edge of the table with both hands, as if steeling herself. "That night, right after I got home from having dinner with Vince, I heard a knock at my door. It was David Scarbray. He told me the FBI knew that Vince had approached me and asked what we'd talked about. I told him everything. I didn't care about Vince. I would have already told Tink what Vince had wanted me to do, only it was too late to phone her. David told me that Tink might be in danger."

Vining fumed. The night of the bust at the Berryhill compound, Scarbray had insisted that Tink hadn't been in danger. So his relationship with Tink had been more than just a way to socialize with the Berryhills and Gig Towne. It suddenly came to her. Scarbray and Madrigal hadn't been interested in Tink. It was

Cheyenne who they wanted intelligence about. Cheyenne held the key to bringing down the Berryhill empire. Tink had been in danger by virtue of her growing closeness to Cheyenne.

Patsy drank wine. "David wouldn't go into specifics but said I could help Tink by telling Vince that I'd changed my mind and that I would help him get access to Tink and spy on her."

"Did the FBI match what Vince Madrigal was paying you?"

"Nan, I didn't do it for the money, okay? Vince's money was nice. Lord knows I needed it, but that's not why I did it. I told David that I had half a mind to just tell Tink to cut off contact with that Berryhill place. To tell her about Vince and the FBI and all of it. David pleaded with me not to. He said it was a way I could help take criminals off the streets."

"Like I did."

"Nan." Her mother looked at her squarely. "I want you to know something. I am inspired by what you did to find the man who stabbed you and who killed those policewomen. The courage you showed. You did a wonderful thing, Nan. The families of those dead women finally know what happened to them."

Vining thought she was truly seeing her mother for the first time. "I always thought you looked down on my work."

"Oh, honey, I am so proud of you." Patsy moved her chair beside her daughter's and took her hands between both of hers. "Let me tell you something. I know I've messed up a lot in my life. I've made bad decisions." She added with an eye roll, "A lot of them. But your old mother's not as big a fool as you think she is. The money that Vince and the FBI paid me was helpful, but I did it because I wanted to do something good. I wanted *you* to be proud of *me*. Then Tink ends up murdered."

Patsy yelped a sob and buried her face in her hands.

"You couldn't have prevented that, Mom." Vining pulled her mother against her and rubbed her back, feeling her bony shoulders against her chest. It always surprised her to realize how much bigger and more muscular she was than her petite mother. "Your intentions were good. Sometimes even the smartest and best-trained law-enforcement professionals can't stop bad things from happening."

"I keep thinking of Tink. I was the last one who talked to her."

"I know, Mom. I know." She gave her another hug.

"And she left me her jewelry. I'd always admired it and told her so. I never expected . . ."

"Tink loved you a lot, Mom."

"There's a bracelet that would look good on you."

"Mom, save your money, please."

Patsy nodded. "I will. I promise. This whole thing has changed the way I see everything."

Vining was thinking that she'd believe that when she saw it when Patsy confirmed her suspicions.

"Although I could use a new car."

Vining let it go. "So, Mom, what did David Scarbray say that nudged you over the edge and convinced you to become an FBI informant?"

Patsy sat back in the chair and grabbed her wineglass by the stem. She breathed heavily, as if struggling with how to frame her words. She was holding the wineglass stem so tightly, Vining thought it might snap. "Because I was in love with him."

"You fell in love with him?"

"No, I knew him from before." Patsy again grabbed Vining's hand and squeezed it. "Nan . . . David Scarbray . . ."

There was a look in her mother's eyes that gave Vining pause.

Patsy tried again. "Nan, David Scarbray is your father. I gave him those clippings about you. I wanted him to know that his daughter was a hero."

FIFTY-ONE

Standing at her bathroom mirror, Vining searched through her hair with her index fingers. Spotting another gray hair, she tried to separate it from the dark strands. It slipped from her grasp. She ferreted it out again, wrapped it around her finger, and yanked. She drew her fingers along it, feeling its coarse texture, before dropping it into the trash.

She'd always wondered about her preponderance of gray hair at age thirty-five when her mother didn't have any at fifty-four. She now knew why after David Scarbray had answered that personal question, one of many she'd asked when they'd met over coffee earlier that day. Scarbray said he'd turned completely gray by the time he was forty.

She finished blow-drying her freshly washed hair. She ran her fingers through it, brought a thick lock to her nose, and inhaled the scent from the new herbal-and-citrus shampoo that she'd tried for the first time. In the drugstore, she'd chosen one of the more expensive brands on the top shelf instead of automatically reaching for the cheap brand on the bottom shelf that she'd been buying for as long as she'd been doing her own shopping.

Somehow her shampoo decision mimicked how she was feeling about her life: turned upside down.

She picked up and read the instructions on the box of hair color rinse she'd also bought. It was designed to cover gray.

Twenty-four hours had passed since Vining and her mother had talked late into the night about love lost and found, paths not taken, and regrets and happiness.

A few hours ago, she'd returned from meeting her father at a Starbucks, where they'd discussed deep personal sagas while seated at a corner table among students with laptops and soccer moms gossiping after spinning class.

Between her mother's and father's separate recounting of times, events, and emotions, Vining had come to some conclusions about where the truth lay. After Patsy had graduated from high school, she took classes at Pasadena City College and had a part-time job as a waitress at Farrell's Ice Cream Parlor in Rosemead. Her high school friends, Tink, Maria Alicia, and Vicki, were all away at big colleges. Patsy was growing distant from her old friends, and felt her life drifting.

One day, three young marines came into Farrell's. They were stationed at Camp Pendleton but one of them was from the San Gabriel Valley and had brought his two friends to stay with his parents for a few days. David Scarbray was one of the friends.

"It was love at first sight," Patsy had told Vining during their talk around the dining room table.

"She was pretty and a lot of fun. Always laughing," Scarbray had said at their corner table in Starbucks.

"I was living with my mom and dad in Alhambra and he came to visit me there. Sometimes I drove to see him at Camp Pendleton."

"After a few months, I left for Officer Candidate School in Quantico, Virginia. I was the third generation of Scarbray marines. It was sad to leave, but . . ."

"It broke my heart to say good-bye." The memory still made Patsy cry. "I dreamed that he'd propose before he left. I was just a girl, full of romantic ideas."

"I promised to write, but I was never much for writing letters."

"Granny warned me not to get too involved with him. I don't regret it. I've never forgotten a minute of it. Later, I found out I was pregnant. You can imagine how my mom and dad took *that* news. Attitudes about that were different then, especially in my parents' house. They talked late into the night, discussing everything from abortion to sending me away to have the baby in secret and then giving it up for adoption to making David marry me. They wanted me to tell David but I refused. I'd come to accept that I was just another girl in a port for him. If I'd told him and he'd rejected me, I wouldn't have been able to bear it. I was determined to keep my baby. At least I had something of him. Something of my one true love." Patsy grabbed Nan's hands. "You were truly my love child."

Nan had wept.

"I bought a plain gold wedding band. I told my friends that his name was David Smith and that he was one of the last marines in Vietnam. He'd been shot down and was Missing in Action. I didn't see my friends that much then, but when I did, I never brought photos. I said it was too painful. That was the truth. I had a few photos, but I couldn't look at them. My parents went along with the story as a way to save face. After a while, we all sort of believed the lie."

Patsy had then dug out the photos to show her daughter.

Vining's father had told her how he'd left the Marines after attaining the rank of captain and had joined the FBI. He'd married a young woman from Baltimore and they'd had three children: a girl who was now thirty, another girl who was twenty-seven, and a boy who was twenty-four and a marine first lieutenant. Scarbray had four grandchildren—five, counting Emily, who was the oldest.

Over his second cappuccino, Scarbray told Vining, "When I thought of my Camp Pendleton days, I'd think of Patsy, the lively, pretty girl I'd dated, and I'd wonder what happened to her."

He became part of the FBI and L.A. Sheriff's Department task force investigating the Berryhills for transporting Fallon Price and other young women across state lines for sex, the suspected murder of Fallon, and other crimes. They'd had Vince Madrigal under surveillance since they'd learned that he was the go-to guy for dirt on the Berryhills and their clients. When the surveillance team identified Madrigal's dinner companion as Patsy Brightly, Scarbray did a background check, uncovered her maiden name, and determined that she was the same Patsy Brown he'd romanced years before.

Tink Engleford emerged as a way for the task force to get deep inside the Berryhill organization and close to Cheyenne Leon, potentially a key witness to the dirty goings-on involving Georgia's Girls.

"Did you lie to my mother to get her to cooperate with you?" Vining asked Scarbray.

He responded without hesitation. "I told her the truth. That I'd often thought of her and fondly recalled our times together. I said I was happy to reconnect with her."

"You didn't tell her that you're married."

"It didn't come up."

Vining couldn't blame him for leading on someone useful to an investigation to get that person to cooperate. She would have done the same.

The previous night, at the conclusion of Patsy's tearful story, during which Vining had accepted a glass of her mother's chardonnay, she'd hugged her mother and said, "I'm not mad, Mom."

Now, in the cool light of day, Vining thought the whole drama was so Patsy. Vining would have handled it differently, but she had always strived to live her life differently from her mother's. Vining was not much for carrying grudges or harboring thoughts of vengeance. She'd discovered her baser impulses after she'd tracked down the creep who'd stabbed her and left her for dead. She'd released her anger about him and many things, finding that it was lighter to live that way.

After Vining and her father had talked—not taking hours, as their law-enforcement background had trained them to get to the facts with brevity—she'd made a call to Kissick. He'd been wandering Old Pasadena with Emily. They came to the Starbucks, and Emily met her grandfather for the first time.

Before they parted, Scarbray heaped praise on Vining's skills as a cop. "You've got great instincts, Nan. If you're interested in coming over to the FBI, a larger organization with a bigger budget and more opportunity, I could get you in."

"Thanks. I'll think about it." While her knee-jerk reaction was to dismiss his offer, as she was happy where she was, she later found herself considering it.

When Kissick was driving Vining and Emily back to their Mount Washington home, Em summed it up with the inimitable wisdom of an adolescent: "That was weird."

Later that night, Vining thought about the sigil she'd created and thrown into her desk drawer at the station. The intention she'd written was: Who is King Getty? Now, she knew.

FIFTY-TWO

So many people attended Tink's funeral service at Church of the Angels' stone-and-brick hilltop chapel that Father Bob Gaestel had to set up chairs on the lawn outside. Tink had touched many people during her life.

Kissick drove Vining and Emily to the gravesite in their car.

"Vicki told me that Tink's two-million-dollar bequest to Georgia's Girls is suspended until it can be determined whether the Berryhills were running a criminal enterprise," Vining said.

"Did you read this about Georgia Berryhill?" Emily handed the brand-new issue of *People* magazine to her mother. On the cover was a photo of a somber Georgia beneath a headline that screamed: I MARRIED A MADMAN.

Vining scanned the article. "I can't believe she got off with only a misdemeanor assault with a firearm charge and she claimed self-defense. Ninety days in county jail and I bet she slips out of that somehow."

Kissick drove through the gates of the old San Gabriel Cemetery and parked. Vining and Emily walked to where Patsy was standing with the three remaining Ramona Girls, their arms around one another's waists.

They separated when David Scarbray got out of a car and walked across the grass.

Patsy offered her hand.

He took it, pulling her close and kissing her cheek. "I

wanted to pay my respects and offer my deepest condolences."

He extended his hand to Granny. "Mrs. Brown, nice to see you looking so well."

Granny mustered, "Thank you."

Words escaped Vicki and Maria Alicia, who stared at him wide-eyed. They managed to mutter pleasantries as they shook his hand.

Scarbray and Kissick shook hands.

"Emily, I won't tell you to be good because I know you know that already. You're a fine young lady." He gave her a hug. "I'll be in touch soon."

Vining didn't offer her hand, but opened her arms and hugged him hard. He felt like something that she'd needed her whole life without really being aware of it. Now that she had what she'd been missing, she realized how deep that emptiness in her life had been.

Scarbray gave her a wet kiss on the cheek. "This is just good-bye for now."

As they watched him get into his car and drive away, Patsy blotted tears and said to her concerned friends, "I'll be okay."

Vicki grabbed Patsy's hand and Maria Alicia took Vicki's.

Watching her mother with her girlfriends, Vining thought of Cheyenne and the desperate means she'd taken to speak for her friends Trendi and Fallon, who weren't able to speak for themselves. She thought of the secrets and lies that can separate loved ones, and the truths and compassion that can bring them back together. That was the enduring power of family and friends, especially girlfriends.

Patsy held out her hand. Emily stepped forward and took it, bringing Granny with her. Vining extended the chain, taking Granny's hand.

   Vining didn't feel quite complete. There was one more
bond in her life. One more thing that was true. Without
turning around, she held out her empty right hand.
Kissick stepped up and laced his fingers in hers. She held
on tightly.